CHR

Neil Cross was born i...
Mr In-Between was published in 1998. He lives and
works in London.

Neil Cross

CHRISTENDOM

VINTAGE

TO THE WORST

Published by Vintage 2000

2 4 6 8 10 9 7 5 3 1

Copyright © Neil Cross 1999

The right of Neil Cross to be identified as the author of this work has been asserted by him in accordance with the Copyright, Designs and Patents Act, 1988

First published in Great Britain by
Jonathan Cape in 1999

Vintage
Random House, 20 Vauxhall Bridge Road,
London SW1V 2SA

Random House Australia (Pty) Limited
20 Alfred Street, Milsons Point, Sydney
New South Wales 2061, Australia

Random House New Zealand Limited
18 Poland Road, Glenfield, Auckland 10, New Zealand

Random House (Pty) Limited
Endulini, 5A Jubilee Road, Parktown 2193, South Africa

The Random House Group Limited Reg. No. 954009
www.randomhouse.co.uk

A CIP catalogue record for this book
is available from the British Library

ISBN 0 09 977861 0

Papers used by Random House are natural, recyclable products made from wood grown in sustainable forests. The manufacturing processes conform to the environmental regulations of the country of origin

Printed and bound in Denmark by
Nørhaven A/S, Viborg

Prologue

It's summer.

The boys, no longer children, not yet men, are dressed in shorts, T-shirts and sneakers.

The tall one, the graceful one, who is called Randall Staad and who one day will save the world by the grace of God, carries a battered blue cooler in one hand, a fishing rod in the other. He leads his friend along a path they have trodden many times before, on many such summer days.

The grass is lush, the soil in which it is rooted rich and soft. Their hi-tops, trailing wet laces, leave temporary, spongy imprints of the soles of their feet − testament to their passage, the distribution of their weight, their leisurely progress towards the river's edge. The fearsome sunlight is made gentle by the pacific canopy of trees beneath which they pass. Ethereal lozenges of green flicker across their skin and clothing.

Soon they come to the river, sinuous and leisurely, the colour of mercury. They set themselves down at the bank. The shadows of clouds passing across the water.

From the cooler, Randall removes two Coca-Colas. He hands one to Frankie. They open the cans and drink deep. It's hot and they're thirsty. They lower the cans and belch fruitily.

They cast off, sit for a while in silence. They rest their chins on their knees and watch the floats bob gently in the muscular current.

They have yet to catch a single fish in this river. There are no fish left in it.

Randall finishes his Coke. He crushes the can, replaces it in the cooler. He lies back, knits his hands behind his head.

'Frankie,' he says.

By now Frankie is reading. Randall does not have to look at Frankie to know his expression. When Frankie reads his brow knits and his eyes flit, left to right, scanning the page with speed and apparent consternation. Frankie looks up from his book, regards Randall from the shadow cast by the peak of his baseball cap. It has on it the Budweiser logo, stitched in yellow thread. It is Frankie's father's cap.

'Yeah?' he says.

Randall's face splits into a wide grin. He lies grinning at the sky.

How do you tell your best friend you're going to save the world?

One *The Giving Ground*

I was an immigrant prodigy. Then I was a soldier. After that I determined to prove a villain.

I'd finished with all of it when I met Isabel, because I was sure I'd seen David McArdle in that car and I very much did not want to have seen David McArdle in that car: the neutral-faced woman to whom I'd handed over the package handing it in turn to him and sitting back in the passenger seat with a flicker of contempt crackling across her shoulders. If you want to know the truth (and what would be the point of this otherwise?), since that escapade I'd discovered whole new heights to which my discomfort was able to aspire.

I was already pretty drunk when she and Nathan decided it was time to meet me. I'd just completed a two-week dry shift, an event habitually celebrated by what my father used to call a bender; four or five days during which one conscientiously did little but drink oneself into a surly temper and (according to him, but he was English and he didn't drink) stagger unshaven from bar to bar reeking of whiskey and piss. He seemed to consider this in some way degrading.

I had yet to reach those giddy lows but I was in a bar. I couldn't shake the suspicion that I was being monitored through the eyes of Christ, through those benevolently bovine orbs set moist and bambi-like in that softly opalescent, wistful visage. There was a large representation of him on the wall, a popular reproduction; white robes and chestnut beard. He had about him all the fresh, pink vitality of one overdosed on carbon monoxide.

I sometimes liked to imagine that he was backing away from me, palms spread in a gesture not of encompassment but appeasement, face set passive against my rage, that tiny Giaconda smile one of embarrassed fear: 'Look,' I liked to think he was saying as he retreated unsteadily on sandalled feet, 'I don't want any trouble, okay?'

I sat in silence with a beer and cigarettes as I and my fellow drinkers, many of them colleagues on similar benders, watched that week's broadcast of CTW on the large screen towards which all of the tables in the bar were angled. As we approached the fifteenth anniversary of the end of the war CTW was becoming exponentially more unbearable.

It was just 'the war' now.

Staad had announced his intention to mark the occasion by speaking in the Temple, something he hadn't done for years, not since the cancer first got to him. The media build-up to this historical watershed was excruciating. I did not believe that Staad approved of all the soft-focus vulgarity perpetrated in his name.

All the same, we were swept along by oceanic sweeps of choral music and epic shots of the Temple, of the Grand Canyon, of a younger and firmer Staad (but still those cheekbones! Still those vengeful Protestant cheekbones!) in slo-mo, shaking hands with the Quorum, each in turn, taking the podium, close-up on those prodigious statesman's eyebrows, the granite quality of the crags that ran deep in the fatless flesh of his face. All this time I ground my teeth and chanted beneath my breath the silent mantra that denied the Lord of Hosts access to my heart.

When at last it was over, I weaved to the bar and ordered another beer, a Hawaiian burger and a side-order of Hi-Cal fries.

Outside was a high summer sunset. The light that filtered through the windows was corn yellow and wholesome, rinsed with pink. Although certain areas of the planet were still prone to meteorological extremes (I had witnessed in central Africa thunderstorms that I swear to God had about them all the apocalyptic fury of tactical nuclear weapons), the South

2

Australian Reclamation, while not exactly New England in the spring, was at least tolerably savage. It was even prone to occasional prettiness. New Winchester, that part of the overall reclamation where I chose to board, was just that touch away from being a hick town down under. Buildings were low, seldom higher than the five- or six-storey budget apartment buildings which ran in ugly standardised blocks, parallel with the main street upon which I was an exile. Nothing stood higher than the administrative or municipal buildings. The streets were wide and traffic was light, sometimes non-existent. Many of us were bussed out to the farms to work our week-, fortnight- or month-long shifts, where we laboured in sunblock and workshirts and Stetsons and boots that laced to the knee beneath the Levi's, doing any one of the hundreds of different jobs that went in to farming the creatures whose recent ancestors had been cows. I liked the work. I liked being outside in sunshine without guilt. I liked the feel of the Stetson on my head, I liked the way I felt when I tipped it back and squinted into the astonishing sunlight. I liked the fact that I could take a break for a cigarette whenever I felt like it, that I could pick a spot shaded by one of those bizarre, incessantly grazing ruminants and just sit and smoke and try not to think. I liked the fact that I worked alone, or with men that did not find it necessary to speak beyond the requirements of the job.

Someone changed channels, and the gathered hordes were spoon-fed their nightly dose of sport – basketball, in this instance. Hideously elongated men moving with gawky grace and astonishing speed in the pursuit of – what? I had never understood sport, not as participant, still less as spectator.

There were few women in the bar – the South Australian in general and New Winchester in particular seemed to attract as *émigrés* the sort of person who still considered it a little unseemly for a woman to drink in public, although their legal right to do so (after a small but rather furious theological debate concerning some remark in one of the Pauline letters, I forget which) was in fact constitutionally enshrined. It's one of

3

the amendments numbered in the hundreds and has about it a rather embarrassed and abashed tone, as if apologising for the necessity of its existence. Three sets of newlyweds had naturally gravitated to one another. There were some out-and-out alcoholics, there were gaggles of working men just off a shift, shouting at the screen and ordering food and booze, there was me, alone in a booth with my cigarettes, my beer, my burger and my newspaper and then there was this upright old woman walking through the door. I felt the little blast of heat follow her entrance, the dying summer heat rushing in, dissipating, leaving a ghost of itself in rippling cigarette smoke that crawled lizardly across the ceiling.

She negotiated the bustle with elegant nonchalance, not a hint of disdain or discomfort. Distractedly, she brushed grit or dust from the lapel of a navy-blue jacket, upon which there was pinned a brooch which reflected exactly the honey-coloured air of the dying day. She seemed to be scanning the bar for a place to sit, perhaps someone she knew. I heard the door hiss open once more, another quick blast of heat, and the woman cast a quick glance over her shoulder. I did not take my eyes off her.

In time her glance swept neutrally but not rudely across me and fell on the three empty seats in my booth. I scowled and scratched sweaty grime from the back of my neck and tried to look proprietorial. I swigged beer from the bottle. Nothing I did seemed to put her off. She headed straight for me, negotiating the crowd like a royal yacht. She paused at the booth. Under her arm she clutched a small patent leather purse. She said: 'Would you mind moving your hat?' I could not have made my body language more unwelcoming if I'd started to pick morsels of burger from my molars with the point of a Bowie knife.

She leaned forward a little and insistently yet still not impolitely tapped the tabletop once with a bony index finger.

'Excuse me,' she repeated, 'but would you mind moving your hat?'

I sat up, leaned over the table and lifted my hat from where I had set it down with the specific intent of discouraging people from sitting near me.

'Thank you very much indeed,' she said, and slid into the booth opposite me. She placed the little leather purse on the ash-smeared, ketchup-stained surface of the table before her and opened it. She began to rummage inside it. Deliberately, I placed the Stetson on the chair next to me. She looked up, very briefly.

I reached into a breast pocket, removed a soft pack of Marlboro and placed a cigarette in the corner of my mouth. The effect was somewhat diminished by the fact that I was unable to find a lighter. I patted my pockets, not without a degree of irritation. I picked up the hat in order to look underneath it. I patted the pockets of my jeans again. Surreptitiously, I looked down and searched the floor. She had stripped me of all human dignity.

Naturally, what she had been rummaging for in her bag was a pack of cigarettes. My humiliation was complete when she produced a gold lighter, snapped the flame on, and offered me a light. I had nowhere to back down to. I accepted the flame with as good a grace as I was able to muster and returned to my newspaper.

I thought I heard her laugh. It was a small exhalation but it was enough to make me blush for what she must have thought of me. I turned the page and read. Mortgage rates on Mary-Jane Kimball had been pegged at three per cent. Rent control had been re-instigated. Also there was some speculation about a reduction in the already low rate of basic tax, to act as a further incentive.

How fucking dumb did they think we were? I'd spent time on Mary-Jane Kimball. Being taxed triple in Australia would have been preferable.

'I'm sorry,' she said. 'Were you expecting company?'

I was visited by the peculiar inkling that this woman was actually trying to provoke me. I glowered at her at her over the rim of my newspaper. She was tall – as tall as me – and her height was accentuated by the fact that she was slender almost to the point of emaciation, although she carried this off with the aristocratic elegance of an old-time *Vogue* model. She had allowed her hair to grey and wore it pulled back in a masochistically severe bun that pulled taut the skin of her face. Her eyes were the most extraordinarily clear blue I had ever seen, have ever seen. They made her face luminous and quite beautiful.

She acknowledged that I was staring at her over the newspaper. When she smiled it was like somebody had turned on a high wattage lamp, like the edge of the sun emerging from behind a cloud.

'No,' I said, 'I wasn't expecting anybody.'

I closed the paper, folded it and placed it on the table.

She nodded that she had heard. 'Good,' she said. She looked briefly in the direction of the bar, raising the cigarette to thin lips and taking a distracted puff. I wished I looked that elegant when I smoked.

I drained the last of the beer and made the sounds and did the things that people do when preparing to leave somewhere. I opened my billfold, ensuring that my smartcard was there. I replaced my cigarettes in my breast pocket. My hand went to lift my hat.

'Oh, please,' she said, 'don't be leaving on my account.'

I made a placatory gesture. I was uncomfortable with my accent. I had and have a bastardised dialect – some of my father's Englishisms (I say 'trousers' for instance. This has often been the cause of much hilarity. Pants will to my dying day be the things you tuck your genitals away in), some military vulgarisms I haven't been able to exorcise completely, and little bits from every job I have ever done and every place I have ever visited. Sometimes I suspect that I am little more than a loosely stitched flibbertigibbet, constructed from the recorded tics and idiosyncrasies of every person I've ever met. My history is in every word to which I give voice and she made me ashamed of this. Her voice was perfectly measured and accentless, effortlessly enunciated with a clipped edge to it. She spoke like American aristocracy.

'I insist,' she insisted. 'I'll be here only a short while – while my husband puts the hire car in for repair.'

That sounded about right. I could picture her, tired from travelling all the way from the sweetness and comfort of the promised land – that kind of wealth, where else could she be from? – here to visit maverick grandchildren intent on making it on their own terms. Here perhaps to threaten the withdrawal of an inheritance should they not choose to return forthwith, leaving dreams of Australian freedom far behind them.

'Don't let me put you off watching your sport.'

She nearly broke my heart when she said that.

'That's fine,' I said. 'Really. That's okay. I'm not much of a sporting person. I mean, I can take it or leave it. You know.'

She laid her pack of cigarettes and her lighter parallel on the flat of the table and, distracted, began to push the lighter this way and that with the tip of her forefinger.

'How refreshing,' she said. 'I swear Nathan would watch sport twenty-four hours a day if he were able. Any sport.'

'Nathan is . . .?'

'My husband. He's . . .'

'. . . putting the hire car in for repair.'

'Exactly,' she said. 'What a business.'

She had made it effectively impossible for me politely to extricate myself. She offered me her hand and introduced herself: 'Isabel Beaumont.'

I took the hand, dry as a bundle of kindling. 'It's a pleasure to meet you, Mrs Beaumont.' I told her my name.

'It's a pleasure to meet you too, Mr Thorndyke. Malachi. What a lovely name.'

'My father's choice.'

'An English immigrant,' she concluded, with a wide and unabashed and incandescent smile. Clearly she recalled my generation's shame, the fashion for inappropriately pious

7

names that turned the English into America's new Poles, the butt of an incalculable number of jokes, many of which had been told in a slightly different form by those very same Englishmen about Irishmen only a generation earlier. 'How many young men of European stock were there named Hosiah, I wonder?' she said. 'Benjamin was never enough, was it, or Michael? You were all Esaus and Hirams.'

'And Malachis,' I added, without any of the bitterness which usually accompanies my hurt shame for my father's best intentions.

'And Malachis indeed,' she agreed. 'Tell me, do you have any idea what it means?'

'None,' I said, 'I never really stopped to consider that it might *have* a meaning. It's just – you know – my *name.*'

'You should look it up,' she said. 'Somewhere.'

'I will,' I lied. 'I'll do that.' I tugged at the loose, bristling skin beneath my jaw (I was becoming a little jowly) leaned forward conspiratorially and confided, possibly with a slightly drunken slur, that: 'I think in retrospect even Dad realised that it was all a little starched collar and stovepipe hat.' I wiped the corner of my eye. 'I think he would much rather that I was called Robert. He always liked the name Robert.' Still, I understand that second and third generations are having it easier . . .'

'Arthur,' she said, 'and Rosemary are very popular.'

I asked if I could buy her a drink. She asked for a Budweiser. I ordered us one each. She lifted the bottle by the neck and took a healthy, unpretentious swig. She made it an act of elegance.

We talked for a few minutes more, and all the while she absently pushed her cigarette lighter this way and that across the surface of the table with a rigid finger. Occasionally my eyes were drawn to follow its arbitrary progress. It began to gather about it a little cake of spilled, damp sugar and a moist crust of drying ketchup. When she lifted it to light a cigarette, she first cleaned the crud away with an opalescent thumbnail.

8

She looked again to her left and let out a small, satisfied exclamation. She half-stood in the booth and waved towards the bar, stiffly from the elbow. An old man in a dark suit acknowledged us with a nod and an affirmatory smile and began to make his way towards us.

He was small and luxuriously dishevelled in an impressively cut navy-blue suit, a heavy wool mix that could not have been more inappropriate to the climate. His white shirt was loose at the neck and grimy. His button-down collars no longer were: one side twisted awkwardly over the lapel of his jacket, the other was tucked under itself like a sleeping swan. His thinning hair looked neatly cut but badly cared for. It stuck up in a little tuft at the crown of his head. I thought he was probably the wrong side of sixty-five. Closer than me to God.

He rested at the booth and wiped the back of a hand across his lips. His face was pleasantly crinkled. He had exhausted marshmallow bags under his eyes and his eyebrows needed a trim. Tufts of grey and black hair grew like desert cacti in the whorls of his ears.

His first words were an exasperated: 'Those *bastards*,' and I was pleased to hear that he was English.

'Calm down,' said Isabel, before introducing us. I bought Nathan a gin and tonic with ice. The bar was out of lemons. When I returned with it to the booth he and his wife were engaged in an intense discussion about the hire car.

'I don't care what she says,' he said to me, after thanking me for the drink: 'They are *bastards*.'

'Nathan thinks that all the incompetence in the world is a personal slight,' Isabel explained.

'Who's to tell me that it's not?' he answered.

Incongruously, she laughed, reached out and ruffled the crown of his head. He nuzzled into her palm like a smug, licentious old moggy.

I was enjoying myself, so when she asked if I would like another drink I was happy to admit, after belching into my rolled fist, that I would like one very much indeed.

9

'You'll have to excuse me, Mr Thorndyke,' said Nathan.

'Malachi, please.'

'All this travel is beginning to get to me. I don't seem to know quite if I'm coming or going. But more to the point nor does any other bastard.' *Bahstad.*

'I told him Hertz,' Isabel said, 'I said: *Hertz*. But he wouldn't have it. The local outfit was cheaper. Now we know why.'

'From now on,' he said, 'I'm sticking strictly to brand names.'

I pointed to myself (my finger was waving unsteadily) and said: 'Marlboro, Budweiser, Jack Daniel's, Levi's, Wendy's burgers, Doctor Marten's, Twinkies . . .'

She admonished me with a half smile: 'The litany of the contented consumer.'

'As you can probably tell,' I said, 'I am at present a particularly contented consumer.'

'And tomorrow there will be Alka-Seltzer and Pepsi Cola,' she said.

'Indeed there will, God bless them all. I lead a very full life.'

Now that the gin and tonic had cooled his ire, Nathan had moved on to beer. He carefully poured the Budweiser into a long glass and took a luxurious pause before taking a thirsty swig, his Adam's apple doing something interesting as he swallowed. He set the glass back on the table with a decisive bump and wiped his hand across his lips again.

I was smiling. I couldn't help it. I was happy.

I lit a cigarette.

'So, what brings you to New Winchester?'

She didn't miss a beat. 'Oh,' she said: 'We're friends of Thomas,' and for a second she focused on me and something bright and faster than light ran the length of my spinal column. With a spasm of the hand I knocked over my beer. It glugged from the upended, spinning neck of the bottle, forming a pool around her lighter.

'Shit!' I said, and made to stand. 'Oh, for Christ's sake,' I said. 'Oh, shit,' I said. I took a shaky draw on the cigarette.

She raised a single, sardonic eyebrow. 'Goodness me. You look like you're having a coronary.'

I felt like I was having a coronary. A heart attack. What do you say, in such situations? What is there to say that doesn't sound rehearsed, that doesn't sound full of false enigma and machismo?

Nathan put a hand on my shoulder and, without menace eased me gently back into the overstuffed chair. He handed me his beer and I took a long swig from it. When he took the glass back, I saw him cleaning the rim with the inside of a shirt cuff. His shirt cuff was really *dirty*, for Christ's sake.

' "Friends of Thomas".' I said.

'That very thing.'

It was a joke code, an ironic means by which to identify ourselves. We might as well have worn carnations in our lapels or a red crescent on our T-shirts for all the sophistication of it. 'Excuse me,' I would say, 'are you a friend of Thomas?' and they would reply: 'I know him well,' or 'Thomas is my brother'. Or some crap or other that always had a thrill of childish play to it because we all knew how absurd the situation was, that there wasn't the need to do this in our father's day, that in our grandfather's youth it would have been unthinkable, unimaginable, the stuff of easy satire.

I scratched my nose. 'I don't know what to say,' I said. 'I'm truly sorry that I can't help you. I don't know how you found me but I'm not a friend of Thomas any more. We had a falling out a while ago. You know how it is. But I'm sure he's got lots of, you know, other friends who would be more than happy to talk to you.'

'We heard that you were particularly close.'

I needed to urinate. I was speaking too quickly and too quietly and I glanced up once more to that rosy, Europeanised Jew in airbrushed tat on the wall, nicotine smoke like Catholic incense curling around him, and wondered what was behind his eyes.

'Look,' I said. 'It was nice to meet you. Really, it was. And good luck. I mean it, the best of luck in the world.' All this as I squeezed sideways from the booth, setting the Stetson square on my head, and making my way from the bar.

It was nearly full dark outside. I could sense the baked-in heat of New Winchester radiating back into space. All that heat.

Like pursuing zombies in a feverish dream, Isabel and Nathan followed me right on to the street. I began quickly to walk away. I could picture my jaw giving way under the strain, exploding outwards in a cartoon cataclysm of wire and springs.

Isabel caught up with me. I could hear the metronomic impact of her inappropriate shoes on the cooling, dusty sidewalk. Hands in the air, I turned. She paused before me.

Over her shoulder I saw Nathan sauntering towards us along the sidewalk. He carried the heavy woollen jacket over one shoulder. One of his shoelaces was untied, and the tail of his shirt had worked its way loose of the waistband of his trousers.

I made to speak and she silenced me. 'Your place or mine?' she said, and again arched a single eyebrow.

This should have made me angry. I should have ranted and screamed and acted like a lunatic and scared the living colours of shit out of this old woman and her husband. I should have made them regret coming within a hemisphere of me. I lifted a finger, went to speak, then felt myself deflate, to fold slightly about myself as if punctured in the navel.

Nathan caught us up. Hands in pockets, he rocked on his heels and gave me an apologetic grin.

She offered me a cigarette – a Lucky Lite, not my brand, but I took it anyway. I couldn't stop my hands shaking.

'We can't stand here on the street all night,' she said.

I exhaled blue smoke. 'Why not? Who's watching?'

'Nobody's watching.'

'Then let's talk here.' The sun was nearly down and the shadows were long and nightmarish. The street was all but deserted. Small groups walked, stumbled, in and out of bars, someone emerged from one of the three twenty-four-hour convenience stores I could see from where we stood, their oxyacetylene gaiety somehow at odds with the season, the exhausted summer.

'Don't be ridiculous,' she said. 'I feel foolish.'

'And vulnerable?' I said.

'Well,' she agreed. 'Well, yes. A little.'

'Then you see,' I said, 'you see how I feel.'

'Let's go inside and talk,' she said.

'Please,' I said, 'Please, really. Please. I really don't want to.'

Without moderating the tone of her voice she said: 'But you're going to *have* to.'

I buried my hands in my pockets and twirled once about my axis, pulling my shoulders tight to my neck and looking at the purple sky, in which could be seen the first glimmerings of the first stars of the evening. I knew she was right, that I was going to have to hear them out before they would accept my refusal, before they would just go away and leave me alone.

'Okay,' I said. 'Let's go to your hotel.'

'That won't be possible. Let's go to your apartment.'

'That won't be possible either.'

'Nathan and I have no hotel. There was no room at the inn.'

I glanced at Nathan. He confirmed with a shrug.

'My place is out of the question,' I said.

'Follow me,' she said.

I let her take me by the elbow and lead me a little down the street, into a convenience store.

After warning her: 'Don't forget the pistachios,' Nathan waited outside.

I felt somewhat unreal, dazzled by the parallel rows of nuts and chips and cigarettes and candy, all in their shiny wrapping, bathed in a light that was heavenly and sterile. Apparently at random, she gathered up a few packs and stuffed them into my arms. I accepted this meekly and continued to follow her down the aisle, a family pack of Doritos tucked beneath my chin. She took a two-litre bottle of Coke, a pack of Tylenol, some Alka-Seltzer, from the chilled compartment some Brockwurst, some mustard, some milk, some bread, all of which she piled thoughtlessly into my already overburdened arms. Upon reaching the cashier at last she tutted, clicked her fingers and walked off, returning with a large bag of pistachios. As the cashier costed and bagged these goods, she ordered three six-packs of Beck's, two packs of Marlboro, one pack of Lucky Lites and a litre of Gordon's gin. She handed over her smartcard before the total had been reached.

Outside the store I passed one of the bags to Nathan, kept one for myself and let Isabel carry the third, the one with the chips in it.

We walked in a line down the empty sidewalk and took a left turn together. All that was missing was the Cowardly Lion and that little bastard Toto bringing up the rear.

As we walked, I talked. 'Where are we going? For a picnic?'

Nathan grinned weakly and Isabel seemed not to hear.

When (rather later than I should) I realised where we were headed, I stopped, bent slowly at the knees and set the grocery bag on the gritty sidewalk.

'Just a fucking minute,' I said.

Isabel seemed to hear this okay. Bag tucked under her chin, she turned to me and raised her eyebrows, both of them this time.

'No,' I said. 'Absolutely not. We cannot go to my apartment.'

'Give me one good reason why not,' she said.

I shifted my weight.

'I think it's bugged,' I said.

Nathan let out a relieved guffaw and even Isabel released a somewhat inelegant honk.

'I have reason to believe,' I insisted, 'that I'm still being watched.'

'What do you mean "still"?'

'I can't have this conversation here,' I said. 'I just can't.

Look, I'll meet you somewhere in the morning – back in the bar. Outside the convenience store. Somewhere.'

The grocery bag tucked under one arm, Isabel wiped a tear from the corner of her eye. 'Tomorrow won't be possible,' she said.

'Fine,' I said. 'That's fine. Tonight's not good for me, tomorrow's not good for you . . .'

She shifted the bag beneath her arm. 'Don't make me insist.'

I tugged at the hair on the crown of my head.

'How many more ways can I say it?'

'As many ways as you like, Mr Thorndyke.'

'Oh, Jesus.' I kneaded the flesh between my eyebrows.

Lightly, Nathan placed two fingers on my elbow. I caught a whiff of Johnson's baby soap. I withdrew as politely as I was able – I don't much like to be touched – but I looked down to see that in his hand he held a slim rectangle of black plastic with a tiny rubber snub of an aerial; a top-of-the-range cellular telephone.

'Don't be concerned about bugs,' he announced.

I met his eyes. 'Excuse me?'

He smiled like a devilish and unkempt schoolboy. 'This is a bug detector,' he said.

'Oh, *is* it?' I said. 'Excuse my ignorance. I thought it looked very much like a mobile phone.'

'What would you suggest it look like?' he scowled. 'A space shuttle? A train?'

I retaliated: 'What if they have bugs that can't *be* detected? You've got no *idea* how small modern surveillance equipment can be – cameras with wide-angle lenses the size of a pin-head. Voice-activated digital recording devices. Stuff which can record the pheromonal shifts in a room, so they know when you're lying even as they listen to you, so they know when you're scared, when you're angry, when you're . . .'

I met Isabel's eyes. She was smiling in something not unakin to amazement.

'Do you know what you *sound* like?' she said.

A conspiracy theorist.

Nathan raised a silencing finger. 'Malachi,' he said. 'I don't want to prick your ego too much, and I won't deny the possibility that such things exist. But if they do, do you have any idea of the cost of such an operation, not just of the equipment involved, but the placement of it, of the man-hours spent monitoring it, of the support systems that support the active systems, and the support systems that support the support systems, and the managerial labyrinth which underpins it all? What do you imagine you've done that would justify such an operation? How often are you even at *home* . . .?'

I made as if to answer. He didn't afford the opportunity.

'And when you *are* home, how often do you have company? And even when you *do* have company, what is it you talk about? Your hilarious smuggling exploits? Your atheism? *Nobody* is watching you,' he insisted. 'Nobody *wants* to watch you.'

I knew he was right. But I was right, too. I knew more about myself than he did – and in a dizzy moment I was thinking about the war and I was thinking about the hospital, and I was thinking about McArdle picking up the package in the car, but not McArdle exactly, about the face in the crowd behind the car, the vision of the huge albino.

I lifted the bag of groceries from the sidewalk.

'How do you know where I live?' I said.

Nathan sauntered off ahead. Isabel took my elbow again and led me on. I was following a stranger to my own door.

'You know how it is,' she said. 'Research. Friends of friends.'

I did not believe her.

Two *What She Knew About Me*

I lived in a one-room apartment on the fifth floor of a prefabricated block. It wasn't large. The mess inside had about it the characteristics of an exhibit, of a creature observed in its natural habitat, its den. The room had a sour animal smell, the stink of me. Towers of pizza boxes, cartons containing dried, mouldering, half-eaten burgers, crumpled cigarette cartons, crushed beer cans, improvised ashtrays, whiskey bottles, wine bottles, unravelling butts floating bloated in the dregs, margarine containers, cracked dishes and plates, arbitrary cutlery and mugs without handles. What clothes I had, shirts, T-shirts, jeans, what had been my good suit and underwear lay where I had discarded them: draped over armchairs, on the floor, stuffed into the corners, across the single bed. There was a pre-war television in one corner. I never watched it. I went other places to watch TV, places where I could be certain the transmission was one-way.

As they stepped over the threshold, I hurried to the window, lifting the blinds I never lifted, and wrestled it open. It took some effort. All the sounds of the night insinuated themselves in there with us. All the comings and goings outside, all the people that carried God within them.

I swept crap from the two armchairs, and began to kick as much mess as I could towards the far corner.

'Please,' said Isabel. 'Please don't bother.'

'I'm sorry,' I said. 'I'm not much of a housekeeper.'

She stepped (somewhat gingerly) into the kitchen area, swept aside some stacked plates and a couple of mouldering coffee mugs and set down the groceries. 'You should see

17

Nathan's study,' she said. She gave me an encouraging smile, but added: 'We should eat the chips from the bag, I think.'

I couldn't believe I was having this conversation. 'Good idea,' I said. 'Here, let me rinse some mugs.' I could find no cloth, but at least the water was hot and – when I was sure nobody was looking – I scratched away at crusted tide marks of coffee with a thumb nail. I shook excess water from my hands and dried them on my shirt.

'Do you have ice?'

'Yes,' I said. Before she could make a move to the refrigerator my heart went cold and I said: 'Here, please let me.' There were things there that I did not want her to see. Even I found the odour overpowering, although not enough to warrant cleaning it. I think I heard her gag as I opened the door.

While all this was going on, I was aware of Nathan sweeping the room with his little gadget. He had a look of childlike concentration on his face, had stooped a little and the pink corner of his tongue protruded from the corner of his mouth. He looked like a mad old man in a municipal park.

'We're free to talk,' he concluded eventually. 'The place is clean as a whistle.'

He and Isabel exchanged a secret glance. I had no idea what it communicated.

I poured us all a generous measure of gin (why not, she had paid) and bid them sit. I moved over to the bed and pulled across it the single sheet in order to cover the shame of my stains. I tossed my hat into the corner. It had begun to feel like a prop.

'I like the hat,' she said. 'Where did you get it?'

'Oh,' I said. 'It was a gift.'

'A ladyfriend?'

Ladyfriend? Good grief. Where was she *from*?

'No,' I said.

Nathan seemed comfortable enough, gin clasped loosely in a hand that rested on the arm of the disintegrating chair. Isabel, however, could not help but give the impression that she was primly but stoically allowing only the minimum amount of her minimal buttocks to make contact with the cushion.

'So,' I said.

Nathan raised his glass: 'Cheers,' he said.

I raised mine in return, said '*Salut*'. Instantly I felt gauche and pretentious. I took a cigarette. She did the same and threw over to me the gold lighter. As I lit, I noticed for the first time that it was inscribed: *With thanks. R.*

She got to her feet and went to the kitchen again, poured herself another gin. She addressed me without looking at me.

'I know you're unhappy about this . . .'

I took a handful of Doritos, on which I miserably crunched between puffs of Marlboro.

'Do you mind?' interjected Nathan, and set the bag of pistachios on his lap. He sat mostly in silence for the remainder of the conversation, grunting assent or otherwise, opening and eating nut after green salty nut in an unbroken sequence, like a looped film. I noted that he had grown the thumbnail of his right hand long and wondered if he had done so with this purpose in mind.

'. . . but we had reasons for coming to you and you alone.'

'Mmmmmm,' agreed Nathan, and popped another nut into his mouth. He was creating a little cairn of empty shells between his feet, and I thought of how Ruth would describe such an artefact were it found ten thousand years hence.

'*We have a code*,' she would say, because she had said it often and I never tired of hearing it said because it testified volumes to the cynicism which she gleefully acknowledged to underlie all fields of academic study: '*When we find an object whose function eludes us, we put it to one side and say: "Of ritual significance." What it means is, "We haven't got a fucking clue what this was for."*'

I had nothing to say.

'Although we've never actually met,' Isabel continued, 'we

have friends in common, and they all speak very highly of you.'

'Hold on a moment,' I said. For the first time I could feel myself becoming angry. 'I'm not happy that they speak about me at *all*.'

'Come now,' she said. 'Only in selected circles. Only amongst true friends.'

I could picture her, Isabel and two faceless but elegantly coiffed women sitting round a coffee table somewhere in the promised land of what had been the United States, the scrubbed clean skies outside, the sprinklers for the clipped lawn, the white picket fence, the sterile carpet, the gravel drive full of gleaming, monstrous automobiles, the cleanliness and the orderliness and the light of the love of God shining down upon them as they bandied about my filthy· name.

'There's no such thing,' I said. I realised that I was standing and felt big and clumsy and foolish.

'Come on,' she said. 'You know that's not true.'

I shrugged. 'Whatever.'

She returned from the kitchen and ground out her cigarette upon a plate on which egg-yolk had congealed to the consistency of mortar. I hate eggs. I only ever try to cook them when drunk and desperate, when they're all my neighbours have to lend me in order to make me go away. Sober, the idea of a yolk sac repulses me in a way I couldn't begin to describe. Soon I'll tell you about the chickens.

'Ruth Felton,' she said.

I looked up sharply and something liquid shifted in my guts. 'You know Ruth?'

'Since we were girls. Well, practically.'

This was designed to put me at my ease, but it did not. I didn't like hearing Ruth's name on this woman's lips, this woman who had called me 'Mr Thorndyke' in that confidently interrogative tone so few minutes before. I sucked in the remainder of the Marlboro and lit another from the butt.

'We're not that close,' I said.

'Mmmmmm,' said Nathan.

'She's extremely fond of you,' insisted Isabel. 'She speaks more highly of you than she does of her own son.'

I did not believe this to be true.

'How long have you known her, now?'

'Oh, I don't know,' I said. 'Seventeen years, eighteen. Since I was a kid.'

'And you met . . . in Israel, wasn't it? During the war?'

I swigged the last of the gin and, rolling the remains of the ice in the bottom of the glass, walked to the kitchen and poured myself a fistful of fingers. 'I was a member of the platoon assigned to guard a dig,' I said. 'She was working on a dig. Some big find or other. This is before they lost so many good men that rejects like me were considered suitable for combat duty.'

Good men. I might have choked on the phrase.

I drained the glass, filled it again. I was drinking myself cold. My hands had stopped shaking and I was no longer afraid.

'You fought, then?'

'Eventually. Not for long.'

'Injured?'

I topped up the glass once more and sat heavily on the bed. 'None of this is relevant.'

'I'm sorry,' she said. 'You're quite right. None of this is any of my business.'

A reflected beam of dirty yellow headlights swept briefly over the uneven ceiling. Flying insects battered themselves senseless on the thin mesh pinned over the open window, blinded by the false promise of the light.

I tugged at my crown. 'So, where do we go from here?'

'Well, *you* go to NJC,' she said. 'You travel in order to see the President's address in the Temple. While you're there, you deliver a small package. Then you come home again. Nathan and I are headed elsewhere.'

'I *bet* you are,' I said. 'No. It can't be done. The refusal stands.'

'It "can't be done"? Nonsense. It's a milk run,' she said. 'You've made far more difficult deliveries.'

I said: 'Don't try to flatter me.'

She seemed to think for a moment, then came and sat next to me on the edge of the bed. I could smell her, smell the powder, perfume and cleanliness of her. She smelled of the glittering new Zion. She smelled of America.

She set her hands in her lap and said: 'Why do you do this?'

I swallowed. 'I don't do it,' I said. 'That's exactly my point. I don't do it.'

'There are easier ways to make money, easier ways to make far *more* money if you're willing to break the law. To smuggle.'

I stood and walked to the window, where I felt absurdly inflated and melodramatic, framed by the halo of New Winchester lamplight.

New Winchester. New this. New that. Everything was New, everything was called New, but we all knew that this was not the case, that what it was, what we were, was worn out and on the brink, despite what Staad had achieved. And like all who loathed him from the pit of their stomach, I had to admit that he had delivered on his promise. Staad had saved the world.

'This is important,' she said. 'This will be the most important document you will ever have delivered.'

I admit my ears pricked up at that, but immediately I was overcome with something like grief for how I had wasted my life. I hung my head and my hair fell over my eyes. That I had endured all that results from refusing to lie to yourself about what to believe, in order to smuggle books.

Books. It even *sounded* like a sob the way I pronounced it to myself. Books that the Church had for one reason or another proscribed. Books that propounded theories, scientific or philosophical or whatever fucking form an unorthodox idea can be given in order to express it, that ran contrary to the Church's concept of the establishment of God's Kingdom on Earth. It was like running parchment for the Cathars. I ran a thriving little cottage industry that specialised in the dissemination of what I can only describe as heretical material. Sometimes it took the form of old movies, copied to disk, like clay tablets unearthed in the savage desert, dating from the time when Hollywood was Babylon. That was an easier, less risky market and often I watched the movies I had gone to such trouble to deliver, although never on my own television. You could never be sure who was monitoring. But mostly it was books. Digitised text, occasionally actual volumes, cloth or leather-bound, even dried and yellowing paperbacks. Some people didn't just want the word. They wanted the artefact. There was really no trick to it, no trick at all. I'd heard tales, apocryphal naturally, of people in a similar line of business who'd had surgery which enabled them to download information straight into their cortex. All cyber bullshit. Cleverness gets you caught. The government has access to technologies far more sophisticated than you'll ever imagine. It was a curious dialect between me and them, the people who wanted to catch me. At border points and – who knows? – elsewhere, they scanned me, monitored me, with equipment it takes months to learn how to use, they looked for cybernetic implants and Christ knows what else, and all the time I had the booty hiding in plain sight: if it was a disk, I'd have it in a little container which contained twenty other disks: photo-albums, games, diaries (faked), even legitimate theology and sanctioned philosophy. One day they'll switch off their machines and get back to patting pockets.

The customers were inevitably desiccated old liberals, 'free thinkers' who belonged to a series of different generations, none of which was mine, who remained useful to the Church to which they paid inevitable lip service. They made for a curious underground, with their bad haircuts and questionable clothes and their politeness even in the act of breaking the law. I have lost count of the number of times I was offered a cup of tea or perhaps a gin and tonic. I delivered to them books with which I would probably have disagreed – I seldom bothered to read them. Books which I would not have understood had I tried. Perhaps books I myself would have banned if afforded the opportunity.

Out of this I had constructed my crusade. Out of this I had attempted vengeance upon that which was not there.

I was a mockery of a human being.

'No document is that important,' I said.

'This one is.'

'To whom?'

I felt her shrug.

'It's a waste of time,' I said. 'It's not worth it. It's just words written by a human being who in the end knows no more than you or I. It's just the same supposition with more syllables.'

The sound of Nathan cracking and eating pistachios, the soft munching of a timid forest mammal.

'It's a piece of the truth,' she insisted.

'I don't believe in that.'

'So I see.' She lit a cigarette and puffed on it, not without anger, crossing her arms and tapping at her lips with an index finger. 'This is why you've spent so much time, exerted so much effort and cleverness for scant financial reward – for something you don't care about?'

I looked at the floor, read the headline of an old newspaper that lay crumpled on the floor – the announcement that a number of dependencies were planning to re-instigate the Olympic games.

'Then I can make you wealthy,' she said. 'I'm willing to pay you a great deal of money. Certainly more than you've ever earned before.'

Although there was no longer much that was funny about the evening I forced a laugh.

'No,' I said.

'Even money won't sway you?'

'What good would it do me?' A tone of mournful self pity had established itself by now. 'What would I spend it on? *Who* would I spend it on? Look at what I've done with my life.' I gestured to the room about us.

'I can see what you've done with your *room*,' she agreed. 'What you've done with your *life* is another thing. I think you've led rather an admirable life.'

I ignored her. I too could be partially deaf when I chose.

'And anyway, what's the bank going to think if all this money turns up unannounced in my account?'

'Well,' she said. 'How are you normally paid? How do you normally account for untaxed credit?'

I tugged at my jowls. Coughed. 'I had a system,' I said. 'I relied on a contact. I'm not willing to do that any more.'

Isabel and her husband exchanged another of those tiny, cabalistic glances.

'We could call it a gift,' she teased. 'An informal bursary.'

'From you to me? What is there to connect us? How should I explain if it's investigated?'

'We'd work something out. I'm not without connections of my own.'

I laughed, coughed, swallowed phlegm. 'I bet you're not,' I said.

She gave me the full-wattage glow of that smile, but this time it was full of savage humour. 'We'll say you saved my son's life during the war.' Even through the gauze of inebriation I was aware that she was toying with me, like a housecat, domestic but full of feral irony, offering you a knitted mouse in the hope that, in thinking it wants to play, you afford it the opportunity of gleefully ripping your flesh with its unsheathed claws.

'I didn't save anybody's life,' I said. 'I'm not that kind of person. They could check that out in seconds. We could give them a laugh: let them look at my war record.'

'Now you're being hard on yourself,' she said. 'It's the alcohol talking. Anyway, there's Ruth. She connects us.'

'No way. No. They'd find out.'

I did not want to hear Ruth's name mentioned again.

Isabel joined me at the window, stood a centimetre away from me. Her face had fallen expressionless and her voice was chilly and precise. She popped her claws.

'I know about Sonny Marshall,' she said. 'I know what you did to Sonny.'

The room went white and I stumbled forward into the window frame. Before I was able to formulate a response I vomited into my hands and staggered to the sink, where I ejected a great deal of the junk food and gin I had recently imbibed. My legs were weak and the room seemed to pitch and roll. I could hear the tide, the oceanic roar of blood in my ears.

When I lifted my head, sniffing back a grey bubble of snot, I could tell that neither she nor Nathan had moved.

'Are you the police?' I said.

'For Christ's *sake*,' she spat.

I rested my elbows against the sink and buried my face in my palms. 'Then who are you?'

'Friends of friends,' she repeated. Comically enough, given the circumstances.

I wiped at my lips. They might have belonged to somebody else. 'And what do you think you know about Sonny Marshall?'

'I've told you all you need to hear.' She held her forehead, thumb massaging temple, a cigarette smouldering away between two fingers. 'You forced me to say that. Do you think I *wanted* to say that? I'd already offered you *money*, for Christ's sake.'

Finally, Nathan had stopped eating pistachios. Perhaps he'd finished the packet, I don't know. He squeezed past me and took a Beck's. I began to giggle. I couldn't stop. I stood there rubbing at my lips and giggling. It sounded like the spirit of an insane child in possession of a grown man.

When the giggles had passed all I could say was: 'Jesus Christ, Jesus Christ,' over and over, and with each repetition of the words I heard their various meanings, their unfathomable connotations, remembered the many contexts in which I had used them during my life, until they became nonsense, until they became meaningless sounds, words without substance.

I ran the cold faucet, stooped under the flow. Chilled water shocked me over the nape of my grimy neck, behind my ears, into my dry and gritty eyes. I splashed my face. My hair fell sodden and dripping over my brow and I swept it back with one hand. 'What an *idiot*,' I said.

She regarded me with a degree of sympathy. 'I didn't want it to come to this,' she said. 'Really I didn't.'

I hung my head and droplets of water rolled down the contours of my face, down that great Roman beak I call my nose. 'What else?' I said. The fearlessness had settled back over me, the inebriate nihilism I well remembered – which I well remembered bitterly regretting on many a bright and hung-over morning and on one morning in particular, one morning when I became scared to know myself. 'What else can you tell me about myself?' My fist closed about the handle of a heavy aluminium pot. I know what my face looks like when I feel like this.

'*Malachi.*' Nathan's voice had about it an arresting gentleness and for a moment I considered sweeping the pan in a wide arc, caving in the side of his chalky, brittle old skull. Just to hear its hollow idiot chime and watch Isabel's face as he stumbled back and down and did not get up ever again. Just to see it hurt her.

I dropped the pan into the sink – into the last watery swirl of vomit – and ran my hands through my dripping hair.

'Give me a minute,' I said.

'I know this can't be easy,' she said.

'Oh,' I laughed and wiped my eyes. 'You know that, do you?'

'I know that,' she said, and she arched her eyebrow once more. She drained her glass and crossed her arms across her tiny breasts, beating out a distracted rhythm with the empty glass.

'I know everything,' she said. 'I know all there is to know.'

27

She told me what she knew, and with a wry little smile let me know that what she knew was of course compiled in a dossier, which was far away, in safe hands. Given the nature of what she knew, she considered this a necessarily prophylactic measure.

'Dossier,' I said, 'is my least favourite word. I never wanted to hear it in the same sentence as my name. I dream about that.'

She agreed. 'It does have a particularly corporate feel to it. Dossier.'

'Well,' I said. 'You know how to talk the corporate talk.'

'And walk the corporate walk,' she said.

Nathan laid a hand on her shoulder and addressed me: 'By any means necessary –', he said. It was a quote I recognised from one of those old movies I had smuggled and watched. I forget which. There had been so many. The lurid primary colours, the speed, the noise, the violence, the witless wisecracks, the energy of a world that had passed away. All that violence and sentiment.

Resignation brought with it a curious relief. I kept saying it aloud: 'Dossier,' and following up with a humourless little snort. As if giving voice would make it real. As if the world would follow the design of the word.

I opened a Beck's and toasted them: 'What can I say?'

She shrugged, walked to the kitchen and filled her glass. She could drink. 'You don't have to say anything,' she said.

Nathan returned my toast: 'Your statutory rights are not affected.'

'How very Christian of you,' I said.

Isabel laughed properly at this. It was like someone had turned the lights on again. Such a smile. I don't know why, I still could not begin to explain, but in that moment, hanging my head in the light of her elegance and beauty and power, I was glad that they were with me. Glad that someone, anyone, had at last come to find me.

★　★　★

28

We drank for a while in silence. It was not uncomfortable. When we were drunk they asked me about Ruth. It was something to talk about. But Ruth wasn't there. Ruth was absent from the conversation, although present in the words.

Sonny was there. Sonny was there in the room with us, Sonny was watching us from the darkness of the corner and they could sense him as much as I. The blankness of his face. A whispering echo of his voice from long ago, from the war, from Cairo: 'Am I awake?'

No, Sonny. No, you're not awake this time.

When it became clear that – naturally – they had no intention of leaving, I offered my bed and they accepted with thanks and not even a cursory grimace. They curled around each other like children, spooning, his knees tucked behind hers, his hand resting protectively against her belly and she made a little, contented smile and a little purr of pleasure and nuzzled her ass into him.

They knew I could not hurt them. I watched them for a long time and then I picked up the jacket of what had been my good suit, patted it into a pillow and fell asleep in the armchair.

Three

```
File code: 100046/macd
Username: sicarius
Password: ******
Last Updated: **/**/**
```

File DMWITRES Located.

Please wait.

File DMWITRES Retrieved.

Warning: This File Has Been Cloaked. Should You Wish to Decloak, Press Return. If You Wish to Quit, Press Escape.

If You Wish to Decloak, Please Ensure That Your Software is Code Protected, and Save Any Files Recently Modified.

Please wait.

Code Accessed and Identified. Print 65385922, Licence Confirmed. Outlet Confirmed.

*** Please Note. Decloaked Files Have Been Encrypted According to a System Restricted to the Use of Government Personnel Only. WARNING. Unauthorised Use of this System of Encryption Constitutes an Offence Punishable By Law. Unauthorised Personnel Should Quit

From McArdle's Journal:

(Final Entry)

As I type at the kitchen table, Naomi is upstairs, busily
preparing for a dinner party from which I cried off, and about
which I lacked the stamina to argue. My daughter is visiting
with us, although I have hinted, as politely as I am able, that I
think it best she does not: I tell her I will pay for her to spend
her vacation broadening her mind with travel. I tell her she
should see as much of the world as she is able, because it is
precious. I tell her that when she was a child we truly believed
that there might not be a world for her to grow up in. Not
without humour (a woman, she is still so young), she accuses
me of becoming a sanctimonious old grouch, she urges me to
get a life, and I hurt inside, I wish that what is about to occur
would not. I wish that it might somehow be magicked away. I
yearn for the days when my daughter was a child. Now she is
grown I miss her even when she is under my roof. I wonder
exactly where she has gone. I wonder where they've all gone,
all those people who feature in the journal that records those
unforgotten days. Even, especially, the man who wrote them.

I know Ruth is headed in my direction and with her a
shadowy figure. I know it will be the one I have met before, if
one could describe it as a meeting. He had about him a tension
which frightened Naomi, as it frightened me, although I
would not admit to it. After recognising me, I remember him
looking past us, over the roof of the car, across the street. He

31

seemed to see something that dismayed him, that rendered him incapable of movement.

I hope it's not that man again, although I suspect it will be. Soon they will come knocking on my door, Ruth and this man who has kept the truth, this anti-gospel, this *bad news*, safe on our behalf, moving it from hand to hand, from land to land. I wonder if he ever had any idea what it was he carried. I suspect not.

I hope not.

So, I must acknowledge their arrival, Ruth and this man, this dismal messenger. I will answer the door to their accusation that I sold my soul cheaply, and surely I must answer their demand also that finally I should meet my responsibility. They cry out for my atonement.

The time has come to recognise that our achievements and our crimes are a creation of a single nature, indivisible. I am very scared.

Four *Desinformatsiya*

I woke at noon with a crick in my neck and something unpleasantly adhesive gumming the lids of my eyes.

I could hear tentative shuffling in the kitchen. My first word of the new morning was: 'Tylenol.'

I prised open my eyes between finger and thumb. Nathan wore a night's growth of white stubble. He looked like a vagrant. He was padding about the kitchen in stockinged feet. I heard a hiss and a glug and he was setting before me a mug of Coca-Cola and two analgesics. I dry-swallowed them and drank the Coke. Tilting my head to drink sent a little spasm of pain down the left hand side of my neck. I massaged my shoulder. 'Jesusfuckingchristohgod,' I said.

He was boiling the kettle. I stood on bambi legs and joined him.

'How do you take it?' he said, cleaning off a coffee spoon.

'Badly,' I said. He didn't get the joke, so I added: 'Very, very strong. Indecently strong, please.'

'Sugar?'

'Lots and lots of sugar.'

He held up the spoon and wiggled it at his ear. 'I've measured out my life in these,' he said. It was my turn not to get the joke so I looked at him blankly. He looked away and made coffee.

Isabel was in the bathroom. She emerged looking exactly as she had the previous evening, her hair pinned back and her straight, below-the-knee skirt and white silk blouse free of wrinkles or stains. I genuinely envied her ability to do this.

'How do you feel?' she asked.

'Like I look,' I answered. 'What about you?'

'Like you look.' She smiled.

Nathan handed me a mug.

'We should leave this morning,' she said.

'It's noon,' said Nathan.

She looked at him snakewise. 'We should leave *today*. As soon as possible.'

I held the mug between cupped hands and blew across the scalding surface of the Nescafé. The room was uncomfortably stuffy, the aircon playing up again. I dreaded to think what it smelled like. 'I can't,' I said. 'I have contractual obligations.'

Isabel spooned sugar into her mug and stirred. 'There are ways round contractual obligations. I took the liberty of contacting your foreman. I'm rather ashamed to admit that I pretended to be your mother. I told him your father was very ill. That you hadn't spoken for fifteen years. He was a very nice man.'

He was not a very nice man at all. He had a belly and a drinker's nose with a distractingly penile tip and after everything that had happened he still used the word nigger, yid, abbo. And he was French. I am English and genetically predisposed to disliking the French. He hated women, the syphilitic old bastard, but he feared them too. I could imagine the effect Isabel had on him.

'You've been granted temporary leave of absence,' she said. 'Unfortunately your pay has been suspended. There was nothing I could do about that, I'm afraid. On that count he was most unhelpful.'

I sat in silence, thinking about my parents, of what they would have thought of the life I'd led, of the things I've done. Of how they had built a new life in a new country because of me. For the love of me.

'Malachi?'

'Yes?'

'Did you hear what I said?'

'Yes,' I said. 'Yes, I'm sorry. I was miles away.'

After drinking his coffee, Nathan left the apartment and

34

returned within minutes at the wheel of a car. As he struggled up the stairs with two calfskin suitcases, I said to Isabel: 'I see they've repaired the hire car.'

She laid a cool hand on my shoulder and said: 'I believe it's called a ruse.'

I looked her square in the face and said: 'You're a very good liar.'

She did not break my gaze, nor remove her hand from my shoulder. 'I had to learn to be,' she said.

'Why?' I said. 'Why did you have to learn?'

'Look at me,' she said. 'Look at what I'm doing.'

I broke the gaze, turned away, began to search for a cigarette. 'I don't *know* what you're doing,' I said. 'How can I know what you're doing when, even if you told me, I wouldn't know whether to believe you? How can I know anything you've told me is true?'

She laughed. 'You can't and you don't. You just have to believe.'

'Very good,' I said. 'You're suggesting that I put my faith in you?'

'All that faith has to go somewhere,' she said.

Nathan laid a suitcase of the floor and flicked open the brass clasps. The Beaumonts had very nice luggage.

He disappeared into the bathroom, emerging some time later shaved, bathed and fresh with *eau de cologne* in a cool linen suit and an open-necked shirt. He had a Panama hat which he removed from a cardboard roll. He had not properly applied the sunblock. There was a white dab of it on the tip of his nose.

'Don't you look quite the thing?' Isabel said. She leaned over him and wiped the little smear of sunblock away. He scowled but accepted the ministration.

Isabel stooped to pick up her own suitcase and closed the bathroom door behind her. When she reappeared, it was in a cream linen trouser suit, which she wore open at the throat, a little pearl choker around her neck. She carried a large pair of oval sunglasses in a breast pocket.

Isabel and Nathan looked at me expectantly. I offered them apologetic palms but did at least brush my teeth before we left.

I directed Nathan to a diner and we stopped for an hour to breakfast. Nathan sounded awkwardly English saying, 'Over easy', and curled his lip in polite distaste at the amount of syrup I poured on my pancakes. I did the same watching him chase yolk about his plate with a corner of bread.

We drove without a break through endless reclaimed farmland, arriving at Docklands sometime in the early hours of the morning. We stopped off at a convenience store, where I bought myself the toiletries I required, then proceeded to the Sheraton. Isabel had booked us rooms.

I was rapturously seduced by the impersonal cleanliness of my room, of the taut bed and the television and the minibar, of the glistening surfaces and miniature soaps of the bathroom. It was a space designed for temporary living which yet had about it no indication of previous occupancy, no sense of having been *used*. Although tired after travelling, I found time to do the things that people have done in hotel rooms since before the mythical biblical census, where Joseph the Cuckold and Mary the Sinless dumped God's bastard in a pile of itching, shit-stinking straw as an introduction to the unfortunate nature of his creation. I picked up the phone and ordered a club sandwich. I left my clothes to be laundered. I took a scalding hot bath – I had only a shower at the apartment – and let the cool angel's breath of the air-conditioning dry me as I carefully shaved. I wiped steam from the mirror with my hand and looked at myself for too long.

Do you know what I look like? Ha! From the top: I have black hair thinning to a vampiric peak, which I oil back because I am sufficiently self-obsessed that privately I imagine it makes me look appropriately Satanic. I have a sallow, thin face, hollow at the temples and the unpleasant eyes I think I've already mentioned (have I mentioned that I seem to have something wrong with my eyes?), and this great ploughshare of a beak. I have bad teeth, the bottom row yellow and stained, like old gravestones collapsing upon one another. I have overdeveloped incisors which I rather like. They are very English teeth. That's another thing – I have never easily been able to voice the word 'orthodontist'. Englishmen use dentists. Or rather don't, in my case. And I'm skinny and inelegant, with a small roll of pasty fat about my middle. And I have hairy feet. So there you are. Malachi Thorndyke. This year's model.

I bunched my bare feet into fists in the deep pile of the carpet and sat naked on the edge of the bed while I ate the club sandwich. I breathed in the cleanliness, the odourless odour of the kind of hotel I'm seldom able to afford. Even the cockroaches were deferential.

That's a joke. The Sheraton was too lifeless to support wildlife. All over Australia things I did not want to think about crept and crawled and scuttled on more legs than was decent, or slithered on no legs at all. Those creatures that were equipped to survive the last three human generations had done so with a sinister glee. I had found things in my apartment that had no right to be there. More than once I had required the aid of my neighbour, Michael, in their disposal. Even though each morning I ritually banged my boots from the heel, putting them on was a daily trial, a triumph of the will. But nothing lived in the Sheraton that did not pay its way.

In the morning my workclothes were set outside my door, laundered and pressed. I took another bath and ordered breakfast in my room, no eggs. While I was finishing it, there were two raps at the door. Isabel and I said good morning, and then she took me shopping.

She took me to a barber and sat, legs crossed, reading *Cosmopolitan*, as a plump old Italian applied hot towels to my face before shaving me closer than I had ever been shaved. He washed and trimmed my hair, shaping it meticulously square at the nape with a cut-throat razor. I found the intensity of his concentration on me oddly hypnotic, and as he combed my hair back into its dracula peak, the teeth of the comb sent tingles of pleasure across my scalp.

She bought me three suits, two casual, one formal three piece, all in shades of neutral grey. She bought me seven white shirts with a conservative, button-down collar. She chose the ties. She was wise to do so. She insisted on a pair of leather lace-up shoes. I had not worn shoes for so long my ankles felt exposed and vulnerable. She had me sized for a hat. I was loathe to lose the Stetson, but she chose a grey fedora with a black band. She made me change immediately into a casual suit.

I felt like a different person, crisp and pressed and bathed. That was fine by me. I had wanted to be a different person for as long as I could remember.

I was born again, crisp and fresh as an apple.

We left the remainder of the clothes (along with my work clothes and beloved Stetson, stuffed into a heartbreakingly loose parcel) while she led me off to buy me some luggage. I accepted what she chose without comment. It was not as luxurious as her own.

She took me for lunch. Sitting at the table, I wondered aloud if I might be allowed to order for myself. She seemed vaguely affronted, and did not speak until her Caesar salad arrived. She said: 'Do you feel better?'

I admitted that I did.

'Good,' she said. 'Have you *always* lived like that?'

I shrugged and sawed at the steak that flopped over the rim of my plate.

'It was a gradual but inexorable decline.'

'Try not to speak with your mouth full,' she said. 'Or to eat with your mouth open. Remember where you're going.'

I looked at her.

'I'm being serious,' she said. 'This is important.'

I speared a french fry on the tines of the fork and said: 'I've done this *before*, you know.'

She sat back in the chair and said: 'I know you have. I know

38

you have but, without going into unnecessary detail, I want to ensure that I've impressed on you how important it is that this goes well.'

I opened my mouth to speak, closed it, swallowed the mouthful of food then said:

'No, *go* into details. Go into all the details you like.'

She rested her elbow on the table, her chin in the cup of her hand. 'It's a film,' she said.

'A movie? Jesus, it must be a good one.' But my testicles had withdrawn. A little biological detail for you.

'And remember not to blaspheme.'

'I shall endeavour not to take His name in vain,' I said.

'Good,' she continued, blithely. 'Look; it's more of a, I don't know, a documentary.'

That was as much as I wanted to know. We ate in silence. After the passage of some time she said: 'So, let's pretend this is a normal meal between two normal friends. Tell me more about yourself.'

I poured Budweiser too quickly. Its frothing head over-ran the rim of the glass and made a damp pool on the starched white tablecloth.

'Oh, *no*,' I said, '– you already know quite enough about me.'

She protested: 'What you *do*, not who you are . . .'

'Oh, no, no, no, no, *no*' I said. 'That's far too cosy a homily for you, Mrs Beaumont. You won't sneak by me that way.' She rewarded me with an indulgent, feline smile. 'What about you and Nathan? How long have you been together?'

'*Married*. Twenty-eight years.'

'Twenty-eight *years*. Is such a thing possible?'

'More than. It merely requires faith in the relationship.'

'Well,' I said. 'I'm not too big on faith.'

'I'm aware.' She laid the knife and fork parallel on the plate. The salad was less than half eaten. 'But you were different once, weren't you?'

39

I chewed steak. Swallowed. 'So how did you and Nathan come to meet?'

She accepted my side-step, but before she replied a look I could neither understand nor properly describe passed across her face. It was almost ghostly. 'A mutual friend,' she said.

'I see,' I looked away, uncomfortable. '– And what do you both do? Other than this, that is.'

'Oh, ordinarily we don't do *this*,' she said. 'This is a first-time thing for both of us. No. I'm an architect and Nathan works in a governmental capacity.'

My smile dropped.

She reached out her hand and took mine. I wanted her to let go. 'The government isn't as faceless an edifice as you seem to presume,' she said. 'It's full of real people, and many of them – many of *us* – find the idea of –' she paused, decided what the hell, continued, '– censorship as abhorrent as you and I. It's absurd that you believe we're all bigots, keeping our manic bigoted eye trained on your every movement. They're only *books*, for goodness sake. They're only *ideas* – many of them absurd ideas at that. It's only a minority who could care less about them. But it's a rabid and vocal minority that it's politic to appease.'

'*Us*,' I said, 'when used in that particular context is my second least favourite word.'

I thought of McArdle, the sour-faced woman handing him the package. And the albino. The albino grinning at me.

Us, I thought.

'Of course, *us*,' she said. 'Ultimately, we're all employed by the Church in one way or another. I design buildings for them.'

'Churches?'

'Good *Lord*, no. I design functional buildings. I was going to say "buildings with a purpose". Imagine.'

'I see.' I pushed the plate from me and lifted the glass of beer: I sipped away the spitelessness. 'So why are you doing this? What is there in this for you?'

'Faith doesn't necessitate the repression of uncomfortable, even contradictory ideas,' she replied. 'Quite the opposite. Kierkegaard . . .'

I smiled. 'That didn't answer the question.'

'– suggested that faith is justified by its very absurdity, by the fact that there are so many other things in which it is far, far easier to believe. Faith requires contradiction in order for it truly to constitute faith. He called such faith heroic. I believe that to be axiomatic.'

'I believe it to be heretical.'

'Such is your right as an atheist.'

'*Touché.* But you still haven't answered the question.'

'And I'm not going to.'

'Which answers it satisfactorily enough.'

'*Touché* in return.'

There was a pleasant pause before we burst into gentle laughter.

'Enough about me,' she said. 'More about you. Are you alone? Is there someone?'

'No,' I said.

'Has there ever been someone?'

'Not really,' I said, but that was a lie. Of course there had been someone. There always is someone, isn't there, swimming languid in the shadows beneath the sunlit surface of our biographies. There is always someone.

I was back from the war, physically mended – physically *reorganised*. I imagined that the things I'd seen and the things I'd done had forged me into a person.

The way she smiled when I made stupid jokes (jokes, jokes, always jokes) and jumped around like a moron, the way her eyes, she had beautiful eyes, met mine for too long when we spoke, filled me, made me want to burst with something I couldn't describe. Something violently incandescent and ineffable, something like a choir holding a single note at transcendent volume. She was – she seemed, I don't know, I *remember* her as being – so beautiful the thought of her still makes a wave of something pass across the flesh of my back, as if fingers had been drawn across me. If I had a photograph I could demonstrate exactly the contours of her face when she laughed, the lines from her nose to the corners of her mouth, the lines in her forehead that would one day become frown lines, the striata at the corners of her eyes. When she laughed something bright exploded just behind my eyes and gravity got weak around me.

I longed to take her wrists in my hands and pull her to me, to twist the short hairs at the nape of her neck and bury my stupid face – my ugly face, the face that was inanimate when it wasn't joking, when she wasn't around – behind the curve of her ear, and breathe deep the transcendent, the holy smell of her, the church-and-incense musk of her neck and I wanted to record, to commit to memory every detail of the skip of her tongue on mine, the way she closed her eyes and groaned the one time we – the one time I was inside her, the agonising slowness of that groan. We were drunk and clumsy and cold and all my patience, all my tenderness was forgotten by the need just to be inside her and I came too quickly, I couldn't help it and I wanted her to masturbate until she was done, for her to do for herself what I was unable to do for her and then I wanted her to turn to me, slow and satisfied and take my face in her hands and say: 'I love you', but she didn't do that, she didn't say that. She just sighed and turned away and I wrapped myself about her and cupped her breast while she slept, her nipple hard beneath my palm. I moulded my body to the curve of her and committed her to memory. The way her eyes juddered rapidly beneath the thin membrane of her lids (Did she dream of me? Has she *ever* dreamed of me?), the way her fingers and the muscles of her calves twitched as she dreamed. The down at her nape. The softness and terrible vulnerability of the soles of her feet, the caps of her knees, the heartbreaking, soft warmth of her belly. But we had been drunk and on the bus in the morning I touched the back of her hand and she smiled and looked sad – sadder than anyone had a right to be and for a moment I was visited by a giddying fantasy of a great wooden table in a great, clean kitchen and newspapers and coffee and pancakes and beams of bright sunlight glittering with the softly spinning motes of our domesticity. And my children, angelic and boisterous in their cotton pyjamas, and my wife insisting on reading the paper before I did and not speaking much before the second cup of coffee, while I ran after the kids and tickled them and made them breakfast and made sure they ate and got them dressed and sent them to school. I wanted to breathe them all in – the beautiful, milky warmth of my children and the familiar, wonderful musk of my wife.

But it was a fantasy and it lasted a second and it was gone.

There was someone else, naturally. There is always someone, and there is always someone else. A better man. He was all that she wanted and he, of course, did not want her. Such are the machinations of Creation, cheap and obscure in their glorious injustice.

There is always someone. But there is always another, one who goes unknown, one who is unknowable.

Ha ha ha.

'There's just me and the Good Lord,' I said.

Isabel looked at me without expression. 'Such bitterness.'

'Sweetness came forth out of the mighty,' I said. 'For the meek and the weak and the despised all that we inherit is this –' I waved my hand about me. 'What's left of the Earth.'

She frowned, and thought. 'You must believe in something,' she said, 'or somebody. We must all have faith in something. If not how do we carry on?'

I lit a cigarette. 'What *is* there?'

She looked at the table and quietly repeated it to herself, testing it for weight: 'What is there?'

Then she caught the attention of a passing waitress and got the bill.

In the evening we got down to business. I sat in their suite.

They had a suite.

We drank glasses of Scotch. Isabel and I smoked a train of cigarettes.

She handed over a small package, small enough to fit in the palm of my hand, and said: 'Here it is. Do with it whatever it is you do.'

I pocketed it and replied: 'There's no trick. If they look for it, they'll find it.'

'They'll have to know what to look for first.'

I tried to look confident. 'If there's a trick.' I said, 'then that's it.'

She gave me my instructions. She insisted that I didn't write them down. I wondered aloud if she was not becoming as paranoid as I.

She said: 'Perhaps.'

She gave me two other things. First a gun, a utilitarian pistol which I could carry unobtrusively beneath a suit.

I declined with a laugh. 'I wouldn't have the courage to use it even if the need arose.'

'It won't,' she said. 'But take it anyway.'

I took it anyway.

Then there was the gold lighter. She lit a cigarette with it then pressed it into my palm and said: 'For luck.'

I bounced it in my palm once, twice, then caught and pocketed it. I thought of all those old movies. I read the inscription once more: *With thanks. R.*

Nathan shook my hand. He patted my shoulder.

'The gadget,' I said, 'The bug detector. It was –'

'It's a cellular phone,' he said.

He had seemed to enjoy sweeping the room with it so very much.

Isabel kissed me on the cheek and I turned and I left the room and I went to bed.

The ship left at six thirty the following morning. When I awoke with the dawn I knew by a change in the quality of the air that they had already gone.

Five

File code: 100046/macd
Username: sicarius
Password: ******
Last Updated: **/**/**

File DMWITRES Located.

Please wait.

File DMWITRES Retrieved.

*Warning: This File Has Been Cloaked. Should You Wish
to Decloak, Press Return. If You Wish to Quit, Press
Escape.*

*If You Wish to Decloak, Please Ensure That Your
Software is Code Protected, and Save Any Files Recently
Modified.*

Please wait.

*Code Accessed and Identified. Print 65385922, Licence
Confirmed, Outlet Confirmed.*

**** Please Note. Decloaked Files Have Been Encrypted
According to a System Restricted to the Use of
Government Personnel Only. WARNING. Unauthorised
Use of this System of Encryption Constitutes an Offence
Punishable By Law. Unauthorised Personnel Should Quit*

Hello, David, How Are You?

From McArdle's Journal:

June 1

Arrived home round midnight. Naomi had waited up. She had been drinking.

The moment I closed the door behind me, she said – How long is this going to carry on? All this *bull*shit.

I told her again this was not a question I was able to answer and she said – I'm your *wife*, for Christ's sake.

I asked her to keep her voice down, to mind her language. I was angry that she had been drinking while alone in charge of Susan.

I sometimes wonder if, as they lie in secrecy and darkness, safeguarding us from the unlikely possibility of assassination, the special agents we never see listen to these conversations. It is an obscurely humiliating idea.

She looked at me with contempt and I went upstairs to bed. I heard the television playing to her downstairs. During the night I woke. Naomi lay alongside but facing away from me. I moved my foot to touch hers and knew she was awake and angry. It was Susan that had woken me. In her pyjamas, her face soft with sleep. I love her most when she's like this, soft with sleep, Captain Howdy clasped in her little fist.

I let her climb into bed. Naomi shifted and tutted, not without jealousy. I curled around my daughter and she nuzzled her little behind into me, rubbing her soft, tiny feet to warm them. I kissed the crown of her head.

– God bless, baby, I said to the top of her head.

– Ssshhhh, Daddy, she whispered. – Peeps now.

Peeps: sleep. One day she will forget she ever said this magical word and I will have to remind her. Perhaps she will have daughters of her own then. I will watch her tickle them, this excited little group of my grandchildren, and she will say – See, Mommy was a little girl once: Mommy was a little girl just like you.

I will be an old man, then, and all this will be over.

June 20

Perhaps because next week sees my birthday, yesterday evening, instead of making an entry in this journal, I found myself reviewing it. Reading over my life. Astonishing, how one becomes accustomed to the world: how the extraordinary becomes commonplace.

I have been alongside Randall now for more years than I had been on this earth before I met him.

I cannot believe that I was ever twenty-two. Was I ever twenty-two? How did I become this man – this *fat* man – unaccustomed to this increasingly protesting body? I have pains in my knees. In the morning they creak. On wet days my knuckles can be so stiff I have to loosen the joints by wriggling them like a children's party conjurer. I take vitamin pills although my diet is superbly balanced. I worry about my potency. My dick seems more wrinkled and shrivelled every time I take a look at it in the bedroom mirror.

This morning Naomi caught me doing just that, after I had showered. I started. How absurd, that it remains possible for me to be embarrassed in front of this woman!

She put a hand on one hip, comically jutted. Regarded me from beneath an arched brow. She said: Taking in the sights?

I patted my belly and ran my fingers through the coarsening, grizzling hair that curls around my navel. I asked if I was running to fat.

47

She said: Goodness me! Do I detect a hint of the birthday blues?

She did, she did. I dressed, a little sulkily, and walked downstairs. In shirtsleeves, I sat at the kitchen table, a fresh coffee at my elbow, hunched over and scowling into this machine. My fingers are too big for its delicate keys. I type awkwardly and hesitantly.

Susan sat opposite me, devoting intense, brow-furrowing concentration to making a concrete-like paste of her breakfast. A spoon and her breakfast bowl decorated with two cartoon characters, a pig in a pink beret and a wolf in blue dungarees, were her mortar and pestle. My wife snuck up from behind and hugged me. She crossed her hands over my belly, nuzzled my ear.

Big Poppa Bear, she said. Going all grizzly.

I liked that.

Naomi ruffled my hair and caught Susan's attention. Who is this? She said.

Big pop *bear*! said my daughter. She incandesced for a moment, before returning, with a frown to whatever task the breakfast cereal had set her about.

They trust me.

Everybody trusts me. Being trusted is exhausting.

It is Randall's task to oversee my own project as he oversees the war. It must cause some vertigo: the logistics of stemming the chaos, stemming the tidal flood of death, to immerse himself in that, and yet to find time for me and my frustrations.

I'm tired, I told him.

We're all tired, he said.

I don't believe I'm up to it, I said.

He sucked his teeth. Perhaps that humility is your most important qualification.

I don't know, sir. I really don't. It just seems too big. So many loose ends. I mean, I know more about building materials, their cost and relative values, than I believed was possible a year ago. And that's a hundredth of my task, you know? An infinite little footnote to the requirements of the job. I mean ask me how, I don't know, marble and concrete compare as construction materials. Go on. Ask anything. Ask about their relative acoustic values. Ask me about the relative values of direct and indirect taxation.

He laughed. Taxation? David, come on, show some imagination. Call direct taxation a *tithe*.

Welfare! I said. Let me talk to you about welfare. Do you know how impossible it is to divorce opinion from fact over anything in a field like welfare? I'm running out of courage. I'm taking policy decisions I'm not qualified to take.

David, he said. Listen to the still, small voice. Find a still place inside. Remember the footprints in the sand.

I said: Sir, are you pulling my pecker?

He said: If you don't want it pulled, take the bell off the end.

That deflated me a little, I guess.

Each to their own, he said. Some to win the war, others to plan the peace. The peace is more important. It needs broad shoulders to carry it.

He had this half grin on his face he wears when he knows he's being hokey, and he knows you know it too. But he knows it works, and so do you.

I apologised. I told him I would try my best.

Have faith, he said, which is Randall-speak for *I've got it covered*.

You're my Peter, he said. You're my rock. I take my strength from you, David. We all do.

Big Poppa Bear. Peter. Collator of grand ideas. Other people's ideas. Planning for this big dream of peace, while the world goes all to shit. Distiller of dreams of paradise.

Another year older.

Date:

Convention of the monthly council, in the chamber. Petersen, Nathan B and I somewhat half-heartedly delivered our bi-annual progress report. There wasn't much to report, just modification of old ideas. Greater theoretical efficiencies. For when the time comes that never seems to come.

What I am doing seems increasingly insane. Every month I address what amounts to a council of war, with other people's ideas for the peace. But who wants to know? The way things are, who really wants to know?

After the council deconvened I needed to spend some time with Randall discussing these problems with the broadcast legislature and the issues we're experiencing with information access. Petersen has tracked down some guy, some rodenty German guy, who seems pretty sure we can police the Net pretty efficiently at reasonable cost. At what Petersen claims is a reasonable cost.

I had some apologies to make too – private apologies about the Capitol Establishment Initiative. I never want to be put in a position again where I am forced to curtail even a fraction of Isabel's working budget.

Randall tried to listen, but I don't think he really heard me. When I'd done he sat on the steps that ascended to the podium.

– Is it ever going to happen, David?

I sometimes forget that Randall is not as tall as I. At the age when I had been a buffoon of a quarterback, paying lip service to the Lord but obeying the commands only of what I remember as a permanently urgent erection, Randall had been no less intense than he is as an old man, a president. He had been luminescent in his monasticism. Nobody who met him ever forgot him, even when he was eighteen and his drive had not yet coalesced into policy. Randall was never a child. He was possessed of a certain knowingness, even before he underwent whatever vision it was that has led us all here, down this necessary and terrible path.

– Nuclear detonation in Georgia, he told me. How could anybody do that after Namibia?

I wanted to go home and hold my wife and child to me for that news.

– We just confirmed the loss of primary supply routes to the mid-east, he continued. We're going to lose ground, there, David. Men can't fight when they're starved and sick.

I agreed that they could not.

The previous morning I had been engaged in passionate debate concerning threatened budgetary restrictions placed upon the Capitol's administrative and executive support structures.

– I don't know what to do, he said. For the first time, I really don't know what to do. I'm praying for a sign, and it just doesn't come.

He looked at me and I couldn't answer. I wouldn't know either, if I were him.

But I am not him, and I too have been praying for a sign. I've being praying, along with Randall, along with everyone else, for a sign that doesn't come.

July 4

On this date we are left with stories.

Sometimes in the evening I tell my daughter stories which Naomi forbids me to tell: stories which contain what I maintain are necessary childish horrors. Stories of babes in the wood and dangerous houses constructed of delicious candy.

When I tell her of children burned in the oven she will think terrible things, she will think of burning alone in an oven in a candy house and she will love me more (she will love me) in her fear because I will not allow this happen to her, I will keep her safe from dangerous candy. The very scent of me means safety to her. When she is scared she sleeps with one of my shirts bundled beneath her face and clasped in her fist. But the things she thinks about will not be as terrible as the things that I am thinking, because I am grown and I know the truth about burning children. I fear for her more than she is able to fear for herself, even in the darkest of her childish dreams, because I know that I am a grown man and a man grown powerful yet I cannot protect her. That if I were to keep her hugged to my breast every day, if I were to sleep with what must seem my infinitely powerful frame curled around her every night (plagued even then with terror and guilt at the thought of nocturnal erections that are not for her, that I swear to God are not for her), that I cannot protect her because I cannot protect even myself. I lie awake at night and think about burning children.

I also lie thinking about protection. There are armed men in my house, my garden, and although they protect me I fear them because they are armed men.

Perhaps it is time to tell my daughter stories of the America which has gone. America has become a story: the candy house that was built on sand.

Shall I tell her how it came to be that America should go the way of the rest of the world? How should I relate to her a tale whose horror she is not equipped to understand, which will never attain its true status even when she is grown because it will be history then, and dead? How shall I tell her about the lights of Las Vegas gone dark, Los Angeles burned and the vast, angry plates of the earth erupted beneath it (God's anger, say some: not Randall), wiping it like Sodom from the Earth. My parents died there. Do I tell her that? If there is one fear she is equipped to understand, it is the loss of a parent. But can she comprehend that I had parents of my own? Can she comprehend that anything existed before she did? That her creator (I have told her that she was made of love. She *was* made of love. By love. She is still made of love. Every molecule of her vibrates with love) was in turn created?

How do I explain all this? Much of the East has yet to be officially reclaimed and mandated (there is some inefficiency and sloppiness. I'm dealing with it), although life after a fashion continues there. We all know the stories of what went on there, the apocrypha of a nightmarish New York and Washington, DC – kids' stories which are true. Robber barons; tiny, medieval principalities established block by block; the first peace-keeping forces massacred; mutilated young soldiers tied by shattered ankles to careening cars driven by amphetamine-eyed young men (Randall wept at that. No bitterness. He wept with love, as if he were watching his own children bouncing along, lifeless and humiliated); rape and murder and arbitrary torture; well-armed, self-appointed warlords in Ray-Bans and narrow-lapelled suits delivering ultimata via the cameras of captured news crews. In a reversion of fairytale, the East has gone wild, resisting the encroaching civilising aspirations of the West – a project hampered by the fact that genocide in the pursuit of civilisation is no longer widely regarded as a viable policy option. Not by us, anyway. Not by Randall and me.

If this sounds bitter and scared (when will I read this back? How old will I be? Where will I be? Will my daughter be with me?), it is because there is nothing we can do. Nothing I can do. We are at war on every front. We are at war with the revenant of what has passed and the dream, the faith in what is to come. I pray that we are the angel and not Balaam. I pray that we are not the ass.

She will ask me why all this and I shall answer – Because people are foolish. People believed that there was not enough, so they fought and killed each other for what was left. When she asks me enough of *what*, I will sit her on my knee and I will stroke the curve of her skull beneath the silk of her hair (her head fits the palm of my hand like the skull of a cat and she nuzzles into me like that, she shifts her weight now and again) and I will say – *Everything*, baby. The Earth was created to provide for us, but people lost faith in its bounty. They got scared that all the riches were running out.

– But there *was* enough, I'll comfort her: There was *always* enough. There will always *be* enough. The world is so much greater than the dumb people had assumed.

If she reads the books, those books which did so much to lead us into this, she will say to me: But it says we changed the *weather*. It says we made a hole in the sky.

I must say to her: We were wrong, honey. It was the sun. All along it was just the sun.

She is a child and perhaps she will see the humour in this, if it doesn't scare her too much. I am too tired to appreciate irony on such a scale, and too tired to get as scared as I know I should be. I am too concerned with the future. I will tell her about the future.

I will tell her that a Great Man was sent to save us all, and that the Great Man chose many people to help him save the world. One of those people was her daddy.

The Great Man said to her daddy, when her daddy was not much more than a boy, that there was a war to come, but that her daddy would have nothing to do with the war. Her daddy was to be a man of peace. And the Great Man set her daddy this task: set about you with these wise people I have gathered to me, and tell me how, when the war is over, we are to make the world all better.

Sometimes I believe we will do it.

There will be the American Reclamations, places where wheat will have ears as big as yours. But the American reclamation project is not an attempt to resurrect America. It will be the spectre of it, a tattered ensign.

When the war is over, perhaps this remnant of a nation will continue to define itself through the shared memory of a culture that was like ten thousand television screens, ten thousand different images which randomly flicker and change, a multiplicitous bounty of sounds and tastes and smells and images, testament to the primary coloured, headlong dash towards suicide into which it led the world. It was all the things that appealed to a child's sensibility. It had wanted to be everything. We had wanted to be everything. America had wanted to be the world perfected, America had called the tune and skipped gaily at the head of a procession and America had stumbled first upon the edge of the precipice.

All over the globe, wherever it is possible and prudent, Reclamations will be established. I have already signed off the development costs, and approved the initial designs for Reclamations in Australia, Japan, the East Coast of China, Northern Europe, Central and Southern India, South and Eastern Australia. I have approved Reclamations that will be semi-autonomous city-states where none before existed: the Pacific Ocean, the North Atlantic, Antarctica.

We will prevail, and we will survive, and finally we will prosper. We will recognise no nation, nor nationality, for we have witnessed the road down which the idolatry of nationalism has led.

Yet, it is the dream of America that will save us.

July 9

Dinner with the Beaumonts.

I wish Naomi would at least *pretend* to like Isabel. I wish she could make that small effort for me.

I wish I felt no shame for my wife. I wish I could accept her faults. I wish I were sufficiently gracious to accept her for not being perfect, I wish I was not so frustrated by her inability to accept that I am not something she does not deserve. She has seen me at my weakest, she has seen me weeping for my mother, she has seen me weeping for myself and the burden of my calling, she has seen me panicking for my daughter's minor ailments, she has seen me screaming down the phone to get a fucking doctor here *now* for what turns out to be mumps or chickenpox and, once, a bad nightmare. She has seen me weeping that another man has been inside her. Yet she will not submit that her faith in me is without ground. She will not allow that I am a lesser man than she thinks.

As ever, all there is to talk about that does not concern the present or the shame of our fear for the future, is that aspect of the past which we share. We laugh at old stories we have laughed at a hundred times.

– Of course, began Isabel, when David and I were together . . .

I could feel Naomi bristling and God forgive me but there was a moment in which I thought how satisfying it might be to strike her.

– I don't think together is *quite* the word I'd use, she said and my anger was coloured by my shame and the pity I felt for her. How can such a love be so lacking in generosity?

What is so terrifying to her that there was a time in my life – twenty-six years of my life – when she was not there?

When I think of Isabel and Nathan, of how they are together, I am sad and I should not be.

That night my wife and I made love. She closed her eyes and whimpered when she came and dug her nails into my shoulders and I slumped on top of her and lay inside her as I detumesced. When I moved to withdraw she made a little groan of complaint deep in her throat and tightened herself around me and I laughed and softly kissed her. She stroked the crown of my head, where my hair is thinning. I remembered for the ten thousandth time that I love her, and fell asleep with my head against the softness of her breast, wondering how it could be that I can forget such a thing as this so unforgivably often.

September

For the first time since any of us can remember, Randall failed to attend the monthly council. As a consequence, the meeting was subdued and inconclusive. Nothing looks good. How can everything go so badly wrong? How can all this effort go to waste?

I thank God I'm assigned no task which has any bearing on the way the war is planned and fought. I cannot quantify human agony on a spreadsheet. I cannot talk of resource management and collateral damage, and I'm proud that I can't. Perhaps I shouldn't be? Perhaps I'm too quick to judge those that are able to do these things, because God knows they're necessary and because I don't know what they endure, in taking the decisions they take.

I find myself hoping, for their own sake and mine, that they suffer agonies of the soul.

After the meeting concluded, Burkhalter sidled up to me and said:

– Some of us are going somewhere else, to talk. We think the situation with Randall requires discussion.

I called him a fucking prick and told him it was faith and prayer we needed, not a night of the fucking long knives and the prick blushed and walked away from me. But part of me isn't sure he wasn't right. Randall has taken on everything and perhaps everything is too much, even for him.

I wonder if I should tell Randall what Burkhalter said to me. I wonder if I shouldn't have gone along to their shitty meeting, just to know what's being said when some of us aren't around. But I didn't.

September

Today I thought about the devil.

Randall had to sanction the execution of three men, two of them officers, for the gang rape and murder of a fifteen-year-old girl, in Malaysia. He confided in me that he has heard reports of widespread cannibalism on the East European front. Cannibalism. How is one to encompass the enormity of such a thing?

He is able to smile when he tells me that in Cairo a clean-up team blew up a hotel because they believed it to be possessed by evil spirits.

– The pity is, said Randall, that it wasn't a half-bad hotel. I attended a conference there, years ago. If it'd been the London

Waldorf, I might have understood why they'd want to do it. Come to think of it, if it'd been the London Waldorf, I might've awarded them *commendations*.

He didn't laugh when he said it. But he looked at me and his eyes were glinting. I could see the striplights reflecting in the meniscus of laughter-tears, and I could tell he was trying his damnedest not to laugh, and that was good.

Six *A Christian Gunman in the Rameses Hilton*

When I think about the war it is Cairo that I remember most vividly. Cairo has not been contextualised in my memory. The sense of it has neither dimmed with time, nor been lent an artificial clarity.

I remember the hunger and the thirst and the enervating heat and I remember the weight of the equipment on my back and about my waist and the gritty concrete dust that coated the uniform, that caked into the week's growth of beard.

It was a dead city which demanded of us a humbled and silent respect. Its streets were numinous and resonant with the ghosts of veneration and submission.

We were not the first to enter. Others had passed through and in an explosion of mission and command had broken the silence for a few bright days. But they were gone now, they had passed on to Alexandria, to Tripoli, to Gaza, to Jerusalem. Silence had smothered the chiming revenant of that brief period of carnival, of their celebration in remaining, for the moment, alive. They had passed on and now some of them were dead. Some of them had been shot, had juddered in gunfire like epileptic puppets. Some of them had been burned and ripped to ragged strips, to tattered olive drab and chunks of hairy meat. Some of them had burst into a fine red mist which rained gentle on their comrades as they fought on, in the heat and the noise and the ringing, swelling chaos, their drilled-in efficiency and the animal pounding of their terror. Some of them had time to call out for Jesus, for God, for their mother. Some of them lay cursing God as they slipped into silence and memory. But here they had laughed: Cairo was the last place they had laughed, in abandoned hotels with American beer and cigarettes, with Israeli and Nigerian whores unofficially flown in on helicopter gunships with whom they danced before and after vigorous and sorrowful fucking, to songs they had loved at high school, songs whose doggerel and repetitive rhythms defined the memory of the last safe time of their lives. They played cards for money and European pornography. They phoned home, a place which seemed more distant to them than heaven, brighter and more beautiful, and they reassured those they loved, those for whom fear and hunger and the fragile belief in the necessity of what had to be done was like the nagging pulse of a vein. They went to makeshift chapels, the house of God in flapping military canvas and they prayed and gave thanks to be alive, for being chosen. Some of them prayed not to die, for this burden to be lifted from them. Cairo had indulged those few days. It had echoed with the life of them and upon the closing of the last of those days had allowed glutinous silence to settle once more upon it, thick and slow as honey.

The Cairo we entered was a great, wise animal, crouched heel to haunch, brooding upon slow and secret thoughts. We flickered in its vast and empty arteries like a cracked projection.

Abandoned cars and mopeds, ancient buses, taxis and bicycles lined the sides of the road. Doors to tenement buildings, to hotels, to department stores hung neutrally ajar. Stripped of function, they hinted at a message coded within the repeating patterns of reflected light and cast shadow. There were mannequins in the window of one store. There were mannequins whose wigs had slipped.

We moved in loose formation through those streets, a securing operation, a bureaucratic afterthought. Tidying up the rear, moving at a dreamlike pace through the exhausted gardens about the Cairo tower, the sorrowful cast of its lost ambition, while the best of men, better men than us, were explosively dismembered many miles away. In formation, we crossed a bridge over the sluggish Nile. Occasionally a head would jerk quickly to one side and we would pause and guns would be raised and hearts would beat thick and heavy in the stillness, but the movement glimpsed in the periphery of vision was always illusory, an infinitesimal flicker, brief as the passage of a cat. We were a pathogen entering a long desiccated cadaver, veins shrivelled to leather, eyes shrunken and dried like fruit. A mummified city.

A helicopter gunship chuttered by overhead. Sunlight reflected from the glass of its cockpit.

We made camp in the vast, deserted Rameses Hilton. The smoked glass of the lobby made of the sun a naked ball, perfectly spherical and heatless. We pretended to clown around. We read the dusty visitors' book, we made in it witless, pornographic entries although in truth we could not tolerate the thought of coitus beneath the ubiquity of Cairo's lidless and neutral gaze. We investigated drawers, we stole trinkets: an old postcard, a fake Swiss Army penknife, a faded photograph of a fat, white woman in a lurid bathing costume, one hand shielding her squinting eyes from the power of the sun. We sought out the kitchen and made use of that food which we found. We ate straight from tins which we discarded on shining steel worksurfaces, where they formed a miniature henge, a functionless, pagan monument to our century. Someone found a supply of cigarettes, carton after unopened carton stacked in some miraculously forgotten or overlooked storeroom. We loaded ourselves with this contraband. In silent elevators we made our way to the top floor, where, filthy, exhausted by the dust and the heat and the palpable weight of time passed, we fell upon beds that had been made long ago and which had lain, waiting, within heat-heavy rooms. We fell asleep fully clothed, two or three to a room, fearing to be alone in the dark in such a place. We discarded equipment in untidy piles alongside beds. We did not speak. We did not post guards. Before sleeping, we sullenly passed round bottles of whiskey.

We were awoken deep in the night by the crack of gunfire

and confused, in a half panic, scrabbled to pull on boots, to find rifles. Above us, on the roof, the gunfire was periodic and considered. It lacked any edge of hysteria. It marked the passage of time. I don't know why I was among the first men up there. I remember that I felt no fear, nor any surprise when we burst upon the roof to find Sonny Marshall, handsome Sonny with his wide and open face and his eyes which glittered with glee for being himself. We fixed him in our sights because we feared he had gone mad – but patient, considerate Halden approached him as he would a skittish horse, one hand raised gently before him.

'Sonny,' he said.

Sonny's flesh was luminescent like polished bone in the moonlight and as he held up the gun we threw ourselves in panic this way and that. But Halden continued to approach Sonny, step by considered step. The cooler wind of the night whipped up eddies of concrete dust which erased the sharp edges of him.

'Sssshhhh,' whispered Halden. 'Sssshhhh.'

'They're smiling,' said Sonny.

Halden stopped a metre from Sonny. 'Nobody's smiling, Sonny,' he said. 'Who's smiling?'

Sonny put his hand to his mouth. 'The people in the corners.'

As if a lover had stroked me, the hairs on my arm stood on end. The breeze fell away.

'Nobody's smiling, Sonny,' said Halden. 'We're your friends. We're not smiling.'

'The people in the corners', said Sonny, 'are smiling.'

I could not look over my shoulder. It was cold. It was colder than it had a right to be.

'There's nobody here but us,' said Halden.

'But I can see them,' said Sonny. 'I can see them whispering my name. They're giggling.'

As he reached Sonny, Halden took the gun from him and gently set it upon the floor. He held Sonny to him, tucked

Sonny's head to his shoulder and for a moment they were transfigured, they shone like marble statuary and I was filled with God in that moment, I was filled with the luminescence of the spirit. But I would not look behind me, into the darkness. Into the corners.

Blake was praying.

Into Halden's shoulder, I heard Sonny ask: 'Am I awake?'

Halden did not know.

Halden had Sonny sedated. We made camp on the roof and did not sleep. Instead we conversed in hushed whispers and chain-smoked stolen cigarettes. Perhaps it was not only I who imagined he heard emanating from the hotel upon whose high roof we had made camp, soft music on the edge of hearing. The subdued tinkling of a cocktail bar piano. We listened for the murmur of distant voices. We glanced into the corners and we feared to hear the sibilance of our names carried on the breeze.

After dawn, acting on Halden's command and the instructions of Buckman the sapper, we set to work. By mid-day we had done, and at one in the empty and dazzling afternoon, Halden inclined his head. There was a dull crump and the Rameses Hilton began to fold in on itself, storey collapsing upon storey until all that remained was rubble beneath a slowly expanding mushroom of dust and debris, like the exhalation of a fetid breath.

Halden was in serious trouble after Cairo. Along with all others involved in the unsanctioned destruction of the Rameses Hilton, I was up on a charge. After that I was assigned to the dig.

Before the posting began I had a week to spend in Jerusalem, which I recall as a nightmare bustle of glaring car horns, military jeeps and wide-eyed Israelis, Arab and Jew, with great, hungry eyes in withered faces, with sun-wrinkled hands. Olive-skinned young men and women in combat fatigues wielded automatic weapons with disdain and indiffer-ence. The Red Cross and Red Crescent postings, the American food aid stations, the sense of more than two thousand years of ululation and ferment, the hissing and spitting of belief and politics that made hell of the holy, an agony of the sublime.

I was able to find him only in the desert, in solitude, that once when I took a jeep out there, as far as I could. I found a good place and climbed for a while, aware of how inappropri-ate it was that a weapon bounced at my hip. I took my rest at a high place, removed sunglasses and helmet, wiped my sweating brow. I surveyed a vast and desolate panorama as the sun drummed down upon me with concussive force. I thought of how he was tempted at a place like this and I followed the progress of a distant helicopter gunship and I wanted to weep. I wanted him to be here, with me, in the flesh. I wanted to smell him and see in his eyes that which I knew would be there – the humour in his love, the love for us flickering, an animate happiness within the focus of his gaze, the corners of his smile. I knew how he moved, I knew the precise intonation of his voice when he taunted his disciples with their ignorance, their recurring lack of faith. There was always laughter there.

I thought about my favourite biblical passage, the verses that summed him up for me: that infinite gentleness and that laughter. The disciples, flushed with their success, crowd around him, an excited, bustling babble wishing to please and impress him. With twenty voices they tell him of their success in casting out demons and he listens, he smiles, I think maybe he draws circles in the dust with a dry twig and he acknowledges them, he lets them say their piece and he loves them for the way they are. When they are done, when they breathlessly await his appreciation – imagine what it is, imagine what it's like for him to smile at you, imagine what it must be like to know that you have pleased him – and he nods, he says *well done* with that nod and then he reminds them:

I saw Satan cast out like lightning from heaven.

Imagine that. Imagine the laughter in his eyes.

Imagine the size of his heart.

There was always laughter in him, right until he allowed them to do those terrible things to him, for what reason I did not fully understand, except that he had done it for love, which was enough. I wanted him to be here, with me. I wanted to protect him. I wanted to smell the sweat of him, the rough cloth of his robe. I wanted to thank him. I wanted him to lie down upon the rock and drift into blissful sleep, curled about himself, helpless as a newborn lamb and I wanted to keep him safe until dawn. I wanted to stand over him and stay awake and guard him. I wanted him to know how much I loved him. It burned in me with the unfocused rage of jealousy.

I stayed up there all night, huddled and shivering. I watched an endless shower of meteors burning away on the edge of the air and I wondered at how old they were, how inconceivably ancient. They had been up there since creation, they had been hurtling through the void even as his feet walked the earth. Their orbits had been in slow decay since before those terrible things were done to him. They had been in the sky when he raised his beautiful, parched face to it and bellowed his death agony before a jealous and demanding God. It came to pass that they were falling now, at the very moment I was present to observe them. After all those years, all those inconceivable thousands of years, it was my eyes before which they were destined to ignite. These things connected me with him: this high place, these incandescent meteors.

In the morning I drove back to Jerusalem and sold some cigarettes in exchange for food tokens.

The dig was around twenty kilometres from Masada, the heroic fortress of which I had read much as a child. It was neither my place nor inclination to question the necessity of the dig's existence, nor the necessity of posting a permanent guard there, watching over this desolate moonscape. We were six hundred kilometres from the nearest front line. In the cooler quiet of the evenings we heard low-flying aircraft, piloted and otherwise, *en route* to distant sorties, weighed down with unimaginable destructive power.

Around the dig had arisen an impermanent village of tents which were stifling in the day and chilled at night. Everything was camouflaged with webbing and drab tarpaulin. It must have been hot work under canvas, all that digging and scraping and bending and lifting. All that scrutiny and recording.

I never entered the dig itself. We weren't allowed to do that, in our big, blundering boots. 'Some ugly grunt in his big, blundering boots?' These were Ruth's words when, bored by the repetitious and uneventful nature of this posting, I requested of her a site tour. 'I don't think so. Now run along, would you.'

She really said that. Now run along, would you.

I was twice her size.

Ruth was Napoleonic, the most extravagantly impatient person I had ever been fortunate enough to encounter. Perhaps fifty when I met her, she was short, broad and heavy-breasted. She wore khaki trousers, army boots and a greasy old fedora which she carefully set before her on the table while sitting with us in the mess. She cut her own hair (with a blunt old pair of kitchen scissors, as I was to find out some time later). It didn't occur to her not to join us at meals. Our discomfort did not impinge on her consciousness. Our presence barely pricked it. She would sit blithely among us, plonking herself boyishly down at the nearest space, ripping off a corner of bread upon which she would ruminatively chew before beginning the meal proper. Sometimes she would bark the monosyllabic request that the jug be passed to her. Without comment she would fill with water both her own mug and the mugs of those who sat around her.

Three unrelieved months into the posting at the dig, I found myself opposite her in the mess. I set on the bench before me a battered aluminium tray upon which balanced my lunch. It must have been a Tuesday: I recall that there was fruit on the tray, a ripe, bruised mango. Many of us were by now displaying symptoms of malnutrition. For weeks my gums had been bleeding. My teeth were beginning to loosen. In the shower a few days before, I'd bent double and with prurient revulsion, peeled off a toenail. It came away with no resistance beyond an insubstantial tug of gummy adhesion. My bowel movements were infrequent and painful. I had haemorrhoids. I'd lost weight, about all the weight I could stand to lose. Despite this I had a firm, rounded little pot belly. We were so thin we had begun to resemble one another. Hunger and proximity were eroding the spurious external indicators of our uniqueness.

Morale was low. Subject to news blackout, we were too isolated even to share and eagerly participate in any of the ten-thousand-and-one wildly inaccurate rumours that commonly served as our sole source of information. In desperation we were compelled to invent our own rumours, which spread and mutated like viruses and came back to us in new and horrifying, mythical forms which we half believed to be true. Something terrible had happened. People were dying again in the streets of America. The inoculation programme had failed: even those previously considered immune were dying. We were losing on the southernmost Caspian rim. Food was running out. There was no more food. Staad had committed suicide in the foundations of the city he had announced it his intention to build. He had fallen on his sword.

I folded rice into pitta and took a bite. I chewed it for a long time. We had been taught this. Chewing was supposed to fool the body into believing it had eaten more than it had. But how could I fool my body? How could I convince my stomach of what I knew to be untrue? My stomach had a direct line to those ancient parts of my brain which remained lizard. My stomach could demand that my will, my self, be erased in pursuit of the imperative that it be filled. My stomach,

67

everybody's stomach, was an animal inside me, a secretly scheming monarch.

'My great-grandfather had a hat like that,' I said, after chewing thirty times. Thirty times. That's how bored we were. 'In all the photos I have of him, he's wearing a hat just like that.'

She regarded me from beneath unplucked brows, indignant at the folly of my frivolity. She met my eyes. Perhaps she saw the thing that's wrong with them. 'This one's something of an heirloom,' she explained, a little brusquely. 'It belonged to my grandfather.'

'He left it to you?'

'While he was still alive,' she said, warming to the subject. 'In his dotage. It was his lucky hat. He had a lucky everything: a lucky hat, a lucky lighter, a lucky *jacket* for goodness sake. A leather jacket. I have photographs of him wearing it at *noon* in the desert. But the hat was his favourite. He wore this hat all over the world. He was an archaeologist, too – an "obtainer of rare antiquities". The old bastard was a bit of a mercenary, but he had a good enough streak to him.'

'You were close.'

'I was young,' she said. 'And I'd read his diaries. He was something of a hero in his time.'

I didn't know why Ruth and I became friends, other than that my initial conversational gambit had touched upon that single spot of sentimentality I was ever to find in her. Certainly we were all bored and certainly there was not one among us who didn't feel the desire for novelty, even so meagre a novelty as conversation with a person with whom one had not spent the last months talking for hour upon vacuous hour. Perhaps she saw something in me, perhaps the intensity of my faith inspired the teacher in her. Perhaps, like many academics, the need to teach amounted to a psychological imperative, a craving. Perhaps there was a sexual motive – perhaps Ruth thought she could get laid out here in the desert, with this malnourished, sex-starved soldier. God knows it was happening. There were five women on the archaeological team, five women and six men. More than once, soldier and archaeologist had slipped past the perimeter fence, along a secret path of whose existence we were all aware, to private places, where they proceeded to relieve their boredom and each other beneath the shooting stars and the bombers thundering overhead in low formation. If this is the case, Ruth had chosen unwisely and anyway I can't believe it of her. Not me. Not Ruth and me.

I had no interest in archaeology, in what had passed. It was that which was to come that interested me. However, over the weeks that followed, Ruth taught me. She contextualised my faith, sketched for me the figure of a man whose movements and words made one sense in the world of first century Judea, and another in the world of mind, the world of the spirit – the world of *translation*.

It was always God with Ruth. Never Jesus.

The will of God was revealed in the process of history. God was in cause, God was in effect. She apprehended His omnipotence in a way that, with the darkness of the desert surrounding us, surrounding this lost, starving little dig, gave rise in me to an atavistic, superstitious fear. She described His immanence in history – how time present contained time past, time past time future, of how everything contained Him, how He contained everything.

She wanted me to learn. I had not been aware that so much required understanding. I just thought of my mother and father, of the first soup they had been offered in America – minestrone, in cracked bowls, with a hunk of fresh bread, of how proud they had been of my name. Of how proud Alan and Rose were to have a child called Malachi who had visions of the living Christ. How their child was able to describe the way Jesus sometimes put his hand before his mouth when he laughed, and how he distractedly scratched at the crown of his head when his disciples bewildered him with their humanity.

One night, assigned guard duty, the silence of the desert was undermined by a profound basso rumbling and, lifting my night-sights I saw a formation of tanks, moving to the north. I watched them recede into the darkness.

Two nights later a bomber came down in the desert less than a kilometre from the dig. Naturally, we raced out there in a battered jeep with exhausted suspension which jarred the coccyx and jostled us as we prepared medical equipment, nauseated at the thought of what we might find. There was nothing left to rescue. We formed a loose circle about the fiercely incandescent remains of the plane and watched it combust, watched the fire pale as the sun rose. Somebody said a prayer for the cremated remnants of the pilots, for the cracked and blackened bones twisting into brittle shapes under the intense heat.

There was a new energy in the air. There came a day when the food drop did not arrive and we waited in trepidation for two days with frighteningly dwindled supplies of rice and water. My lessons with Ruth ceased and she became increasingly withdrawn and foul of temper. It became clear that there was conflict amongst the archaeological team. They engaged in public argument, huddled close under the sky, jabbing fingers at one another, miming exasperation and fury. Pointing at the dig. Saying things I could not quite hear.

It ended in a flurry of confusion. Under cover of darkness a transport helicopter landed just outside the perimeter. It was flanked by two gunships which hovered menacing in the air above it, wasp sillouhettes against the astonishingly complex sky. A group of men emerged, a general I didn't recognise, and a civilian in clean cotton desert-wear. Although the civilian wore a hat and dark glasses, and kept a handkerchief pressed firmly to his face, he moved in what seemed to me to be a half-familiar way. They hurried to the site, bent almost double, shielding their eyes as the thundering crump of the rotors raised a storm of stinging sand. The men were guarded by grim-faced soldiers who avoided eye-contact with us as they passed. Passed this curious, half-asleep, raggedy platoon burned brown and cracked by the desert. Two of the bodyguards carried between them an HRCV, one handle each. Bringing up the rear was a three-man camera crew. The recording eye of the lens passed across us and we were ashamed, bags of bones with gums that bled and eyes grown too large in our heads.

It was Ruth who met the men, shaking their hands in turn and nodding her head. The bodyguards turned their Neolithic contempt upon us, forcing our eyes to the floor. Some returned to their tents. I hid in the shadows and watched. The camera recorded everything: Ruth in profile greeting the men; Ruth's gait, still waddling despite her loss of weight, as she led them under the rope barrier and into the dig itself.

For perhaps half an hour nothing happened. The gunships described a wide circle about the camp. Then they returned to hover over the transport and there was movement from the dig. The men with the HRCV emerged. They were surrounded by archaeologists, camera crew, bodyguards, the civilian man and Ruth, as close to frantic as I have ever seen her. It seemed that everybody was trying to talk to everybody at once, gesticulating and pointing and shouting and massaging frustrated temples. All except the men with the HRCV and the bodyguards, who made stoic progress through the bustle, professionally expressionless. The entourage made its way to the transport, whose ponderous rotors began slowly to spin, to pound the desert air. The HRCV was loaded on board, then a contingent of troops made its way into the camp, Ruth and others snapping impatiently at their heels, and began to shift the archaeologists' belongings from the tents to the transport, lugging boxes of books and laptop computers and rucksacks. I was unable to tell if Ruth and the others were trying to hurry or impede the troopers' progress. Whatever: within five minutes, Ruth and half the archaeological team had boarded the transport and it had departed, accompanied by the furiously buzzing gunships.

She didn't say goodbye.

Those archaeologists who returned did so silently, a forlorn group in their practical clothing, their boots scuffed and scarred. They returned to their tents and immediately began to pack their own belongings, their books and their photographs and their scribbled papers, the markers of their temporary lives. One of them, a man with a clownish mass of ginger hair, bald at the crown, with whom I had exchanged not even a cursory 'good morning', emerged from beneath the flap of his tent carrying a camera. He looked over his shoulder and said something. I think it was: 'Fuck it,' but I couldn't be sure. He began to take photographs of the external construction of the dig, of the tents. Turning, he saw me standing in the shadows. He photographed me.

The following morning we were commanded to return to Jerusalem, leaving the dig to be reclaimed by the desert. Since I had seen it last, Jerusalem had been dropped and it had shattered. It was a city in fragments. Transports landed with increasing frequency. Food distribution points descended into riot which, denied access to the more benign but more costly non-lethal weaponry with which they had learned their trade, paramilitary police contained with the more traditional baton, gas and rubber bullets. The numbers of the wounded, provided with second-line emergency treatment before being shipped off to a more distant place, a better place with better facilities, seemed to increase daily. There were so many of them. There were so many of us. Traumatised young nurses and medics formed blank-eyed cabals in bars and requisitioned hotel foyers. There was brawling in bars, there was praying on street corners, there was a palpable craving for sex. It felt like the edge of the end of the world.

After a disorientating week there I was mobilised on to combat duty, despatched to the East European rim of the Caspian basin. I remember my face, reflected in the window of a transport as I boarded: expressionless, yearning for home.

I rejoined Halden and Sonny Marshall and the others.

They'd been on the front line for a month. Men I knew were dead. Men I knew had died in ways I did not want to contemplate.

Sonny Marshall had thrived on it. His eyes were phosphorescent.

My war was brief. I was introduced to streetfighting. I participated in bitter guerrilla skirmishes, whose nature – irrespective of the satellite-linked laptop computers which bounced on our hips and from which we were directed, individually or in groups, from command centres safely behind what we called a front line (even though it was not; there were dozens of front lines, hundreds, some of them theoretical, a psychedelically shifting Mandlebrot-generated map of imagined and coveted territories), irrespective of the cameras in our helmets through which our progress and conduct were monitored, or of signature weapons and gas-masks and belief in just cause and Holy War – had barely changed in three hundred years.

I chanted his name as I fought, as I thought about fighting: Jesus, I said, sweet Jesus, sweet holy Jesus.

The first man I ever saw die was killed by Sonny, on the ground floor of what, in a previous life, had been a department store – before it had been radically recontextualised into a looted and burned remnant. He was wire-thin in ripped, stained Nike hi-tops, greasy 501s and much-torn, fur-lined parka. He carried a semi-automatic assault rifle manufactured in Birmingham, England. His fear made him an animal, a crouching, hopping, yelping chimpanzee, chattering for his life in a language whose words we did not understand. Sonny shot him in the throat.

Three days later, I killed a human being. A sniper. (As if that was all he had ever been. As if he had come thus into being.) He and two others, situated in other buildings, had effectively pinned us down in the street, crouched behind the wheel-less shells of cars, in doorways. We feared being cut off, surrounded, massacred. There was some panic, not much.

I was alone when I kicked open the door and burst in on him, because I'd left Dobbs on the stairs with a fucked-up leg and shrapnel in his ass and Buckman dying in the lobby. How elastic time can be. I seem to remember that I hesitated for hours, but there can have been no more than half a second of it. As the man I was about to kill began to stand – it all seems so slow! – I imagine him climbing lazily to his feet, raising the gun at his leisure (he too wore a parka, the fur-trimmed hood thrown back, and his hair was long and his beard heavy, and he wore fingerless woollen mittens and his fingers and face were grimed black), when of course he leaped with the speed of shock and fear and the urgency of his desire to live. He saw no expression. My face was encased in the ubiquitous gas-mask, its reflective, Munch eyes. I emptied a clip into him. I made him jump and leap and convulse like current was passing through him. Observe the splatter pattern on the walls.

It did not mean much.

For a moment, before Sonny led me from the room, I bent heel to haunch and scrutinised the thing I had made, my head tilted to one side.

Four days later I walked into a grenade.

We thought it was all over; we thought all the killing and the dying was done. Numbed, we advanced slowly along a main street, I don't even know what street, nor remember why the decision hadn't been taken to carpet-bomb the fucking place and have done, past the smoking houses and cars, the remains of an industrial town fallen into decay and now catastrophe, past the scattered dead we did not allow ourselves truly to see and for whom not even memory can manufacture significance. I have no idea what happened to whoever it was that threw the grenade. I cannot picture him. I never think about how old he was, nor how scared, still less about how much he must have hated me. I do think about it landing in the rubble on the road just before me, though. *That grenade is Chinese*, I thought. Halden and I began to look at each other in what I'm sure would have been a comical double take if the grenade hadn't detonated. Halden took the brunt of it: patient Halden, extinguished in a divided instant: Halden, distributed in a whipping storm of pieces across the street, into the air.

And there was me, behind him.

Time.

I seem to see Halden expand, erupting from within as if something has been forced into him under unendurable pressure. Then I am hammered by a titanic concussion. For a confused moment I imagine I've been hit by a car. Then I realise that I'm in the air, that I'm flying. Nothing makes sense. The ground rises up and knocks from my lungs what's left of my breath.

I'm aware of panic, of shouting, of gunfire. I have to take cover. I'm wet. I've lost control of my bladder, perhaps my bowels. I try to find my feet. There is a ferocious noise in my head. I can't feel my legs. I lift my head to identify whatever it is that pins me to the floor, whatever it is that prevents me from finding my feet and crawling towards safety. I look down.

I look down, and not all of me is there.

I seldom dream of that grenade or of Halden bursting open all over me, of my body all torn open down there. Sometimes when I'm awake I find myself remembering a foot, still in its boot, lying across the road, and I remember a feeling of something growing within me, like a flower opening inside the cavity of my chest.

In truth I hardly remember it at all. I have some difficulty believing it happened. My experience of combat was so short, I was so ill-prepared for it, so scared and so hungry and so desperate not to die. I can't imagine that such a thing can have occurred.

I sometimes wonder if I'm alone in this. I've witnessed the fact that people who lived through the war remember it as a *real* experience, more real than the lives that were to follow.

I often dream of Cairo, but they are confused dreams,

75

dreams in which the roof of the Rameses Hilton is the high place upon which Christ is tempted, and Christ in the dream has the guileless psychotic innocence of Sonny Marshall, of my good friend Sonny. There is never a Devil in the dream. Just Christ and his temptation. Considering a silent, haunted city for his kingdom.

The voyage was long, but Isabel had booked me in a club-class cabin (far above the waterline) and so I slept and read thrillers and watched television and dreamed of not much at all: not even McArdle, not even the albino. I looked out of the porthole and I watched the sea. The ship docked for two days at New Edinburgh, the first of the great floating reclamations and the only one which I had yet to visit. In the heat of noon I watched from the upper deck as it rolled over the horizon, an inconceivably vast, water-borne insect of metal and glass. I remembered the quiet triumph with which the completion of this first seaborne reclamation had been announced. Staad's drive forcing vigour back into the exhausted world. How I had hated him as I mended. As they mended me. As my stump grew a taut little polyp, transluscent and traced with veins.

I had a good time in New Edinburgh. I enjoyed exploring it. It was an impressive piece of engineering, plugged deep into the seething heart of the planet, but I can't say I'd want to live there. I didn't mind the ocean, the ocean is one of those things that has never scared me, so long as it was a thing across which I moved. To be stationary upon it struck me as somehow unnatural.

To be stationary anywhere no longer seemed natural to me. The aftermath of war had made travel easy. There were thousands like me, tens of thousands, for whom the chaos of the post-war world represented a kind of freedom. At first I luxuriated in the asinine idea that I was running from my past. Shamefully, I'll admit that I'd learned much from sentimental songs about drunken strangers with broken hearts. It's a role I enjoyed trying to play for a while, until I was forced to realise that I lacked the taciturn bitterness required to play it well. There was no real story – no story I could tell – but I insisted on naming my pain, on regaling every stranger with whom I fell into inebriated conversation with every detail of her.

With every telling of the tale she became more beautiful and more cruel. It was from an ever greater height I fell.

Inevitably I came to acknowledge that she was not responsible for what I felt, that she was as fragile and weak and meagre as I. She was a stranger whose memory I sought to fashion after my own image, according to the peculiarities of my own demands. So I learned to shut my mouth and I didn't speak of her, because when I spoke of her I told of myself.

Even so, the day remained rare that I didn't think of her. Remained? Remains.

She's still there, still here, a half-created ghost, an unformed essence inside me.

But it was not her who fuelled my rage and my self-pity. It was him. It was the memory of him, my one and only true love, ha ha: the object upon which I had projected all that I needed to see. That's all he was; a blank screen, a paint-by-numbers messiah, an interactive fucking saviour, a nothing, and yet I could feel the place where he'd been, I could place my hand flat on my belly and cup the hollow there and I'm ashamed to admit that more than once I prayed: I begged him like a lover: I humiliated myself like a lonely widow conned from her life savings by a man who feels nothing, before whom she will nevertheless prostrate herself, at the cuffs of whose trousers she will desperately tug, which she will kiss and wet with her tears. I cursed him and I swore at him and I wept and I begged him to come back. It was like being sane yet willing oneself to be mad and it didn't work, although sometimes I wonder if madness wasn't the result. Sometimes I wonder if all this stuff, all this tangled and bursting stuff behind my eyes isn't just the mess of insanity. I think of the people I've killed. There, I've said it, the *people* I've killed. God help me. People who no longer exist because of me, people who are photographs and melancholy anecdotes because of me.

Movement lost any spurious shred of romance. By the time I settled on the South Australian I'd worked half the reclamations, and half the shipping routes between them. I'd even worked the freight-dirigibles for a few months. I'd applied myself to a series of labour-intensive, low-skilled, low-waged jobs for a succession of large corporations, each of which wanted me to believe that it loved me. This despite the fact that it was, for instance, paying me a subsistence wage for spending eighteen indescribably dismal months contracted not to leave the Antarctic environs of Mary-Jane Kimball.

It was this that precipitated the breakdown: Malachi in the Big House, wearing his coat back-to-front for a while.

The company that loved me refused to pay for this little excursion to la-la land because, although it was of course insured – by one of its own subsidiaries, which not only loved me, but wanted to look after me as well – it successfully argued that the ease with which I bypassed its psychometric testing procedures indicated that I'd perpetuated against it a deliberate falsehood. I was advised that I was fortunate not to be sued by the company for loss of investment. That's exactly how much it loved me.

I hated Mary-Jane fucking Kimball. It was a filthy, throbbing, neo-industrial pit of claustrophobia and resentful paranoia. It was populated by those for whom the vigour of survival – of being *chosen* – had long since worn thin and rotten. All that remained was faith, the same cheap determination to *carry on* that you could find scuttling beneath any rock. Except on the Antarctic Reclamation, of course. It was just too cold there for anything with more than two legs to scuttle. It was just so unbelievably fucking cold.

After the Mary-Jane Kimball farrago I landed a job with the catering division of a commercial liner which did the long haul between three reclamations and America, picking up this here, dropping off that there, taking along for the ride a paying smattering of the idle rich along with the wide-eyed and the itinerant. I didn't last long. They had a problem with my personal hygiene. Just because I wasn't obsessive about it. It wasn't like I was a *chef*, for Christ's sake. It wasn't like I came into contact with any *food*. I was a porter. I carried things. I did a job which twenty or thirty years before would've been done by a machine, and done better. I was supposed to be proud of that, and to love Jesus. That charlatan.

That *cunt*.

Of course, all the time I was practising my vocation, dealing unorthodox Christs and new Gospels to the Godless and the heretical. I was good news. Even when inactive, I would lie in a rictus of terror, obsessed by the thought of what the Church would do should I be caught, by what God would have them do. Of all His many great and glorious secrets, this was one I was happy that He maintain a while.

But I wasn't scared this time. We left New Edinburgh and that night I ate alone in the restaurant and was joined by a married couple and their squabbling adolescent progeny. I was very happy and animated. I talked with them and of course I lied to them: they talked with me and of course told the truth. They were taking the kids to see America. They wanted the kids to know their roots. The whole family was enraptured that they were shortly to witness Staad's address in the temple. And of course there was the shopping to be done afterwards, ha ha, and there were restaurants to visit (cue the patting of burgeoning gut. What greater testament to Staad's success in saving us than the comeback of the gut? Not the beriberi distension of the hungry, but the genuine article, real fat, one-hundred per cent genuine excess bodyweight, the real thing. Perhaps by the time these adolescents had grown and married and sired children the world might have decided once again to hate and fear fat, to consider it ugly. But not just yet. We were still in love with our fat, those few of us who had it.)

They were called Ted and Laura, my companions, and they were fine people. Part of me actually liked them, the part adjacent to that small piece of me that wanted to *be* them, for my spirit to grow diffuse and dissolve into them, to experience their fondness for one another.

The morning arrived upon which we rose early and crowded on the deck and craned our necks and politely shoved our beloved neighbours aside in order to catch a better glimpse of America, scrolling towards us over the horizon, as if being delivered on a conveyor belt. The shimmering halo of its lights, even as another new dawn fades.

Upon our disembarkation, there were porters to carry our luggage, there were waitresses to bring us snacks as we queued at customs. My heart was not hammering as we shuffled like refugees, tired and slightly displaced by arrival. My heart did not hammer even as I reached the desk. A woman in semi-military uniform and ash-blonde hair pinned sexy and chaste at her nape took my smartcard, checked the information thereon. My voice did not break when she looked brightly up at me and said:

'Place of birth?'

I replied: 'Bristol, England.'

She smiled yet wider, this marvel of orthodonty, as if she had heard that Bristol, England was a fine place to be born. She handed back my card and said: 'Please proceed to baggage check. Follow the signs and enjoy your stay.'

It was only then that I began to experience the first weakening of my knees, the first longing for a cigarette. But this was America. This was not a place where one could blithely produce a Marlboro and happily puff away on it as if it were the most natural thing in the world, which of course it is.

I stood before a long table and watched as a man, a kid built like a man, with a geometrically precise parting in his heartbreakingly lustrous hair, opened my suitcase. Another kid in a man's body, this one with an almost comical shoulder width, watched my face as kid number one went through my things. I knew the cool gaze of hidden cameras was trained upon me. I really began to feel it. I forced my hands to stay still by locking them behind my back, but not before I had folded a stick of gum into my mouth, coaxing moisture into my throat.

Those new suits, unzipped from their bags and unfolded, patted down.

All the while he's talking, deceptively casually: 'So, what brings you Stateside – business or pleasure . . .'

'Oh, pleasure,' I say – 'Well, I hope. You know.'

He looked up briefly from inside my case and he laughed sympathetically. He was a very friendly fellow. 'Sure,' he said, 'I know.' He lifted my camera and opened it. He ran an index finger around its interior, held it to the light and scrutinised it: 'Visiting family?'

He asked this just as I was forming the thought: *What on Earth can people smuggle in cameras, for Christ's sake?*

'Friends,' I said. The next line was the clincher: 'Old war buddies, mostly.'

'Sure,' he said brightly. I prayed that he would not ask where I fought, because I cannot lie about that, about that I can be nothing but truthful, and I did not wish to stutter and blush and stammer, as I knew I would. But he didn't ask that. Instead he carefully replaced the camera – every bit as carefully as he ensured that his silent and heroically shouldered young assistant refolded my suits correctly.

Then he picks up the box of assorted disks, the box where it is, whatever it is, hiding in there in plain sight, and he holds up the box and he says:

'Now, is there anything in here you want to tell me about?' He rattles off the legal spiel, the script, asking me if these media contain material or materials which are or which I believe might be in contravention of the Seventh Amendment of the New Constitution.

And of course I answer: 'I hope not!' and he smiles and replies: 'I guess you won't mind if I take a look?', and I nod: 'Go right ahead.'

I stand with a benign smile on my face and try to will the sweat back into my pores, stand as firm as the temple, concentrate on not rocking on my heels. He selects a disk at random, slips it into a drive bay, taps a key or two on the keyboard, selects a file from the menu. The file opens and he runs through some of its contents. I know the disk. It's a family album compiled for just this purpose. Stills of me in uniform, film of my mother as a young parent, wheeling me in a tricycle along the seafront of an English town. My mother is embarrassed before the camera and as she approaches it, she sticks out her pink tongue and says: 'Bum,' before her face fills the screen with a fuzzy white blur. She can't be more than twenty-five in that piece of film. Imagine that. Your mother can be twenty-five. More film of her, taken by my father to record the moment the Thorndykes finally arrived at the American shore. She is tired now beyond even the slightly desperate gaiety of the first clip of film. The camera testifies to the hollow of her eyes as she takes her first nervous steps onto the promised land, with her silent child at her side, clutching her hand. The camera records the first free soup and fresh bread of America. And there is me, a slight, silent child perching without movement upon his mother's lap, gazing steadily at the lens. There is already something wrong with my eyes.

The customs kid removes the disk, replaces it in the box, withdraws another and I feel for all the world like somebody has kicked me in the folding pivot behind my knees. I'm forced to disguise this near collapse by patting the pockets of my suit and withdrawing another stick of gum. It is the disk. It is the disk Isabel gave me and I can't even roll my eyes in despair because there are eyes everywhere, there are eyes fixed upon every aspect of my behaviour, there are eyes looking at my eyes.

I chew gum and try to look polite but impatient, as if I am tired and longing for a shower, which is not altogether untrue.

Again he accesses the menu and examines the long list of file names scrolling before him. I wonder what they are: Isabel never told me and I'm wondering frantically what I'm going to say if he asks me what's on this disk because of course I have no clue, I have nurtured no desire to know what's on it, I'm afraid of what's on it because I'm afraid of the lengths to which Isabel went to ensure that exactly what she wanted to happen to it happens to it, and now look, here I am, about to be busted at customs like a teenage drug mule. I watch helplessly as he opens a file and studies what unfolds.

His smile falters at the edges then collapses as if his lips have become unendurably heavy and I am about to think, fuck it, and punch him and run, when he says, quite seriously, making me dizzyingly cognisant of where in the world it is that I am: 'Thank you for what you did for us, sir,' and his eyes well – I swear to God. His eyes well as if he is about to cry.

I swallow and say: 'Which, um, particular . . .?'

He makes a sad, brave smile and swivels the monitor and replays the snippet of film he has just watched. Primarily it is film of Ruth, of Ruth in her grandfather's fedora. She carries as a pointer a mahogany cane. As she talks she is pointing at and tapping things with it, but there is no sound (he is wearing a little ear plug) so I can't hear what she's saying. Then the camera pans across a line of faces, a line of thin, uniformed men with hollow cheeks and dusty, sun-bleached hair which sticks up in tufts and sways like grass in the desert breeze. They are arranged haphazardly outside their tents. Some of them smile and wave and goof around for the camera, but most do not. One of those that does not is me. I am shocked by the power of recognition, I am shocked by how emaciated and enervated I am, how obvious is my dissipation. My image turns and faces the camera for a full second and I stare at myself down this tunnel of years as if I can see myself from both directions, as if he is looking at me as I look at him, as if he is blankly curious to see the creature he will become.

I can't speak. Too much is happening inside me.

'Were you a POW, sir?' says this crisp blue-uniformed cocksucker from under his luxurious hair, and as I look at him I realise that he is of course too young to have fought, that he has been sentimentalised by the constant harping of the television about the anniversary of victory, its constant iteration of the lion-hearted sacrifice we had made, that we had all made for the love of God and the love of Christ and the love of our fellows. For the love of Staad.

And I am somehow able to answer him, despite the roaring in my head: 'No,' I say, and if I look distant he imagines it is because my thoughts have drifted back to another time, 'No. There were just some hungry times, I'm afraid.'

He swallows and nods and, sweet holy Jesus, slips the disk back into its case. He closes the lid of my suitcase and pats its lid twice. His eyes are still moist and I see that he is bursting with tenderness for me, for this ugly man who had offered his all to allow him to be here, proudly rooting through people's underwear and occasionally sticking two or three fingers up somebody's ass. He smiles and says: 'Please pass through, and enjoy your stay sir.'

'I will,' I assure him. At the final gate, after I am x-rayed and photographed and God alone knows what elsed, my gun is handed back to me, a fresh clip of ammunition in the breech. I sign for it and slip it into the empty holster at my waist and as I do so I am swept into the maelstrom of arrivals, I am surrounded by people weeping and people hugging and couples kissing and men shaking hands and people blinking, bewildered, people being helped with their luggage, and I pass stores: fast food restaurants, Irish pubs which serve black beer and salted peanuts, clothes stores, drug stores, stores positioned to encourage one to spend from the moment one arrives to the last seconds before one leaves, because we now understand that it is a duty, not an indulgence to spend, it is a duty to enjoy the fruits of our labour, and then I am passing through the doors to the port and outside, where at the sidewalk there awaits a great line of taxis, into which people in all their thrilling variety are helped by the best dressed, most courteous taxi drivers who ever lived, the cars are winking under the new sun and I catch myself laughing, I catch myself looking at the beautiful sky and

I catch myself swelling with the love of America, and I want to explode, I want to *do* something, I want to *buy* something, because I'm here, because I've not been caught and because there is still no finer, no more exciting place in the world in which to be free.

Seven

```
File code: 100046/macd
Username: sicarius
Password: ******
Last Updated: **/**/**
```

File DMWITRES Located.

Please wait.

File DMWITRES Retrieved.

Warning: This File Has Been Cloaked. Should You Wish to Decloak, Press Return. If You Wish to Quit, Press Escape.

If You Wish to Decloak, Please Ensure That Your Software is Code Protected, and Save Any Files Recently Modified.

Please wait.

Code Accessed and Identified. Print 65385922, Licence Confirmed, Outlet Confirmed.

*** Please Note. Decloaked Files Have Been Encrypted According to a System Restricted to the Use of Government Personnel Only. WARNING. Unauthorised Use of this System of Encryption Constitutes an Offence Punishable By Law. Unauthorised Personnel Should Quit

Hello, David, How Are You?

From McArdle's Journal:

Date:

Something has happened.

Randall cancelled the scheduled council. He summoned
five of us — Isabel and Nathan Beaumont, Frank Shaw, Oscar
Petersen and me. Oscar and I were the only two members of
the Quorum whose attendance was required. This alone was
extraordinary, and should've alerted me to the fact that
something of moment was about to occur. He'd invited only
his favourites. His little cabal.

Greeting us from the podium in the empty and reverbative
council chamber, he looked grave and graceful.

When we were seated and silent, he said: Something has
happened.

We exchanged glances, the five of us. There was some
murmuring. He silenced us with his hand.

He said: God knows there can't be one among us who
hasn't come to wonder during the last months if our prayers
would ever be answered.

All at once I remembered what he is all about. After all the
months of agonising over the logistics of feeding people when
there is not the food available to feed them, of keeping them
well when there are not the resources to treat them, of
planning for their future once the war has ended although we
cannot know how many of them will be alive to share in that
future, of all the tortuous demands of the war, which we suffer

in the pursuit of the wider vision. I remembered that Randall is a man of God, that the intensity of his vision is not merely remarkable.

He introduced Ruth Felton. She had been waiting unseen and unheard in the aisle, just behind us. As he spoke her name, she walked past us, and took the podium. Randall stood aside for her, then sat. She was uncomfortable in formal wear, denied the infantile comfort of her stupid hat. Why am I writing this? It doesn't matter. It doesn't matter what she wore.

I don't know what to think. I can't remember how to think. As I type, my tiny daughter sits on my lap and watches the screen, the scrolling letters, the winking cursor. Fascinated, she is breathing hypnotically through her mouth because she has a slight headcold. Primly, she sniffs back a little trail of snot. I want to crush her. I bend and I kiss her head, a big smack of a kiss and she wriggles on my lap and says, crossly:

– Dad-*dy*.

– Baby, I say.

She giggles. We say this a lot.

– No, *Daddy*! she says.

I nuzzle her head with the tip of my nose. It bends on her skull, left and right. She smells sleepy.

– Who's my baby? I say, and smack her again with a kiss.

Naomi passes the door of the study. She is carrying freshly laundered towels. I can smell them. They smell of the life the world is dreaming of.

– Don't get her over-excited, she says. It's nearly bed-time.

– She's okay, I say, She's being good.

My daughter swells with pleasure. She repositions herself on my lap and I do not want any of this to be happening, I do not want any of these thoughts to have room in my head.

3 am

I could not sleep so I came downstairs to smoke one of Naomi's cigarettes. It's been so long since I smoked. I feel giddy and nauseated. Naomi was lying with her arm across my chest and when I shifted from beneath her she smacked her lips and opened one eye a crack and said something very quietly. I leaned forward and put my ear to her lips. She was asking me not to go. She was warm. She loved me. I stroked her hair the way she likes and soon she was asleep again. She had one palm tucked under her cheek and her lips were squashed together and open a little. I could see her front teeth.

I can't get it out of my head. It's like I have an engine up there. Pistons and heat and steam. But not one clear thought. Just this lurching inside me every time I try to think. A lurch inside, like I am falling.

[section deleted]

[Ruth Felton] stepped down from the podium. Randall took her place.

I hardly know what to say to you, he said. Except: God is with us, in this room. God is with us. This is His work.

That's all I remember. Perhaps when I am an old man, reading this journal, reading back over my life before I die, perhaps by then I will have convinced myself that I remember clearly every word of what Randall said, because memory is more creative than many of us dare admit. But it was only this morning – yesterday morning (God, it's so late, I must try to sleep, there is so much I have to do tomorrow). I know that every word is lost to me. I can remember a dull metallic colour, like pewter, before my eyes. And this lurch inside me, like the room was an aircraft, crashing. That I was falling.

I saw him weaken. I watched him struggle with something that threatened to unleash itself and toss his frame within the maelstrom of its unravelling.

When he had gone we formed an undignified babel.

I remember it as chaos.

I remember spoken prayers.

Ruth took to the podium once again. She yelled over the babel.

She said, There are no doctrinal implications to these events.

I have never liked Ruth, although I have tried, but I have never liked her less than in that moment. I found myself muttering, perhaps a little too loudly because Nathan turned and gave me an odd look:

Fuck you, you fat little dyke.

There was not one there among us who did not murmur something. I guess it might even have sounded like a rustle of assent, even if it was not. None of us knew what to say, not even Isabel. She must have been behind me, somewhere at the edges of the council of elders, somewhere on the periphery of this mass of confusion and disbelief.

I think it was Petersen, maybe Frankie Shaw, who said: What the fuck is this? What is this bullshit? This is bullshit, right?

She said, Listen: this is really happening. Much as you would like Him to, God does not adapt Himself to fit your design nor accommodate your whim. I suggest you remember who is here to serve who.

Fuck her. Fuck the fat, arrogant little dyke bitch. Fuck her.

But she was right.

Fuck her.

Item

Present: Isabel Beaumont, Nathan Beaumont, Franklin Shaw, Oscar Petersen, David McArdle, Ruth Felton.
Location: A Public Bar.

Jesus, said Isabel. This is a nightmare. I don't believe it. I don't believe it.

I reached out and took her hand.

Don't fucking *touch* me, David.

Nathan, I said.

Nathan shrugged. He was very drunk. He had been very drunk for two days. We had all been drunk for two days. We had hardly left each other's company.

Come on, I said. Isabel. Frank. Oscar. Come *on*. Let's just see it through. Let's see what happens.

Isabel: Don't be a prick, David.

I stood too quickly. The table toppled. Glasses smashed.

I told her to fuck herself. I told them all to fuck themselves. I left them there, wild-eyed and drunk. And scared. I mean really scared. Scared right down to the secret places inside them.

Scared of what?

That, all along, we've been wrong? That this is all based on nothing?

Or that we've been right? That we've been more right than we thought was possible.

Scared of which? I don't know.

I don't know which is more terrible.

I don't know anything.

At night, I jerk awake before slamming into the earth. There is a roaring inside me, like a hurricane which cuts me off from the silent, protected world in which my wife, oblivious and loved, curls like a child, imprinting her body and her musk upon the mattress.

I can't pray.

I've never been weaker and more confused, not even in my helpless, hairy nudity and impotence before my wife's long-ago betrayal with Richardson.

How obsessed I was by fantasies of revenge, how eaten with loathing for what I could not help but imagine as his humiliating virility, his bestial fertility.

How, even now, I feel betrayed.

How somehow it is worse than falling.

Date:

At last I know what is troubling Naomi. This evening she began to weep while preparing supper. I set my papers on the table, removed my spectacles and took her in my arms. I planted small kisses on the nape of her neck and said – There, there, whatever is the matter?, but she didn't stop. Instead she really broke down. She began to convulse and draw in shuddering sobs, like she had when the Richardson thing came out. I was a touch discomfited. For a moment, I feared for her sanity.

When she turned to face me and told me about the new baby inside her, I felt her shy from me a fraction. I was ashamed that she harboured this fear of me, regretted that I had ever displayed towards her anything but the kindness and tenderness she deserves. Perhaps she sensed this because she snuggled tight to me and pressed her face to my chest and I played with her hair.

She sniffed – Why are you laughing?

– I don't know, I said, Why are you?

– Don't make me laugh, she said. You'll make me cry.

– You're not making any sense, I told her. You're a crazy woman.

She pinched my arm, gently enough, and I rubbed the palm of my hand over her belly, over the little seed sprouting in there.

Date:

[the following is a transcription of an incomplete longhand text.]

[When the] helicopter touched down, I could hardly [believe] that she had burrowed and toiled in such a hellish place for so long. I almost warmed to her, [but] not quite, God forgive my vanity.

I [regret that I] was not responsible for the organisation of the airlift. Somebody has some explaining [to do]. How inappropriate that on such an occasion we should be afforded all the dignity of a side-show, a troupe of travelling players arriving under the gaze of starving soldiers. So [conscious] was I of the picture we made, the four of us accompanied by the absurd retinue of bodyguards and camera crew barking instructions –

[extract incomplete]

There was little sense of the ceremony or dignity which surely was demanded. All I recall is hurry, something on the edge of panic, as if like circus clowns we passed between us something soaped and slippery which we dare not drop. [I am aware] that this moment will assume its due significance as the years pass, but I am troubled that this significance will be an illusion borne of vanity, of a longing to have been present at great events. How absurd that, as I stood and shook Ruth's hand, in the stinging storm whipped up by the rotors of the transport helicopter, all I was able to think about was whether she might have heard what I called her during the council: how ridiculous that I [entry concludes]

Jesus. Oh Jesus. Forgive us.

Eight *American Pornography*

Of course it was all bullshit.

America did not exist. It was an *idea*, a kind of pornography. After a spasm of intense personal engagement, one was left with helpless disgust for one's weakness, for one's capitulation to this glossy, posed promise which traded on the recurrence of desire.

This wasn't America because America had gone.

That which remained continued to bear the scars of the preceding generations, the last of America: the insurmountable racial and economic tensions which had beset and bested the land of the free, of the plurality of cultures that had been allowed insufficient time to forge a cohesive identity, if such a grand design had ever truly been possible and which had been complicated by the decision to allow into the borders huge numbers of immigrants: European, Asian, East European, African. A burgeoning sense of united Americanness was created by the very perceived threat to it. Logical argument – that, since the nation's infrastructure was decaying along with vast numbers of its erstwhile populace, large-scale immigration was an economic and social necessity – had failed to fully convince a country grown dangerously if understandably insular.

Appeals to the Christian spirit fell on stony ground. America was not Job. It did not believe and love and worship *despite*. It believed *because*, and the big because was that it was scared. Terrible things had happened to the world with a sequentiality in which it was difficult not to infer design, and in design retribution.

Marcion was right – the God of the Old Testament is a

committed barbarian, but what he did not add in a footnote is that fear is a lower and more human attribute than love and tenderness and generosity and forgiveness. Who needs a God that forgives? What use is he to everyday life? What does it matter what we do if some doddering old fuck is magnanimously going to take our sinful and selfish shoulders at the end of time and say: 'Don't worry, child; it's all forgotten'?

But a God that'll wipe out your family, that will cause your husband and daughter and neighbours and friends to be made hideous then dead by rude, malignant buboes which defy treatment with the super-antibiotics upon which new, multitudinous strains of voracious pathogens have learned actively to thrive: a God who will silently preside over an instant and inexplicable terminal currency collapse: a God that can watch China eradicate the population of Japan with a delightfully designed supervirus which itself had expired in 36 hours, making the Islands safe for doomed financial exploitation: a God that can create a genius sufficiently fucked in the head to develop genetically targeted weapons: a God who can preside over the bleak comedy of the use of these weapons by men to whom this filth represents a means to purity: a God that can nudge military satellites from the sky, cracking like eggs in the lower atmosphere in order to distribute unintended payloads of weapons-grade plutonium: a God who can allow the food-chain to be savaged like a rat in the jaws of a terrier by agricultural techniques of staggering shortsightedness and ineptitude, ultimately providing a culture to nurture the very beasties against which such techniques had been designed as prophylactic, resulting not in excess, not in profit, not in plenty, but in not *enough:* a God who had created humanity in His own image and yet could sit back and watch it starve and burn and waste away: a God who would preside over the birth of children delivered from the womb without brains, with vestigial and ambiguous genitals, without bones, without eyes, with too many eyes, with too many limbs, with too many bones: a God who could see His ostensibly beloved creation descend into a war that was a result not of ideology but panic: a God like an autistic savant who creates a work of genius which has no meaning to him, whose fragility and perfection are not qualities he recognises or to which he ascribes even cursory value and which he is thus able to rip up, discard and forget: *that* was a God worth worshipping.

Fuck the love crap. I want mine. The ontological equivalent of panic buying.

Such was the presiding Christian spirit which accompanied my family's arrival in America: such was the Christian spirit which broke the heart of my father and turned bloodless and bitter the mouth of my mother, whose atrophied, vinegar womb had borne only dead children and me, the visionary prodigy of whom she was so selflessly proud. At first they had decided to call their child Robert, after his maternal grand-father, but they instead named him Malachi, fearing their entry visas might in some way be contingent on quantifiers of their Devotion. He was an oddly intense and gentle child who could recite the Beatitudes by the time he was eight, and by the age of thirteen was equipped to dissect the argument of an atheist with the cool logic of his faith, even if forced to use Pascal's Wager. He was subject to dreams of Christ sufficiently intense to qualify in the eyes of some as visions. Once, at the age of eleven he had gasped at the dinner table and his eyes rolled ugly in their sockets and passionately he addressed his parents in a guttural language neither they nor, later, he could identify or understand.

Little England – the British enclave – represented to my father a noble and progressively high-minded attempt by the Government, which was as yet not synonymous with the Church, to preserve on foreign shores those cultures which were dying in their emptying homelands. To my mother it was a ghetto, a repulsive and soulless parody of Britain, just as elsewhere there were parodies of France, of Taiwan, of Poland. 'I can't live in a *theme park*, Alan,' she said. Since I was childishly incapable of understanding what she meant, this must have been during the first years. We lived in two rooms in a block. My father would leave Little England each morning by train. He taught English-speaking adolescents the virtues of Marlowe and Salinger, of John Donne and Harper Lee, texts which have subsequently been withdrawn from national curricula and quietly banned. My mother would catch the commuter ferry across the bay, where she was PA to an anti-Semitic middle manager to whom the current downshift in the market for sports footwear (which was being diluted by the inconvenient visitation of wide-scale premature death amongst its target demographic) represented a thrilling challenge to his legendary capacities for market-identifcation and -adaptation. And I would walk transposed English streets to my little Anglican school for gifted children, where I would sit all day in studious concentration, beneath the desk my left ankle gently locked behind the right leg of Nicola Barton, for whom I nurtured an inexpressible and agonising pre-pubescent love about which I still occasionally dream.

I wonder what happened to Nicola.

Thus, the Christianity which met this transposition of much of the rest of the world was a function of fear. The individuals who comprised America feared pain, they feared starvation, they feared poverty, they feared disease and they feared surprise changes to the television scheduling. America the *gestalt* entity feared subsumation within influx, sublimely neglecting to reflect upon the fact that it was a nation of immigrants founded on land-theft and genocide.

It was not the soil of this ruined memory upon which I disembarked but rather the Golden Corridor, the independent state established by the Church along a swathe of what had been the American East Coast. But this wasn't America: this was New Jerusalem, wherein sat the Temple, snug and secure, dead in the centre of New Jerusalem City, magisterially squatting over the city like a barren toad in holy robes. The entire journey to NJC (courtesy of a train that bore passengers only, no freight) was a hypnotic observation of rushing swathes of greenery; of intermittent forest of such sweetness and fecundity as to moisten the eyes; of small towns comprised of large houses and wide streets upon which passed sweet kids on bicycles and adolescent girls with braced teeth and long, brown, tennis legs. And whiteness. Everything was white that wasn't green, even the people: the blacks were white, the few hispanics were white, the Asians, rarer still, were white, the semites were white. The cars that weren't white were black, and the cars that weren't black were red. They glinted delightfully even when the sun of New Jerusalem crept briefly behind the occasional pretty cumulus.

None of us, not one person I knew actually thought of these meagre few hundred thousand square kilometres as New Jerusalem: we were hooked, we were inculcated with the brand name. What this was, was *America* – an idea of America which had lodged in the soft tissue of our brains like a sliver of glass.

I knew it was a lie. These communities were model towns inhabited not by the hard-working, well-rewarded but the super-rich and ultra-favoured who found their employment in NJC itself, spending their working day in any one of the administrative and executive bodies which comprise the political organs of the Church. Their children were beautiful because they were rich (itself a sign of God's favour). The grassland and the lawns and the forest through which the silent train sped were cosmetics applied to a celebrity corpse, a false micro-ecology constructed at prohibitive expense – justified by the labour it provided in the maintenance of the fecund illusion, the perpetuation of green and white, the colours of prelapsarian, consumerist Eden.

My carriage was not empty. I had a window seat, so both the fat woman next to me and the people on the wrong side of the carriage apologised delightfully as they leaned over me, crushing my newspaper, to catch the first glimpse of the city through artfully placed clearings in the forest: a distant flash of white, consolidated by another, longer glimpse, and soon it revealed itself, pure and white and beautiful.

It is not a large city but is without question comely, designed with love and logic. It is comprised of concentric bands, a witty acknowledgment of cosmologies past. The exterior three bands are residential: wide, tree-lined avenues which shelter grand, detached houses, heated swimming pools in generously appointed gardens, fragrant with fresh-mown grass, the pleasantly acrid, atavistic aroma of the family barbecue. This is the most expensive real estate in the history of the planet. The first of the three inner rings is dedicated to commerce: with wide boulevards designed for strolling visitors; hotels and malls and restaurants. The second circle is administrative, the guts of the Church throbbing serenely away behind elegant white walls and reflective, blast-proof glass. The inner circle is an elysian park, an architectural paradigm of circularity. Deer run in this park, skittish and Christ-eyed. At the summit of a gentle slope, elevated to a position such that it may be gazed upon from any point in the city, there rises the pristine body of the temple, the ethereal glow of its stony whiteness pleasingly juxtaposed by the grandeur and gravitas of its neo-classicism, of the massive marble pillars which rivet it to the earth. The temple, the symbol of our unity and our humble excellence in the service of God.

New Jerusalem City, New Jerusalem.

I scuttle through it like a crab.

I stepped from the train, heaving my suitcase on to the platform with some difficulty. Sullenly unwilling to surrender it to a moon-faced bellboy with the demeanour of a hotel porter in a light comedy, I heaved it all the way out of the station. I found a cafeteria where it was possible to smoke. It was not full. I took a window seat. I ate a Danish, drank three hundred cups of coffee and smoked all the cigarettes I had not been allowed to smoke on the train. Soon I began to display symptoms of cardiac arrhythmia, my papery heart skipping too lightly just beneath the skin of my chest. I worried myself half to death that I was about to die.

Some show-off bastard in the booth opposite sat alone, smoking and drinking coffee as he flicked intently through a black New Testament with which, he was at pains to make abundantly clear, he was very familiar. He indulged himself with a private little smile when he came across a favourite passage. I didn't need to peek over his shoulder to guess that he was reading Luke. The insipid and the sentimental love Luke; those who have difficulty nailing together two pieces of wood and enjoy classical music favour the gospel of John. If you want my advice, avoid friendship with anybody over the age of fifteen who is fond of Revelations, because they are dangerous and insane and they might hurt you.

I watched him with hypnotised revulsion for a few minutes – I could tell that he knew I was looking at him. No doubt he fancied that I was admiring and approving his devoutness. His private little smiles became littler and more private. A cold shudder of disgust broke the spell. Hurriedly, I got the bill and made good my escape.

It was going to be an exceptionally long four days.

One of the enduringly hilarious aspects of Christianity was that, even now, it was something practised by the majority as a kind of hobby. I never understood that: Islam means 'submission', Judaism kind of demands it and moreover expects nothing in return, but that's understandable. This is, after all, *God* we're talking about, this is the instigator of the laws of physics, a system so elegant that one can stir milk into coffee and observe the revolution of a galaxy. This is the universal, primal creative force, this is a being beyond being, created *ex nihilo*, a being even a fragmentary glimpse at the tiniest portion of true understanding of which would pop all the neurons in our little head like the bulbs in a string of Christmas lights. This is the everything before which you are nothing, this is the thing in which, if you truly believe, it is surely imperative that you surrender your heart and soul in their entirety – look at

Abraham, willing to skewer his progeny for no reason other than that it was demanded of him: look at Jesus, the charismatic human being Joshua bar Joseph, look at him praying – sweating blood – in Gethsemane for this terrible burden of death and humiliation to be taken from him.

People just don't seem to get the hang of this.

Oh, they understood during the war, they understood when they were hungry and they were starting to show the first signs of fever, they were faithful then, but it was faith as another aspect of this inculcated consumerism: they prayed because they wanted something. They wanted to purchase their life on easy terms. With the passing of crisis, so passed this intensity of belief. Christianity remained largely nominal. Most of us went to church, but most of us went to church because it was expected of us. What the Church represented was a loosely strung chain of norms and prejudices to which the populace at large largely adhered, to one foaming-at-the-mouth degree or another: family was good, crime was bad: work was good, indolence was bad: homosexuality was bad: sex before or outside marriage was bad; the termination of an unwanted child was not just bad but abhorrent while the execution of criminals was considered worthwhile, if sometimes distasteful: swearing was bad: *we* are more humble and civilised and more advanced and generally better all-round than *them*, whoever they might be. Beards were suspect, even though Jesus had one. And so on. It was a broad church, all right, and as the old cliché goes, it's all in the vast and largely unread document which defines our culture: the homophobe will quote Leviticus, telling us that for a man to lie with another man is an abomination unto death, neglecting to further inform us that two or three verses later we learn that a) shaving one's beard or b) mixing different cloths in one's choice of *ensemble* are similarly deserving of capital punishment and eternal disapprobation. What they believed in was each other: each other and Jesus, that gentle big brother in the sky.

I could live with that. I could live with them, with their

stopping-off at the garden centre on the way back from church, communion with the monstrous and furiously primal kinetic drive which is God not sufficient to put their mind off the leaky guttering. I could live with that, because I had to, despite the far from infrequent urge to stand astride a table and denounce them all as hypocrites and empty vessels who should open their eyes to the grandeur of that which they professed to worship.

I admit this is a somewhat paradoxical urge in an atheist who gets his kicks passing on banned books which suggest that Jesus was queer, or if not that he was fucking Mary Magdalene (but that this is quite legitimate because he was married to her also).

But NJC was different. One was not a tourist here, one was a pilgrim, and the old and the young alike had that oily metallic gleam in the eye that testified to the true thing, to the kind of faith that heals diabetes and which endows lamentably lame songs with legs, with a militaristic passion, and sentimental trash with disproportionately emotive power. Listen to them singing 'The Old Rugged Cross' and disagree with me. Give it a try.

The men were smart and sober-suited and the women were friendly and sociable and pretty in a way that precluded any hint of sex. Imagine his righteous, sweating humping and her unsmudged lipstick, her smooth foundation, her cool, dry, powdered thighs and belly, the pumiced feet she locks around him. They utilised the word 'community' more frequently than anybody in history had ever found necessary. Male and female found it easy to weep, especially when praying aloud in groups.

And their kids? Their kids were fucking *freaks*. Their adolescent girls positively revelled in the fact that their parents' love for them was such that mom or pop was willing to give up a free evening in order to chaperone her on one of her pheromone-free dates with whatever buck-toothed gimp she deemed acceptable (the more perversely devoid he was of the trembling imperative that he get his hand up her sweater, like, *now*, the better). These girls were not embarrassed by the fact, let alone the presence of their parents, a phenomenon for which my father had prepared me before it actually happened, and which I didn't believe ever would until it did. Ova nestled in their teenage bellies like shiny little ball bearings. Those few who were truly beautiful were creatures of unearthly sexlessness.

And the boys. Jesus, the *boys*. They dressed like their fathers through *choice*. Neat, sober suits and short hair cut square at the nape. Not one of them found it necessary to grow their hair to any great length, nor to colour it any way other than that intended by God, nor to pierce any part of their body, nor to have any part of the same tattooed or branded or in any way mutilated in the pursuit of fashion. They believed that having two friends round to watch a film and perhaps drink some fruit-juice punch was 'a party'. They did not consider it necessary to listen to music their parents did not understand precisely because their parents did not understand it. They *washed*. The movement of a bus across a pothole or the abstract consideration of a passing ankle did not give rise in them to an erection the size of a house with similar architectural tenacity.

Now, even in the depths of my childhood Christianity, I had understood the necessity of adolescence. As I say, my father had prepared me for it and, being a precocious and somewhat bookish little shit, I proceeded to read round the subject. When it began I recognised the symptoms immediately – the first sign was existential despair in the school lavatory, the sudden realisation that I was actually going to *die*. This profound train of thought was immediately derailed by the discovery of a lusciously purple zit on my forehead. I remember it, it's one of the moments of my life I remember with utmost, indeed suspicious clarity. *Here we go then*, I thought.

Then I did this: I went home and – you won't believe this, but it's true – I warned my parents by unveiling my first pimple that I was entering the undiscovered country of burgeoning adulthood, and apologised to them in advance for any discomfort, shame and/or heartbreak of which I might prove to be the cause. I mean, I was joking, but I still said it, precocious little turd that I was. They laughed, like they were supposed to, but I could tell they knew I meant it, too. Believing I'd done all that could realistically be done by way of preparation, I then proceeded to go joyously apeshit for a number of years. There are things I stopped doing, such as going to school other than when absolutely necessary, such as going to the church which had become emblematic of the stifling 'system' of which I had recently become so very aware. I stopped not doing the things I wanted to do, such as drinking and smoking cigarettes and pumping my poor body full of every dubious drug I could get my hands on. I became crazed with what seems, in celibate retrospect, an insane and permanent lust, my cup ranneth over, so to speak. The first time I touched the skin of a girl's breast I ejaculated in my pants despite a preparatory hand-job half an hour earlier, in the cinema toilets. I'm afraid to say I grew my hair long and tried to grow a beard. I wore sunglasses both indoors and after dark. I introduced myself as *Mal*, an abbreviation I had previously been unable to abide, but soon I was granted a plethora of nicknames to make this ugly truncation redundant. I learned that I had an unsuspected talent for violence, which I recognised immediately as a temporarily valuable commodity. I got a criminal record and a reputation. I was invited to leave the nice Anglican school for gifted youngsters and was packed off to a school that was somewhat less nice and full of somewhat less gifted youngsters. I had more friends than I would ever have again. As an adolescent, I was a great success. As an adolescent, I was fucking *fantastic*. I really had what it took for adolescence. It was a triumph. But the point is, at no time during this fondly remembered period did my faith desert me: my faith in the institution of the Church was about the first thing to take temporary leave of absence (later, of course, to become somewhat more permanent), but the faith itself remained. Indeed it burned with an added intensity, since like all adolescents worth their salt, I saw the world as being comprised of two opposed factions: 1) blind, docile hypocrites who understood nothing about anything and 2) me.

There is nothing like the perception of hypocrisy to fuel one's righteous teenage ire. 'I come not to bring peace but a sword.' I used to quote that a lot, although I did not understand its significance until many years later, in the Negev desert. It sounded good, though, when I was forced to justify smashing the chapel windows with a claw hammer and subsequently assaulting the arresting officer.

There was no such eructating passion in the freakish adolescents accompanying their shining parents to NJC, other than that roused by the aforementioned norms from which universal truths were inferred (*why* is it good to work? The politics of that are just so transparent, don't you think?) Just this stern, Protestant smugness in a starchy, stoical faith.

I was going to have to stand it for four days, and I did not know if I could.

I took a cab to the Sheraton, stopping off on the way at a liquor store to treat myself to a bottle of single malt. I imagined prices at the hotel would be what we call prohibitive when we are the kind of person who resents spending money while being congenitally incapable of stopping.

This time it was a real bellboy who took my bag (a student, naturally, of wealthy parents, earning vacation money and equally valuably, 'life experience', the handsome, hideous little bastard with his easy grin and enthusiasm for his temporary servitude) and I lumbered awkwardly in his cheerfully subservient wake resenting how much he would be earning by the time he was twenty-five.

Before the latch had snapped shut on the door behind him I had popped open the whiskey and taken a refreshing draught directly down my open gullet, smooth as silk, not touching the sides.

As ever, in this sterile place, I was acutely aware of a fragility in my sense of self. I was in clothes I did not commonly wear, speaking, when I spoke, in a way I did not commonly speak, surrounded by people to whom I did not commonly come any closer than necessary, far from home with nobody to call and affirm that I was still the person I had been when I left. I kicked off my shoes, turned on the TV and sat on the edge of the bed, taking another swig from the bottle and extracting a cigarette from its pack in the elegantly efficient way I can never seem to manage in public. I watched a sitcom about an endearingly inept and situation-prone wealthy family whose collective bacon is saved on a regular basis by their sardonically wisecracking chef Nelson, a neat old black man with a halo of endearingly silver hair for whom the series was named. I watched ten minutes of a discomfitingly informative documentary about the lives of Australian creepy crawlies, which I pretended to myself I switched over because it was boring rather than frightening and abhorrently fascinating. I came in twenty minutes late to a film I had seen twice before and enjoyed both times: an ex-military specialist is ousted from his new life of monastic solitude in a shack in the western badlands in order — naturally — to do 'one last job'. One of the Chinese reclamations has fallen under control of an unspecified terrorist force. He must lead a team of experts: 1) the gum-chewing, handsome kid who specialises in communications 2) the impossibly beautiful, impossibly athletic and unusually firm-breasted woman who can kill a man with a look, a little finger or a karate-kick which shows off her legs to best advantage 3) the wise, black explosives expert who's tired of killing but knows there's a job to be done 4) the cynical and unshaven ex-criminal who is a) the only person to know the maze of secret tunnels underlying the reclamation through which the crack team must gain entry b) clearly in love with the aforementioned killer woman c) going to betray the team for money and d) ultimately going to save the day and make it all right, although he cannot get the girl since not only does he not regularly shave, he is shorter and less spiritually attractive than her, and what's more, he smokes. With a sardonically redeemed smile and a cigarette he accepts this as the natural order of things.

The villain is an elegant Englishman with an aquiline nose, an attractively receding hairline and a nice line in suits. For some reason all villains are Englishmen with aquiline noses and usually the hairline and suit thing. You never see a short, fat, French villain with a little pink smudge of a proboscis, or if you do he's wiped out by the *proper* villain before the first half an hour is done. It's no wonder I'm paranoid. I look and speak like my culture's popular conception of a villain, and I find it vaguely troubling that the popular opinion should be so justified.

I searched my memory for the opening soliloquy of *Richard III* because, becoming drunk, I was under the temporary illusion that I was as clever as I promised to be as a child instead of this shambling mess, and I wished to revel in its appositeness. My attention was distracted by the film's justly celebrated car chase, and held by a number of explosions and not a few gun- and fistfights so I forgot about Shakespeare. By the time the credits rolled I had become righteously drunk and toyed with the idea of phoning Ruth, who lived relatively close-by, and to whom I had not spoken for close to eighteen months, not since the McArdle thing. Swigging from the bottle, I spilled a little down my chin and wiped it away with the back of my hand as I weaved to the bathroom, cursing myself aloud for allowing myself to think about McArdle.

I watched a little MTV, wondering why all the new bands were such shit, remembering that when I was a kid you could hear the words and sing the tune, then I remembered some words and a tune and began to sing them. It was an old song when I was a kid and I never really understood it then, but I loved it:

And I don't care what you're called, I sang.
Tell me later if at all, I added.

Very loudly, I agreed that: *I don't care for words that don't belong,*

Tum-te-tum-te-tum-te-tum, I decided, then:

I could wait a long, long time before I hear another love song, I bellowed with red-faced volume, and opened my arms to the air in a grand gesture of surrender or encompassment to which only the television was witness and then fell backwards onto the bed. I propped myself on one elbow, lit a cigarette and drank from the rapidly emptying bottle.

'You are a fucking drunk,' I told myself.

'Fuck it,' I replied cheerfully, by way of consolation, and puffed stoically on the cigarette.

I sat up and finished the bottle. It slipped from my numb hands and fell with a satisfyingly cushioned concussion on the pile of the Sheraton carpet.

'Fuck it,' I recited happily. 'Fuck it, fuck you, fuck me, fuck fucking Marlboro, fuck fucking her, fuck fucking Ruth, fuck fucking Isabel and fucking Nathan, fuck this fucking minibar, open you fucking bastard, there, fuck the fucking Church, fuck it all. Fuck McArdle.'

For a moment this cheerful litany of condemnation paused and as always I was sober deep down. I looked in the mirror, at the pallor and the idiocy of my inebriation, my drained skin and my hair in a peacock's tuft at the crown and the eyes that people do not like to meet and inside my skull I saw McArdle projected, sitting hunched in that car trying not to look like himself, the contemptuous woman to whom I had delivered the package sitting with barely repressed fury alongside him, as if she can no more believe that they are doing this than I can and the only word I can voice in my head is: 'Jesus', because soon I know I am going to be visited by thoughts that are too big for me and I watch him turn the key in the ignition and that is when I become aware – not scared, but aware – that I am being watched and the hairs on my nape stand alert and I look up and around me. Directly across the street moves a busy, anonymous crowd intent on its own business. Like sweet water flowing about a chalky boulder the crowd parts about the unmoving figure of a huge albino who dwarfs them in every dimension but who they do not seem to notice. He is wearing a navy-blue suit tailored to encompass the raw power of the width of his shoulders and his skin is of an angelic pallor. His hair is a mane pushed from his brow, tumbling thick and lustrous and proud down his back and it is he who I feel looking at me and when my eyes meet his every muscle in my body spasms and I fear collapse. His eyes are an impossible neon red. He smiles at me. It is a hideous, ravenous smile and I look away from it, from that moist, salacious cavity cropped out with glistening teeth.

He grins and I look away but the car is gone, McArdle is gone and when I look back to the albino so too is he.

I picked up the phone and banged out a number.

'Hello, Ruth,' I said.

'Excuse me, who is this?'

'It's me,' I said.

'Malachi? Where have you been? Are you calling me up drunk?'

'I'm scared,' I told her.

'You're shit-faced,' she informed me.

'I am that,' I agreed. 'Have one with me. Go on. Have a drink where you are.'

A pause. 'Oh, why not. Just a second.'

I waited with benign patience until she returned. She would be drinking water. Or mint tea.

'So,' she said. 'My prodigal pupil. What have you been up to? I thought you'd forgotten me.'

'Don't be dumb,' I said 'I haven't forgotten anything. Not anything. Not a fucking thing.'

That's all I remember.

In the morning I woke up and very much wanted to die. I was on the floor, half dressed, a Sheraton towel scrunched as a pillow beneath my head. The patch of carpet over which I'd spilled the last mini-gin from the minibar was sodden and offensively malodorous: the stench made my stomach clench like a squash ball in a fist and I ran, bent double to the bathroom, where I howled and strained and moaned and swore and ejected a thin, brownish bile that adhered like egg-yolk to the corner of my mouth.

Miserably, I sat in the bath and ran the cold shower over myself.

After drying myself down, I went and lay foetally on the unmade bed, holding my belly, sticking out my yellow tongue and muttering to myself: 'Jesus fucking holy Christ, you fucking idiot,' in exactly the manner I had intoned to myself on innumerable, not dissimilar occasions. I went hot, cold, hot, cold, and I shivered and shook and venomously cursed myself. Soon, but by no means soon enough, I began to feel a little better.

It became necessary to risk a cigarette. By the time I'd half finished the Marlboro, I was beginning to feel somewhat less bestial. It was then of course that the terrible chill of post-inebriate anxiety made my bones flash silver and I crouched, wrapped my head in my hands and said 'Fuck' a few times more. I remembered phoning Ruth, I remembered telling her that I was scared, and that was it. Every time I thought about what I might have told her my limbs tingled and strength drained from them and it was imperative that I say 'Fuck' again. I was in an agony of self-reproach and jerky paranoia. I stomped to the bed, pulled the covers over my head and said 'Fuck' some more. I said 'bastard', as well, for novelty, and once or twice I said: 'shitshitshit shitshitshit*shit*.' But mostly it was just 'Fuck'.

I lay on my back, removed the sheet from my face and smoked some more cigarettes. I was very thirsty and had never been less hungry in my life. When I could stand it no longer I dressed for breakfast, at which point it occurred to me to seek out my wristwatch. I realised for the first time that breakfast would in fact be an early dinner. It was five pm. My first day in this terrible place would soon be over. Red-eyed, I made my way to the restaurant, where I drank several cups of coffee on an empty stomach, followed by a rictally grinning walk to the bathroom, where I immediately threw it all up in one impressive roar.

Clearly, a satisfactory recovery from a hangover of biblical proportions was going to require a serious degree of application. I stepped outside and strolled the wide New Jerusalem boulevards for a while, breathing in air that tasted like the coolest, freshest water you've ever drunk. I bought two cans of Coke and some candy from a newsvendor, along with a newspaper. After an hour I made my way back to the Sheraton. More coffee, a couple of cigarettes, a medium-rare steak with fries, a dish of Ben and Jerry's. It was seven thirty. For a while I made a show of reading the paper. Flattening out the centre pages, I caught the attention of a waiter (another dumb fucking student) and ordered a whiskey sour. God, what a whiskey sour can do for you when you need it most.

Late into the evening I fell into fascinating conversation with a man who introduced himself as Eric Howson. The conversation did not start well, but picked up after a drink or two. Eric Howson ('As in house & garden.') was a doe-eyed and soft-spoken little God-botherer who had some trouble taking his eyes off the floor. He was eager to see the President's address. He was not normally one for drinking, but his wife, daughter and son-in-law were out taking in a show and, well, it was a special time. 'Special time.' He said that. Within minutes he was talking about faith healing. Faith healing had a constitutionally ambiguous status. I got the idea that Staad had no time for it. Staad believed in science. Staad believed that science, properly applied, was the means by which God had granted us the ability to regain perfection, to raise ourselves from our fallen state.

Eric, however, was very keen indeed on faith healing. He had seen it in action. He had seen the lame made to walk, the blind made to see – stuff we've all heard about a million times. (Incidentally, I had yet to meet somebody who had *themself* been made to walk or made to see. In my case, for example, it had taken a two-month stay in hospital while I grew this new leg: a moist, pink bud which sprouted from my hip, wriggling like a baby's finger, like a maggot munching its way out of me: a two-month stay, a lot of physiotherapy and exercise, not to mention some serious counselling. Maybe they've all set up a little community somewhere, those who have been so healed. Maybe they all live together, doing all their walking and seeing alongside people who understand why they get so damn excited about it all the time: 'Look! I can see a flower! God, it's so *beautiful*.' 'You stay there, honey. I'll walk over and pick it for you.')

Anyway, Eric had seen all this. Eric was keen to impress on me that he had witnessed miracles on a basis which one could safely call regular. But Eric had a problem (he confided after his third whiskey and soda on the rocks). Eric was one of these quietly brave fellows. He'd won a purple heart for something he did in Angola, something upon which he was modestly unwilling to elaborate. Since coming back, though, he'd had this problem. Eric had a morbid fear of goldfish. It verged on the obsessive. He could hardly bear to say the word. He voiced it like a stammering admission of guilt.

It had started, unexpectedly, as a mildly phobic reaction to a fish his youngest daughter, now married, had brought back from school to feed during the summer vacation. He had hated that fish, the metronomic popping of its mouth, the idiot glare of its eyes, the discoloured, whitish patches on its belly. The gossamer thread of its turds, streaming gently behind its obscenely tight, fishily undulating anus. He had ordered his daughter, Bethanie, to keep the fish in her room, out of his sight. But Eric couldn't help himself. Day after day, he found himself sneaking into Bethanie's room, with all its frills and flowers, with all its gingham and lace, where he would perch on the edge of her bed and stare for hour upon flesh-creeping hour in rapt disgust, his being monopolised by a single goldfish swimming endlessly and malevolently round and around its limited universe.

There's more, much more, to this tale of degradation and terror, but I'm not here to make a fool of Eric (put it this way: the fish died, there was a problem with a flush, there was a funeral attended by a traumatised and sobbing daughter, there was a replacement fish to buy . . . Basically, things got a lot worse). Eric seemed to me to be a good man. He loved his family and his country – he had fought for both. But most of all Eric loved God. Eric loved God with a tender humility that beguiled and saddened me, like the sight of lovers kissing.

Eric, who had gone hungry during the war, who had left the family he loved to travel far away, who had undergone deprivation and duty with good grace, stoicism and faith, had resorted to faith-healing to cure him of this piscine morbidity. Eric passionately and unequivocally believed in the power of the laying on of hands.

The laying on of hands had failed.

Eric loved God more than anything. Eric lived his life for God. But Eric did not love God as much as he was frightened of goldfish.

That's how I got through my first day. Eric Howson got me through it. Eric Howson's life was a parable.

I left him alone, drunk, sometime after midnight.

I would have loved to have stayed longer and talked some more about fish, but the next day I had work to do.

Nine   *What I Did On My Vacation*

What can I say? I can only recount what transpired, acknowledging from the outset the restriction imposed by my viewpoint. I believe there was a Great Design: Staad's design, Isabel's design, whoever's. It doesn't matter. What does is that there was not merely chaos, panic, entropy and the urge to preserve oneself in the face of it.

I want to believe.

This is what was supposed to happen: on Thursday, I was to go and see the two pm showing of some movie, I forget exactly which, some sentimental war trash about how great we were. You know the stuff – Christian nobility in ripped fatigues and four days' growth, squinting into the middle distance. After watching the movie (don't ask – I didn't. I just did as instructed), I was to dine alone in some Italian restaurant. A table had been booked in my name. As I began dessert, I would be surprised at my table by an 'old acquaintance', who would say: 'Good Lord, Malachi?,' and I would look up and say: 'Ted?' I would stand, we would shake hands and be delighted so see one another. Ted would join me for a very brief conversation. We would make a date for lunch the next day which of course neither of us had any intention of attending – but there was nothing illegal about avoiding dinner with somebody you had encountered by accident. Whatever was on the disk, he was to leave with it. Unless I was busted in the subsequent hour or two, I'd be safe, at least as safe as I could realistically hope to be. I was to hang around for a couple more days, go to galleries, a museum or two: Isabel had suggested the War Museum and I'd agreed. If I was under surveillance, which she assured me I was not, then I at least should behave like a pious veteran, take an interest in the war whose end I was supposed to be here to commemorate. On Saturday she had booked for me the cheapest available seats in the Temple – 'cheap' in this instance being a defining example of the relative concept. I would sing at the top of my voice (I sing very well) to stirring and inspirational hymns. I would close my eyes when prayers were said. I would look awe-struck and moved when Staad, the cancer-ridden old bastard, shuffled to the podium to deliver his first public address for many years. Quite possibly it was to be his last. It was a commonly held opinion that he wasn't long for this particular world – that since Lydia had died, since he'd witnessed the first flowerings of Christendom, he was content to give up the ghost.

He had led us to the Promised Land. Unlike his predecessor, he had been suffered to abide there a season.

All these pilgrims, all this piety. It was a freakshow. They were an audience of wretched voyeurs, hypocrites come to feast their eyes on the spectacle of a dying celebrity. This is what Staad had become: an idol. It was confidently predicted that the television broadcast of the Address in the Temple would pull in the largest audience since the announcement of victory fifteen years before. The world would be watching this wise old man, his prodigious might slowly failing, bid it farewell. It would know then that it moved towards a future made possible by his vision, but no longer shaped by it. Dying, Staad was giving us back the world.

On Monday I was to begin the journey home. I would swear to myself, as I had sworn to myself a dozen times before, that this had been the last time, that clearly there were things going on that I had no wish to know about or be involved with. And in six months I would be back, and I would never know why.

That is what is supposed to have happened.

Here's what did.

I made it to the movie. It was not a good movie, but it

killed an hour or two and I felt safe in the dark, chomping down on a family-sized tub of salted popcorn. After the movie (we won it in it. Again) I walked two blocks to the designated restaurant. I ate Carpaccio Al Picere, which I did not enjoy, followed by veal kidneys with mushroom, which I did, very much. I ordered apple pie and cheese for dessert because I liked to consider my sense of humour self-referential and full of insidious, bitter irony. Look at me, I thought with Mephistopholean glee, the anti-Christ devouring a symbol of your goodness.

Unfortunately, two courses on top of that huge tub of popcorn had rather soothed my appetite. I dined at a very leisurely pace. As I swallowed the final mouthful, Ted had yet to arrive.

I sat for a while, dabbing my lips with a napkin, wondering what I should do. I ordered a second dessert, exaggerating to the waiter exactly how delicious the first had been and what a scandalous appetite I had. Protesting far too much, but there we are. The second round of pie and cheese was extraordinarily easy to linger over. Halfway through, I took a long pause and peeped round the restaurant. My belly was beginning to strain against my belt in a most uncomfortable way.

I wondered what Ted looked like. I imagined him as a rotund and gregarious man in a houndstooth jacket. I pictured him keeling over with a coronary two blocks away, or slipping beneath the wheels of one of those monstrous automobiles, whose 'lightweight' construction, measured against the chassis of the human body, is another fine example of the relative concept.

I finished the second dessert. Ted was in police custody by now, telling them my name and where to find me, the chickenshit moron. No: Ted was a *policeman*: Ted was some twisted double agent, some super-Christian sociopath who'd set me up for a fall. I began to really hate Ted. I was furious with Isabel for ever trusting him, the duplicitous, red-faced bastard in his tacky suit and flashy watch. Then Ted was dead in a back alley with a government-issue bullet buried in a brick, having passed through the back of his skull and out through his face. Ted's cheery smile was spread all over the sidewalk.

I had to get away.

I didn't though. I ordered a bottle of house white and lit a cigarette. I forced myself to drink slowly. I'd give Ted half a bottle before I went. In the end, I gave him the full bottle and a couple of glasses of decent brandy before admitting that he really wasn't going to show.

I considered disposing of the contraband. It might have been wise to do so – things might have worked out better for me. I don't know, I doubt it – but anyway, the truth is, I was too scared to dump it. I was too anxious to take an executive decision. I needed to be advised what to do.

I kept remembering that albino, the incalculably knowing ugliness of his smile, like he was announcing his intention to eat me all up. His big, pink, wet, lolling tongue and his teeth, the same yellow-white as the mane of hair that swept back from his brow.

I left the restaurant and took a circuitous route back to the Sheraton.

Arriving, I was clumsily inarticulate requesting that my smartcard be charged with my keycode. The receptionist regarded me without suspicion or contempt, which I found suspicious. I desperately hoped that I wasn't about to bump into Eric Howson. I couldn't face the thought of that fish. It had already kept me awake half the night. I collided shoulder-to-shoulder with people coming in the opposite direction and made courteous and subdued apologies which were politely accepted.

Sharing a mirrored elevator with an elderly couple, I looked at the floor, the ceiling, anywhere but at them or their reflection. I found myself following irrelevant trains of thought that I very much did not want to follow: had anyone ever *fucked* in this lift? I shifted my weight uncomfortably. There were security cameras in the lift, I knew. There might be film of whatever clean-limbed young Christians had done to one another in here: crisp, digital images with an accompanying soundtrack of her stifled groaning and his low muttering. Get the right bellboy, I thought, and you could rent, maybe buy this stuff. After all, most of them were college kids. I don't care how pious. Give a couple of college kids access to film of some pretty young girl being vigorously seen to by her husband (or whoever, I thought, and I had to shift my balance again), and they're going to make the most of it. There must have been many couples who'd done it in here, in a hurry. Perhaps even the newlyweds I'd observed through the corner of one twisted eye the previous evening: the girl in the black evening dress, with her over-sophisticated haircut, her long, flawless neck. On honeymoon in the American dreamstate. Trying to be pious rather than passionate, but not fully succeeding because they are young, they are in love, and they are human. A late night, a restaurant, some wine. Perhaps *last night*. I'd watched them leave, after all, and it seemed to me that they'd finished enough wine to sufficiently disinhibit them. In the elevator, he is unable to wait for the still-novel and unfamiliar feel of her. He urges her, begs her to bend and grab the handrail. She says no, but she has a wild look about her, slightly drunk and a little childishly devil-may-care, and then she says yes, okay, but *hurry*, and she laughs behind her hand. They're hurried and agitated. He lifts her evening dress. I'd watched him lean across the table and laugh, touching her knee briefly, and I wanted to kill him. I wanted to smash his fucking teeth right down his throat. You could see he was in love with her, and she with him. But he was too young and too handsome and too fucking happy. She wriggles awkwardly from the pretty underwear purchased by friends as a wedding gift. Her hands are shaking as she hurriedly stuffs the panties into her purse. Then she presses her cheek to the mirrored wall and urges him to hurry, which helps him to. He steps behind her, bends his legs a little at the knee. An almost defecatory crouch. He grins more lasciviously than seems possible for such a young face. But this expression is not young. It is the oldest face there is.

It doesn't take long. Five or six seconds. Nevertheless they're just in time. As the elevator stops a bellboy enters . . .

This is one of the most inappropriate erections I have ever endured. Which is saying something.

I let myself into my room and went straight to the minibar. I took a drink, swallowed. I wanted to think – but for the moment all I could bear in mind was the camera in the elevator, and which bellboy seemed the most potentially corrupt. Resigned to myself, I went to the bathroom. As the elevator stops a bellboy enters . . .

The story had a thousand variations. Sometimes people surprise you, Sonny had said, sometimes they do just what you want them to.

Soon I was able to stop thinking about it. I poured another drink.

There was nothing else to do, nowhere else to go, so I drank a little. Isabel knew where to find me if she wanted to.

Unfortunately, however, Isabel wasn't about to find me, and nor was Nathan, because Isabel and Nathan were dead. I just didn't know that yet.

I filled the tooth glass from a pint of whiskey and worked my way through a pack of cigarettes. I watched two syndicated sitcoms without seeing them. Then came the news. Isabel and Nathan were the first story. They were headlines. The anchorwoman, auburn hair piled high and solid above her gamine neck, fixed me with a stare of neutral gravitas.

With the commonly extraordinary diction of the news-reader, putting stresses on words where no stress is warranted, she enunciated: 'Good evening. I'm Hannah Blackwell . . .'

Cut to second anchor: 'And I'm Paul Jones.'

'. . . bringing you today's news on CTW Syndicated.' Cut to the CTW News Network logo, a five-second blast of the network signature, four chiming notes of orchestral urgency and gravitas. Cut back to Hannah: 'Our lead story this evening is still breaking,' she told us. To illustrate this, she ruffled a sheaf of paper as if it had at that very moment been handed to her, for all the world like we weren't all fully aware of the existence of autocue.

We knew all about Hannah. Hannah was a big celebrity. Hannah was very beautiful, and had led a personal life gratifyingly rich in tragedy. At the moment, she wore one of her signature expressions: one eyebrow raised slightly, the other frowning. Hannah the professional anchorperson, fighting the flood of emotion presently being endured by Hannah the caring human being. Hannah suppressing her own sadness to her greater charge: Us.

Hannah loved us, and we loved her in return. This expression was an index that something Tragic had occurred. It was her *Children Die in Plane Crash* expression, and it was very endearing.

'You join us on an evening,' she said (after a little swallow), 'when, poised for celebration, the Government is instead plunged into tragedy. Three of the Government's lesser-known, but greatly significant figures – Frank Shaw, and husband-and-wife, Isabel and Nathan Beaumont, died today . . .'

My head snapped up so hard it hurt.

On screen there was footage of a horribly mangled car, of emergency vehicles with flashing lights, grim-faced policemen forming a barrier between curious pilgrims and the aftermath of Isabel's brutish extinction.

I put my hand over my mouth.

'Details are still coming in,' Hannah reminded us, 'but Nathan Beaumont, who is believed to have been at the wheel of the car at the time of the accident, is understood to have had a history of coronary disease. More details as they arrive, but first: Paul, what impact are these terrible events likely to have on the President?'

Cut to second anchor. Paul is younger than Hannah. His friendly gravitas is belied by his soapy smooth skin, the potential for twinkle in those boyish brown eyes. Paul is single. He is not as famous yet, as Hannah, and not as touched by tragedy, but he has allowed the cameras into his beautiful home and admitted that he is still searching for lasting love. Beneath a photograph of him, casual in white cable-knit sweater and jeans, leaning on his tasteful mantelpiece, I remember the legend: '*Sometimes I do worry that I won't find the right woman. My love life seems to come second to my first love, reporting the news!*'

'Good evening, Hannah,' he said, pretending he's talking to her when of course he's not, he's talking to us. He's telling us that Isabel and Nathan are dead. He's telling us that they've had the life smashed from them: that she is no longer able to say to him: 'Don't you look *just* the thing.' That he will no longer pretend to scan rooms for bugs with a cellular phone. 'Well, it's of course difficult to say for sure, but I think it's safe to say the President will take this tragedy particularly hard – especially coming as it does on the eve his long-awaited Address to the Temple.'

Cut to Hannah. Sympathetic nod. A little moue. 'Sure. So, Paul, for those of us who might not be as familiar as we should be with the workings of government,' (*This is why we love Hannah*, I thought, *she's one of us*.), '. . . could you perhaps fill us in on the gap these people will be leaving behind.'

Cut to Paul. 'Of course.' Looks straight and unblinking at the camera. His eyes might be a little moist. 'Well, Hannah. The truth is: you might be forgiven for not being familiar with the names Isabel Beaumont, Nathan Beaumont and Frank Shaw. But although none of these remarkable people ever chose to stray far into the spotlight of public attention, it's true to say that each of them had a lasting effect on all our lives. Today we have witnessed the tragic death of three figures who each played a truly critical role in the institution of the Church as a functioning reality. In fact Franklin Shaw . . .' cut to a photograph of two smiling, crew-cut young men dressed in swim-shorts and life preservers, each of them bearing an oar.

One of them is recognisable as Staad, something grim already established behind his toothy, slightly gauche grin. He has his arm, impressively muscled, about the narrow, pale, freckled shoulders of the other kid. The other kid has jug-ears, but he's laughing none the less. He's an old man, now, and dead. '. . . was a childhood friend of the President. It was a friendship which was to endure for many years, in fact, poignantly, Frank Shaw was to prove loyal to the very end of his life. He was a man who made no secret of his early doubts concerning the young Randall Staad's expressed mission to reunite the Christian faith under the famous "ecumenical umbrella" . . .' Cut to a clip. An ageing man, barely recognisable as the kid in the photograph, makes himself more comfortable in a high-backed leather chair. He is dressed in slacks and a cardigan with leather buttons. His face has grown kindly, his ears larger, hairier, fleshier. The clip is extracted from a documentary, the kind that's shown in 'Modern History' class. The Rise of the Church. The Theocratic Imperative. Shaw laughs throatily, a good old smoker's cough, an impressively phlegmy rattle. He looks gnomish and irreverent, rubbing at the side of his nose with a gnarled index finger.

'Well,' he says. He's laughing at the question that's just been asked. Eyes gleam from deep within the shadows of laughter lines. 'That's some question. That's really some question. What can I say? You have to remember, this is all a very long time ago and Randall and I . . . well, we were buddies. I didn't know he was going to be *the Great Randall Staad*, y'know? He was just Randy, this clever kid from the back end of Baker Street, or wherever it was. We met when I was thirteen and he was twelve. He was one of those kids . . . well, he wasn't one of *anything*, if you know what I mean. Nobody ever knew anybody who was like Randy Staad. I mean, on the one hand, he was kind of a . . .' He rubs the edge of his nose with an index finger and laughs. 'No, hang on. I need to be careful how I put this, don't I? He was, you know, a straight A student, a decent athlete and God-fearing too. It wasn't too fashionable to be God-fearing in those days. So in a way, Randy wasn't cut out to be popular with *everybody* – this clean-cut American kid. But he wasn't like that. Randy *was* friends with everybody. Everybody loved him. He'd do anything for anybody. He'd help, y'know, the kid who was the school nerd, the kid who got bullied real bad, he'd help him with his math or his geography or whatever, he'd take time out to teach this kid. And once . . .' Shaw barks a great laugh, scratches at his forehead. He looks at the camera with a little apprehensive mischief: '. . . can I really say this stuff?' He shakes his head and says: 'Okay, okay. Well, Randall wasn't *squeaky*, you know. There was one time . . . well, this one kid, he was giving a hard time to this other guy who wasn't, like, one of the in-crowd, he wasn't one of the popular kids. Well, of course, this poor kid who's having the hard time, he's a friend of Randall's, but he won't tell Randall about what this other kid's putting him through. And when Randall gets to hear . . . Jeez. He blows his top. He doesn't even wait until lunch. He leaves his own class, just as everyone else is sitting down, and he strides to the class where this guy, this bully, is. He apologises to whoever's taking the class, he nods to apologise, I guess they're kind of taken aback, why is Randy Staad in their classroom, y'know, and Randy, he walks up to the bully. The class goes quiet, Randy makes this kid stand, right in front of his classmates, his buddies and girls he has a crush on or is dating and . . . well. Randy just punches this guy once, and down he goes. And Randy, y'know, much as everyone loves him, well, you can't *do* that sort of thing, and he's suspended from school for a couple of weeks. I guess the incident's still on his school records somewhere.' Shaw shakes his head. 'We used to go camping together, camping and fishing. He loved to fish. Still does, if he can find the time. It was while we were fishing that he made, y'know, the announcement . . .'

Interviewer, off-screen: 'How old were you at the time?'

Shaw: 'Oh, eighteen, nineteen. Out of short pants, y'know.'

Interviewer: 'And you can remember the words he used?'

Shaw: 'Well, gosh no. To tell the truth, I wasn't really listening. I was concentrating on catching fish, not doing too well at it. The rivers weren't well stocked in those days. Randall says something like: Frankie. I've had a revelation. Naturally, I think there's a joke coming, I think he's going to say something like, oh, I don't know, It's been revealed to me that Lucy Masterson is interested in you romantically, so I looked at him and he looked kind of serious, the kind of serious you look when you're trying your damnedest not to laugh, so I said, can I say this? – I said something like, "Revelation my ass. You dickweed." '

Off camera, an explosion of laughter. Shaw looks past the camera and laughs, as if to say: I did, I really said that.

Interviewer: 'And what was his reaction?'

Shaw: 'If you want to know the truth, he laughed right out loud and threw a handful of maggots at me. And he said: "Thanks," but he wasn't laughing when he said it. Not too much anyway.'

Cut. A later scene. Shaw is sober and still.

'So, can you pinpoint the moment of your conversion?'

'To the second. Right to the second. Randall and I had fallen out of touch for a while, a number of years – I was making public service broadcasts and he'd – you know – he'd taken his own path in life. That's how I saw it. I followed what happened to him, I followed his career through newspapers and television, even a couple of books which were written about him in the early days. Pretty bad books, if you want to know the truth. I didn't believe those books, but didn't much believe in Randall's calling either, although of course I knew *he* did. Lord knows he'd done enough by the time he was thirty-five to prove how serious he was – and although I never believed he could achieve what he wanted (I mean who believed it was possible in the early days?) it never seemed odd to me that Randy Staad should be out there, trying to save a world all gone to pot. I was kind of proud of him. Anyway, it turns out Randall's going to speak in my home town, address some rally or other. It wasn't too good a time in my life, if you want to know the truth. It wasn't too good a time in anybody's life back then. My first wife, Mary. Well, she wasn't one of the strong ones, she'd passed away the year before and . . . Anyway. It was a beautiful day, there weren't many beautiful days back then, you're too young to remember, but it was a beautiful day and the crowd – jeez, the crowd was *huge*. I remember thinking – all these people have come to hear *Randall*, and for the first time it began to dawn on me that, y'know, something really *serious* was going on with this guy. There were news crews from all over the world, there were helicopters everywhere, there were police, there was security, all these *beefy* guys in dark glasses – but when Randall took to the podium, this *silence* descended. Even the breeze died down. There was this feeling of peace, this peace which came from an *incredible* strength, an incredible *faith*. So there was this hush and I craned my neck to see him and I thought – there's something *different* about him. I couldn't put my finger on it, but there was something about him I'd never witnessed before, not in a man. I wrote in my journal,' he laughs at himself, 'it's a little overwritten, but those were days which deserved a little overwriting. Anyway, I wrote: *He had about him the nobility not of a man, but a great idea.*' Laughs again. 'My buddy Randall, I got the feeling he'd already stepped out of the world and into history. And as soon as he opened his mouth, I *knew*. My heart opened and I let Jesus in like a cool breeze, I knew he'd been waiting there all along, waiting for me to let him in. Waiting for all of us, waiting for the world, and that was what Randy was doing. He was bringing Jesus back to the world.'

End of clip. Back to the newsroom, back to Paul. 'Frank Shaw went on to join Randall Staad's campaign, and to record it for posterity. He went on further to document many of the historically significant moments of Randall Staad's early years as President, perhaps most importantly the darkest and most difficult days of the war, which make up such an important part of the National Archive. After the war Frank Shaw was to become Executive President of the CTW News Network.' Paul allows himself a little confirmatory nod to us. *Yes, he was my boss.* 'And I know that Hannah and the rest of the crew will join with me in breaking with tradition a little and adding our personal tribute to Frank. He was a fine man to work for. We at CTW loved him for his kindness, his wisdom, the personal emotional support with which he was always so very generous, and which helped so many of us through some difficult times. But above all, we will remember Frank for his sense of humour. Even under the considerable strain sometimes involved in bringing the news to your door, Frank Shaw, Senior, never once lost his playfulness or his sense of fun. He brought so much light into all our lives, here at the CTW network studio. We extend our sympathy and love to Frank's beloved wife, Paula, whom we have all also come to love and admire, and to the fine children he leaves, Sarah, Mary and Frank Junior. Tragically, Frank's first grandchild was due to be born on December 21. Paula, Sarah, Mary, Franklin Jr, you are in all our hearts and prayers today. God bless you all.'

Paul gathers his thoughts. It's Nathan's turn. There's an old, still photograph of him. He's wearing a tweed suit, brogues, holding a pipe. His hair is blowing in the breeze. He's standing in front of some old statue. This is an English photograph – like a pastiche of an England which, had it ever existed, is now certainly long past. He looks about twenty-one. A young fogey. 'To Nathan Beaumont the Church owes an incalculable debt,' Paul tells us. Much of what came to be the structure of the world under the aegis of the Church is the direct result of what the President has described as "endless late nights in smoke-filled rooms with Nathan, screaming at him in frustration, and getting screamed right back at in return".'

I slapped my thigh, laughed out loud. I couldn't believe it. Nathan hadn't seemed that smart to me. He'd just seemed like this slightly doddery old fool who wasn't too clever with his shoelaces.

'Mr Beaumont was thirty-eight and a bachelor when the President introduced him to Isabel Wade. Ms Wade, two years older, also unmarried, was an architect who had been brought to the President's attention several years earlier. Like Frank Shaw, hers was not an easy appointment. The President described the process as "a necessary, but an extended and occasionally frustrating wooing". Ms Wade and the President were to enjoy a close, personal friendship. Ms Wade was the chief architect for New Jerusalem City. She had the capital mapped out when there were still those who saw its establishment as a dream which would never be fulfilled. Many of the Church's most instantly recognisable buildings are constructed to her design, the Parker Tower, Roehm Hall, the Callow Memorial Building. Perhaps most importantly, she was responsible for proposing what form the Temple should take, when the time indeed came to see it built.

'Both Isabel Wade and Nathan Beaumont were dedicated to their professional lives – yet, shortly after introducing them, the President described the pleasure he took in witnessing "one of the greatest real-life, straight-out-of-the-movies love affairs you could ever hope to see". The pair were publicity shy, so it was fitting that their moment of public recognition fell on the day of their wedding, a ceremony conducted by the President, who joked in an interview that he had "wanted to put the seal" on what he had started.'

Cut to a clip: news film. Staad, the new President of an unmandated country in a world falling apart, is conducting a wedding. We do not see the bride and groom – just the President, much younger, saying: 'I am honoured to be here today. Seldom have I witnessed such a powerful tribute to the truth which underlies that easily voiced sentiment: that two people might truly be brought together by God.'

Cut to a photograph. There are four people in it. In the centre, Isabel and Nathan, now Beaumonts. She is wearing an ivory wedding dress, holding a bouquet. Her hair is blonde and pinned at the nape. She is young and tall and slender and elegant. She is beautiful. To her left, the President, sober and proud, his jaw a little tilted. His hand rests paternally on her shoulder. To her right, Nathan in a morning suit. He has loosened the wing collars. His cravat is at an angle. To his right stands David McArdle. This photograph was taken years before he began to run to fat, years before I passed on to him whatever it was I passed on to him. I cannot formulate thought. I am rigid, the passive recipient of images I am unable to contextualise.

We see the photograph for a few moments more, in silence.

Cut to Hannah: 'Well, Paul, I guess that photograph just about says it all.'

Cut to Paul. 'It certainly does,' he agrees. 'Sadly, Isabel and Nathan Beaumont leave no children. It might be said that it seems somehow fitting that a husband and wife so dedicated to one another and the Church should be taken at the same time, together with God in death as they were in life.'

Cut to Hannah. 'A sad day,' she says. Her big brown eyes are brimming. We watch her steel herself, settle her wonder-fully formed shoulders over her deep personal sadness. 'Now,' she says on a slightly broken but rising inflection. 'Other news.'

I remembered the wedding. I'd only been a kid, but I remembered it. There was an almighty media fuss around Staad's officiation. I suppose it must have made for a little positive propaganda, when things weren't going nearly as well as they might, and ongoing military skirmishes were beginning to consolidate into outright world war. My parents watched it. They told me to stop playing and be quiet for a while, so I must have been reading a book or something when it was broadcast. I don't remember my mother commenting on the bride, but I'm sure she must have. Isabel looked so very beautiful.

My mother, fixed to the screen, admiring a woman who would one day compel me to come here, to this city, this hotel by using everything she knew about me. A woman before whose will I was powerless, in whose company I would spend a very few hours, and in whose death I felt a sense of loss whose enormity I did not understand.

I drained the glass. I took the pint of malt from atop the minibar, sat on the bed clutching it in one hand, glass in the other. I remained without thought, or rather, with so many trains of thought running at great speed simultaneously that I was incapable of isolating one and following it through. I took a few more drinks, set the bottle back on top of the minibar, settling it neatly right in the stain its base had made on the varnish, and went to the bathroom to clean my teeth. My mouth felt foul. I washed my face, combed back my hair, dusted off the fedora but left it hanging on the hook because the sky was darkening and the sun had lost its threat for the day. I slipped an unopened pack of Marlboro into my pocket. Beneath the base of the standard lamp which stood in the far corner, casting a warm ambient glow upon the proceedings, I slipped the disk. I straightened my necktie and left the hotel. I went for a walk.

The streets were crowded with people to whom the deaths of Isabel and Nathan Beaumont were of only tertiary, sentimental interest: *the poor President, to lose three such good friends at once – Y'know, for a second or two I really thought Hannah was going to cry. She tried not to show it, but I could tell. You could see she really loved that guy. That old guy, the boss guy. – Didn't he seem so nice, and the woman, the architect lady, she looked so happy in that photograph, the one they showed – You know that wedding . . .? – That's the funny thing, I do, I remember it on TV – You know what? You know what I was going to say? I remember it too! Been a lot of water under the bridge since then, but I still remember it. Clear as day. It's funny how these things stick in your mind – . . .*

They drank *espresso al fresco.* They walked arm in arm. They laughed and they looked at each other.

I wandered through a small park, sat on a designated smoker's bench, but did not smoke. I couldn't feel my hands. I was aware only that no one else in this city was alone, and that these happy people would hate me for the blackness of my heart. They would have been right to do so, because I hated them back, and I still did not understand why. I pitied them the emptiness of the belief from which they extracted such idiotic comfort. They had nothing to hurt me with and had nothing it was possible to envy other than a commodity I no longer desired. That, and the occasional romantic attachment which engendered a passing pang of sadness, before I remembered that, like every passing pleasure, it would extract its price.

I watched the sky for a while. The stars were coming out. Then I watched a skinny girl, nine maybe, unsteady on roller skates, her father, in shirtsleeves and loose tie, just behind her, half-stooped and jogging, ready to catch her should she stumble. I thought again of Eric Howson and his goldfish. The girl lost her balance and, sure enough, her father was there. She fell right into his arms. She giggled. He took her beneath the arms and lifted her into the sky: 'I'm gonna throw you to the *moon*,' I heard him shout, and she play-slapped at his hands.

There were a couple of payphone booths just outside the park. I entered one, patting my pockets. I did a mime-show of exasperation and embarrassment, exited again and stood outside, hands bashfully in my pockets. The man with the roller skate daughter passed me. She was breathless and flushed and laughing.

'Excuse me,' I said. 'Excuse me, sir.'

The man stopped and turned to me, in a friendly enough fashion. This is a real friendly place. We're all here together. There's no such thing as a stranger. He didn't seem real. He was like a famous photograph of a father.

'I'm sorry to trouble you,' I said, 'really I am. Believe me. But – oh, this is *really* embarrassing. But I need to phone my wife back at the hotel. The thing is, I've come out without my smartcard and I've got this birthday surprise all prepared, she thinks she's going to the theatre but she's not, where's she's actually going, only she doesn't *know* it yet, is this restaurant a block away. All her family are there, her mom, her pop, her sister, you know. This is a big deal for her family, and I've been running around like a madman trying to organise all the last-minute problems; now all I've got to do is call her at the hotel, tell her *not* to meet me at the theatre after all, but to come along to this *restaurant* I told you about, where we've got this big joke all lined up, she's going to meet me there, but it's going to be all *dark*, you know, like it's empty and nobody's there and ... the thing is, I've been in such a panic running round trying to organise everybody, it's not until now I realise I don't have my card and ... oh, let me tell you one thing: I never want to spend another Christmas at her folks' place house ever *again*. *Believe* me. That's if I don't just go right ahead and kill myself before her mother gets to me.'

He waited for me to stop ranting. I rather enjoyed it. I almost managed to convince myself that the scenario I recounted was entirely true. I knew I was doing well when he placed a fraternal hand on my shoulder. When I finished, or let myself run out of breath, he laughed sympathetically and made a pained little face. His daughter did it, too. She tilted her pointy little chin and scrunched her little freckled nose for me. 'No problem,' he said, and already he's reaching into his pocket, withdrawing his billfold. 'That's somewhere we've all been at one time or another.' He looks at his daughter and says: 'Huh, honey?' She grins and agrees, grown up as you like.

He steps into the booth. He's holding his smartcard.

Whatever central agency monitors our movements by monitoring the use of smartcards, this call will be recorded under his name. It's the unique whorls of his fingers authorising the use of the card. It's his PIN number. It's his life on that card, his medical and employment history, not mine. If anybody is looking for me, by monitoring the use of my card, they won't even know yet that I've left my hotel – not until I use my card to gain entry.

I became aware of him looking at me a little quizzically.

'I'm sorry?' I said.

He's grinning ear to ear. 'Boy, do *you* look worried,' he said. 'Don't be. She'll be fine.' He patted my shoulder again. 'Go ahead and dial.'

I thanked him politely but not too effusively as he stood aside and let the door of the booth close on me. Peripherally I was aware of him whistling out there, his hands in his pockets, his daughter with her skates slung over one shoulder.

The phone was answered on the eighth ring.

'Hello,' said Ruth.

'This is a big ugly grunt in big blundering boots,' I said. 'Please call me back on this number.' I gave her the number three times, put the phone down. I opened the booth door and handed the man his smartcard, explained that my wife was calling me back. I thanked him again — after all, he'd just broken the law for me, a minor infringement, but it was a good and Christian thing to do. I said goodbye to him and his daughter. I had my eyes fixed on their retreating backs even as I snatched up the receiver on the first ring.

I was so pleased to hear her voice. Really, that was all I wanted, all I'd planned on. Now we were speaking, I didn't know how elliptical to be. If they were monitoring her calls — and how was I to know they were not, how had I ever known? — then voice-recognition software, if set to the task, would recognise the print of my intonation in a tenth of a second, and despatch representatives of the New Constitution to do to me whatever it is they did to people like me. On the other hand, if the call was being monitored by just a *person*, some low-paid operative who spent their working life monitoring the conversations of the kind of person whose conversations were deemed worthy of monitoring, then perhaps ellipses were no bad thing. Or perhaps they were trained to respond to the specific cadence of the ellipse. Perhaps my being obtuse would set all the alarm bells ringing in their bored and corporate little skull. Perhaps nobody was listening, perhaps there was no one out there. But I didn't know. I just didn't know. All this was component of my thought processes at this time: like ticker tape whipped up by a tornado.

'Have you heard?' I said.

'Yes.'

'Do you believe it was a crash?'

A dry pause. 'No. It wasn't a crash.'

'Jesus, Ruth.' I kneaded the knob of flesh between my eyes, 'I think I'm really in trouble.'

'I think you really are,' she said. 'But try not to panic.'

'I can't think straight enough to panic. Jesus, I need to piss.'

'Are you charging this call to your own card?'

'Of course not. No, I'm not.' I was kind of jogging from foot to foot. I really did need to piss. It was beginning to hurt.

'Good,' she said. 'That's something. I can be in the city in an hour, an hour-and-a-half. I'll meet you somewhere.'

My legs went weak with relief. I needed to piss even more urgently. I was childishly reassured by Ruth's decisiveness. Ruth had always helped me. A certain childish logic dictated that she always would. The trouble was, of course, that it was Ruth who'd gotten me into all this in the first place.

'Jesus, Ruth,' I said. 'Jesus, thank you. Really.'

'Sssh,' she said, a little sharply. 'Hold on, we're not done yet. Do you have it on you?'

'Have what?'

She lost her patience. She snapped: 'What do you fucking *think*?'

The world made a lazily sinuous, reptilian shift beneath my feet. An anaconda, adjusting its coils, made lethargic in its long digestion.

'You *know* about it?' I said.

She sighed. She was forcing herself to be patient. Ruth would attempt this only in a crisis. Once, at the dig, some of us had found ourselves volunteered to assist in a little shoring-up operation round back of the dig proper. It was something to do. There was a pretty bad accident. It sounds odd now I say it, but while we were shoring up the walls, the ground beneath our feet more or less opened up. Everything went to hell for a while. Most of us fell into the hole. The scaffold collapsed, along with a good proportion of the structure it had been erected in order to support. Things weren't as bad as they first appeared. The hole turned out to be a crater that measured maybe two metres at its deepest. Moreover, nobody was too badly hurt, but we weren't to know any of that at the time. After a few seconds of exchanging glances between us – did you *see* that? – we set about implementing a grim but surprisingly efficient rescue operation. We heaved and levered at boulders, dug at rubble with bare hands. We called out the names of whoever we thought might be buried. There was a lot of dust circulating. It got in your eyes and nostrils. There were a couple of guys buried down there, but it turned out they were okay. They were dusty and shaken, and we joked with them nervously as we pulled them from the hollow scoop in the rock in which they'd crouched, laughing at them because we were glad they weren't dead or seriously injured. The worst of it was, as the scaffold collapsed, an archaeologist, this bony young Scandinavian guy none of us had much time for came down with it and ended up impaled on a pole. It went into him through a kidney and out through his navel.

It was pretty nasty to look at, especially since he kept making these spooky little noises, like he was asleep and having a bad dream. Impalation isn't all you tend to think it might be. Whatever foreign object has pierced the body tends to staunch blood flow so long as it stays *in* the body. This Scandinavian, though. Something major had been majorly severed and was whipping and wiggling like an unmanned little firehose just inside the exit wound. Every second or two he treated us to a little black geyser from around about where his navel had been.

Ruth volunteered a somewhat bewildered young corporal. She coaxed him into applying pressure to the severed artery. She was very calm and patient. She had to tell him three times what to do before he'd do it, the chickenshit, and when he did, he looked away with his eyes screwed tight, and his lips pressed all white together, like he was unblocking a lavatory. It smelled, I suppose. Then she hurried off to get her hands on some medical supplies and radioed out for a helicopter.

The following day, she tore into the corporal like a pitbull terrier. I seem to remember that he cried.

My hands were cold round the phone.

'Malachi,' she said, slowly, in that voice. 'I know this is difficult, but please try to focus. It's important that you do that.'

She was scared.

'No,' I said, sniffing back half a sob. 'I don't have it on me. Not on me, not right now. I hid it. Well, kind of. I put it somewhere a little safer.'

The click of a philosophical tongue against a palate. 'You're going to have to go and get it,' she said. 'Right away. I'll meet you at – where do you know?'

'I'm in a park,' I said, I leaned over a little, craned my neck. 'The south entrance to Eleanor Roosevelt park. In a phone booth.'

'I'll see you there in an hour. Don't bring any friends.'

I made an involuntary little noise.

'Be calm,' she said. 'This isn't good, but things could be worse. You're in public and that's a good thing. Keep to the crowds as much as you can. I'll be with you very soon.'

I thanked her and put down the phone. I attempted to return to the hotel in a manner that might be described as a stroll. However, my body was temporarily unable to perform as commanded, even with its usual equivocal grace. Periodically my head would twitch spasmodically to the right, as if I were glancing over my shoulder to see who might be following – something I was in fact concentrating very hard on not doing. I felt grotesque and soiled, as if the people who noticed my passing (how many noticed me? How many people and how many security cameras were there, recording this humiliatingly grotesque parody of relaxed pedestrianism?) could smell my corruption, the way a moth can smell sex.

I had no wish whatsoever for the crowd to be alerted to the secrets of my heart.

At least the elevator was empty this time. I did not believe myself capable of sharing its confines with another being. My dexterity decreasing each time, it took me three attempts to open my room door.

I stepped inside, closed the door carefully behind me. I leaned my shoulders and the back of my head against the flat comfort of its corporate anonymity. I closed my eyes, and concentrated on my breathing, slowing my heart, unclenching my fists. I took a good couple of minutes to do this. When my respiration had slowed a little, I opened my eyes, resolved to apply some logical analysis to my unfortunate predicament.

But there was a man in there. There was a man in my room.

I will not be the first person to comment on the extraordinary nature of human behaviour. Nobody is able to predict how they will behave in an unprecedented circumstance. Those who dream of bravery are revealed as cowards, and vice versa. We have the neurotic who, under pressure, becomes a natural leader, whose calmness and ability to think under extreme pressure saves lives. We have the mother who lifts a collapsed sedan from atop her child. The accomplishment shatters bones in each thigh and punches down the jagged ends, along shins, past popping kneecaps. We all have examples. The hero of Angola, capable of bravery in battle, but helpless in the face of a little fish. The acrophobic who hangs by a hand from a sixtieth-storey window to rescue a kitten. The gentle man, and generous, driven to violence by sexual betrayal. The loyal woman who proves capable of such betrayal. We all have examples. So, the truth is: I can tell you everything I did in this room, but I would be lying if I tried to tell you how I did it.

There was a man in my room who wanted to hurt me. This I established very quickly.

He wasn't what you'd call immense. In fact he was narrow through the shoulders, somewhat cartilaginous at wrist and ankle. His fingers were very long and tapered. He wore a simple, gold wedding band. I put him somewhere in his early-to mid-thirties. His face inclined to the gaunt: hollow cheeks and lipless mouth. His eyes were very dark brown, beneath sardonic eyebrows. His skin looked smooth as talcum. It didn't look to me like he could grow a full beard. And he wore this expensive haircut. Immaculately conditioned chestnut hair fell from a neat parting and across his brow in a floppy fringe. Conservative with a hint of dandy.

He dressed like old money: understated, dark grey three piece with an indistinct brown check. Tie secured with a pin. Brogues.

He looked like the kind of brilliant young professor of economics who is beloved by his students for his easygoing nature and hated by the hookers he regularly picks up in the nearest small town for exactly the opposite reason.

He looked like a psychopathic fucking *vegetarian*, for Christ's sake. He had this supercilious tilt to his jaw to which I very much took exception.

I was engrossed in taking exception when he decided to point the pistol between my eyes.

It wasn't even an impressive gun. It was what I'd heard a special kind of man describe as a 'lady's firearm' – capable of dropping a man only at very short range, and then rarely to lethal effect.

Other than pointing at me a pistol which might have been chosen with the intent of subtly deriding my masculinity (or as a signifier that the man who was pointing it at me was some kind of sexual deviant. A ballistic transvestite. A pervert vegetarian with a penchant for lady's handguns) he was sitting back, legs crossed, in an armchair. His socks, I was far from surprised to note, were silk.

Set on the carpet alongside him was a black attaché case. I should have been devoting my attention to the gun. I know that. But my eyes kept sliding back to the attaché case. Coupled with his unusual choice of firearm and aristocratic haughtiness, it had an almost dictatorial lure.

Its very unspoken presence compelled one to imagine exactly what such a man might carry in it. This process was more terrifying in its implication than the gun which he was indisputably pointing at my head.

Given all this, I was unexpectedly intelligible, even louche, when I said: 'Aren't you going to show me a badge and read me my rights or something?'

He shot me.

He lowered the pistol a degree or two, and he shot me. Imagine someone taking a good swing at your femur with a mallet. You'd go down like a bag of cement dropped to the sidewalk from the back of a truck.

I rolled around for a while. Although I was trying to think, I couldn't stop the sentence 'Jesus Christ, I've been *shot*' from circling my head like a toy plane buzzing round a wire. There was no pain as such, not yet, because I was flooded with endorphins. I could see the blood, though, so it didn't need to hurt much to get my attention. The little lady's round from the little effete lady's sidearm had managed to blow quite a lump of meat from my thigh.

Also, I pissed myself.

As if it was a real annoyance to get up from the comfy chair and come hurt me some more, he stood, pocketing the gun in a shoulder holster. I found myself hoping to God the holster wasn't *embroidered* or anything. An embroidered holster would be a truly bad thing. As he approached me, I was endeavouring to crawl towards the door, but it just wasn't happening. I couldn't get the crawling thing together at all.

He watched as I struggled to my knees, fell over. Then he reached out a fastidious foot and tipped me on to my back. I felt like a beetle, right down to the fact that my good leg continued to wriggle in the air for a moment, as if independently still intent on crawling away.

He gazed down at me with academic neutrality. Then he kicked the hole in my leg a couple of times. I did a lot of begging.

He kicked me in the ribs a few times, mechanical little punches that hit like golf clubs. I tried to turn within the flurry of his kicking and crawl away some more. He kicked away a buttressing elbow and I fell flat with my face buried in the carpet.

He said: 'Please what?'

'Please don't.'

'Please don't what?'

'Please don't hurt me any more.'

'Hurt you how? Like this?'

I began to take him for something of a corny bastard, because naturally, he started all over again. Kicking me, edging round me with these precise little insect movements.

I curled foetally. He interrupted his kicking. After getting back some breath, he drove his heel into the wound on my thigh three times, each time with a manifest increase in resolve. Then he turned and wiped his bloodied heel on a corner of Sheraton bedding while I flopped and shuddered like a landed fish.

He said: 'Remove your sidearm and pitch it toward me. Then . . .' he dropped the heavily blood-smeared corner of bedding. 'Oh, put your hands behind your *head* or something. Make like you're harmless.'

He seemed a touch perplexed, like a great deal of his concentration was directed elsewhere.

The world came at me in waves. I told him it hurt too much to move.

'Let's not get into a discussion about the theoretical limits of pain,' he said. He nibbled on a thin, bloodless lower lip, as if too engrossed in the search for a misplaced set of keys to give me much attention. 'Because it's an argument I'll win. Just do as you're instructed.'

I did as I was instructed. It wasn't easy, but I was able to grasp the gun Isabel had given me and skip it towards him across the carpet.

He kicked it to the far corner. He stalked round me a couple more times, giving forth with a couple more kicks to my head and ribs before tipping me on to my back again. I lay flat, staring at the ceiling.

He stamped on my mouth. Something in the hinge of my jaw made a noise. He rubbed thoughtfully at his sculpted little chin, calibrated his posture and allowed himself a satisfied grunt of self affirmation just before he kicked me in the testicles.

I snapped shut like a cigarette case. I bit my knees. I rocked like a neonate.

He waited serenely until I had unwittingly given some signal that I was again able to hear. Then he hitched his trouser legs and crouched.

'*What* are you saying? *What* are you asking me to do?'

I sobbed into my knees. I didn't want him to see my face all crumpled and wet.

'Well, you certainly said *something*,' he chided me. 'You said "don't", didn't you?'

I told him I was sorry.

He allowed for a short, reflective silence. Eventually, he said: 'You're not trying to *lie* your way out of saying "don't", are you?'

I assured him that I was not.

'Well,' he said, the corny bastard, 'I must admit I find it hard to believe anyone could be quite that stupid. Evidently the mistake is mine. I accept that without reservation. Now,' he said, 'let's get down to business.'

I didn't want to get down to business. I wished my father was here, who had never landed a blow in anger in all his life. Whose honesty and intelligence and insight had made a good man of him, and killed him in the end. My father died of disappointment. It was a terrible affliction for which there remains no cure.

'Okay,' he said. 'I'm about to ask you where it is. I suppose you'd better think about telling me.'

I had arrived at an unmistakable, if disagreeable reckoning. The police, in the normal course of their duties, utilised non-lethal weaponry: happy gas, immobilising foam suds, stun guns, anti-traction liquids: any number of ingenious devices designed to maximise apprehensive potential while minimising the risk to human life.

This dashing blade had already shot me. The other stuff probably constituted torture, which of course stood in stark contravention of the New Constitution. It was my legal right not to be tortured. That idea didn't seem to worry him unduly.

This for a crime which, now I really had to think about it, seemed a relatively minor one. More of a Constitutional infringement than a crime. More a misdemeanour.

Moreover, had he wished to extract testimony, it would have been the work of moments to inject me with an agent which, once it took hold, would compel me to spill the beans whether I wanted to or not, what little beans I had. And to tell the truth, I wouldn't have minded, not if my eagerness to co-operate was allowed in mitigation. But instead he shot me and kicked me and stamped on me.

He wasn't a policeman, from whatever division – or, if he *was*, he was taking his instructions from a command sufficient to grant him *carte blanche*.

He was going to kill me.

I reasoned with him to give me a second. I told him I couldn't *think*. I told him I was thirsty. I told him I was *sorry*, for Christ's sake.

'I can hardly hear you,' he said. 'Sobbing into your fucking knees like a fucking *queer*.' Positively irritated by this, he said: 'Get up and go sit in the armchair.'

I looked up from my foetal crouch to see him run fingers through his hair. His coiffure fell neatly back into place, just like in the adverts. The glossy tracks left by his bony digits evaporated like the sweaty print of a palm.

His patience snapped. He bellowed: 'Get off the fucking *floor* and into the fucking *chair you pussy piece of shit.*'

It took me a while.

He took a seat and enjoyed the show. He watched me drag myself to the chair. Fall to the floor. Lift myself.

'Once more,' he said. 'You almost made it that time.'

In extremis, we are beasts. He had taken from me even the illusion of free will. He had disabused me of the notion that my mind and body are anything but one and the same. In doing so, he had reminded me which obeys the demands of which.

I read about an experiment once, a long time ago. It was an experiment with monkeys. They took a female monkey and her baby, still young enough to be suckling her and clinging all day to her back or belly. They put the monkey and her baby in a featureless little cell with metal walls and floor. The floor could be heated like a griddle. Once they had closed the door on the monkeys, the heat was turned on. It was never long before the adult female embarked on a display of real discomfort. With the baby securely but fearfully clamped to her underbelly, she would explore the cell with great anxiety, searching out an exit which did not exist. Egress was not part of the design. By increments, her discomfort and anxiety would turn to pain. Urgency would escalate in the direction of panic. She would begin to leap from foot to foot, a little like she were dancing, her pain and her fear expressed in a monkey smile. Unaccompanied by the soundtrack of her screaming, in a film she might even look kind of cute. *She looks so human, dancing like that.* But only if the lens doesn't come too close, because each time she hops from one foot to the other she leaves behind her a sizzling, sole-shaped smear of skin and fat which instantly bubbles and boiles away on the barbecue the floor has become. Eventually there comes a moment when she concedes that there is no possibility whatsoever of even a fragmentary second's relief. Her agony cannot be overcome. Neither can it be tolerated.

This is when she sets her infant upon the floor and stands on it.

There isn't one amongst us who would not do the same. There isn't one amongst us whose first sensation wouldn't be relief. Guilt is a luxury enjoyed by a decadent species. Nothing persuades like pain.

But what kind of mind could conceive of and execute such an endeavour? To introduce a simple creature to an environment designed for the inducement of pain, and expect it to behave in any way other than that commanded by its nature. Where is the purpose in that?

After an interval, I succeeded in lugging my weight into the armchair. I sat, after a fashion. I let the cool wall take the weight of my head. With a sleeve I wiped away sweat and snot and blood. Each expiration inflated a bubble of mucus which clogged one nostril.

The room had taken on the attributes of a glossy photograph advertising a luxury hotel left abandoned to the wind and rain.

But not him. Every spiky line of him was in focus, strutting priggishly on spindly joints.

'Oh, well *done*,' he said.

Prick, I thought.

'Now, tell me where it is,' he said, urbanely. 'And all this can stop right away. I'll make sure you're processed through the proper channels.'

The extremity of my situation is illustrated by the fact that, for a moment, I received this pronouncement with a swell of joy and gratitude. In a matter of a very few minutes, he had made that which I once feared above all else, being 'processed through the proper channels' the thing for which I hoped against all hope. I thought of the monkey and I thought of Eric Howson and his stupid fish, and the girl with the roller skates, the way she wrinkled her nose for me, copying her father. I projected these images on an imaginary screen just behind him. They cast him into silhouette.

'You're too late,' I said. 'I already passed it on. I passed it on about twenty minutes ago. No more than that. Half an hour at the outside. A block or two from here. I just got back. I'm sorry.'

A silence fell that was not at all measured. He lowered his head and a shadow passed over the sun. The room's colour faded as at the pressing of a hidden button. Vibrant shades softened to monochrome.

He walked to the window, pulled aside a drape and glanced at the world outside. When he turned to face me, the sun reappeared. He was recast as an indistinct blob, shifting liquid within the flare of light.

'Now,' he said, 'you and I both know that's not possible.'

I sniffed back the annoying bubble of snot, wiped at my nose.

'You have a problem with your intelligence,' I said, without inflection. I didn't want him to go picking up any double meanings. 'Shoot me up all you want,' I invited him. 'Kick me around some more. It won't make any difference. I don't know what's on the fucking thing. I'm not *interested* in what's on the fucking thing. Certainly not to the extent that I'd get myself shot for it. *Jesus*. Look, I don't know *who* I passed it on to. I can *describe* him if you like. Drive me around and I'll point him *out* to you. I've got nothing to gain by lying. I don't know who you *are*. I wouldn't like to speculate why you decided it was worth shooting me. I mean, Jesus, get some *perspective*.'

I gestured at my damaged leg. 'How important can a book *be*?'

'It's not a book,' he said, diverted. He scratched at the corner of his mouth, passed a hand through his hair. 'Jes-us,' he said, wearily. 'Jesus. You know: I think you might be telling the truth.'

He placed the barrel of the pistol against his lips. He didn't move for a while. Then he gyrated spikily towards me.

'On your knees,' he said.

I went very clammy.

'I just got *up* here,' I said.

He lowered the gun at me. 'Get on your *knees* you mother*fucker*.'

I made rapid, pacifying gestures, movements with my hands that said: *Okay, okay,* and set about lowering myself to my knees. I was losing a lot of blood. My leg and crotch were sopping and black with it. It was smeared all over me. There were bloody handprints on the walls, where I had steadied myself.

'Hands behind your head,' he said.

He marched over to me and dug the barrel of the pistol hard into my skull. He didn't say anything. He just stood there, quite silently, quite content. He just seemed to enjoy digging the barrel into my head for a while, the way somebody stands on the top deck and enjoys the smell of the sea.

My hands were laced at the base of my skull. My head was lowered. There is no more humbling position in which to find oneself. Through the corner of my eye I could see the tips of his brogues. He seemed to be entirely without scent. My hair was sweated into spikes. My face was wet and screwed into a Japanese mask: the anticipation of pain.

I thought about what we must look like, should some accidental stranger burst in to save me. Two perverts made for each other. Mai Lai in the Sheraton.

He said. 'You have until the count of three. One.'

I lost some control. 'Please,' I said.

'Two.'

I felt the incremental increase in pressure against my skull, the infinitesimal displacement of air as his lips formed the final syllable: 'Thr . . .'

I screamed. What I screamed was: 'Okay!', although it was not. I was weeping a little. I held out my hands at the level of my shoulders, a plea of surrender. I kept saying: Oh dear Jesus, oh sweet Jesus, oh dear Jesus.

He said: 'Don't dick me around.'

I turned my head a notch, made eye contact. I said: 'Jesus Christ has sucked my cock and swallowed.'

There is probably a clinical name for his reaction: that tiny burst of cognitive static which is the result of confidently expecting one manner of response and receiving quite another. The momentary blankness while you quickly adjust to an unexpected context.

Of course all this happened in no real time at all. Like someone said to me once, it takes a hundred times longer to tell than it actually took.

I don't deal well with the specifics of humiliation. Like someone else once told me, I have a problem dealing with anger. I had been crouched like a flea, my legs bent beneath me. When I released that tension, I was launched into him with surprising velocity and violence. I tucked my head tight to his bony hip and hammered my shoulder into his spindly midriff.

His gun didn't discharge or anything. It just flew from his hand and went spinning and landed on the bed with an inoffensive, domestic plop, like a patent leather purse.

It was all kind of inelegant. He went lurching back (I picture his arms windmilling and his eyes wide and his mouth idiotically agape but of course I couldn't see his arms or his face because I had my head tucked into him and anyway my eyes were screwed tight shut and I could see lazily rotating mandalas of psychedelic complexity). His lower back crashed into the minibar.

There was a moment of bleak slapstick. The cabinet and the wall behind it allowed him first to correct his balance.

When he had done so, he threw himself upon me. I was on my knees. His momentum threw me on to my back. He landed on top of me. The floor, solid enough beneath the deceptive epidermis of pile, punched the wind from me. I gagged and dribbled and made dry puking actions. He took the impact on his knees. I heard them crack. For a second neither of us moved. The stuff inside that makes us not want to die was pulsing away, bypassing pain.

He was breathing very quickly. I had trouble drawing any breath at all. He was on his hands and knees. I lay flat beneath him. I held the waistband of his pants in one fist, a bunch of rucked-up shirt-tail in the other. He tried to scrabble away. He was light, but fast and lithe with all these wiry muscles. I just couldn't hold him down. He found his feet, if a little precariously, and took a floundering, Frankenstein step towards the bed, where his fallen gun lay.

I held on to him. He dragged me like a net bursting with a heavy catch, right to the edge of the bed. My good foot sought purchase on the carpet, but naturally there was none. My nails bit into flesh. He bled from ragged, chickenskin weals just under his ribcage, but he just kept driving himself forward. I couldn't stop him.

I lifted myself like he was a pull-up bar. He began to slow. The extra weight was too much. He reached out a hand. He strained. He looked like his face was going to burst. Tendons in his neck like piano wire.

I put my head under his rucked-up shirt-tail, like I was glancing under the flap of a tent. He was no longer odourless. I put my face into his crotch. I shifted my head to an angle my neck had not been designed to entertain.

Along with a double fold of fabric, I took into my mouth as much of his genitalia as I was able to accommodate. I bit down hard. Even through his clothes, it really was a most unpleasant textural experience. There was a little crunch and some mysterious popping.

I hadn't noticed how silent we'd been until I heard him scream. It was like walking from a soundproof booth into the flightpath of a jet.

He didn't so much fall to his knees as fold in on them, not unlike a card table about to be stored away until next Christmas. He laid his hands flat on the bed, fingers splayed and rucking at the covers. I don't know how close he'd got to his gun, but it didn't really matter. He was screaming too much to notice.

I'd made him the monkey. The pain had expelled all the mind from him with a blast that shattered his eyes from the inside like office-block windows. The empty hollow of his skull was walled in surgical silver which reflected an interrogative and blinding luminescence: the absence of the thing which came in time to think, and to conclude that it was. In its stead there reverberated the screams of a long dead creature: the revenant of the first ape driven insane by recognising the face in the pool as its own. Behind its reflection combusted that identical sun, dying from the moment it was born, and so far away. A billion years of apes, grinning like mooncalves to demonstrate fear and servitude.

I bit until my teeth met. I worried my head from side to side, as if denying something I was secretly pleased to have done. I worried at his generative organ like a terrier with a rag. He contributed an oddly orgasmic bucking and the chimpanjee shrieking I think I already mentioned. He tried to punch my head but the angles were all wrong. The punches were weak and ineffectual. He tried to gouge my flesh, but he had these neatly clipped little economist's nails. The best he managed was to rake at some scabs of incipient dandruff, perhaps some lubricative sebum. He bucked his hips like he was fucking me but he wasn't. He was trying to force me away from him, but I was heavier, I kept pushing forward, chewing at him, until he fell back.

I heard the air expelled from him. I heard the concussion as his head hit the wall. I had to let go for a moment. I didn't want his unbalanced weight ripping the teeth from my head. But after he had fallen, I dived on top of him and I bit him again. It occurred to me that I was *goring* him. I considered the idea magnificently satisfying, as if I was a lion of the African savannahs caught in the act of establishing dominance of the pride. I *wanted* to gore the motherfucker. I wanted to bite his balls off and his miserable little cock and I wanted to spit them out like undercooked chicken. I wanted to smash at his solar plexus until it shattered, to dig my fingers into the fissure and force open his fucking ribcage like an elevator door. I wanted to root round in the warmth of the cavity and rip out his heart quickly enough for him to witness its last redundant fibrillation before creation dimmed and the life in his eyes faded away.

I admit to grinning at the idea, even as I bit down on him, but in my defence: it was an original grin. It was more than lips spreading over teeth, but it did not denote amusement. It was the grin which gives the lie to our protestations of love and altruism by illustrating that what we are, is *ravenous*. We carry the fear of the dry season in the whirl of our genetic code. Our fear of death is located in the obligation to expel agonised globs of half-living things: the sightless things which squirm inside us in their terrifying billions: ancient things, older than the creature which bears them, testament to a cretinously blank teleology: to replicate in the direction of a future whose sole purpose is to be that towards which we replicate.

The coiling things which contain all the past and the possibility of the future, were once assumed to be a parasitic infestation of the testes. It is an understandable misapprehension.

Our mind is not an indicant that God cohabits our flesh. There is no divine spark which flickers unextinguished and persistent within the moist viscosity of our interior. Heaven is a chasm, unoccupied, except by the passing agonies of transfiguring elements. Our soul, that splinter of divinity lodged within us, flickering with the memory of a luminescence so fierce we dare not look upon it, is an epiphenomenon. It is an unexpected side effect. It is the surface tension of our brain.

All this hurtled past the rear of my eyes with the kinetic rhythm of an express train, proof if one were needed of the grotesque intellectual acuity to which we are often prone in times of physical stress. All these familiar thoughts rattling round the same familiar old track. There were other thoughts, too, while all this was going on, flashes of memory for which there exists no word, scents of a mysterious potency, which I could not begin to articulate.

Suddenly, hot, gluey liquid flooded my mouth. It spurted through gritted teeth, flooded my mouth, into my gullet.

I hope to God it was blood although I acknowledge that it doesn't make much difference what it was.

I tried to swallow, but there was too much and I began to gag and suddenly I became inappropriately but terribly embarrassed: sprawled on a hotel carpet, ripping the testicles from the body of a man to whom I had yet to be introduced. All this warm goop continued to ooze like tincture into my larynx. I gagged and coughed some more. I opened my mouth. I lifted my head, took a breath, coughed, and vomited a packet of his own interior liquid all over him – along with a tiny package of my own enzymes, already industriously and dutifully intent on beginning the process of ingesting this bit of him, and making him a bit of me.

He wasn't moving much any more. He didn't even cup his nuts, as I had expected he might. He just stared at the ceiling. There was a lot of blood, his and mine, splashed and smeared all over the place. We looked like a couple of mud wrestlers. It was pretty gruesome.

Now and again he would say: My God, in a tiny little whisper. It was a voice like looking at someone you love and remembering with a jolt of absolute clarity why you love them. My God, you say, in exactly that voice. They might be shaking out an umbrella, or they might have spilled a cup of coffee and are embarrassed and flustered, they might smile at you halfway through a conversation with their mother on the telephone, it doesn't matter, but you look at them and are staggered by the awesome nature of the thing you feel for them. He said 'My God' exactly like that. I wonder what he was thinking.

He'd crapped himself. I felt bad about that. I wanted to tell him – I'm sorry you had to go and crap yourself, on top of everything else. That's really too bad, that you have to go and crap yourself.

Stuff was smeared all over my face. It was clogging my eyelashes. It was bunging up my nostrils.

I crawled to the bed, got some purchase, took three big breaths and lifted myself to my feet. I saw that we'd made a big, dark smear on the carpet, like kids playing with a big pot of paint. I also saw that his face didn't look as I had expected. It had the opalescence and blissful expressionlessness of a Catholic canvas depicting the early martyrs.

I speculated that this expression reflected a euphoria generated by a mortally increased flood of endorphins, a kind of last-ditch effort. It is a reaction exhibited by prey: the wildebeest, brought to its knees by lions after an obviously desperate struggle, seems at the last to sit quite contented, all cow-eyed and dopey, as the lions rip strips from its shanks.

Over the catastrophic somatic rampage, all the pumping and the hammering and the exuding, and the inhalation and exhalation, all the sweating and seeing and the bleeding, I too was draped in a shroud of beatific calm. I thought this was interesting in itself. I observed that my self seemed to bob slightly behind me, like a buoy tethered to a boat. My brain had shunted my sense of self to one side. It had encouraged my intellect to keep itself occupied with irrelevant speculation while my body got on with the business of doing anything it could in order not to die. I had sent myself off to play like a bothersome child. I was kind of grateful to myself for that. It was a pretty impressive trick. If you want to know the truth, I was grinning like a buffoon, like a hillbilly inbred, and I was muttering to myself: 'Very clever, very clever.' In retrospect, I don't want to know what I must have looked like to him, all smeared with his blood, swaying over him and repeating 'very clever', with a big soppy country grin on my face.

At that moment, I was flooded with so much of whatever it is which causes relief, I bore him no malice. I was just pleased that it was him on the floor and not me. I kind of liked him for being weaker than me and letting me get my teeth to his balls and rip them away from his body.

I looked at him for a while, until I regained some sense of solidity. I raised my hand to my eye and flexed my fingers. What I perceived my fingers to be doing corresponded very satisfactorily with what I felt them to be doing. I was aware of a distant psychic percussion, like war drums beyond the horizon and I knew that something, soon, was going to start hurting me very much. A more familiar set of perceptual parameters were about to establish themselves.

I wondered if he was going to bleed to death and save me a job. I didn't know. I thought he probably would, eventually (I wished he already had). I worried that blood might start dripping through the ceilings. Split-splatting on the private dinner of the young couple I'd found the time to imagine fucking in the lift a few hours before. With this thought, the world as I knew it established itself another increment.

I wanted to say something to him, but I didn't know what. I didn't know whether I wanted to apologise to him for what I'd done to him, and what I was about to do, or whether I wanted to taunt and humiliate him. Neither seemed appropriate.

I said: Can you hear me?

He rolled his eyes. He said: Jesus. Jesus Christ.

I said: Can you move?

He said: Hurts.

I know, I said. I know. Look, can you make it to the bathroom? I can't carry you. You shot my leg all to shit.

I can't do that, he said.

You've got to help me here, I said. You've got to help me to help you. Come on, help me.

Come on, now, I repeated. You know you can do it.

He does it. He rolls over. He farts as well but I try not to pay too much attention to that, because he's crawling on his hands and knees, his elbows are shaking with the effort and he's dripping spots of blood in a splattering trail, and I can't stop seeing him as a menstruating old dog crawling to the side of some suburban road to die. I don't want to think about him farting as well.

I know if I make a move towards one of the pistols he's going to know it, and he's not going to take another step towards that bathroom and make things more difficult for me than they already are. So I watch him make this slow progress, this almost heroic plod towards the reverberative, tiled interior of the hotel bathroom. When he's almost there, I limp towards him. I tell him, well done, well done, and as I do so I lift from the minibar a half full bottle of whiskey which our impact had toppled but not sent rolling to the floor. I clasp my fist round the neck of it.

The bathroom isn't large. It's an Ur-hotel bathroom. Mirrors and tiles, a shaving point, a toothglass, a white bathtub with integral shower unit, chrome handrails and a white shower curtain hanging from a rail. There are towels: lots of fluffy white towels imprinted with the Sheraton International corporate logo. I remember the design being featured in news broadcasts a while ago. They'd paid a comical amount of money for a couple of squiggles and a rectangle. Still, as long as they were pleased with it. The bathroom remains subtly scented with faeces, soap and eau de cologne. He crawls right on in there. A hand closes around the edge of the bathtub and he lifts himself a little. He kind of hugs the bath. He rests his cheek against its coldness and I wonder if it reminds him as much as me of the world we have left behind: me, of course only temporarily. Certainly there is a relieved softness about his face that makes me not feel too bad about beating down on his skull with the whiskey bottle. It makes an interesting sound: a depressingly prosaic concussion slightly lifted from the every day by the acoustic qualities of the windowless, tiled bathroom. The first blow is enough. He slides slowly down the bath like an invertebrate. It's an impression accentuated by the smeary trail he leaves across the tiles as he slides back across them, like an eel upended from a bucket. I step out of his way.

I suspect that he's still not dead, although he might be. I bend at the waist and give him another blow with the bottle. It is slightly more tentative. I observe him closely, looking for signs of a reaction. There are none, although I scrutinise him for what seems a long time. I just do not trust him to be dead. The whiskey bottle is a less fragile club than many movies would have us believe, it does not shatter like sugarglass in a bar-room brawl. As with any club of comparative weight, it's possible to kill with a bottle. But I needed to see the skull wet and wrecked before I would accept that he was dead. I suspected that his head might prove more resilient than the bottle, for all that the intellect it contained might be extinguished. And I just didn't feel up to beating down on him until either the bottle smashed or his head did.

Instead, I took a long drink from it. A pool of mellow fire inside me. I wanted to drink it like beer, to knock back that last half-pint: temporary oblivion to celebrate deferral of the eternal.

I took another long swig, then set the bottle on the cistern. I bent, took him beneath the armpits and set about lifting him. My bad leg kept juddering and sliding precariously beneath me (I thought of Elvis and Ed Sullivan), but he wasn't too heavy and I didn't have far to hoist him. Once I'd gotten his head and chest into the bathtub, the rest of him just slid in after them. He settled in the tub, finding his own uneven level, like a semi-set liquid.

I sat on the john to catch some breath. I took another drink. Then I sighed, slapped my thighs at a long job nearly completed. I walked into the mess we'd made of the room, over spongy, tacky patches of carpet, and I retrieved my pistol from the floor. I took it to the bathroom, the door of which I took the unnecessary precaution of kicking closed behind me, and I laid it on the cistern while I took two towels and folded each of them into quarters. He was laid out flat in the tub and his eyes were conveniently closed. I took one last look at his face to fix it in my memory because it would not be there very long, then I pressed the two towels to his face with one hand, eight layers of padding to absorb some of the velocity and some of the blast, and I blew most of his face apart with three shots.

He didn't twitch or anything, so I concluded that he might well have been dead already, but at least I'd made sure. The bathroom filled with cordite smoke, soon sucked away by the super-efficient extractor fan. I turned my face away from him, reached behind myself and took in my fist a handful of shower-curtain. I ripped it from the rail. Half the rail came away from the wall. There were a couple of tiny avalanches of plaster. Face averted squeamishly, I draped the curtain over his body. It didn't mould to the shape of him, it wasn't designed for that. I weighed it down with a couple of bars of soap and my own bottle of anti-dandruff shampoo.

I still didn't much trust him, and had the thought not been so icky, I swear I'd have prodded him with a stick or something, even though I knew that beneath the weighted-down shower curtain and the sopping wet towels, I'd broken his head all to pieces. I still had to walk backwards from the bathroom. I'd seen one movie too many. It was too easy to picture him sitting right the fuck back up again, casting aside his shroud and shuffling out behind me, with his face all gone and everything. The idea of the shroud didn't help much. In fact it made it worse in a way. I didn't have to look at him – but I had to think about him, just like I'd had to think about what he kept in his attaché case. I couldn't even decide whether or not I should close the bathroom door. After a moment's irrational deliberation, I compromised on leaving it ajar. I still didn't much trust him to stay dead. Right until I left the hotel I was half expecting him to sit up – either a dreadful shambling automaton, or possessed of vengeful malevolence.

I suppose I was in shock. I'd undergone an experience I wasn't equipped to contextualise. I had just murdered a man. I was in some degree of real trouble. I was shot and bleeding and beat. The people I was working for were dead. The man who

I'd murdered had tortured me and certainly would have killed me.

Instead of trying to process all this, I worried about him coming shambling and moaning after me from the bathroom, wrapped in a shower curtain.

When I was thirteen, my father had reluctantly capitulated to my swaggering insistence that I could happily, indeed casually, sit through the television screening of a horror movie which involved hordes of shuffling undead zombies munching on the succulent flesh of upright young Americans. I watched it right through, doggedly and not without pride, but I slept with the light on for a good few months afterwards.

The film contained no scene in a hotel bathroom, not as such, but nevertheless, as I sat on the bed and lit a cigarette, I wondered if the two things might not in some way be connected.

Ten

```
File code: 100046/macd
Username: sicarius
Password: ******
Last Updated: **/**/**
```

File DMWITRES Located.

Please wait.

File DMWITRES Retrieved.

Warning: This File Has Been Cloaked. Should You Wish to Decloak, Press Return. If You Wish to Quit, Press Escape.

If You Wish to Decloak, Please Ensure That Your Software is Code Protected, and Save Any Files Recently Modified.

Please wait.

Code Accessed and Identified. Print 65385922, Licence Confirmed, Outlet Confirmed.

*** Please Note. Decloaked Files Have Been Encrypted According to a System Restricted to the Use of Government Personnel Only. WARNING. Unauthorised Use of this System of Encryption Constitutes an Offence Punishable By Law. Unauthorised Personnel Should Quit

This Document is Not Password Protected.

Hello, David, How Are You?

From McArdle's journal:

Date:

Since my return from the Holy Land, I am a pariah.

It's as if contact with the mystery of my precious cargo has somehow corrupted me, scarred me with the mark of a dreadful future. I feel loosened within time, like a ghost flickering behind myself as I walk these endless marble corridors. I am mocked and terrified by the echoes of my own footfalls.

I'm treated like Judas: the betrayer, allowed to sup at the table, necessary but despised. I sometimes fear that I am losing my mind. I can confide in nobody: not the man I fear to betray, not the colleagues who already feel betrayed by me.

I have done nothing save perform a task that was set me. It was a difficult task I had no wish to perform, which I fulfilled through love of the man that set it. How can loyalty be perceived as betrayal?

To what, or to whom, is my loyalty directed?

How am I to encompass this question?

Time feels fragile beneath my feet, thinning ice over a swift-flowing river. I consider that holy thing. I cannot feel him, or even evidence of him, in it. Instead, he reveals himself through it, a relic, a clue unravelled through time, at one end of which is his world, at the other, ours. I can feel the vibration of him, a faint, throbbing echo of his presence. But the gap between us remains unbridged.

Surely this opposes faith: to clutch with the intellect what does not reside in the heart.

If it is the opposite to faith, then how can it be used to justify faith? How can it be right? Because the man who has brought us here tells me it is right. He tells me it is God's will, and I must believe him. If I do not believe him about this, then I can believe him about nothing, and the reality we have constructed must fracture and craze about us.

I must act as if I believe Randall to be right, because for Randall to be wrong is too terrible a thing to contemplate?

Worse than the victory of death over God?

Oh, Jesus.

Yes. Because I have followed Randall. We have all followed Randall. I believe we fear to be wrong not because we fear for our souls – I am no longer so sure if it is humanly possible to believe, to fully believe, all or even most of the time. It is, however, possible to yearn. And, in the face of this collective yearning failing to come through, what do we have to fear?

Humiliation.

This is a terrible thing to say, probably blasphemy, but who am I to talk of blasphemy? Certainly, it is unkind to my remarkable fellows to suggest that we fear the mirth and disapprobation of our fellows, and those who will follow. Perhaps the most powerful and enduring emotion is not love, or hate, but the base fear of humiliation. How humbling. Men who fear death on the battlefield go to it because, dead, they are lions.

Perhaps this is why God chose such a death: a triumph of the scorned, the powerless and the humiliated, of those who cannot choose but to submit.

In the story. This is what God does. The story is all, said Ruth, over the telephone, before I left to meet her in the Negev, to oversee the transportation of the body of a man who, in his lifetime, did not wander more than 100 kilometres from the place of his birth.

It is impossible for me to record accurately feelings I can't understand, or to justify my actions. I pray that my humanity is mitigation enough.

Perhaps my recent compulsion to record is a neurotic attempt to render these things definitive. I don't know. What I do know is that, since taking this decision, I have accumulated three hours of video footage, and many more hours of audio recordings. The source of both of which is, more often than not, surveillance equipment. In the case of audio recordings, I wear this equipment secretly about my person.

Five of us know. Of those five, not one is fully supportive of Randall's actions, myself included. The degree of our disagreement I can most ably illustrate via the following transcription, extracted from a meeting which took place between eight and ten pm, within the last week. I will not record the venue, but will remark that it was neither a private residence (we fear surveillance), nor a public place. The recording from which this transcript is extracted was, of course, taken without the knowledge of the participants. The transcription, and any inaccuracy within it, is my own.

Those present were:

David McArdle (DM)

Ruth Felton (RF)

Isabel Beaumont (IB)

Nathan Beaumont (NB)

Oscar Petersen (OP)

Frank Shaw (FS)

RF – I can't believe your reaction. What century do you suppose this is?

IB – Reaction to *what*, exactly?

RF – To fact.

OP – Fact, bullshit. There are no facts in all this. Just some bullshit line you spun, that Randall took. Hook line and . . . Jesus, Ruth. What have you *done*?

RF – I haven't *done* anything. If your faith can't accommodate *history*, it isn't faith, and that isn't my problem. Don't lay responsibility for *your* neuroses at *my* door.

OP – Oh, *fuck* you. Fuck *you*. Look at you. You fucking . . .

NB – She has a point, Oscar. She has. If what she says is true, then there *is* some personal re-evaluation to be done.

IB – Some '*personal re-evaluation*'? As opposed to what, exactly?

NB – Political re-evaluation . . .

IB – (inaudible)

NB – Fine. It's your decision. But what can you suggest as an alternative? Abandonment of the entire *project*, for instance?

IB – (inaudible)

NB – I'm sorry?

IB – Two of the words I used were 'monstrous' and 'indefensible'. Would you like me to spell it out? Would you like me to write it *down*?

RF – Listen to yourself! Listen to your choice of words! Since when has the *truth* been indefensible?

IB – When it's not *true*!

RF – Oh, come on, Isabel. You of all people. Don't fall into denial. You've seen the evidence. David has seen it with his own eyes. You can't deny the truth of it. You can discuss the *meaning* of it until the cows come home – but not the *fact* of it.

IB – Why couldn't you leave well alone? Why couldn't you leave everything as it was? What makes you think you have the *right* . . .?

RF – The right to *what*? To the *truth*? My *God*, Isabel.

OP – The right to fuck with God.

RF – I'm not *fucking* with anybody or anything, Oscar, least of *all* God. If anybody can be said to fuck with God, it's the wilfully ignorant. Isn't it more monstrous to choose ignorance over knowledge? Isn't denying the fact of history denying the fact of God? Do you believe in God because you *feel* it to be true, or because you *need* it to be true? You sound like one of those assholes who wouldn't believe Jesus was *Jewish*. This is the same thing, Oscar, the same argument. What I'm saying, what I found, is *undeniable*. Must we have a sophomoric discussion on the difference between fact and truth?

IB – Sophistry is no defence.

RF – Where's the sophistry? This is quite the opposite. Here are the facts. Make of them what you will. There's no sophistry in that.

OP – I can't *believe* you, Ruth, coming on with all this 'fact and truth' bullshit.

RF – Interesting construction. 'Fact and truth bullshit.' I'll say it again: I've presented facts. I don't see any misdemeanour in that. Quite the contrary. Any problem you have with the real world is your own, by definition.

IB – (voice raised): You're telling us it didn't *happen*.

RF – I'm telling you it didn't happen exactly the way you *imagined* it. There's a big difference. It's *your* misapprehension, and that's for you to deal with. It's doesn't alter the ontological *fact* of God a single *iota*. Above all, we should impress on our memory as an infallible rule that what God has revealed to us is incomparably more certain than anything else: and that we ought to submit to the Divine authority rather than to our own judgement.*

*Some days after this conversation took place, I took the opportunity to ask Ruth if she had been quoting somebody in the above passage. She looked at me somewhat askance and replied: 'Descartes, from his *Principles of Philosophy*. Why?'

It seemed obvious that asking this question had aroused in her some suspicion. In retrospect, I believe she already suspected more about what I was up to than she ever led me to believe, even later. As such, this unremarkable conversation marks my own crossing of the Rubicon. It was like passing the event horizon around a black hole. Seeing Ruth's suspicion, or knowledge, of the course of action to which I was committed somehow made me acknowledge it as being real. There was no going back. Strange, how we are able to acknowledge such moments while continuing as normal. As I recall, I responded 'Descartes, huh?', and Ruth replied with a prosaic shrug, as if refusing to apologise, and said: 'Whatever weapons are at our disposal.'

IB – Something *opposite*? Like, *it didn't happen*? That's pretty opposite.

RF – Like suggesting that *part* of it didn't happen in quite the way you *imagined*. You find your apprehensions to be mistaken, and now you presume to question God? There's a *word* for that.

IB – You're saying he *died* and they *buried* him and he *rotted*!

RF – But I'm saying that, before that, he walked the earth after . . . his first death. Does the fact that the mechanism behind this was ingenuity – *inspiration* – rather than miracle make it worthless? Does it render his entire mission redundant? Do you no longer see God in Him, this excellent, this most beloved, this most humble, most perfect servant? What about the Sermon on the Mount? The healings? The scourging of the temple? Because one element of the story (a single, historically suspect element) is disproved, you would disregard the entire *message*? You'd disregard *God*?

IB – I'd do no such *thing*. But where is *God*, Ruth? Where *is* God? In this *story*?

RF – Exactly. *God is in the story*. God is in history. You're making the wrong kind of demands on this document – and the wrong kind of demands on God. One should never presume, *never*, to make demands on the Divine. Look at yourselves, making demands that things be just the way you'd like them! That's not faith, that's *petulance*! Where's your humility? Where's your *submission*? His will is more terrible than you can begin to comprehend and it's your place, your function, to bow to it, to fear and to worship and obey: not make *demands* of it. You're a disgrace before the God you claim to worship, petulant children screaming for the return of your comfort blanket. You're a disgrace. Grow *up*. This has *happened*. It happened a long *time* ago. It's *always* been the case. *You* were wrong, not God. Not Jesus. *You*. The mistake is yours and yours alone. To demand that things be otherwise is to bow before a false God. That's idolatry. Creating a God in your own image.

IB – Jesus. Stop. Can we stop for a *moment*?

DM – We should maybe get a drink. Coffee? Tea?

IB – Do you have whiskey?

DM – Sure.

IB – Whiskey please.

OP – Make that two. Jesus H. Does anybody have a *cigarette*?

FS – I got a cigar. David, would you think me rude if I were to ask for a large glass?

DM – Of course not. Nathan?

NB – I wouldn't say no a Scotch either.

DM – Sure. Ruth?

RF – Just a little iced water. I'm parched.

The following is extracted from the transcript of a meeting which took place the following day. Circumstances were similar to those documented above, with the exception that Ruth Felton was not present. The meeting took place at a different location.

Once again the transcription is my own, with the identical caveat.

11.43 pm

NB – We're here to minute the position we find ourselves in. To continue, if I may. Item One: We have no choice but to concur with Ruth Felton that the specifically spiritual significance of this event, if it has any . . .

IB – If it *has* any?

NB – . . . *if it has any* is a matter for individual conscience. Item Two: We stand poised for a significant political achievement: the reclamation from chaos of a large percentage of the globe. No matter what else has happened, no matter what individual spiritual doubts have been engendered and expressed within this group, this is a *remarkable*, an *unprecedented* achievement. It would be foolish at this juncture to question the very faith upon which it was first constructed. If we *were* to act upon an event the nature of which we don't fully understand, we risk everything. We have no right to do so. Ergo, we must of necessity take no action against the President.

FS – Jesus, Nathan, I don't know. I really don't.

OP – So, we should be hypocrites and liars. Reject everything we thought we stood for.

NB – Not *everything*.

OP – Everything that *matters*.

NB – I'm saying that you must make a difficult, but *necessary* decision on behalf of your neighbour. Your fellow man. Et cetera.

IB – To lie, that they might live.

NB – Exactly. Exactly that. Your faith is a matter for yourself. Above and beyond that, you have an *obligation* to your fellows.

FS – Jeez.

NB – Remember how terrible God can be. Remember Job. Remember the lamentations of David. The agony of the Israelites, forty years in the wilderness. Jesus praying that the cup be removed from him. It's those who serve him best who suffer the most.

IB – That's not my God.

DM – Realistically, even if we had a mind to act, we couldn't. Short of staging a *coup*, there's nothing we can do.

NB – *One* thing we can do is stop thinking of *ourselves* and what *we're* going through.

FS – He's right, Oscar. Isabel. You know it. We got no choice.

OP – All right. All right. Goddammit. We have no choice.

IB – Not at the *moment*.

NB – What does *that* mean?

At this point, the recording ends.

February 9

Six weeks into the new year, another year: my first journal entry since Christmas, since Naomi was taken to the hospital. Already I can sense spring, sense the fresh warmth of it on the edge of the cold morning air.

Astonishing, humbling, how rapidly things can change.

Although it has been won, the war is not yet over. It will go on for too long, far longer than it should. These things do. People are still hungry, people are still sick and there are people all over the world who are maimed and lost and alone and scared. Even as I write there are men dying, there are terrible things occurring and God knows what sorrow fills me at the thought of it. But the war is won, and soon it will be over. I have seen the plans, I have seen what will result from our labour, from the collective genius it has been my privilege to witness, and to some degree harness and direct. I know it will all come to pass, that the world will have been pulled back from the brink, that when the time comes for me to die, it will be in a world where food is once more abundant, where the cankers and tumours of disease are eradicated, when the world is united in its love of God and I can think: *Christendom*, and allow myself some small pride for having played a role, however humble, in its establishment.

When there is a good day, I can believe that.

But most nights, it's Randall I see, it's Randall I hear, the day he led us into that blindingly sterile room, and told us: We are witnessing the end of history. The point at which science and faith meet.

Even Ruth is scared now. She has about her the expression of somebody who has just walked alive from a plane crash.

I have stolen the film. I have copied it, replaced it. Connors, the doctor, tall, deeply tanned, in surgical white, mask pulled down across his throat, addresses the camera, addresses us. He is a very handsome man.

As we are all too aware, cloning from dead matter is not an easy process. It's like trying to blow life into a tiny flame; blow too softly, the flame dies. Blow too hard, you extinguish it. But blow just right, work right alongside the flame, and together you can make it alive.

Two months ago my wife was taken into hospital. For a reason we will never understand, my second child, my son, made a judgement upon the world to which we fervently wished to welcome him, and found it grievously wanting. He died, still inside my wife's warm, living body.

We called him James, and buried him in the first days of the new year.

After successive attempts, says Connors, the first complete DNA sample was extracted from the fourth rib on the left hand side. He allows himself a smile, a flash of perfect dentition, weathered crows' feet at the eyes. Sparkle of blue.

There's a certain poetic symmetry about that, he says.

Eleven *The Passenger*

The matrices of our lives are infinitely intricate, a vast filigree of cause and effect. Everything and everyone is linked to everything and everyone else: everything that happens is the result of everything that has ever happened, since time erupted with a scream of rage into the pacific void. Time past is contained in time future, and time future in time past.

But I didn't care because I wanted somebody to blame. The ludicrous position in which I found myself was clearly not of my making. With Isabel and Nathan so recently dead, it seemed churlish to hold anybody but Ruth responsible. That fucking *bitch*, I thought, for getting me into this.

Not without difficulty, I lay on the bed and struggled from my sopping, stinking and soiled clothing.

The leg wound wasn't critical. Objectively, I had to admit it was really little more than a good-sized, but shallow notch in my thigh. I didn't think anything major had been severed. The bleeding had been retarded by a black snotty lump that was offering to coagulate, though not quite making good on the promise.

It wasn't about to kill me, but I'd lost and was continuing to lose more blood than could possibly be good for me. There was as yet little pain, but clearly it would very soon become the source of what a doctor would inevitably call some acute discomfort.

I made a temporary tourniquet of a necktie, limped hurriedly to the wardrobe, removed my luggage and searched for the little traveller's first aid kit. There was stuff I needed in there – a small length of bandage, pins, sticking plasters, some rehydration salts. There was a tube of antiseptic cream.

I don't think the cream had been designed for application on raw flesh. Besides, I don't believe I was able to root around inside those burned, raggedy lips.

Instead I made my way to the bathroom. Naked, daubed and smeared with blood, I padded back to the marble wash-basin. I took the opportunity to examine my reflection.

I looked like the aftermath of a high-speed collision. Witnessing this appalling sight engendered in me bravery sufficient to flip a passionately committed, rigid middle finger at the body of the man under the shower curtain. I called it a bastard. I wanted to hit it with something. But that was too creepy a thing to get into.

Instead, I rolled a facecloth into a sausage, stuffed it into my mouth and bit down on it, in the hope that, should I do something in the process of cleaning the wound that *really* hurt, I might at least avoid biting off the tip of my tongue. I wet the corner of a clean towel, spoke a muffled word of encouragement to myself and succeeded in smearing a thin, pinkish wash over my thighs and lower belly. Then I poured whiskey into the hole. If you've ever watched a movie and wondered what that feels like, don't. I whimpered and mewled and shouted and screwed up my face and pounded down on the washbasin with the bottom of my fist. That's what it feels like.

Before the stinging had even begun to abate, I bandaged the wound as tightly as I was able. It wasn't adequate, but it would have to do. At least it arrested further blood loss.

I washed blood from my face and hair and mouth and neck, bending right the way over the faucet. My mouth was cut up inside and a little swollen, but not so much that I had yet come to resemble a product of the wrong kind of small farming community. I rinsed with Listerine better than I had ever rinsed in my entire life.

What felt like a dinnerplate's worth of tissue bitten from the edge of my tongue was probably a tiny nick, but these things are relative. I just knew that my tongue was going to balloon and loll from my lips like that of a recently exerted German shepherd.

Once my mouth was minty fresh, ha ha, I washed and rubbed with towels until my skin had about it a temporary but gratifyingly vigorous and healthy pink glow.

The mattress and bedding I laid across the spongy, soggy carpet – soon it would begin to smell unpleasant in here – and using it as a platform, I dressed in fresh clothes. My hands shook, especially knotting a new necktie. I was clumsy and hurried. I buttoned the jacket and put on the hat then stiffly half-clambered over the mattress and bedding to regard myself in the full-length mirror. I looked surprisingly okay. My skin was unappealingly grey, offset with angry red blotches, but at least I was presentable. Nobody was going to begrudge me a little dermatitis. From a metre or two, I looked fine. Except for my eyes. They belonged to something small and mean and hungry, the kind of thing Canadians would caution you that you didn't want snuffling around your campsite in the dark, most especially if you had young children.

I settled the disk in a breast pocket, took a sequence of deep breaths, counted to three with my fingers, and stepped into the hallway. Nobody shot me. I took the elevator to reception and shuffled out into all that dark marble and chromium and smoked glass and leather busy with new arrivals with too much luggage. A very dapper and exquisitely polite but tired and tearful old man of Eastern European origin was dealing with a booking problem. His well-fed wife (who, I learned as I passed, had a problem with her colon) was sunk into a sofa, clutching a little purse atop a vast lap, gazing ahead like a traumatised refugee. Couples with young children smiled stiffly and politely, throwing occasional sidelong 'wait till I get you alone' glances at boisterous and over-tired offspring. Families, not a single member of any of which produced a gun and shot me. Everybody didn't produce a gun and shoot me, even the hotel employees. Everybody didn't even look at me.

The door was opened for me by the old man who embarrassed me by calling me sir.

On my way out, I met the young couple over whose imaginary antics I had whiled away a masturbatory minute or two that very afternoon.

I tipped my hat in greeting. Of course, neither of them was as perfect as I'd remembered. His earnestness did not allow for much playfulness or humour. He ordered coffee with the dark decisiveness of a general capitulating at the last possible moment to the imperative that he command a nuclear strike. He said hi, and shared with me the grave tidings that it was good to see me. He had the kind of handshake that squeezes your hand like some dreadful machine designed to calculate the precise kilo-per-square-centimetre ratio at which your fingers will liquidate. His expression was that of a man looking into the eyes of his fellow sole survivors of a bloody and hard-fought battle on some unnamed, faraway hill in a distant land.

He was kind of scary.

When he had released me from the fraternity of his grip, I took his wife's hand in mine. But a few minutes before, I'd killed a man. He was in my bathtub right now, dead as they come, and I was feeling evil and predatory. I met her eyes and grinned the wrong kind of grin at her, it was nude and ravenous, and she returned it, inquisitive and humorous at first. Then I saw the faintest flicker of response. She probably wasn't aware of it herself. I let her hand fall.

I hoped they'd had a good day.

They'd wandered the galleries. Post-war stuff, mostly.

I wondered how they'd found it.

They'd been waiting a long time to see it, he vouchsafed, in his scary way. As if that was any kind of an answer.

Well, I told them, and looked at my watch.

Sure, he said, and selflessly relented, commanding me to have a nice evening, in a what-the-hell, they're-good-men-and-everyone-needs-to-go-ahead-and-cut-loose-once-in-a-while manner.

171

Gratefully, I hoped they did, too, knowing that they wouldn't have half as nice a time as I could for them, in my head.

Tomorrow, I thought, tomorrow at the latest, somebody was going to find my stiffening roommate. I could imagine this couple's repugnance. How he'd shaken the murderer's hand in his own. Her detestation – and perhaps a little guilt, the kind she could admit to nobody, not even a religious counsellor, for that moment of communication. As if she'd been unfaithful. Except she wouldn't say that. She'd say: like he *assaulted* me. You could just tell there was something *creepy* about him. It was in his eyes. Y'know. Right there in his eyes.

Nobody shot me from any of the vantage points afforded to them by my limping on to the sidewalk. I turned a corner and nobody shot me again. It was my hope that everybody would continue not shooting me for many happy and fulfilled years to come. But in my bath there was the cadaver of somebody who had been told that the time for not shooting me had passed. I doubted that he was alone, although I hoped he was.

I made good progress, all things considered. I felt better, wearing a hat. Elsewhere, hats were a practical necessity until somebody got round to making the sky all better, but here they'd become *de rigueur*.

Anybody who was actually going someplace wore his hat, even at night. So I wore mine, and felt protected.

NJC retained an enforceable dress code. For women: no skirts above mid-thigh, no halter tops or swimwear, nothing which reveals the midriff. For men: no shorts or bare chests, and no sandals (this last perhaps a tad ironic). This was the kind of law nobody was likely to break, or enforce: who in their right mind wants to saunter about like they're dressed for a suburban barbecue when everybody else looks like they're dressed for a wedding? And who in their right mind was going to prosecute some pretty young Christian girl, happy and hard-working and married, for innocently displaying a little more of God's beautiful creation than strictly she ought?

It reminded me a little of how I remembered downtown Paris. I passed coffee bars and restaurants, places that sold mementos of your pilgrimage. The merchandise ranged from affordable to exorbitant, but everything delighted in an assured tastefulness. It lacked vulgarity. There were, for instance, few pictorial characterisations of Christ. The Church frowned upon such idolatry. One suspected this to be more of a question of waspish taste rather than theology. There were many Church histories available in assorted formats, from the interactive to the hide-bound, various (tasteful) pictorial characterisations of the President and manifold collections of his speeches, once again in multiple format. His war-time speeches were by some margin the most popular.

For all the Government's ecumenical generosity – for all that, if you were a Jew you were not denied access to a synagogue, for all that if you were Muslim you were constitutionally encouraged to pray to Mecca five times a day, for all that Catholics could worry at their decades of the rosary and mutter their dark confessions – here in the Capitol it was imperative that the Church represent itself as prototypical: an irreproachable spiritual and intellectual assemblage.

It was the City of God: craggy granite which bedecked an abstraction of such thoroughness that it could indulge the existence of other sentiments, while never actually endorsing them. There were many routes to God, but only one Road.

This was all well and good but for the fact that the one purchase I needed to make just at that moment was a sanitary towel to soak up my embarrassing flow.

I located the same bench outside Eleanor Roosevelt park. A family of four, probably North African, two parents, two teenagers, occupied one of the benches. The woman had a shoe in one hand. With the other, she massaged the arch of a foot. The man listened attentively to one of the children, a boy about thirteen, patiently explaining something directly into his ear. When the boy had finished, the father frowned, as if in incomprehension, then he laughed out loud at the joke and took the boy, who was grinning widely, under his arm and with the other hand knuckled him on top of his head. The girl, at the far end of the bench, leaned over to see if her mother was done yet. She was hungry and bored and her father and brother were embarrassing her.

No cars were parked by telephone booths. I'd agreed to meet Ruth in an hour, but I didn't know exactly how long ago that had been. I'd fitted a lot in. It was safe to guess that I was late. I supposed that, as a precaution, she was circling the block until I turned up.

I hoped she was circling the block. I hoped she hadn't got herself all dead and messed up in my memory like Isabel and Nathan. Ruth was pretty much the best friend I had.

A year or two after the war ended, I, along with tens of thousands of others, found employment constructing the twelve satellite towns designed to provide for NJC – to provide raw materials and a workforce which could not afford to live in the city itself. The work was hard, but there was some satisfaction in seeing an entirely new city rising from the churned-up mud. For a while I was happy. Soon I was working in an office, processing information and dealing with the manifold logistical problems inherent in such a project. I wore a tie and a suit and tried to make a normal life. I fucked up very badly. When the walls of my life began to crumble, it was Ruth who took me in. She gave me a job. I looked after her house and grounds. She lived all alone, outside the city. She couldn't afford to pay me, but she'd made an arrangement with somebody she knew, registered me as her responsibility, and that's where I got better. It was a grand house, with eight bedrooms, six of which, for the duration of my tenure, remained unoccupied. Furnishings were spare. Ruth didn't much go in for luxury. There were objects of value, though: things she'd dug up, or traded for other things she'd dug up: statues and Sumerian tablets, little Greek figurines, the twisted faces of Mesopotamian devils.

I spent a spring there, and a summer, tending to her garden, which was big enough to contain the foundations of an entire block of prefabricated apartments of the kind I'd latterly left behind me. I constructed a rock garden and excavated a pond to which she introduced fish and lilies. Upon finding the first frog residing there, I rushed breathless to the study. She looked over her shoulder, under her spectacles, and told me she was glad I was so pleased. I wandered back to the garden a little sulky and resentful.

I trimmed back hedges and mowed the lawn, front and back. I washed and waxed her car. I kept the garage clean. I cemented a little area of garden for her to set out a table and chair in the summer and drink iced tea while she read. I fixed her leaking roof.

Occasionally I cooked for us in the evening, but mostly this was a task she undertook. She liked plain food, and at each meal she said Grace like she meant it. I respected that because she was Ruth. I closed my eyes, tipping my head so the tips of my fingers rested against the space between my brows. She'd tell me about the day she'd had – University politics, students who were in or out of favour. The only guests she ever brought back while I was there were a bunch of postgrads, one Sunday, as autumn began to downshift into winter. They were served one course, ladled from an enormous tureen, with bread and some good enough wine. I joined them, and after an awkward first few minutes establishing just who I was and just what it was that I did ('Malachi and I are veterans. When this man was three or four years younger, he'd have sold all he had for a plate of stew like this.' I agreed, but added: 'Except back then just about all I owned was a fake Swiss Army penknife with all these useless useful attachments, and a pair of genuine Ray-Bans which made me look like the nerdy kid brother of a Colombian coca lord in a TV movie. I traded a whole carton of cigarettes for them before I even looked in a mirror and when I did, I looked like a Wanted poster.' Laughter) Dipping bread into the stew, I was surprised to find myself conversing with these bright young things as normal and everyday as you like, even flirting a little with one of them. This is when it occurred to me that I'd got better. To this day, I believe that to be the sole reason Ruth invited them back – to show me how much better I was. Of course she never said and I never asked.

There were no more lessons. What would happen is, I'd take a bath before supper, put on some clean clothes. After eating, we'd sometimes talk for an hour. She told me a little about herself, that she'd never married (but not why), where she'd grown up, some of the things she'd found in various holes in the ground in various parts of the world. I talked about what had happened to me since I was wounded. I told her about the weirdness of the hospital on Crete: how it felt like it wasn't quite there, how sometimes everybody seemed a little grotesque, like characters in a children's book or a feverish dream. I told her about Sonny, how his cartoonishness and his visits and his sex stories had kept me sane, until he was remobilised to the mess in Eastern Europe. How he'd emerged eighteen months later with the same light in his eyes and a chest full of medals for the terrible things they made him do. How for the remaining two years of the war I was deferred from combat. The Caspian Basin burned until there was nothing left to burn, and soon they needed our bodies to start repairing things. Of course I never told her everything I did. I never told anybody that. Isabel knew, though. Isabel knew what I did.

But mostly I'd retire to her study. It was the biggest room in the house. The books soaked up as much room as they did light. They lined every wall, floor to ceiling. They were arranged haphazardly, in no particular order I could see, which made for good browsing. She had a more extensive library on disk but she told me that the physical and the digital played dual roles: with the latter, one accessed information: with books, one communed with wisdom. Information and knowledge, she said. It would serve me well to learn the difference. She was of a different generation, though, and sentimental about old objects.

More often than not, she'd join me, reading or tapping something into a laptop, the sound of it as comforting and soporific as rain on the window of a cosy and familiar house. We'd sit in an entirely companionable silence, which she would sometimes break by disappearing to the kitchen to brew a coffee for me and a mint tea for herself.

The aroma of mint tea always evoked for me our time spent together at the dig in the Negev desert. The things she taught me.

At night, the dig was almost silent. There was little to do and certainly nowhere to go. Most evenings, people wrote or read letters. Cards were played for imaginary stakes, fantastical and dizzying, which yet somehow lacked the comparatively visceral thrill of playing for matches you could pile up as you won or observe ebbing away as your luck changed. A couple of the archaeologists had a thing going with a couple of the men, and occasionally it was necessary to pretend not to hear one or the other or both scrambling quickly in the direction of whatever rendezvous has been arranged. By tacit agreement a blind eye was turned to this. None of the archaeologists did anything for me, to tell the truth. Even deprived as I was, I preferred to consider myself abstinent. That way I got to feel a little pride for not getting any. Once, assigned perimeter duty, something to which we actually looked forward, things were so monotonous, I happened across two of them *in flagrante*. I have to admit I was fascinated. It was easy for me, equipped with nightvision, to establish myself in a dark corner from which to observe them. It was interesting, but not what you'd call erotic.

I visited Ruth two evenings a week. She'd brew a pot of mint tea. She kept her tent semi-lit, with an Anglepoise lamp set on the folding table, pointing down. It made the tent subtly mysterious. This impression was accentuated by the walls, which rippled and billowed in the night breezes, and occasionally snapped taut with a crack that made the heart leap.

I'd sit at a the folding table, on a folding chair, the Anglepoise lamp pushed to the far edge.

Deep beneath her eccentric bluff and bluster, the combat fatigues worn with embroidered waistcoats and of course her grandfather's hat, I detected in Ruth something that occasionally made me nervous. She had about her an anarchism that had little to do with insubordination. Something impish and elemental flickered within her, and would not be tempered. It was most visible while darkness insinuated itself silently just beyond the walls.

Ruth had a thing about St Paul. Of his somewhat strained relationship with and impact upon the movement Jesus had left behind, she once told me: 'The erstwhile Saul of Tarsus proved to be possessed of an unguessed-at genius. He understood the imperatives of product placement. He tailored Jesus to the demands of the market and sucked all the life from him, along with his Jewishness. It was Paul who created the Jesus we know. His letters are the earliest extant records of the life of Jesus. They predate the first Gospel by sixty years.

'However, even though the Jesus of the very earliest Gospel is recognisably Pauline, we are still able to apply some historical contextualisation, to extract from the Gospel accounts a hint of the real man.

'He wasn't *meek*. He wasn't *passive*, he wasn't another mystic too interested in the next world to bother himself with this one. That's not *Jesus*, Yeshua bar Joseph. It's the Christ which Paul repackaged and sold on to the Romans. It's the anodyne neuter he rebranded for a more popular appeal. Paul knew his market and like all the best salesmen, he had faith in the product. He believed in its potential to become market leader, if marketed accordingly. And Paul wasn't just a good salesman: he was the Alexander the Great of salesmen. He set out to conquer the world with his pitch, and he succeeded.'

She poured boiling water from a kettle into a teapot. She placed the pot on the table before me, then passed me a mug of the kind you find capping a Thermos flask. I thanked her, even though I wasn't too keen on mint tea. Ruth didn't drink alcohol, except a glass of sherry once or twice a year. She didn't like me to smoke. If I really needed a cigarette, I had to smoke it outside the tent. I didn't mind doing that. It made me feel like I was about ten. Occasionally there was a skirmish close by and you could see the flashing in the sky and sometimes hear a muffled concussion. That wasn't often, though.

'It's necessary,' she said, 'to tease apart the two characters: the one in the book and the one in the world. Of course, they can never be fully separated: one informs the nature of the other. It's like stripping a painting, layer by layer, removing what Paul added, the new colours, different perspectives, until we're able to see the outline of the original: an undoctored image of the man who actually walked this country, before he was consigned to the half-life of narrative, and the humiliation of exegesis.

'In order to begin to separate the two characters, one might merely apply this maxim: Jesus taught the Kingdom. Paul taught Jesus.

'Jesus preached, prophesied or announced either the doctrine or the actual establishment of the Kingdom of God. The Kingdom was specifically a political as well as a spiritual entity. Indeed, to the observant Jew – and he was the most observant of Jews, even in his radicalism – the two were indivisible concepts. The Covenant with Israel assured this. It's not going *too* far out on a limb to posit that Jesus believed his mission to have in some way already established the Kingdom – but this is speculation. The nature of the Kingdom of which Jesus spoke is obfuscated by the writers of the Gospels, largely because there was some embarrassment in recording that Jesus Christ, the Son of God, proclaimed the establishment of the Kingdom of God, shortly before the Romans shut him up by nailing him to a tree.

'For his early followers, reconstructing his mission in the light of his death, it was necessary that certain of his pronouncements underwent a degree of diligent recontextualisation simply because they had failed to come to pass, at least in the way that had been anticipated. The logic of faith dictated that it was the *anticipation* which was in error, since the prophecy by definition could not be. That's the genius of faith. There's just no arguing with it. Jesus Christ, the maelstrom of righteous fury, had foretold – had threatened – that the Temple would be destroyed and rebuilt by him in three days. Quite apart from being a strong candidate for stamping the final seal on his warrant of execution, this prophecy is notable for the fact that it did not come to pass.

'How did the early Christians account for this? Through *revelation*. It becomes retrospectively *obvious* that when he spoke of the Temple, the house of God, Jesus spoke of *himself*, of his own death and resurrection.

'So, given the retrospective nature of the Gospels – written on the *a priori* understanding that Jesus Christ was the Son of God incarnate, that he died for all our sins, and through him alone might we find salvation – and given the politic first-century editorial policy of maintaining as much distance from specifically Judaic concerns as was possible, we'll probably never know for sure quite the nature of the Kingdom as it was proclaimed and understood by Jesus.

'What does remain certain, however, is that his concern was Israel, right there and right then. He wanted an end to Roman occupation. The Jews had already endured an astonishingly unfortunate history – in the circumstances, no wonder Gentiles were somewhat baffled by Jewish adherence to an all-powerful, all-seeing, all-knowing God, who claimed to hold them in special favour but nevertheless appeared never to miss an opportunity to compound the misery of their lot. That just wasn't what gods were *for*. Come the time of Jesus, a significant proportion of the Judaic population had had it all up to *here*. Demands were being made for salvation. Who can blame them? There were many claims to the Messianic mantle, a few of which were sufficiently successful that the Gospels found it prudent to slanderously diminish their claim.

'This is the case with the Baptist. Even posthumously, John was a cause of great consternation to the early Christians, because in diminishing him, it was necessary that they tread on eggshells: they couldn't come right out and denounce the man by whom Jesus had been baptised in the Jordan without compromising that very baptism, which marked the beginning of Christ's ministry. So they wheeled in the big guns. They brought in God the Father.

'It's one of the subtlest black propaganda jobs in history. You have to admire them. What happens is: ritually purified, Jesus emerges from the waters of the Jordan. A voice is heard. *This is my son*, it booms, *in whom I am well pleased*. It's widely rumoured in academic circles that an early editor red-lined the subsequent sentence, which is believed to have read: "*That one, over there. The young one with the wet hair. Not the hairy one with the thing for insects.*"'

She searched my expression. 'That's a joke,' she said. 'But it illustrates my point well enough. The stature of the Baptist was subtly diminished and the nature of the relationship between him and Jesus firmly established: John was a great man chosen by God to prepare the way for the messiah. In fact the relationship between John and Jesus wasn't so clear-cut. It's quite possible Jesus was an ambitious upstart, whose faction formed from a splinter of the Baptist's own. Certainly the Lord's prayer pre-existed Christ's ministry. It was John's before it was his. He taught us to pray as John did.

'It's ironic, but one can say that Jesus' fame is predicated on his singular lack of success as a messiah. One might strip down what we know about him to a few key events: a very provocative donkey ride into Jerusalem, a few upturned tables outside the Temple and the next thing, the Romans punish him capitally. Great liberators don't get themselves nailed to crosses – but great religions can be forged in blood sacrifice. But this is a theory I reject. I believe Jesus knew *precisely* what he was doing. To portray him as a failure is to misunderstand him entirely.'

The tent snapped in the desert wind. I sipped cooling tea. 'Then what did he do? Invite execution or submit to it?'

'Both and neither,' she said. 'But each plays its part. Absolutely. Oh, he was *scared*. But he was *cunning*, Jesus. He was a clever and cunning man. He inspired love in his followers. He was as humble before God as he was defiant towards Rome. "Render unto Caesar that which is Caesar's." There's no capitulation in *that*. There's the most callous contempt for the hubris of this man whose image adorns this meaningless currency: "Let Caesar have what is Caesar's. It has no meaning to us. But Israel is not Caesar's, and we will no longer suffer the odium of his presence."

'Can you *see* him now? He means so much more, like this. He's contradictory and complex and elusive. He's witty, he's *clever*, he's wise in the Law to a *breathtakingly* audacious degree – to the degree he can claim to obey a stricture by *reversing* it! That's not a bad trick, whichever way you look at it – and not everybody looked on it favourably, you can count on that. He could spin a good yarn. That's a laudable rabbinical tradition, and they weren't speaking emptily when they addressed him thus. Unless you ascribe him to the more esoteric end of the Essene spectrum or similar (which I don't), there's no reason to suspect he was anything but a loving husband and father. Certainly the Gospels don't specify otherwise.'

This shocked me from my half-hypnotised reverie. 'Come on. I don't think it says anywhere that he was *married*.'

'Nevertheless, he probably was. The fact that the Gospels don't mention he was married shouldn't suggest to us that he was not – in much the same way that their failure to describe the colour or texture of his hair shouldn't lead us to conclude he was entirely bald. You get what I mean. They record what was *remarkable* about him, where he *differed* from the norm. To be unmarried was to be very different *indeed*, and would certainly have warranted more than a passing reference.

'As it happens, there's a good chance that the marriage at *Cana* was his own.'

She read my expression, not without mischief.

'Oh,' she said. 'Some heroic historical detective work has gone into this. Would you like me to simplify for your unschooled and eager mind?'

I told her that would be very kind. She laughed. She was enjoying herself.

'Not at all. No trouble. Basically, the theory goes like this: The Marriage at Cana. Bustle bustle, busy busy, you know what weddings are like. Dreadful occasions. What we know is this: Mary, Jesus' mother, is very edgy about the wine. The wine's running out and she's not happy. She keeps badgering her poor son about it. He's pouring wine for people, and all the time his mother keeps bothering him about the wine running low. Eventually he steps outside and performs a miracle just to make her shut up and leave him be for a while. Okay? So far, so familiar. Putting aside for the moment the miracle itself, we ask the question: You're at a wedding party. Do you worry about keeping the glasses of the guests topped up, do you pester your beleaguered son about not being diligent enough in pouring drinks, to hurry up and pour, already, *unless you're the host?*'

She paused. Her smile grew heavy and fell. 'He was a dutiful son,' she said. 'He did what was expected of him, to the spirit and the letter. He was remarkable. He was marked from the moment of his conception to lead a great life. He was all these things I've talked about, all these funny human things writ large and splendid by his nature. He was capable of fear, though. When he wept in Gethsemane, it wasn't for effect. A man that great, so full of fear – but fuller of the love of his God. And he was betrayed. And they hurt him.'

The walls of the tent snapped in the wind, and cast the shadows in motion behind her head, in the corners. We sat in silence, not looking at each other. We knew he was with us. I could feel the peace and the ferocity of him. The gentle slowness of his eyes and the quickness of his grin. His aching plea that, should it please his Lord, this bitter cup be taken from him. He stood at my shoulder.

When Ruth continued, it was very quietly. 'They hurt him terribly,' she said. 'They beat him and they broke his body and they mocked him in his agony. King of the Jews and two of his wretched followers.' She paused again. She was thinking. She picked at a loose thread on her desert fatigues. Then she tilted her jaw, and she regarded me from beneath her brow. It was an unsettling look, it had about it the dispassionately intense enquiry of a fox. My arms broke into goosebumps. She opened her mouth and spoke in a voice I had not yet heard. It was the voice of the passion that drove her, the fear that she might never know God, however she prayed, however much she read, or dug, or catalogued, or meditated or extended love to her neighbour. It was the voice of something expelled from paradise, grown weary and certain of the world. 'What we should not forget,' she said, 'is that he did not have at his command only knowledge of the law, and charisma, and quick wit and piety and bravery and humility. Because he was cunning, too. He was sly, and he was cunning. His schemes were devious and convoluted to the point of wickedness. I shouldn't say this,' she said. 'But I will. What we shouldn't forget is that he had something of the devil in him.'

We were frozen in this tableau while her portable alarm clock, propped on a folding table next to her camp-bed, next to a pile of library books, a spare pair of spectacles and some indigestion tablets, beat away a little time. She leaned forward so that her eyes were half a metre away from mine, unblinking and animate beneath the inadequate light powered by the outdated generators chugging away on the perimeter of the camp. Her hands clasped her knees. She scrutinised me closely, without embarrassment or humour, then she clapped: once, sharp and shocking, and barked a single laugh.

'Faith's as personal as it is doctrinal,' she said. 'What point otherwise in free will? God contains multitudes and it is absolutely incumbent upon us to confront God as an individual. Investigation and supposition don't constitute apostasy. One should struggle with the unformed essence of one's faith, one should determine to find shape in it, and definition. It shouldn't be something you passively receive, like a report on the news telling you that there is a living God who's come to save you, and now for the weather.

'I see the divinity of Christ's mission manifest in history, in the ongoing unfolding of Creation. I acknowledge this Christ, this aspect of an incomprehensibly inclusive God. But Jesus the man? I *love* Jesus the man. I would so like to have met him. The more I learn about him, the more I'd like to spend an afternoon, listening to him spinning a tale, making a fresh point with an old, old story.'

I understood what she wanted. I wanted it too, although we were talking of different men with the same name. But I asked her anyway, because I could tell she wanted me to.

'What would you say to him? What would you ask?'

She took a small sip of tea. 'I'd ask him outright if I'm correct in my surmise of his cunning.'

I laughed and said: 'Go on. I can tell how much you want to. Give me an example of the low cunning of the Son of Man.'

'Oh, there was nothing *low* about it. However, to illustrate: political ferment was a continual frustration to the administration of the Roman empire, so they weren't slow in quashing insurrection at the first glimpse of it. Insurrection was one thing, internecine squabbles between rival factions of some backwater religion quite another. The Jews were allowed to administer Judaic Law. What they did with their odd God was entirely up to them – as was what they did unto one another, up to a point. Jesus might have defecated in the temple while denouncing the sacred name of God and Pilate would not have batted a reptilian eyelid. Nor would he when furious crowds ripped Jesus to little pieces and stamped on his remains for this *inconceivable* blasphemy.

'I've already indicated that the hands of Jews are clean of Jesus' blood. However, I'm sure there were a few individuals, largely jealous would-be Messiahs, possibly even the Baptist, if he hadn't have gone and lost his head, who wouldn't have minded too much to see him dead, but as a race they were unfairly implicated in a crime without precedent. And for that little lie, generations later, another crime without precedent was perpetrated on them. But that's not what we're talking about.

'It wasn't a couple of bored Legionaries and some Pharisees with their noses put a little out of joint who came to arrest him in Gethsemane. It was upwards of *two thousand men*, a cohort. These aren't soldiers like you. These are *real* soldiers. Veterans of God alone knows how many military campaigns, defensive and invasive and up to their knees in entrails. Two *thousand* soldiers. Now, a group of men that size doesn't sneak around a small town like Jerusalem without being noticed. This isn't a small operation. It created a God al*mighty* commotion. It wakes the entire city. Children cry and mothers comfort them. You can fill in the details. Lights go on. Windows are barred, etc. etc. etc.

'Do you believe it possible that even the most wet-behind-the-ears and politically naive Governor would go to the administrative trouble of sending out two thousand armed men in the middle of the night to arrest a doe-eyed hippy and his twelve like-minded compatriots, camping out in their rich friend's garden?

'Of course not. Jesus said it himself: he came not to bring peace but a sword. When the arresting hand was placed upon him, it was one of his most beloved followers who drew a sword and struck off a Roman ear. If this was a novel, a close reader would be compelled to ask: why is he carrying a *sword*, this man who is so devoted to his leader, who teaches only peace and the turning of the cheek? Consider his behaviour in the temple, the spilling of the moneylenders' tables. In order to understand, you've got to set aside the gentle Jesus, meek and mild, they taught you about in Sunday school. You've got to think about *people*. Imagine how politically explosive it was that he fulfil a prophecy of liberation by entering Jerusalem astride an ass, and picture the riot that must have accompanied his subsequent disruption of the customary routine at the temple. *People*. Always people. Can you think of a single historical example in which one could say with any authority that the kind of person who made money by selling and lending money would passively accept such an act? Commerce protects itself with violence, of one kind or another. Especially then. Did these men, these lenders, clap and laugh to see this lunatic making chaos of their livelihood? Come *on*. Imagine the surprise, the outrage, the violence and the passion of it: the anger and the bloodshed that must have resulted. Jesus was not displaying humility and passivity. He started a *riot*. It was the declaration of power – of *mandate*.'

I set the empty cup on the rickety table, poured myself another from the pot.

'But he was arrested and executed,' I said. 'Where's the cunning in that? Accepting the will of God is one thing. Setting yourself up for a fall is quite another.'

'You're forgetting a fundamentally important point which should always be at the forefront of your mind. *Jesus wasn't a Christian*.

'None of Jesus' *followers* were Christians. He doesn't know a New Testament is going to be written in a few years, let alone that he'll be the protagonist. He's an observant Jew. He'd consider the idea of Christianity an outrage, an *appalling* blasphemy. His concern, his primary and overwhelming and driving concern is the Kingdom of God, the cleansing of the temple, adherence to Scripture and the immediate withdrawal of unwanted, idolatrous Italians.'

She pre-empted my interruption.

'Bear with me. We have established that Jesus was aware of his impending sacrifice. We can be confident in ascribing validity to this, given that his terror in the garden has the rather lovely narrative awkwardness of an event we would rather had not happened, but unfortunately did. It is essential to the Plan that they come and take him away.

'We admit there is a Plan. We should also conclude that Jesus is in the garden that night, waiting to be arrested, not because he has supernaturally prophesied that tonight is the night, but because he has chosen this night. He has studied scripture and prayed, he has prepared for this mission all his life. Everything he has done in the preceding week, the entry into Jerusalem, the riot at the temple, the threat to the temple, it no longer looks careless and ill thought out. Quite the contrary. All of the events of his life have led him here, to the Mount of Olives.

'So,' she said. 'Given all this, bearing in mind his application and the meticulous intelligence he applies to everything, given his *humanity*, I'm going to ask you a question. Who was the most important disciple, and why?'

I thought hard. After the passage of an acceptable number of seconds, I said: 'Peter. He trusted him as the foundation upon which he could build his church.'

'He didn't *want* a new church,' she reminded me. 'He was more than happy with the religion he had. God was as real to him as I am to you. So – no, not Peter. Poor Peter. I suspect he was a bit of a buffoon.' She took my hands in hers and she squeezed them. She shook her head, *no*. 'No. Not Peter. The most important disciple was Judas.'

I must have looked offended. She looked gratified.

Then she exhorted me, once more: 'Step away from it for a moment, step out of the story. It's too familiar. We lose all sense of narrative consistency. For a story to be true, to have any value to us, the people in it must *behave* like people, even if they never lived. This is what gives the parables their power, all their mystery and poetry. Look again at the parable of the Prodigal Son, this time from the perspective of the dutiful son, the son who did exactly as his father instructed. Suddenly, you're no longer looking at a tale of paternal mercy, but at a horror story, where the dutiful are punished and the reprobate rewarded. The Prodigal Son is a *terrifying* story – but one can understand something of its particular resonance to an obedient Chosen People labouring under the yoke of rapacious idolaters. It rings true. You can't paraphrase a parable, but there's much to extract from it.

'Even if we don't fully understand the motivation, any action taken within a narrative should *feel* right; like the father welcoming back the prodigal in the way we would like our own father to greet us in similar circumstances, with generosity and forgiveness and love. We must believe that it's the kind of action a person, with all their inherent complexities of motivation, might take. So. It was necessary that Jesus be crucified. He spent his ministry preparing for his death: perhaps for the *spectacle* of his death, but that's another story. Okay? Picture it. The Last Supper. Thirteen men, twelve followers and the one they follow. He makes a new covenant with bread and wine. He announces that one of those present is to betray him – in an ambiguous way, but that's for another day as well. This is the point: There are *thirteen men* present. Once Jesus had identified the individual intent on betraying him, it would have been the work of seconds to restrain him.

'Against twelve men – at least some of them *armed*, remember – an unmasked traitor stood no chance of escape. But they don't restrain him. They don't tie him up or beat him or kill him. They don't jeer their disgust and spit upon him and curse him. None of this happens. Instead, they sit back and let him go.

'In what way can this possibly make sense, outside the dictates of a fairy tale? We can say that it is not truth, that it is a story, a tale attached to the reality – but in this instance, I'd tend to apply the maxim: the more apparently inexplicable the tale, the more likely it is to be true. Lies tend to simplicity. So, we're left with the question: why was Judas allowed to leave? The only explanation is that surrendering Jesus to the authorities was *part of Jesus' own plan*. God's plan, if you will.

'No other explanation for letting Judas go reflects the behaviour of human beings as we know them – even if this is extreme behaviour. And it is. It is extreme. When Jesus identified Judas as the man who would betray him, he wasn't making a prophecy. He was issuing an *instruction*. It was an instruction of such forbidding nature it could only have been entrusted to the most devoted of his followers, a man sufficiently heroic and selfless to surrender to history a memory of himself as cowardly and greedy. A man willing to sacrifice himself in order that his master might do the same, to more exalted effect.

'It was a terrible, terrible task to set someone who loves you – and it was an act of indescribable love to bear that burden, to undertake that task. Without Judas, no betrayal, no symbolic sacrifice, no paschal lamb. We may never understand exactly why the Messiah schemed to have himself humiliated in the most terrible way imaginable, but we can safely conclude that he *did* plan it. He considered it necessary and you and I believe he was correct although we might disagree as to why. 'What we are left with is the simple conclusion: no Judas, no salvation. Ergo, Judas is the most important disciple.'

'But that's just *logistics*,' I said. 'The way you talk about it, there's no genius. I don't see any cunning. He's set the right man to do the right job. That's cold intelligence and patient planning. I wouldn't call it cunning.'

'That's not the cunning part.'

'Then what is?'

'*His concept that power can be exercised without being demonstrated*. He bowed the entire Judean Administration, the efficient Romans, the conservative Sadducees, the money lenders, the whole of the city of Jerusalem, to the dictates of his will. He had them jumping through *hoops* for him. *He made them fulfil God's prophecy*. The might of Empire performed for him like circus poodles, obeying his dictate – which was God's also. When they came for him, it was at the time of his choosing. He was scared all right. He did his share of weeping. How terrifying to surrender oneself to the knowledge of imminent, terrible pain. All of it was his will, although not his desire. They whipped him and stripped him, and I wouldn't speculate on the pleasure there was to be taken in knowing that when he did indeed confront Pilate, that the Governor was his inferior in every way, that he didn't suspect the triumphant depth of contempt behind the questions the bleeding Christ threw back at him.

'When Pilate asks: "What is Truth?" this Jesus could have replied: "Where is power?" '

She smiled, sadly. The weird melancholy of witnessing a sunrise. 'His cunning was in the knowledge that they couldn't beat him. That with God on his side he didn't need an army behind him to defeat the Romans. That they couldn't defeat him even by executing him.

'He knew they weren't able to kill him.'

She looked about herself. Abruptly, the discussion was terminated.

'I don't see it,' I said. 'That's not the Jesus I know. It just doesn't feel right.'

She handed me my cap. 'You don't have to agree with me,' she said. 'I was sharing an opinion with you. I didn't intend to pass it off as fact. I wouldn't dream of interfering with your faith, Malachi. The apprehension of the living Christ is a deeply personal thing. God manifest in Christ is every colour and every age and each gender, every possible sexual orientation.'

'You say that,' I was epically frustrated, 'but you don't believe it. You don't feel it. Compared to the other stuff you say, it's doctrinal spiel, the same kind of bullshit you hear spouted every day by people whose claim to faith is founded on . . . oh, I don't know. The usual bullshit. Fear. And the rest. Bigotry.' I was visited by two unwelcome images: Christ on the cross. His hair hangs over his face. On his mouth there is a smile of secret triumph. And Christ, the Pied Piper.

'And, surely, it didn't even *work*.' I said. 'I mean, a few years after he died, the Romans were there and the Jews weren't.'

'Oh, but I think he came close,' she said, and marked an increment between forefinger and thumb. 'I think he got about as close as it was possible to get.'

'Was he God?'

'God was in him, I don't doubt that. As to his fundamental nature – who can say? That's the issue. It's never been a satisfactory aspect of the Christian faith. Not who, but *what* was this man, whose survival of the cross changed the course of history?

'But here's the rub, here's the central irony, here's what you should reflect upon when you need to remind yourself of the awesome, incomprehensible nature of God. Remember that the Jesus of the Bible and the Jesus of history are not one and the same. It's central to the nature of my faith that I see God's will manifest in what was to become of him: that, whatever the fate of the physical being, Jesus became a half-fictional character in a profoundly important but little-read book, in which half-fiction, speculation and editorial amendment contain Truth of the most fundamental nature. God is revealed in History. The Bible *created* our history.

'That history dictates that Jesus be elevated as far as is possible – to become a component of the Godhead. But here's the irony. It's an honour whose abhorrence he would scarcely have been able to encompass. It would be a crime on a scale too great to be imagined. Jesus, who served God like no other before or since, would have been *appalled* by what God did to him.

'In humiliation, he found triumph. In deification he found humiliation.

'God suffers for us in ways we can't imagine.'

I stood. I had my cap clasped in my fist. I couldn't respond. Then I said: 'What comfort can you draw from *that*? It seems worse than atheism.'

She said, 'It's liberation. It's free will, as God intended us to have. Only if we admit that God is too great to encompass – that the best we are able to conceptualise is that there is something which it is beyond our ability to conceptualise, which we grasp at with stories and analogy – only then are we able to cast aside the idolatry with which we commonly demean him. Our existence to him, to it, to this unspeakably vast, primal *enormity*, is correspondingly infinitesimal and fleeting. Yet, seeing this, we acknowledge that, although we cannot account for his actions, he encompasses and creates and transcends what we perceive to be good and evil. He loves us, he cherishes each one of us, each individual. Thus one becomes both infinitely meaningless and infinitely important, because one is important *to* the infinite. I find that thought comforting and beautiful.'

I had a headache. 'Not notably orthodox.'

'Oh,' she said. 'A poor attempt to share what is, after all, ineffable.'

I smiled. 'I'll dream tonight.' I lifted the flap of the tent. Before I passed through the portal, she called my name.

I waited.

'Yes?'

She had me wait while she rooted around in a trunk she pulled out from beneath her bed. She removed a book and handed it to me. *The Lives of the Historical Jesus*.

She told me the scholarship was outdated, but the reasoning was classic. She told me this was a good place to begin.

I thanked her and delivered a mock salute, which she seemed to find amusing enough, and I stepped out of the tent under the awesomely cloudless sky of the Negev desert, the book clasped in my right hand.

'But keep it to yourself,' she said. 'I'm not a lending library.'

I thought little enough of it at the time.

In retrospect, I was able to isolate the act of pocketing that book and leaving her tent as the moment it all truly began.

Twelve *The Analogical Convalescence Unit*

I waited on the bench until I began to fear a repeat of the delivery in the restaurant: that every assignation I made would be a no-show. I didn't know what I'd do without Ruth to help me. I didn't want her to be dead. I wanted her not to be dead so she could help me not to be dead either.

She was twenty minutes late. So many tourists, so many hired cars. The traffic had been heavier than she'd anticipated.

She pulled up to the kerb in a big, fuck-off Volvo estate that looked about a hundred years old. She honked the horn once and gave a little wave through the windscreen. My heart expanded like a party balloon and I waved back. Only her nose and eyes and the top of her head (her dry, mousy-brown and greying hair) appeared over the dashboard. I clambered into the car, favouring the bad leg rather dramatically. Before I could say hello or even close the door properly, she was pulling away. I struggled a little with a recalcitrant safety belt. We had stopped at a red light before she said: 'Well, I'm glad to see you're not dead yet.'

I eased my head into the rest. She didn't look much older. The bags round her eyes were a little puffier and her cheeks were softer and more old lady-like, but she affected exactly the same no-nonsense haircut and practical clothing.

I thanked her for the sentiment, then I told her that a man in my room had shot me in the leg and tortured me. She took this like grave but expected news, without taking her eyes from the road or changing her expression. She just nodded sagely. Then I told her that I'd killed the man who shot me. What she said this time was: 'I see.'

I enquired politely what exactly was happening to every-thing and she replied that now wasn't the time to ask. I knew I'd get nothing from her. I asked her if we were going back to her house (a safe place, my little animal senses told me, a safe place to get better and hide yourself away from whatever's going to eat you). She afforded me a sidelong glance and her lips thinned a little. She said: 'I don't think so, do you?'

I took out a cigarette.

She said: 'I'd rather you didn't do that.'

My voice broke. It went high with outrage. 'Jesus, Ruth,' I said. 'Jesus Christ. Come on. Jesus. At least let me have a cigarette. Somebody just *shot* me.'

'Oh, go ahead,' she said. 'Do whatever you want. Inject heroin.' She reached out, touched a button. The passenger window rolled down. Puffing away, I felt sullenly justified.

'How bad is it?'

I blew smoke from the window. Eddies of it in the slipstream. 'It's not nice. It hurts like a bastard. I need to clean it, and I need to stitch it a little. It keeps opening. I feel it opening and closing as I walk, beneath the bandage. I've lost blood. I need treatment.'

After a few minutes, we drove into the suburbs. Streets wide and lined with trees. It was less busy. Ruth pulled to the kerb alongside the kind of local store which looks like a family business but is actually a global franchise.

She told me to wait in the car and returned with a few bagged items, which she passed to me through the passenger window. Three cans of Coke. Two packs of Marlboro. An okay bottle of whiskey. A pack of sanitary towels.

'All my favourites,' I said. I studied the folded instructions within the blue box of sanitary napkins. I removed a towel, unbuttoned my trousers, and applied the still-cool pad to my thigh, staunching my unfeminine flow.

She looked askance. 'Do you have to do that here?'

I looked askance right back at her. 'Yes.'

She clicked her tongue against her palate. 'Well,' she said. 'Be quick about it.'

I kept my silence and got on with it. When I was safely decent again, I said: 'Where are you taking us?'

She pressed her lips together. 'Nowhere just yet, I thought we'd just drive for a while.'

I chucked her left shoulder. 'You romantic old fool,' I told her. 'You have the sweetest ideas.'

'Fucking right,' she said, with the same fixed expression. 'Fucking right.'

I sat back. The leg was really beginning to hurt, to throb like the tentatively introductory drumbeats of a dental abscess.

Ruth said, 'Are you okay?'

'Sleepy,' I said.

'Stay with us, now,' she said. 'I need you with me.'

'Five minutes,' I said. 'My leg hurts. I'm tired. Five minutes to rest my eyes.'

'No more than five minutes,' she said. 'I need you with me. I'm going to need you to be strong.'

'I will,' I said, 'I will be strong.'

I fell asleep with my leg pounding and throbbing like a vagrant telling you his life story, third time over. It wouldn't shut up.

After I got myself all blown up, they helicoptered me to Crete, just outside Iraklion, to a place of safety – an asylum in the old sense, an enormous, rambling old hospital which overlooked the coast. They flew broken people out there, made them better, then sent them back to get broken all over again.

Our recuperation was not hurried. We weren't processed like battery chickens. We were tended. It never felt like I was really there. The crumbling colonial environs had a dreamlike quality. Temporarily reliant on a wheelchair, I could take in the sun, read on the patio, sit and watch the sea, read, or attend counselling sessions (group and individual).

I was encouraged to attend group meetings. I tried my best.

I really did. I let myself get wheeled to a big room, bright and shadowless beneath the Mediterranean sun. It was filled with misshapes and near write-offs trying to encourage one another along the road to recovery.

The first issue to deal with was our anger at God for allowing this to happen to us. It was a natural reaction, the counsellor assured us. It's something we all experience at some time. You could call it a *natural response*. Because of this, it wasn't really a sin. Even so, it was something we had to get over. Re-establishing our relationship with God was a checking-in station on our journey to health. All of us in the room were at different stages, so he wanted to get the ball rolling by asking some of the more familiar faces in the group to break the ice for the new attendees, to tell us what had helped them come to terms with their injuries.

'Okay,' said this guy.

He was a pale, waspish Presbyterian type. Somewhere along the line, he'd surrendered his eyes to the cause. He wasn't about to get them back. There wasn't much they could do for eyes back then. He didn't seem too unhappy about it, though, because he knew it was all part of God's plan. He was assured that he had surrendered his eyes because God willed it. If God willed it, it was both necessary and good. He therefore didn't feel embittered by his blindness. Instead, he felt blessed. He felt *rewarded*.

He leaned forward while he told us this, then he sat back, crossing his legs and arms. He was wearing cotton pyjamas, a towelling gown and slippers, all of which had been shipped over to him by his wife. He tapped one foot as if impatient. Then he said: 'Look at it like this,' and proceeded to explain exactly how he claimed to look at it: 'Imagine this: some scientist makes a discovery, this discovery that's going to change the world forever, for the better. Some great, long sought-after secret. Nobody knows exactly what it is, but they know it's going to be just *great*. Because it's such a big secret, the scientist decides he has to code it, so that's what he does.

He puts it in an unbreakable code. But this scientist dies. All the other scientists, they know the secret's there, but they don't know exactly what it is, and they know the code can't be broken. They speculate, they argue, they break into factions about what exactly the secret is, and what the code means.

'But the humble scientists, the ones who loved the dead scientist the most, and honour his vision, they forget about arguing and get on with studying the code in order to understand it. They know that, if they do, the world will be a better place.

'That's how I see God's plan. It's a good secret written in a code nobody can break.'

He sat back and crossed his arms again. Two weeks later he woke screaming in the night. They came for him, stuck needles in him and took him away. We never saw him again.

That's when I began to think I'd go mad if I didn't get away from there.

By now, I was nearly all better and happy again, except I wasn't. My leg had almost completely regrown. Soon it would fill exactly the space I perceived as being in use by my phantom limb, marking the end of the delusional triplication which they'd assured me was common, but which would take a little getting used to. No kidding. I spent weeks enduring a cognitive battle with some ostensibly lower but nevertheless persistent mental processes. For all that my eyes and hands and indeed nurses told me otherwise, for a season I was effectively the proud owner of three legs. One of these was the fond and familiar old limb I'd first sprouted when I was a gelatinous blob about the size of a walnut and which had stayed with me ever since. The second was the regenerating limb over which I had been warned not to expect much conscious control in the early stages. (I was glad to take their advice and not look at or think about it too much because some patients found the regenerative process disturbing. Big surprise.) Third, the leg that wasn't there any more. It wasn't anywhere, any more. Most of it got spread like a fresh bucket of piss all over the teetering walls of some mortar-damaged house I would never be able to identify even if I got the chance to see it again. The gritty wind would have abraded away the last faint stains of it by now. I imagined, or hoped, that somebody had taken the trouble to lift the still-booted foot, from which protruded that pornographic little knob of ankle, and toss it in a fire. If not, then something had certainly scavenged and made a slim meal of it by now. I didn't mind that too much. What bothered me sometimes was that it might be stored deep in some unthinkable nest with pale grubs burrowing blindly into the gamey meat of it.

Whatever had become of it, the memory lingered on. For months I experienced intermittent attacks of bad cramp. It started in the sole of my foot, which spasmed and locked into shape like a malformed hand straining to make a fist. My calf and thigh followed. Each fibre of muscle contracted and screamed like nylon wire.

Except it didn't, because the leg wasn't there.

I know there is a biological explanation for all of this, although I'm not sure exactly what it is. Whatever. The result was that, despite the empirical evidence cited by the epipheno-menal freeloader which was my mind, a fundamental compo-nent of my brain remained utterly unconvinced that the leg was simply not *there* any more. It was fizzing and popping with frustration because something, it couldn't quite work out quite what, was just not right. It was incapable of incorporating such a radical amendment to the form for which it could conceive no alternative: without the one true form there was void: completeness, or complete absence. This provided an opportu-nity for a vulgar little Cartesian interlude. Having your mind observe your brain getting something so terribly wrong is a disquieting experience, a precursor to the madness to which the most casual epistemological enquiry can lead, if we are not careful. Here be dragons, if you're in the mood.

It should hardly need saying that mine proved to be a rather more troublesome phantom than was common. Many freshly limb-asymmetrical patients experienced the occasional unscratchable itch, which I suppose must be irritating enough, in its own way. But not me. Whatever the fundamental nature of the pain I experienced in a limb objectively gone on to make its own way in the world, it sometimes saw me throwing myself in frustrated rage from one side of my convalescent bed to the other. I raged and hissed and spat demonically at nurses who rushed to my aid.

As the new leg established as its own the site of the phantom's malicious haunting, so ended its merciless and unjust persecution. It faded away as if it had never been, which of course it had not. As I had been assured, once there was muscle tissue in which to manifest, the cramps did not recur. My mind and my brain forgot their temporary difference and got on with the job of maintaining a sense of somatic and psychological unity.

In hospital I had too much time to think.

I was instructed that the treatment for which I was scheduled (there was a waiting list. It was a very fashionable injury) was the genetic equivalent of taking a balled-up rubber glove and inflating it into the shape of a hand. This wisdom was issued to me by a broad-shouldered, narrow-waisted consultant who wore a crisp white shirt (open collared), and Levi's beneath his white coat. I reckoned him to be just the right side of sixty, but with a full head of alarmingly romantic steel-grey hair and eyes two shades darker. It was as if God, in a moment of whimsy, had decided to breathe life into an image from the jacket of a very bad romantic novel. A fully-accessorised human being whose movements were assured of commanding respect in much the way a truck will assume your willingness to get the fuck out of its way.

That squashed up old glove didn't only contain the *potential* to be hand-shaped, he told me: that was the shape it *preferred*. It would actually *seek out* that shape. Fold it into a ball and straight away it would try its damnedest to unfold and shape itself like a hand again. 'Your genes are like that glove,' he told me. 'Your body knows its shape. It knows there's supposed to be a leg attached right about here' (he indicated the rude stump with the end of a pen). 'Your body wants to find its shape again, just like that glove. We're going to help it along. All it needs is a little encouragement, a little jump start, and it'll do most of the work for us. There's nothing new about this. Lizards have been doing it for years. It just took us a while to find how to hit the right switches.'

I smiled brightly and nodded an enthusiastic affirmative. Thank you.

In fact I began to wonder if he expected to be congratulated on his analogy. Perhaps he was holding out for one of his patients to suggest he enter it to a Surgical Analogy Competition, in order that he might be modestly dismissive but humbly gratified to be so rewarded by a patient whose interests he held to be so much more important than his own. (Such as his abiding love for seventeenth-century metaphysical poetry, the Shakespearian comedies, or whatever else it is people do in their spare time, who are born to be actors who play doctors, but by some ontological administrative error, become real doctors instead.)

Or perhaps because he was a doctor with a full complement of legs and I was a private recently demoted to one, he simply assumed I was stupid.

I told Sonny all about this.

Sonny had enjoyed a brief stay in a different ward of the same hospital. He'd caught some shrapnel in his back and broken an arm, but by the time I was close to being fully healed, he was enjoying a month's recuperative leave, billeted in a requisitioned hotel in town. He came to visit me two or three times a week. He always brought something along with him: he'd swagger in, bursting with life and distribute chocolate bars or cartons of cigarettes, tossing them on the edge of a bed as he passed. It was the corniest thing in the world, done in the corniest way. That was why he did it and why we loved it.

His broad face was full of artless glee. The Greek sky never got so blue as Sonny's eyes, beneath a lick of corn-yellow hair. He radiated an inherent positivity that temporarily charged those around him. He had the widest smile I ever saw, a distillation of such audacity and charm that even his sins were endearing, and thus many and varied. Sins just seemed less sinful when Sonny committed them. He was my closest friend.

Of our favourite nurse, Sonny claimed: 'I gave her a good time. Swear to God. All it took was this,' he mimed a surreptitious, sideways nod of the head in the direction of an imaginary cupboard. 'You can always tell,' he said. 'They work so hard, these poor girls. They're so dedicated. But there comes a point in every girl's life when if she don't get what she needs, she'll go *insane*. She didn't grunt or groan or whisper my name, or anyone else's for that matter. She just *smiled*. She just had this big grin, like she was so *relieved*.'

He slapped the knee of my good leg and rocked in his chair with delighted laughter.

None of us believed him, but – despite the fact that the nurse of whom Sonny spoke had tended us with unfailing good patience and tenderness, had eased our discomfort and our pain and had never made any of us feel like anything other than an individual, unique human being who it was a pleasure to know – we all dearly wanted to believe it was possible to lead her to a cupboard, hastily tugging at her own buttons, we all longed to believe that she ached for someone like Sonny (someone like us) to come along and relieve her.

What we believed to be true and what we wished to be true began to merge, until it was not possible to see her without imagining her offering a soft, white breast and an excited nipple to Sonny's lips, or sinking her teeth into his shoulder to mask her grateful whimpering.

Because the pleasure he took in relating his adventures was ruddy and innocently eager rather than muttered and lewd, we wanted, pretended and finally came to believe that Sonny's life was one, long, bawdy novel which had been interrupted by war only as a function of plot.

We all loved him. We even secretly appreciated his ability to intuit and exploit our predilections.

'I swear to God,' he said through that semicircular slice of shit-eating smile. 'Hand on my heart, it was her. Short hair, black, kind of shiny. Tucks it behind her ear, like so. The one with the legs and the attitude.'

I had seen this woman perhaps five times – in Sonny's company only once. I knew nothing about her, other than that her position was senior but not medical. I assumed she represented whichever charity it was put money into this place. I didn't know her name, nationality, or even ethnicity. I'd caught her eye once, very briefly, as she passed aristocratically through the ward. It was Sonny who turned to follow her progress with a knitted brow and a stifled little moan. I prayed she knew it came from him and not me.

That was it. Nothing was said – except that, perhaps a week later, Sonny pulled a tubular framed, canvas chair to the edge of my bed. I'd never seen him so excited. He spoke softly and urgently. He knew all the aphorisms about God and details. He dressed up a lie just enough to allow you to believe it if you really needed to.

What he told me was this: the previous evening, after visiting, he had for various elaborate reasons let himself into a disused office at the rear of the building, on the lower floor. He stumbled across the woman and her husband. They were dressed up 'for the opera or something'. She sat on a desk, her back to the wall, her evening dress hiked to her waist. Her legs wrapped around her husband's back. Her eyes were rolled up in their sockets. They were not hurrying. Sonny made sure I knew exactly how shocked he was: 'You've got to understand,' he said. 'All this takes a hundred times longer to tell than it took to happen.' The woman's eyes rolled down and she saw Sonny, stood, mouth agape behind her husband's shoulder. She gasped. Sonny saw her nails bite deep into the man's shoulders. The husband stopped the movement of his hips and slowly turned his head. Seeing Sonny, he displayed polite surprise but no shock. He was extremely courteous. He withdrew from his wife, stood back ('tucking away the old man'), and greeted Sonny. For her part, she adjusted her dress, without taking her eyes from Sonny's.

The man watched her do this, wriggling to ease the skirt back over her hips and thighs, and quietly asked Sonny if she was not beautiful.

'I mean,' Sonny said: 'What would *you* say, in this circumstance? I can hardly tell the guy the woman barks at the moon, can I? Luckily, he's not lying. She really is. So I say, "Yeah, she really is." I have to cough into my fist before I can speak. And before I know it, I'm in a goddamn conversation with them. He says: "She has such beautiful breasts, don't you think?"'

She still had not uttered a word. Silently, she accepted the ministrations of her husband, as he asked for Sonny's assessment of her breasts, the line of her throat, her thighs. In order for Sonny to fully appreciate her, it was necessary that she undress. She did this as her husband requested; 'Just take off the dress now, honey.' When she was fully naked, the husband had her lie flat and stroked the lines of her, 'as if she was a goddamn sports car, and all the time she's arching her back into his hand. She's practically *purring*, for Christ's sake.' Finally satisfied that he and Sonny were of a mind, he courteously extended an invitation to Sonny. 'Like I'd proved I was a connoisseur, so it was polite to hand her to me for a while. Let me road test the engine. Check out the handling.'

I called him an evil lying motherfucking pervert with a filthy mind.

He smiled wider and told me he hadn't reached the good part yet. 'You got to allow people a little fantasy,' he told me. He told me strange times called for strange measures. This woman and her husband had enough worries running this place. They just wanted to play at being decadent for a while. After Sonny was done with her, she stood, put on her dress, nodded at him politely, kissed her husband's cheek and left the room. Sonny and the husband stayed behind. They were instant friends.

'Just as well,' I said, 'you sick bastard.'

'Quiet,' he said, 'listen.' They two had made love in the room twenty times, maybe more, and nobody had ever caught them. They'd decided that, if anybody ever did, they'd do what they'd discussed, unless she gave the signal otherwise. They'd never really expected anybody to walk in, and if anybody ever had, he'd never expected her to actually go through with it. It was just a fantasy. He expected her to give the signal right away. But she hadn't. 'Luckily, it was me who found them,' said Sonny. 'Somebody who knows how to behave with a little decorum when the situation demands.' Then he leaned forward, tipped me a conspiratorial wink and told me: 'I set you up. It's your turn next.'

'You fucking moron,' I told him. 'Go fuck yourself.'

'Not a word of a goddamn lie,' he protested, wounded, 'and shit on me if I'm not the best friend you ever had for putting an opportunity like this your way.'

Although the husband and Sonny had struck an impressive post-coital rapport, he hoped Sonny didn't mind that the events of the evening could not be repeated. He thanked Sonny for his understanding. He told Sonny how fortunate they were that it was he who discovered them, since he could not bear the idea of some eager vulgarian pawing rapaciously at his wife's body. 'So I told him about you,' said Sonny. 'I told him that my good friend Malachi thinks his wife is an angel, and that he trembles with admiration and awe every time she walks past. I good as told him you'd treat her like she was the holy grail. As soon as I told him, I could tell he started to get hot all over again. She came past to check you out this morning. You're on. Thursday night. I'll tell you how to get to the office. You're not supposed to let them know that I've told you this. I'm supposed to trick you down there with some story or another. Your surprise is important to them, y'know? So play along. That's all you have to do.'

I called him a motherfucker, but my heart was pounding and I felt sick. This was not a normal place and these were not normal times. And she *had* walked past my bed this morning.

I laughed out loud to show him I could take a joke. I called him a sick bastard.

He frowned, looked concerned and said: 'Are you telling me that, for all the things you've seen and been made to do, for all the terrible things you've seen done to people, you can't believe that something like this can be true, even when it's your friend telling you about it? Jesus. That's sick.'

It was all very good-natured. I never went to that room that night, because I wasn't that stupid. I thought about it a lot, though, I admit that. I wished it could be true, and occasionally convinced myself it was, if only temporarily and as a means to an end. I knew what Sonny had done to me.

Good old Sonny. He did us good with his stories and his lies; he opened up to us the possibility of a finer and more exciting world, a brighter place where magic lurks in the mundane if you have the child's eyes to see it and the foolhardiness to grasp it. Except the devil was an angel once, too, and three years later they found Sonny floating face-down with the fish nibbling his eyes, and I was never even formally charged for doing it.

The throbbing wound in my leg reminded me of that hospital the way the smell of Ruth's mint tea evoked the dig in the Negev. Time seemed to be rushing at me from every direction.

Ruth asked me if I felt better. I told her: 'A little.'

We stopped outside the kind of house to which advertisers believe we all aspire. Situated back from an already quiet, tree-lined avenue: a regal, white structure arranged in immaculate gardens. Approached by a gravel drive. Apple trees in the garden.

'This is it,' she said.

I lit a cigarette. 'This is what?'

'Oh, *very* tough,' she said. 'This is where we're going.'

Despite the *ad hoc* treatments I had self-administered and although it was temporarily strapped and bandaged, the injured leg had stiffened and I had lost an abundant measure of blood. Moving it as I got from the car was an exquisite discomfort. I was feverish and clumsily spastic as I shambled the length of the gravel path in her wake. I followed her up the driveway, to the wooden door with brass fittings. I leaned against the doorframe. I was wet with perspiration.

She rang the doorbell.

Nobody answered.

She rang again. Again, we waited. Ruth clicked her tongue, then pressed her finger to the buzzer and just rang. Ceaseless ringing bounced around inside the house. I shifted uncomfortably.

The external voicecom lit up, framed in faux brass.

A woman's voice, sharp as a paper-cut: 'Yes?'

'It's Ruth,' said Ruth.

There was a pause. It was full of something.

'Ruth, I really don't think it's a good idea for you to *be* here, right now.'

Ruth looked at me and raised her eyebrows.

'Naomi,' she said. 'Please fetch David.'

'David isn't here.'

Ruth spat venomously: 'Oh, stop being such a *child*.'

There was another, much longer pause. It was followed by the woman addressing someone else, *sotto voce*. We heard her hiss: 'This is my goddamned house. I don't want your mess all over my goddamned *house*.'

The door opened. There was a man behind it. He was a big man, still powerful although past sixty and long run to fat. He was David McArdle.

I hated him. I had hated him for a long time, for many years. But there had been a time when I had not hated him.

Many years before, when I was thirteen, he had paid a visit

to my school, the special school for gifted kids. It had won some award, topped some poll. This visit was televised. There was as yet no all-out war, but things were pretty bad. We were gathered in the assembly hall. Cameras at back. Out front, nervous, thrilled teachers in Sunday best.

David McArdle was introduced to us by the head teacher. As he took the podium with his big, confident, artless tread, I knew I was secure.

He spoke to us of many things. Because this was Little England, he made a few jokes about soccer and what he called 'real football'. Then he told us about how proud he was of our school, of our teachers, but most of all, of us.

He said: 'When I was younger, it seemed that all anybody ever talked about was the generation gap, how kids grow up too fast, how we didn't listen to the wisdom of our parents' generation, how we were out of control and would come to no good. I guess pretty much through all of history, parents and children have been having this conversation. But what I've got to say to you today is this: look where it got us.

'Growing up, becoming an adult, used to mean putting away your dreams. Putting away your dreams meant putting away your notions of fairness and honour and dignity. It meant looking out for number one. Where did it get us? It got us right here.

'I guess all of you here know, Jesus said to suffer the little children to come unto him, and for generations, people have been telling us that the key to the kingdom of heaven is to be as a child, to think as a child, and for generations people have nodded sagely and completely *ignored* this wisdom.

'No more. You want to know something? You're a special generation. You'll be the first generation to become adults in a new world. Now, I'm not saying it's going to be easy. Nothing worthwhile is ever easy. But looking at you, I'm looking at the future, and looking at you, and meeting and speaking to hundreds like you, I know that future is going to be a fine one.

'You're here to save the world. Now, that might sound grand, but it's true. Without you, without your integrity and your vision, we'll all be lost. Soon, sooner than anyone here can imagine, including me, it'll be time to hand the world over to you and to people like you, and to say: Those who came before you didn't do too good a job. Please look after the world.

'Because of that, it's my job to *listen* to you. Remember, I'm here, we're here, to work for you, because in your hands lies the secret to the keys of the kingdom of heaven.'

There was more like that, endless amounts of hokey bullshit, and if you want to know the truth, I cried. Ninth row back, third seat from the aisle. He was like a vision. It was kind of like having St Peter up there, Jesus' big, slightly oafish lieutenant. I felt cherished. I felt like it was all *for* something, all my parents' work and sadness, all their unutterable patience with me, their love for me despite my manifest oddness, my claims that an angel stood guard at the head of my bed while I slept.

When I was seventeen, along with God alone knows how many tens of thousands in Little England, my mother contracted a virulent strain of anthrax that was doing the rounds. She died hideous and stinking and humiliated. My father died a year later. I think he'd just had enough. No other person is more deserving of the descriptive euphemism, 'passing away'. He just seemed to loosen the catches which married him to the world, and died. At eighteen, I was three months out of basic training, billeted to central Africa, where I buried bodies with a bulldozer and cried when I got drunk.

Sometime during all this, Jesus began to slip away from me. But there was always McArdle. I always remembered McArdle. He was the guy the president chose to make announcements about these new advances which would be applied as soon as the war was won. Reclaiming the world for the family of humanity. Announcing that education bonds could be taken out with the Government, the Church, which could be redeemed in time to pay for a family's further education needs. All this while the missiles rained on Azerbaijan, while I was bulldozing bodies in Africa. It was always McArdle who spoke of the golden future while our teeth loosened in our skulls and we grew thin and we got turned into things that were barely human: Staad was like Moses; we trusted him (we had no choice but to trust him,) to guide us through the wilderness. Yet so confident was he of God's design, he allowed his favourite disciple to paint pictures for us of the promised land. McArdle was the rock upon which the Church was built. McArdle was us. He was everything we aspired to be.

All those years down the line, when I had already become filthy with corruption and betrayal, to see him accepting a banned text, turning his back on the dream he had dreamed on our behalf, was worse to me almost than the loss of my God.

And looking up, over the roof of the car, and the albino, vast and flickering with amusement and malice, the crowd parting and passing him without knowing he was there, something numinous and immortal uncoiled within me, and I knew we were damned.

McArdle glanced at Ruth and me. He crossed his arms in a manner that did not indicate welcome. He looked like he wanted to gather me up by she scruff of the neck and stick me in the garbage. He looked like he could still do it if he really wanted.

I caught a stray scent from the house. Fresh laundry, cooking. All the secrets of his domesticity, his real life.

The real life of David McArdle.

I could not believe this was happening.

He and Ruth regarded one another. He glowered down. She glowered up.

'Ruth,' he said. His voice was deep, measured and very reasonable. 'You know you have to leave here. You know that.'

She sighed: 'Don't be a such goddamned prick, David.'

'Jesus, Ruth,' he said, measured but aggrieved: 'if there was something I could do, you know I'd do it. You know that.'

She looked so small, craning her neck to look up at him. For the first time it occurred to me that she was just as helpless as me, and just as lost.

'And where do you suggest I go?' she said. 'David: If we don't address this right now, I'm never going to see my home again. Do you understand that?'

McArdle rubbed at clipped, grey hair. He was solid, fleshy and jowled. He must have been strong when he was young – one of those men who can crack walnuts in the crook of an elbow. He was in shirtsleeves and brown corduroys. He wore wire-framed reading glasses. He wore *slippers*, for Christ's sake.

'Oh, Ruth,' he said, and there was something like exasperated tenderness in it. 'You know we can't have this conversation here.'

'Naturally. Let's have it inside.'

'That won't be possible.'

I said: 'Jesus fucking Christ.'

He swivelled his gaze. Our eyes locked. He spoke to Ruth, but pointed at me. 'And you can tell this little prick to back the fuck off.'

I don't mind admitting that I'd nearly had it by now. I was about one step away from over-reacting.

Ruth glowered at me over her shoulder.

'Fuck *you*,' I said.

'David,' Ruth insisted. 'Frank and Isabel and Nathan are *dead*.'

He shrugged his shoulders and lowered his bullish head.

'Fuck,' he said. 'Fuck fuck fuck fuck.' Half-heartedly, he thumped the frame of the door. Then he stood aside to let us in.

Four of us in his hallway. At the end of it, in an open doorway leading to the kitchen, stood his wife – the woman to whom I'd handed the package all that time ago, and who had in turn passed it to her husband (apostle and hypocrite). She had been wearing a hateful expression.

From her immaculate appearance, it was possible to extrapolate an entire life: properness and the fear of disorder, dreams of dirt and asymmetry. She was younger than McArdle by perhaps ten years, and put some effort into looking younger still. She was slim and trim and exercised, and her hair was neat, flattering her heart-shaped face. She regarded me with transfixed revulsion, her mouth curled in disgust. Here I was. All the dirt she'd worked to expel.

I was exhausted, in pain and disoriented. I rubbed at my sallow and sweating brow with the sleeve of my shirt.

McArdle led us through to the sitting room. Large. *Generously proportioned*. Off-white, deep pile carpet. One wall lined with books, photographs and porcelain. A large television.

In the middle of the room stood a girl, clearly McArdle's daughter. She was younger than I would have expected, perhaps twenty. She had seeded late in her mother's grudging womb. Like everything in McArdle's life, she was beautiful. She had her mother's trimness, but none of the stiffness. Wide-eyed and unsure, she greeted us with self-conscious, practised grace, and stood at her father's side with a kind of defiant compliance.

I looked around the room.

He invited us to sit, and did so himself, in an overstuffed, floral armchair. Elbows on knees, he buried his big face in his hands. He rubbed at tired eyes, and muttered something to himself. Then, to his daughter: 'Honey, how about making us all a hot drink? Does everybody want tea? Coffee?'

She stood. Her hand was at her throat in a hurtfully vulnerable little gesture. 'Of course,' she said and, in a parody of social intercourse, she looked at us in turn. Tea? Coffee?

I looked at him in wonder and shook my head. Tea or coffee. Jesus. 'I'd like a drink,' I said. 'A drink drink. I mean, would that be possible?'

From between his fingers he looked up at me with a slow-burning contempt. 'Susie, honey,' he said. 'Take Mr Thorndyke the whiskey, would you? And a glass.'

It did not register as a surprise that he knew my name.

His daughter smelled like summer. She smelled like the dream of your first kiss. She looked at me like I was an insane and dangerous old man, which of course I was, and retreated to the kitchen. After archly excusing herself, Naomi followed.

It was just Ruth, McArdle and me. I removed my jacket, laid it on the sofa, and sat on it. The wound continued to leak a little and I didn't want to get McArdle's sofa all bloody. Ruth and I sat alongside one another. Her feet dangled above the floor. I slumped back, and cradled a tumbler of whiskey. I drained then refilled it. I wanted a drink very badly. To kill the pain.

He stood and began to pace the room. I asked if I might smoke. He told me to go ahead, what did it matter. Then he said: 'I haven't had one of those in fifteen years.'

I offered him the pack. He shook his head. 'It's a little late to start again now.'

Then, he said: 'Would he really do it, Ruth? I know we *talked* about it. I know we took precautions; but when the chips are down . . .'

Ruth barked: 'Oh, don't *lie* to yourself, David.'

'Excuse me,' I said. 'Excuse me. Who's "he"? Who are we talking about?'

McArdle rolled his eyes. Ruth patted my knee and said, 'Randall.'

'Oh,' I said. 'Randall.'

She patted my knee again, squeezed it once. 'The President.'

'Oh,' I said. '*That* Randall.'

There is a certain perverse joy to be found in having one's most extravagant paranoia so massively trumped by reality. So it was the *president* who'd sent a man to kill me. It was the *president* who killed Isabel and Nathan and the other guy, the one who'd been his lifelong friend. It wasn't just the Church, nothing so simple as that. It was the man with his name above the door. Of *course*. This was an opportunity of the sort one might be afforded once in a lifetime, if one is outrageously unfortunate, and I sat back in the armchair and closed my eyes and revelled in it. I had never imagined my hour of vindication would be *quite* so vindicating. I wasn't paranoid at all. All the while, I had been *underestimating* my predicament. What do you think about *that*?

A grin spread across my face. 'Sweet Jesus,' I said.

They ignored me. This was old news to them. They bickered. Ruth accused McArdle of being blinded by the comfort of his hypocrisy, which I thought was a good line. It landed like an open-hand blow and he said: 'You sanctimonious bitch. Jesus, you always gave me a pain in the ass. You always did.'

'And for my part I never harboured a secret longing for you,' she replied. I thought, take *that*, motherfucker, write that one down and post it to Randall. I was enjoying myself. 'There's only me left, now. And Malachi.'

He pinched the bridge of his nose. 'I won't do anything that might jeopardise my family.'

'Oh, you jeopardise them just by knowing what you know,' she said. 'Come on, David. You were never a coward. You were never that.'

She waited a long time for a reaction. Then she said: 'If you do nothing, Randall will kill us all. Including Naomi and Susan. You *know* that.'

Randall will kill us. There's one for the scrapbook. I lit another cigarette.

He put his fists into the small of his back, bent back. Click click click. He made a grizzly face. He was a big, handsome man. I wondered if I'd have liked him if circumstances were different. Or he me. Almost certainly not.

He opened his eyes and stood there, fists behind him, staring at the ceiling.

'You know it's true, David. I know how difficult this must be. But Randall will do it. He'll kill me. He'll kill you, and he'll kill your wife and child. All he has left is his place in history. It's all he cares about now.'

He tugged at his loosening jowls. 'You know what you're asking me to *do*?'

Her face lost its passing tenderness. 'It's demanded that you humble yourself, David, it's being asked that you prostrate yourself before history and allow it to judge. You're being given a chance to atone for your actions.'

'It's a terrible thing to ask.'

'It's a terrible thing we did.'

'I did.'

She left him to reflect. I drained the glass. When I had poured a third triple and replaced the bottle on the carpet, he surrendered.

'Oh Jesus Christ almighty. I know.'

He buried his face in his palms, dragged down the lower lids of his eyes with the spatulate tips of his fingers. When he spoke again, it was with decisive urgency: 'I made a contingency plan,' he said. 'The first thing is, to get Naomi and Susie away from here. I have a property in Greece. They should ship out tonight. You should go with them.'

She ran her fingers through her short, thick helmet of unflattering hair. 'I can't ask that,' she said. 'I can make my own arrangements.'

'Oh, bullshit,' he said. 'I *need* you there. There's nothing more you can do here. I need you with my wife and *daughter*.'

'I feel like I'm running out on you.'

'Jesus, Ruth. Just *listen* to me, okay?'

She half-laughed. 'I'm sorry. Go on.'

'Okay,' he said, 'I don't think Randall can afford to try anything before the speech: not if everyone's together. He can't do anything to you if you're with Naomi and Susan. And he can't do anything to them if they're with you. Not after Isabel, Nathan and Frank. That would just be too much. All being well, that gives us three days' grace – and all being well, in three days it'll be too late for him to do anything.'

For my part, I said: 'And what about me? What should I do?'

She patted my knee again.

McArdle said: 'I'm going to need your help.'

I laughed. 'Fuck that,' I said. 'None of this is anything to do with me.'

He looked down at me.

'Are you an *idiot*?'

'No,' I said. 'So fuck you.'

He clenched his fists at his side.

Ruth held up her hand.

'He doesn't *know*, David.'

McArdle's expression mellowed.

'You don't know?'

'I don't *want* to.'

He laughed astringently. 'Yeah. Right.'

'The less I know the better for me. Somebody already *shot* me, for Christ's sake. Here,' I said. 'In the leg.'

He massaged the back of his neck. It was all getting very tense and unpleasant and I very dearly wished I was at home, in bed, far, far away.

'Right,' said Ruth. She levered herself off the sofa, faced me and held out her hand. 'Give me it.'

I sighed, reached into my pocket and produced the disk this had all been about. I handed it to her.

'Give me ten minutes,' she said.

'With great respect,' I said, 'I don't care what's on the disk. I really don't. I just want to go home and for everybody to leave me alone.'

She smiled. 'Of course you do. But give me ten minutes. Fifteen. Indulge me.'

I sat back and waved her on. 'Go on, then,' I said. 'I can't stop you.'

She wandered to the home entertainment centre, switched

on the TV, found the video channel ('Channel seventeen,' said McArdle), slipped in the disk and pressed *play*.

On screen, there was a flicker of static. Ruth stepped back.

McArdle put his head round the door and shouted upstairs. 'Susan! Susan, honey?'

There was a faintly interrogative response. 'Nothing, baby. Just to say that you and your mom better stay upstairs now, d'you hear? Don't come down here for a while.'

He pulled his head back into the room.

'I don't need to see this,' I said. 'I really don't.'

'Just watch,' said Ruth.

The static cleared, replaced by what was clearly a home recording. The picture quality was superior, but the camera jumped and skipped, in inexpert hands. The shot panned round a generic sitting room, possibly a hotel suite. In the room were five people, standing shoulder to shoulder. I recognised Nathan, McArdle, Ruth, Frank Shaw – all of them younger. There was another man, whom I half-recognised: a fleshy, jowled, disconsolate-looking man with balding, bushy red hair combed into a low parting.

After the initial pan shot, each of those present introduced themselves. The red-haired man reminded me that his name was Oscar Petersen. His area of responsibility was transnational law enforcement. I didn't think we'd have gotten along.

When the introductions were done, Isabel stepped before the camera. She too was younger, but her face seemed harder than the face of the woman I had met.

My heart skipped.

She introduced herself. She told us that she had been nominated by the group to act as spokeperson. She gave us the date of what we were about to see. Seventeen years ago. Then she asked for our understanding and forgiveness, before fading away. Cut to a new shot. A desert. It is the dig in the Negev.

I'd seen this footage before: the camera panning over the exhausted face of hot, bored and half-starved young soldiers.

The tumult of the helicopter landing, the disembarkation of the civilians, one of whom I now recognised as McArdle, shaking hands with Ruth, stooping in the dust storm whipped up by the thumping of the rotors, alternately holding shut his billowing cotton jacket and keeping his hat on his head with one hand and pressing a handkerchief to his mouth and nose with the other.

A new scene: the interior of the dig, which I had never seen, and in which I had never much been interested. I saw now that the dig centred on a large cave set in the rockface. Although the cave itself looked natural, niches had long ago been carved into the walls. On each rough shelf there lay an ancient cadaver in a discoloured and rotting shroud.

Upon the floor is set a frame within which had been reassembled an ancient, incomplete human skeleton.

The camera closed up on Ruth.

Seventeen years later, she stared back at herself, devoid of emotion, as her recording spoke. 'Unfortunately the ossuary was not secure and the contents, over the years, have been subject to a degree of animal disturbance. This is only to be expected. This is an old tomb. As you can see, several bodies, fifteen in all, all male, were deposited in this chamber. All showed clear signs of violent death, and most showed indications of previous violence: old fractures, missing teeth, and so on and so forth. Once we were sure we had isolated the correct body, the process of reassembly was necessarily painstaking and thorough, subject, in the weeks subsequent to completion, to DNA tests which confirmed that these are the mortal remains of a single individual.'

Off camera, a voice: 'And you're sure it's him?'

'Oh, I'm sure this is him,' she says, a little brusquely. 'Final confirmation of the hypotheses was provided by a number of codices we came across during the course of the dig, which not only confirmed what we had already suspected, but went on to supply some further, surprising detail.

'Note also the very obvious damage to the right and left

femur. There is no extant damage to the wrists or hands consistent with the hammering-in of nails, so one must conclude that he was in fact tied to the cross, by his arms at least.'

Suddenly, everything was different.

Thirteen

```
File code: 100046/macd
Username: sicarius
Password: ******
Last Udpated: **/**/**
```

File DMWITRES Located.

Please wait.

File DMWITRES Retrieved.

Warning: This File Has Been Cloaked. Should You Wish to Decloak, Press Return. If You Wish to Quit, Press Escape.

If You Wish to Decloak, Please Ensure That Your Software is Code Protected, and Save Any Files Recently Modified.

Please wait.

Code Accessed and Identified. Print 65385922, Licence Confirmed, Outlet Confirmed.

*** Please Note. Decloaked Files Have Been Encrypted According to a System Restricted to the Use of Government Personnel Only. WARNING. Unauthorised Use of this System of Encryption Constitutes an Offence Punishable By Law. Unauthorised Personnel Should Quit

Hello, David, How Are You?

From McArdle's Journal:

Date:

Following discussion with my fellow witnesses and, more importantly, with my wife, I present what follows because I recognise that it is my duty to do so.

I have spent many days and sleepless nights reflecting on those events related by the journal which follows, ruminating upon what exactly it was I did or did not do. As yet, I'm no closer to any answer I feel able to live with.

My own response to what occurred can be of only peripheral interest, and can perhaps be better imagined by the sensitive reader than I can suggest by my clumsy hand. I recognise however that it is incumbent upon me to provide a context for those images which otherwise would be allowed to speak for themselves, without the mitigation of context. My wife is correct: I cannot allow that.

It is my fervent and heartfelt prayer that, in reading the words which accompany these images, you are able to find room in your heart to forgive us. To forgive me.

Although some sequences, notably the final one, were appropriated by others within the group, the filmed material to which this journal is an accompaniment was collated largely by myself. It was I who had access to much of the primary material.

It has of course been necessary to edit those filmed materials, presenting only key events.

What follows represents to the best of my knowledge and ability an entirely factual account of what transpired. Any inaccuracies are my own. If they exist, they should be attributed not to deliberate falsehood but to the fact that, even though it strives to record actual events, this diary, any diary, is no more than an individual testament.

I commit myself to God's forgiveness. I pray that, should I have done a terrible thing, He will understand.

Date:

At noon on (date) Randall summoned me to his office. He greeted me without shaking hands and made an enquiry as to the well-being of my wife.

She is sick to her soul, I wanted to say. She is eaten alive with unbearable remorse for a sin that is not of her making. Her child is dead and she is half insane with it.

Good, I said. She's good.

Randall nodded, distracted. I sat like a child before his desk. I had my hands knitted in my lap and my head bowed. He couldn't keep still. He spoke for some time. I don't remember a word. But sitting in that chair, in his office, my hands clasped in my lap, fixing my gaze, which I feared would betray me, on my interlaced fingers, I thought: This evening I shall go home to my wife and child, Randall. I shall eat a meal with my family, I shall play with my daughter for a few minutes before she goes to bed, if she isn't already asleep when I arrive, tired out by her own boundlessness. And I will discuss with my wife the events of her day and as many of those of mine as I am able, and perhaps we will be able to make love, in that fond and reassuring way that has its roots in something a million miles hence from passion. But how can you expect me to do that?

I looked up and he was still speaking. He spoke for a long time. It occurred to me that he was barely aware of my presence. I was merely a person to whom he could relieve himself of the intolerable pressure to share his revelation. The light was fierce in his eyes, and animate, but I did not believe it was God who was its source.

When he was done, he bade me follow him. We took an elevator to the top floor of the building.

On the top floor, a hospital has been constructed. It is secure, accessible only by those with Code Clearance White. Inside there is a long ward of perhaps twenty rooms. The hospital is white and sterile. It is unimprinted by occupation. It is reverberative and without odour. Its white tiles and chromium door handles are unsmudged by human sweat.

Once we had passed the security door, five centimetres of blast-proof titanium, Randall led me to an office, three walls of which were book-lined. The fourth wall consisted largely of a single window which overlooked the half-constructed city outside.

The city looked very beautiful. The sun was at its zenith. The reflective whiteness and quiet serenity of the finished buildings, contrasted with the mud and the muck and the dust and scaffolding and the earth-moving equipment, the human sweat and labour being put into the completion of the still-skeletal buildings which radiate from the hub of the Temple like heat from a child's sketch of the sun, and which had begun as dreams and sketches and Profit-and-Loss projections, was quite moving.

Before the window was set a desk. Of solid, scarred mahogany, it had been old and valuable before I was born. Behind the desk there sat a man. Although broad shouldered, narrow waisted, miraculously toothed, and stunningly coiffured in natural, American blond, he was not less than sixty. He wore faded blue Levi's, a leather belt, and a white shirt, open at the collar. His sleeves were rolled to the elbows. His forearms were very muscular. Fine grey hair nestled between his clavicles.

Randall said: David McArdle, Doctor Curt Connors.

Connors nodded, smiled, shook my hand. Requested that I call him Curt. His handshake was too firm. I will not be dominated by another man's handshake. I squeezed back, impassive, until he released his grip.

Curt just arrived from Crete, said Randall. He was surprisingly proprietorial about the doctor, as if he was a long lost friend he was keen for all his new friends to love. I did not like to be made to feel like a new friend. He said: He's been working in a field hospital out there.

Okay, I said. That's great.

The doctor smiled. He said: Somebody had to help put those guys back together again.

I smiled right on back.

Surreptitiously, he massaged the squeezed knuckles of his right hand.

Randall threw an arm about the Doctor's shoulders. He chided me: Don't let this guy's modesty fool you. Because of him, we're putting men back together who, even five years ago, would have spent the remainder of their lives dealing with severe disabilities.

Connors laughed dismissively.

He led us through to an ante room, in which we were made to wash down and don surgical clothes. When this was done, he led us through another door, through to a windowless laboratory. It was very white. It was full of electronic equipment for which I have no name. There was a metal table which shone drab silver beneath the purity of the lights. Upon the metal table, the skeleton was laid.

Against the metal, the bones looked very old. I thought they might crumble to powder with a gentle touch.

Recorded by security cameras set high in the corners of the room, we looked at the bones for a long time.

Under their neutral gaze I felt myself elongate like a cartoon man. I thought I might faint, but I didn't. I just kept looking at the bones, over which stood Connors, inappropriately proprietorial. Arms crossed.

It was Randall who broke the silence.

Can you feel it? he said. Can you feel the truth of it?

Connors took a long bone his hand, lifted it. It was brown and yellow.

He said: Medically, we have found nothing which substantially contradicts Doctor Felton's initial hypothesis. There are however, a number of things to add. For example, this knitted fracture here is consistent with a single, extremely violent blow – as if somebody had reached up and . . . He mimed the action of striking above his head. He said: At some point, somebody did him significant damage. It would have taken time, considerable time, for a fracture such as this to successfully knit. Considerable time, and considerable expertise. He would have been in great discomfort, but somebody was there to nurse and care for him.

He placed the bone back on the table, in approximate alignment with the remainder of the skeleton. Not all of him was there. Time had done that. For all those years, he had been crumbling away.

The doctor said: These remains would seem to bear out that information contained within the Codices which came into Doctor Felton's ownership. It appears he was in his late forties or early fifties at time of death, possibly older. Not a bad old age. Given the circumstances.

Very quietly, Randall said: May I?

I hated the way Conors stepped to one side and said: Of course. Please, and indicated with his hand that the President should go ahead and touch.

Randall lifted the skull. He was tender. He was awed. He held it in his hands and let out a breath. He lifted it and gazed into its sockets. Its balloon had thinned. It was almost translucent under the pitiless lights.

Do you feel it, David? he said, Do you feel the truth of it?

He required no response.

Connors held the tip of a ball-point pen to the skull. See how the front teeth cross, he said: crowded together by the pressure of his wisdom teeth descending. He had crooked teeth. One can almost picture his smile.

Yes, said Randall. Then he said: Beautiful. Tears spilled from his eyes. They landed on the skull. Like rain in the desert. Like the first sign of rains come to end the famine.

He began to shudder. His shoulders were bent like an old man's. He was an old man. My God, he said. My God, my God, my God.

He sobbed there for a while. Then he faced me.

I've spent many weeks praying in this room, he said, over this body. Praying for guidance. It's time, David, he said. He's brought us here, to this world. He has led us towards the establishment of His kingdom on Earth. This is the end of history. The ultimate marriage of faith and science.

Perhaps he was unable to read my expression. He regarded me through his tears. He leaned towards me. He spoke through a small frown, as if confused as to why I had not grasped his point.

David, he said. We're going to bring him back.

Date:

After concluding the previous entry I got drunk. I sent out for a pint of whiskey, which Rachel produced, wordlessly, within fifteen minutes.

Rachel deposited the bottle without comment. She has served me so well, with such little recognition. Note to self: I must thank her more. Perhaps I'll buy her a gift. A little something. She will appreciate this, I'm sure, since I have relied so unfairly on her to choose my gifts on anniversaries and birthdays.

I had a bewildered sergeant drive me home. I told him to tell his wife and children how much he loved them as soon as he was able. I was very drunk. He said that he would. I'm afraid I've caused the genesis of an anecdote about myself. Of course he will relate the story of his strange evening. How I commanded him to leave his post and drive me home. He will relate me as a drunken and sentimental ogre, and he will be quite correct. This is how I behaved.

I have never believed in the devil, although there are many that do. I considered Satan to be a means by which simpler people in simpler times explained away the evils in their lives. I am no longer so sure.

At home, I draped my drunken arms around Naomi's shoulders and hugged her until she told me she couldn't breathe and I was hurting her. I told her I loved her.

Love is a miracle. It is a miracle which is so very common, even now, even in the middle of all this mess, we forget that God is there, in the space between us. The closer we are to one another, the closer He is to us. He is that which warms the spaces between us. When we say: I love you, He is there. He is right there.

Date:

Ruth is one of us now. The six of us gathered together in a room which wasn't as secure as I had claimed. I had activated all of the internal monitoring devices. I have begun to collate these fragments of information with an obsessiveness which I'm not yet too ill to recognise as having its genesis in a deeper malaise. I am engaged in an operation to shore the walls of my own existence.

The meeting was a success, inasmuch as an agreement was reached. Whatever the nature of the body Ruth Felton dug up in the Negev desert, Randall's proposal transcends hubris. Effortlessly, it vaults blasphemy. But there is nothing we can do about it. We fear to destabilise the body politic, and we fear what Randall, full of Messianic vigour, would do to us if we were to do so much as voice our opposition.

We are scared of Randall. We are scared of his power. We fear his freedom to do as he wishes. We fear his vengeance.

I even felt a touch of sympathy for Ruth Felton when it fell to Frank Shaw to voice the accusation. For the love of God, Ruth, he said, why couldn't you have left well alone?

She did not answer.

Petersen presents a real problem. He protested that, much as he might wish to, he couldn't be like the rest of us and stand back and watch an act he could find no word for, other than evil. He wasn't able to do that, and although he'd come here in good faith, willing to be convinced, he hadn't been, and he would be a liar to himself if he were to do anything but take any action he believed necessary in preventing this crime against God.

Where pleas to reason failed, the threat of violence didn't. I hope I might be forgiven for expressing some of the dislike I've tried not to feel towards this man, the vulgarity of whose views once caused Randall to wonder aloud who had managed to insert a bug quite so far up his ass. The memory made me helplessly sad. I told Petersen to keep his goddamned mouth shut. I told him that if he placed my wife and child in jeopardy with his big mouth, I'd rip his fucking head clean off his shoulders and shit down his neck. I told him I didn't trust him to keep his goddamn mouth shut and if he wanted to know the truth he was giving me a pain in the ass and it was all I could do not to put my fist in his face right there and then, so help me God.

He found this convincing.

Briefly, I toyed with the idea of erasing the above incident from this testimony. In the end I decided not to do so. My vanity is of no importance. Perhaps my outburst might provide a little comic relief for somebody who has to watch this unfolding, sometime in the future. Perhaps it might indicate a little of the strain we are under.

Date:

Randall gathered us in one of the debriefing offices.

We sat, six of us spread over three rows, before a screen perhaps twice the size of a large domestic television set.

The screen was full of Connors, the doctor, in full surgical regalia. We observed in silence as he scraped a gleaming scalpel across a portion of the incomplete skeleton of a man who had died over two thousand years ago, under the aegis of the Roman empire.

Connors provided the narration which accompanied this recording.

After successive attempts, the first complete DNA sample was extracted from the fourth rib on the left hand side. As we are all too aware, cloning from dead matter is not an easy process. It's like trying to blow life into a tiny flame; blow too soft, the flame dies. Blow too hard, you extinguish it. But blow just right, work right alongside the flame, and together you can make it alive, and get from it all the warmth you like.

The next shot was in close-up.

Magnified many dozens of times, a tiny, beautiful thing spun slowly in liquid, like an isolated galaxy. This single cell became two, four, eight, sixteen.

The translucent bundle continued to divide before our eyes, taking its first steps towards humanity.

The sole thought I was able to formulate was: How do I get hold of and copy that piece of film?

Date:

Had it been conceived of man and borne in a womb, the child's size indicates that it would be about two years old by now. It was cultured less than two weeks ago.

Dead DNA coaxed into unnaturally rapid expansion, I find the speed of its growth unnerving. I sometimes believe I detect a sense of purpose in it.

Each time we endure footage of the child, floating unconscious in ersatz amniosis, breathing God's air through a mask, each time we witness the neonatal kicking of its feet, movements of a child much younger than this one appears, I am almost compelled to exclaim that no more can be endured, that it must end now.

Last night, I went home to my wife and child and shared with them a wordless dinner. I am not so preoccupied that I don't appreciate Naomi's patience. In fact I appreciate it all the more because she is of course in no position to know quite how much I need it.

Nevertheless, as I loaded the dishwasher, she said: I assume you intend to come home at some point in the future, or do you intend to just keep sending your body and hoping we won't notice?

I slammed the door of the dishwasher and said: Not now.

I told her I was stressed. She put her hand on her hip, like she does, and told me she knew, and that made me laugh. I rolled my bunched shoulders. I wish I was home more, I said. More than anything in the world, I would like to spend a while helping my favourite baby daughter bake a cake for her mom. You too, honey? You wanna bake a cake sometime soon?

Susan's nod was tired, even a little shy, like I really have been gone too long. I told Naomi: I'm sorry, things have been tough lately. But it won't be for long. Really. All I want to do is come home and spend some time with my family. As soon as I can, you try and stop me.

No, she said, I won't do that. I won't try to stop you.

Date:

Although we know that by now he has the body of a man in his early to mid-thirties, we have seen no footage of him since he was a child. We have been granted no access to him. Only Randall is allowed that privilege, Randall and the doctor who birthed him.

Randall awaits the moment when the spirit of the Lord will descend and take up residence in this, the body He adopted the first time He walked the earth. From that moment of union between spirit and flesh, God and man, faith and science, past and future, we will see Him rule the peoples of the world from the seat we have prepared for Him in his new Jerusalem.

Randall believes.

Date:

This represents my first journal entry for the five days since non-essential personnel were evacuated from the Capitol building.

Since then none of us has left this place. It's easy to forget that there is a real world out there still. We have clothes and food delivered, but even so our hygiene has slipped more than a little. It's difficult to pay attention to anything other than this interminable watch over an impenetrable, blank hospital door.

Randall has been locked away in the hospital unit to which we are denied access, for six days and seven nights. There has been no communication from him.

Last night, as we settled into sleeping bags, Petersen said: But he's been in there so long. What if it's us that's wrong? What if all there is standing between us and the love of the Lord God made flesh is a goddamned locked door?

There are no doors to God's love, I told him.

I know that. That's not what I meant.

I know what you meant. But I don't care. Just shut up. Let us get some goddamned peace.

Date:

Today, on the eighth day, Randall emerged from behind the blast-proof door to the empty hospital. He had become an old man. His breath and his body and his rumpled, greasy clothing smelled bad. He had taken a little water, but not eaten. He was confused. He was stooped and weak and uncertain of his footing.

He looked at us with the illusion of canniness. I knew you'd be here, he said. I knew the strength I found was not all mine. I knew you were here.

I said, Sir. Please. What's going on in there?

Praying, he said, with a wicked smile for his craftiness. He tests us to the last. He tests the mettle until it can be tested no more.

Oh, Jesus, said Petersen. Will you look at him.

Randall regarded us with wisdom for our childish folly. The body must endure, he reminded us, in order that the soul might be freed of its concerns. The body must be subjected to the discipline of the spirit.

There was no pity in Isabel's voice. It was she who had courage to voice the sentiment: Stop now, Randall. Stop it now.

Isabel, he said, and he stumbled forward a step. It was I who caught him. I helped correct his equilibrium. My skin crawled at the touch of his filth, the unwashed and despairing stench of him.

He did not thank me. He addressed Isabel. I need your faith, Isabel, he said, I need your faith and your strength. I have undergone moments of weakness. Without your love, I might have despaired.

For the love of God, said Isabel. Look at yourself.

He looked at her afresh. He squinted as if she were an unfamiliar specimen in a bell-jar. He said her name as if it were unfamiliar.

Randall, said Nathan. His voice had about it the insistent gentleness I will always remember him for. You are not a young man. If you don't eat soon, you'll become sick and you'll weaken and you'll die. Do you understand me? You're confused. You're malnourished and dehydrated. It's time to come with us.

Randall shuddered with the effort to stand. His finger shook as he admonished us with it. Oh, the tempter is wicked to the very last, he said with a sly old grin, like he well knew exactly what it was we were up to. Very well, he said. Very well.

He made to shamble on. His feet shuffled but he made no motion.

One of us had to do something. It was me. One moment more, and it might have been any of us. It is important that I record that thought.

I said one word: Enough. I shoved Randall to one side. He was desiccated as a leaf, without substance. This time it was Frank Shaw who caught him. Frank took Randall's insignificant weight as the President railed to my back that I was not ready for the glory I would come to look upon, that I should return before I was blinded by the light of the glory of God.

But I did look upon him. I looked upon him, and I was not blinded.

The ward, into which I had walked once before when it was

shining and sterile and without habitation, was in darkness. The darkness was richly meaty with the odours of enclosed habitation, like an animal's den. Like a zoo.

Light was thrown from a single room in the darkness. It fell across the obscure corridor. I did not stop to question that the room which was the source of the light was where I would find him. I could not. Whatever makes me a person had deserted me.

I came upon a small room, about which I remember little more than squalor. There was a soiled bed. The air was thick and yellow with the feline reek of urine, of sour sweat and faeces. I leaned against the door frame, bent at the waist and vomited sour liquid into my mouth. Filthy as the room was, I could not bring myself to expel it. I swallowed the bile. Took it back into myself, and stood straight.

I saw him. He lay on the bed, half-curled on his side. His nakedness was concealed by a once-white sheet, from which protruded the slender legs he had drawn up towards his chest. Through the skin, the knobs of his ankle bones glowed pastel white.

He looked like I had always known he would. His natural grace was the perfection of our nature.

He was built as tenderly and delicately as a yearling. His limbs were lean and without flaw. The line of his neck and throat, before they disappeared into the thickness of his beard and the thinner scrub on his chest, had the regal perfection of a swan. His hair was long, and darker and thicker than I had thought it might be. It had never been cut. Knotted strands of it partially obscured his face. His beard was darker and curlier and coarser than I had ever pictured. The wiry hair obscured the soft fullness of his lips. He contained in his form all of nature. His skin was pale and flawless.

His skin was pale and flawless because he had not yet been exposed to the light of the sun it had been His Father's will to burn.

I was without movement. I stood a metre from him. With a single step and a gentle hand, I could reach out and brush my hand against his skin.

I wept.

I fell to my knees. I uttered words of welcome and worship. Apology. I spoke nonsense. The sobs of a desperate child, half joy, half terror.

His eyes fell upon me.

I looked up and into blankness. There was nothing behind them.

For a few moments he watched me pray to him. Then he mewled. Viscous white spittle adhered to the corners of his mouth and the leading straggles of his beard. He attempted to shift his position but his co-ordination was poor. He moved like a retarded child. He grinned. His mouth split back savagely from his teeth. His front teeth were already crowded together but none was chipped and worn, or blackened and stained and cracked. His teeth were perfect. His tongue, pink and wet, writhed uselessly, independently, inside his head.

As I watched, his brow knitted. He was stimulated by the novelty of me. Under the yellow stained, rank sheet, his hands were busy. He concentrated. He looked almost confused, intent on a goal he did not quite understand. Perhaps it was the disgust hitching in my throat that caught his attention. He was looking into my eyes as he spasmed. His empty eyes rolled white in their sockets with the wordless ecstasy of it.

Much of the thin white rope of seminal fluid came to rest on his taut belly and upper chest. Some came to earth on his spindly upper thighs. Beads of it were caught in his body hair. They glistened under the lights, first white, like pearls, then grey, without colour.

He regarded me from beneath his brow, from behind the greasy curtains of his hair. His eyes shone with an idiot's glee. His sniffed the hand with which he had pleasured himself. His mouth split open like ripe fruit, exposing the moist, pink flesh inside him. He grinned at me with the lewd joy of a monkey. His beard was wet with saliva.

I am aware that it was not necessary to strike him. For that unnecessary action I will continue to pay for the rest of my life. But strike him I did. I drew my hand into a fist, and I drew back that fist from my body and I brought that fist down upon him. With the very first blow, his nose shattered beneath my knuckles.

He screamed. It did not sound like a person. It sounded like the ripping of metal, or the death agony of a sea creature, a whale or a dolphin. Or a dog, the second it is hit by a car. He screamed like an animal *in extremis*.

He knew neither where or how to move. He moved in all directions at once, and thus did not move at all. He described wordless panic on the bed. He howled and screamed. The sheet bunched up under his circling legs. His hands went to his face. He buried the pain into his palms. I circled the bed. I stood in a drying curl of faecal matter, his or Randall's. I reached out a hand. I closed it around a wrist, fine as a puppy's fetlock. I pulled his hand from his face. Doing so, I half-lifted him from the bed. He protected himself with all the little strength he had.

His hair and beard and skin, his eyelids and his brow, were dark and smeared with his blood. A point of bone had broken through the skin between his eyes. I tried to punch him there again. He struggled away. I hit his cheek. I think it broke, too. I can't be sure.

He bent over himself, tried to burrow into himself on the bed. I punched him a few times more; body blows. I know I broke ribs.

At some point, he stopped mewling and screaming. At another, later point, the rage drained from me. For a while, I stood there sobbing, slapping him with the flat of my busted hand.

Then I laid him out, gently, on his back. I put a pillow beneath his head. His lips were all swollen and split. He'd bitten through them in his fear. I brushed the sticky, matted hair back from his face and took his throat in my hands. I stood there for a long time, squeezing.

I feared that he might open an eye and look at me. I could not bear to face that accusation.

I have no recollection of Isabel, Nathan and Frank joining me. I know they stood in silence and watched me kill it, because they have indicated as much. The truth is, I had probably beaten it to death long before I took it upon myself to squeeze the life from it. Nobody has ever said anything about that. It's never been discussed and I hope to God it never will be.

Odd, that such a situation, should result merely in an

embarrassed silence. When it was done, I stood back from the bed. I fought an urge to look at my hands.

It was Isabel who was first to speak.

Poor Randall, she said.

Fourteen *The Fever Programme*

The film came to an end without fanfare, just a snap, crackle and pop of static. It wasn't too professional a presentation.

For a long time I couldn't move. To tell the truth, I couldn't think. It was like somebody had hit the mute switch in my head.

What followed I remember with some detachment.

I stood, pulling the pistol from its holster. In the act of turning I raised it to the level of McArdle's head. My hand was shaking very badly.

'You son of a fucking bitch,' I told him. My jaw felt wired shut. I spoke through clenched teeth. 'You fucking son of a fucking bitch.'

He just sat there, hands loosely crossed in his lap, palms up. He was looking at his knees, like he didn't give a shit one way or the other.

Ruth got to her feet. She stood between McArdle and me, very calm. To tell the truth, I could have stood on my tippy-toes and still blown the bastard's head to nachos and gravy, so she didn't achieve much, other than stand in my force-field and exude calming vibes.

'Malachi,' she said.

'Jesus!' I said.

'I know how hard this must be for you.' It was a line I guess she must have heard from the movies, possibly some daytime soap she happened to catch herself watching, because Christ knows it sounded strange coming from her mouth.

'You hypocrite son of a bitch,' I said, over her head. 'You lying, hypocrite, motherfucking liar son of a bitch. I want to be sick.'

'Malachi,' she said.

'I'm not kidding,' I said. 'I really think I'm going to throw up.'

She observed this nonsense with the doleful complicity of a bloodhound.

'Ruth,' I said, 'what did you *do*?'

She made this sad smile. 'Have you never done anything you regret?'

There was this guy called Sonny, I said. Except I didn't. 'Nothing like that,' I said.

'Nothing like *that*.'

'Nothing like what?'

'I don't even know. I don't even know what to call it.'

'It was a warning,' she said. 'From God.'

'A warning from *God*?' I began to laugh, then I began to cry. Then I began to laugh again. My nose got all snotty. I wanted to go home.

McArdle stood. Unfolded. With the palm of one murdering hand, he rubbed at a hairy forearm. 'You cocksucker,' he said slowly, as if greatly fatigued. 'You have no idea.'

'Of what? That you're a lying, hypocrite son of a fucking bitch? I know what you did! I saw what you *did*.'

He leaned forward, towards the gun, and he said: 'Then tell me. Tell me what I did.'

I wanted to pull the trigger. David McArdle. Living embodiment of the idyll they had assembled from the fragmented, smoking jumble of the world. The man only a degree of whose corruption and depravity had been revealed to me when his wife took from me on his behalf a smuggled package, the contents of which the Governing Church of which he was representative had elected to prohibit. Handing it over, recognising him, I had come to know him for a hypocrite and a liar. Only a hypocrite breaks his own law. But I was not equipped even to speculate upon the scale of his dissolution. And now I knew, with direct, startling clarity, that had been this very film that I had delivered to him: a security camera whirring quietly, high in the corner of a defiled hospital room: his broad back bent over that wretched thing: his big, protective, statesman's, *father's* hands beating and beating at that powerless, defenceless thing, beating it and beating it, the unendurable pitch of its wailing, its frenzied, vain attempts to retreat from the deluge of blows that fell upon it, smashing at its fragile ribs like a pile driver, the unpardonable frenzy and the way he wrapped the filthy, bloody knot of hair in his hands and punched and punched.

The angle of the camera was such that we could not see McArdle's face. Just his broad back and his lowered head and the dead thing on the bed, twisted in an idiot's rictus, the final, tiny testament to a dreadful absence. And McArdle's hands, heavy at his sides. The exhausted rasp of his breathing.

The gun was wavering enthusiastically.

I said: 'You fucking bastard. You *hurt* him. You didn't have to *hurt* him.'

McArdle growled at me. His old man's lips peeled back from his imperfect orthodonty: 'Tell me who I hurt, you twisted little cocksucker. Take the weight off my goddamned mind, because I go to sleep every night wondering, and I wake every morning wondering. I'll go to my grave wondering. So go ahead and tell me who it was.'

The injured leg began to judder beneath me. I wanted to tell him what he'd done. He had taken in barbarian's hands the last bleak echo of something good and he had pounded and shattered it with his fist, he had squeezed it by the neck until its tongue poked black between its teeth and its exquisite fingers curled in claws and its feet got all crooked, like fucked-up hands. I had the proof. I'd had the proof in my hands, all along. McArdle was my proof.

In answer, I wanted to put a bullet through his face and watch the vehicle of his intellect describe Rorscharch blobs on the neutral walls of his lovely home, hung with framed photographs and his wife's insipid, passionless watercolours. I wanted to leave a flap of face on his hollowed skull.

'You're a goddamned thief,' I told him. I began to sob, just like I had sobbed in his presence when I was thirteen, for precisely the opposite reason.

His brow furrowed. He stared at me with indeterminate emotion.

Ruth said: 'It wasn't even a *man*, Malachi. It was –'

He kneaded his brow. 'Ruth's right. It was a warning from God.'

'Oh, fuck,' I said. Even now, he could talk about God with all the attendant tenderness and sadness of one who has betrayed but still loves. I wondered at his guilt. I wondered what it would be like: to appreciate the magnitude of one's hypocrisy and yet continue living. It appeared to me in that moment that perhaps he actually did love his family in the way he had led us all to believe. Perhaps it was for the love of them that he carried on. Perhaps he loved them more than he hated himself.

Judas took his own life but Peter, who heard the cock crow in counterpoint to his denial, had lived to evangelise the world.

To what degree was Peter's ministry driven not by the love of his dead Lord, but by the memory of his own cowardice and betrayal?

I looked down. My injured leg was bleeding prodigiously. I felt myself weaken.

I said: 'My leg is bleeding.'

Ruth took my hand. She led me to the sofa. I sat heavily upon it. I looked up at McArdle and said: 'I got shot.'

Ruth hushed me. She even brushed some straggles of sweaty hair from my brow.

I know this is going to sound strange, but if you want to know what happened next, I fell asleep. It was just like some caretaker inside decided to shut the system down before it overloaded and got all broke up.

I woke only a little while later. The leg was still hurting me like a royal bastard. It was good and stiff. I was shuddering and shivering and shaking, running a fever. My clothes were kind of sweated through. Ruth had a hand on my shoulder. McArdle had gone.

'Look at you,' she said. She sucked her teeth.

'I don't feel too good,' I said. 'I think I'm going to puke.'

On cue, I graced her with an impressive dry-heave, like a cat trying to present a fur ball.

'David's with his family,' she said. 'He's left us alone to talk. But first I think we need to make you better.'

'Please do,' I said. The room was lit a funny colour. The subdued pattern in the drapes was doing a slow, fluid waltz, like the first stages of a peyote hallucination.

'Okay,' she said. 'You remember your field medical training?'

'Some.'

'Me too. Some. You're going to have to remind me of anything I've forgotten.'

She asked me to remove my trousers. If you want to know the truth, things had gotten pretty bad and she had to help me do it. I popped the buttons, lowered my zipper and arched my lower back. She helped me slither and slide from them. Some of the fabric was a little stuck down. It felt like removing a sticking plaster that had been there a hundred years. I have to admit I did a little yelling.

She was muttering to herself. She looked at the wound, then winced and looked away for a couple of beats. She whistled through the little gap between her front teeth.

She said: 'I didn't know it was this bad.'

I pinched my nostrils. 'I did tell you. Once or twice.'

She jutted out a bottom lip, selectively deaf to any possibility of criticism. 'How on earth did you manage to walk?'

I shrugged. 'How does it look?'

'Like modern art.'

I laughed. The ceiling seemed slowly to respire. Inhale. Exhale. The room was set all at an odd angle.

'Very well,' she said, resolved. She clapped her hands together, once. Alongside her on the carpet there was a metallic green case about the size of an overnight bag. It was marked with a red cross in a white circle. When she opened it, I let out an appreciative little gasp. Inside were rows of very exciting looking bottles and shiny chrome implements, all set in foam. It was like a fucking field hospital. It was to the family first-aid box what *foie gras* is to a Whopper with cheese. It was the first-aid box to die for. If you see what I mean.

'Wooo,' I said.

She furrowed her brow. 'Impressive, isn't it? David has one in practically every room. Lift your shirt tails.'

I looked to the ceiling and did as she asked.

'This might hurt for a second.'

The needle was about a metre long. She jabbed it into the meat of my thigh just like she was checking to see if I was cooked through. True enough, it hurt for a second. I bucked and yelped and cursed and hissed. After the passage of a few moments, though, the pain began to recede. After a minute or two, I was pretty much a pain-free individual. She had administered a dose of Co-morphenol, a complex (and profitable) analgesic, the discovery of which, twenty years previously, had been heralded with a fanfare not dissimilar to the discovery of penicillin. It was a treatment which made dying of stuff they couldn't cure a relative pleasure, and which made being blown to meatballs in ketchup by small arms a comparatively temporary discomfort. It was non-addictive, non-habit-forming and, gram for gram, about a thousand times more potent than morphine. I recognised its effects like you recognise a scent you haven't come upon for twenty years. I was still sensible of my body. I was even sensible that there was pain. It just wasn't pain that actually *hurt* any more, if you see what I mean. There was simply a constant, gentle reminder that I shouldn't be moving that particular leg in that particular way if I knew what was good for me. The rest of my body might as well have been wrapped in a duck-down sleeping bag. Most of me actually felt pretty gorgeous, if you want to know the truth.

'Jesus,' I said. 'This is mean shit.'

She handed me three red gelatine capsules and three tiny white pills. Somewhat reluctantly, I palmed and dry-swallowed them. They went down easy enough. They were field uppers, stuff to balance me out. She didn't want me floating around in an opiate haze for the rest of the night.

Meanwhile, she produced a smaller syringe. I watched, stoned and fascinated, as she jabbed it into the lips of the wound. That part of my brain we were discussing earlier kicked in again, and I was interested to observe myself twisting away. She held me down and pushed me back.

'You're supposed to whisper words of comfort,' I told her.

'Dean Martin is alive,' she said.

Next, she cleaned the area of the wound with a square of wet, antiseptic fabric. When it was rusty and soiled she scrunched it up, dropped it to the carpet, took another from an aluminium dispenser and began to wipe again. She repeated this until my leg was clean, and had the delightful bouquet of fresh lemon. Then she took a small aerosol and shook it vigorously. It rattled like there was a ball-bearing inside. Then she sprayed the wound all over with plasti-skin.

'There you go,' she said. 'That's the rough stuff all done.'

While the semi-permeable membrane dried over the still porky-pink wound, she strapped a powered unit beneath my armpit, and set up a portable drip.

Finally, when the plasti-skin had dried to a vibrant blue, she took a box of little chromium clips, like the mandibles of robotic ants, and clipped closed the lips of the wound.

By now I was beginning to feel the benefits of the uppers. I asked for my cigarettes. She passed them to me without comment. Before lighting up, I pulled on my blood-crusty and sweat-clammy trousers. Tentatively, I stood in stockinged feet.

247

The leg held very well. Smoking, I walked up and down the room for a while. I could just about feel the depth of the carpet pile beneath my feet. I continued to favour the injured leg, but it no longer looked or felt like it was going to collapse beneath me.

I took a seat again, lit another cigarette. My heart fibrillated like a paper flower.

I said: 'I take it you were joking about Dean Martin.'

It proved to be a long, somewhat awkward and entirely sleepless night.

Ruth made it clear to me that, whatever happened, it was imperative that McArdle's wife and daughter should be evacuated at the earliest opportunity. I thought it an interesting choice of words.

Whatever we thought about McArdle, neither of had much of a wish to infringe any more than necessary upon his final evening with his family, so we retreated to the kitchen. She closed the door behind us.

It felt institutional in there. It had the peculiar quality of light and the characteristic acoustics of a hospital waiting room late at night. Bad news had been delivered. Upstairs, there was subdued muttering, modest consolation.

In my fist I carried a bottle of whiskey which I opened as I sat, stiffly, at the big, wooden table. I set the bad leg straight before me. Ruth set about making coffee.

Ruth had long ago recognised the hopelessness of counselling me not to drink. Instead, she asked me with genuine interest how I managed to stay sober. Where did I put it all? I said: 'I'm not sober.'

I told her I was in a state with no name: the nameless not-drunk stage people drink themselves into when things around them become a little too fraught, a tad too emotional. To make the point, I poured another inch.

'I'm in "my world has fallen to pieces" mode,' I told her. 'The end is nigh. The sky is falling.'

This made her laugh. I'd seldom managed that. She called me an asshole. Then she said: 'Like; "My wife has left me"?'

'Exactly,' I said. 'Or "my husband wears my panties".'

She sat at the table with a mug of black coffee on a coaster before her. 'My son has pinned a poster of Judy Garland to his bedroom wall.'

I sprayed whiskey when I laughed. She grimaced. I wiped my lips, then leaned over and tilted the lip of the bottle to the rim of her mug.

She half-closed her eyelids to indicate: Go ahead, and I poured a measure into the coffee.

She lifted the mug and toasted me. I clinked it with my tumbler.

Then she said: 'Don't think too badly of us.'

I said, truthfully: 'I don't know what to think.' Then I said; 'All the time, at the dig, you were digging him up. You *knew*. You were brushing off his bones with a fucking *toothbrush* or whatever it is you use, and you still . . . I mean. You would come to the mess tent and, you know . . . *eat* with us. You still talked about him. Like it was all real.'

'It *was* real,' she said.

I guffawed like an eighth grade jerk. 'Yeah. *Really*.'

'I *told* you all this,' she said, not without a degree of what I considered a rather hardhearted impatience, given the circumstances. 'I told you all this at the dig. What he was, who he was, has *always* been subject to debate. Always. That's the nature of the faith. It always has been. If he was God, why did he allow himself to be humiliated and murdered by his own creation? If he wasn't God, what was the nature of his *relationship* with God?'

I waited, but she did not, as I had feared, launch into a sermon. There was no more. I said: 'Sure. Okay. *And* – what if there *was* no relationship with God? What if there's no God to have a relationship *with?* What about that? What if it was all just lies and bullshit that somebody made up? Doesn't that just about put an end to the debate?'

She fixed me with the familiar, intolerant glower.

'Not at *all*,' she said, spitting out the words like feathers. 'What that does, is explain it *away*. There's a sizeable difference. Nobody *made it up*.' She said this last as if it were the most preposterous suggestion she had ever heard in all the many years she had been obliged to debate with oafs. 'Tell me this,' she said. 'Tell me just one thing; who in their right mind would make up a God that *inconvenient*?

'If you're going to invent a God, in *any* century, under *any* mythos, under *any* cultural circumstance *whatsoever*, you don't invent a God who does what *Jesus* did: a God who delivers a message entirely contrary to the one you were expecting, moreover a message which you in no way can be said to fully understand, who then gets himself murdered by the very forces from whose yoke you very much wish to be liberated, leaving you bereft, confused, frightened and probably not a little embarrassed.' She glowered at me huffily, as if she resented every word of what she had to say. She sipped coffee with scandalised resentment. 'If you set out to *invent* a God,' she said, 'I don't care *who* you are: you invent a God which people can understand: a vengeful God, a God who liberates, a God who punishes your enemies. You might say that the history of Christian faith is an account of the distress caused by the controversial nature of Jesus.'

She was beginning to get warmed up: really to motor. It began to dawn on me that, in some obscure fashion, even after seeing what I could still not believe I had really seen, she was still somehow offended by my lack of faith.

'Even his *miracles* weren't unique. We know that priests of the Isis and Osiris cult were healing the sick, the lame and the blind long before the birth of Christ. They cast out demons. They even walked on water – although I suspect that particular trick was prone to occasional failure.

'There are even those who believe that the crucifixion and apparent resurrection was a deliberate attempt on Christ's part to associate himself with the Osiris mythos, to graft some Egyptian salvific ideas to his native Judaism.

'Whatever. We'll never know. What remains is that any examination of his historical and cultural context is inevitably hazardous to misguided notions of his uniqueness.

'Again, much the same can be said of the Osiris cultus. Before Osiris was sacrificed, only to rise again, there was a "last supper", where his devotees ritually partook of his flesh and blood in the form of bread and wine. The knowledge of this caused an almighty stink among the early Church fathers. One of them, Origen, wrote that the Osirian last supper was the devil ridiculing Christianity thousands of years before it was formed.'

'Go figure,' I said, with some weariness. I disliked the fact that Ruth always seemed compelled to put me on the defensive. She was a bully. There is no other word for it.

I said: 'So, Jesus was just some guy who did stuff like other guys, and got lucky because somebody put him in a book. What are you left with?'

'With God,' she said.

I laughed. A little fleck of spit landed on the table, next to my whiskey.

'With God,' she insisted, with something that seemed very much like venom. 'With God and His love for us. At the *very* least, the very universality of the Jesus narrative discloses God's love of His creation.'

'You can say that even after *this*?'

'Even after this.'

'You're crazy.'

'Perhaps.'

That really was too much. Her inhuman confidence in her elementary correctness appeared to have taken on the attributes of clinical denial. I erased the bubble of saliva with an index finger. It made little smears on the woodstain. Then I got a little exasperated and uncomfortably het up.

'There's no *perhaps* about it,' I said. 'Your logic is faulty. No,

I'm sorry, Ruth: your logic is *fucked*. Completely. What you did, all of you, was the craziest fucking thing I ever *saw*.'

She bristled, hunched over her shoulders like a defensive hedgehog. She retaliated, quietly, but with the same degree of single-minded insistence.

'What *Randall* did was crazy. What *I* did . . .' She paused, anticipated my response to whatever claim she was about to make, changed tack. 'Listen to what I did.

'Since it finally acknowledged that the Gospels didn't contain anything *like* the unadulterated truth, the academic and theological consensus has been that the historical Jesus, to a greater or lesser extent, doesn't matter a good God-damn. Pardon my French.

'I urged you, all of seventeen years ago, to put your faith in *God*, in God's love for you. Your awe of Him should reflect the unrestrained, *ferocious* love He has for you. Your love should be absolute and unconditional. If nothing else, the story of Jesus is a paradigm of this. Without that, merely worshipping the inaccurate narrative portrayal of a man who died – by whatever means – over two thousand years ago is effectively idolatrous. The story of Jesus, bastardised and corrupted as it is by history, is the means by which one should find a path to God.'

I mumbled something disrespectful which she contrived not to hear.

'When I was a young girl, my grandfather passed away. I loved my grandfather very much, for all his faults. He was a good man. During the course of his life, he'd been to strange places. He'd led a rich life, seen and done some very unusual things, as well as claiming to have slept with a great number of women. But that's beside the point. He left me with two things: the first was his hat. The second was a collection of artefacts of various antiquity and ethnicity, none of which he considered, for whatever reason, to be suitable for a museum, or indeed academic study. Chief among them was a codex, a kind of book on a roll. He'd picked it up at some illicit dig in the Languedoc. There were some *very* shady stories behind his possession of this artefact.'

She fell silent for a few moments. She always seemed to, when discussing her grandfather. A shadow fell across her face. Her eyes softened.

'The codex contained the claim that Jesus survived the cross. So far, so familiar: this is a tradition which goes back about as far as the cross itself. However, alongside this claim and some fanciful nonsense about the survival of Jesus' bloodline, the codex specifically named Jesus as 'the Egyptian' whom Josephus identifies as leading an armed insurrection in the Holy Land around twenty years after the crucifixion.

'There is abundant apocrypha concerning what befell Jesus after his survival of the cross. This, however, was not one with which I was at all familiar. It so happened that his identification as the Egyptian aligned itself with those theories that his ministry was influenced by the Osiris myth. It's not beyond the realms of possibility that, if he had been some syncretic rabbi, synthesising Judaism and Osirism, that he might indeed have earned himself this nickname, if only disparagingly. There were so many would-be Messiahs doing the rounds, this would have been a convenient way of differentiating him from all the others. No matter. That's incidental.

'I read on. The codex went on to identify the place where Jesus "the Egyptian" had died and been buried.

'Imagine that. Imagine how I felt. Like my grandfather and Lord alone knows how many generations before me who had owned and known the contents of this fragile antiquity, I kept it to myself.

'One is driven to wonder, when fate puts one in such a position, if one might not somehow be an instrument of God. Then one begins to wonders if one is going insane, giving even passing thought to such superstitious nonsense.

'It was many, many years later, when I was no longer a young girl, that it occurred to me that perhaps that idea wasn't quite so insane. It seemed to me that perhaps I had the means by which to pull Randall back from the brink of apostasy – claiming a direct, personal mandate from God.

'Clearly Randall was doing good work, possibly even God's work, and who's going to step in the path of a man who has history on his side? But even so, he had no right or justification in making any claim to a unique and unprecedented relationship with God. But I saw him moving towards exactly that! Over the months and years, I watched him drift further and further towards this perilous dementia. Imagine what he could have *done* to the world. We all know that power tends to corrupt, and absolute power corrupts absolutely – but Randall was drifting towards the kind of power that hadn't been enjoyed since the Pharaohs, the Roman Emperors at their most decadent. Nobody needs to be told what Joseph Stalin or Mao Tse-tung did with an ostensibly salvific doctrine once the power to administer it fell into their hands. It's a *tiny* step from saviour to tyrant, and Randall was in real danger of crossing the line.

'So I decided to tell him what I knew. I thought it was in my power to shock him from his mania, to make him consider that he might be fundamentally *wrong* about himself. I wanted to shake his faith to its foundations. I wanted to terrify him, to confront him with the possibility of his own insanity, his own apostasy. I wanted him to understand that he was not, and will never be like unto God.'

'You wanted him to cut out the bullshit.'

'If you will. No matter. It didn't work. I didn't know it, but he was already too far gone. His belief that he retained a hotline to Jesus had already passed far beyond the rational.'

Again, I was taken by her choice of words. *Staad's* faith had 'passed far beyond the rational'. But not hers. She was still holding on in there, steadfast in her insistence that her own faith was grounded in discriminating sagacity – even while being thoroughly mindful that Staad was manifestly fruit-loopy in *his*. And it was the *same* belief!

'Then by your own standards,' I said, 'what you did was as arrogant and misguided as Staad.'

'Oh, I recognise that *now*,' she said. She couldn't seem to resist saying it in a manner which indicated that I was in some way at fault, and that her patience with me was beginning to wear very thin.

'It was arrogance beyond reason. I committed *exactly* the same sin as Randall. But I hope it was a sin which can be forgiven. It was committed with the best of intentions.' She snorted horsily. 'It must be said that as a Machiavel I was a catastrophic failure. I neglected to bear in mind that God doesn't need me or anyone else to intervene on His behalf.

'In the end, all I wanted was to remind Randall that certainty is a heresy. Faith is a *process*, not a state. Faith is an adventure.'

'White water *rafting* is an adventure,' I corrected her. 'Faith is something utilised by the needy in pursuit of something they can't attain by other means.'

She sucked in her cheeks. She decided not to say something. Instead, she said: 'Clearly, that will remain a matter of difference between us.'

Her response indicated that she was by now attempting at least a cursory degree of diplomacy. After all, this can't have been an easy conversation for her.

In recognition of this, I held up a hand. 'Okay,' I said. 'There's just no point at all in going round and round. Whatever you did, and whatever justification you choose to give for doing it, you *did* it. That's *it*. Over and done. No going back. I know what I think about it, and now I know what *you* think about it. So there we are.

'What you *haven't* told me is why Isabel and Nathan and (what's his name?) Frank, went and got themselves killed and why some freaky geek shot my leg and stamped all over it in Room 315 of the fucking *Sheraton*. I mean, I *know* you were probably getting to the point, but I'd really like to know what's going on. If it's not too much to ask. Since I got *shot* and everything.'

She watched me rant, calmly watched me look away from her in a mime of frustration. She sipped at her coffee. Her throat was dry. I heard her fighting the croak in her voice.

'We were about to admit what we did. What Randall did. What David did.'

'Admit it to whom, for Christ's sake? Your therapist? The *National Enquirer*?'

'No.'

She stood up, drained the dregs of the coffee, went and poured herself another. When she returned to the table, she held out the mug like a diminutive street performer. Obligingly, I poured in another slug of whiskey. She put the steaming coffee on the coaster and rubbed at her tired and gritty eyes.

'I mean, we were going to tell *everybody*,' she said.

She told me about it.

Staad's valedictory speech, his official goodbye to the world he saved and which yet loved him, was in two days. It would attract the biggest television audience in post-war history.

Isabel and her little cabal of apostates had arranged for one of the five copies of the all-time, hot-dog snuff movie of which I'd just been given a sneak preview to be delivered to Frank Shaw. Frank Shaw would arrange it that transmission of the President's speech was interrupted. Instead, the viewing public would be treated to a home movie which promised to be something of a blockbuster: hubris, resurrection, insanity, and, by way of a finale, a violent deicide.

Ruth wasn't joking. They were going to tell *everybody*.

Hannah the news-reader had been instrumental to this strategy.

It is instructive of the limitations of the imagination that I found Hannah's complicity harder to believe than the rest of it. Betrayal on that scale fell well within my frame of reference.

I was shocked.

She had been willing to do it for the platonic love of Frank Shaw, dear, dead old fucking Frankie. Naturally, she hadn't known *exactly* what she was doing for him; it was just that, if Frank asked, it would be done. Frankie had never asked anything of anybody, not in all the years she'd known him. Frankie had been a *giver*. She had only wanted to give in return.

I wondered if she would have forgiven Frank, once she came to know what it was he'd asked of her.

Another of her personal tragedies. Jesus, how much could this woman take? She was an *angel*.

'That's really good of her,' I said. 'That's a real risk for her to take at this stage in her career.'

Ruth looked at me askance. 'Jesus,' she said. 'Get a *grip*.'

She went to the bathroom. Too much coffee. When she got back I stared at her as she gazed down into her mug. Despite everything, I felt protective towards her. I wished she'd get herself a better haircut or something. Her hands were very small and calloused, hardened by digging and scraping and brushing dirt and whatever else she did. She didn't wear any rings. She was an old woman, or would be soon.

What I said was: 'So, after seventeen years, you decided to *tell* everybody.'

'That's the essence of it.'

'And,' I said, 'why the fuck would you want to do *that*?'

She shrugged. 'It certainly wasn't our original intention. What we had agreed was that, while we were alive, we'd keep the film in circulation. Five copies. That way Randall could never hurt us.

'Provision was made that the contents of the film and our own journals should become known once we had all passed away. Preferably of old age. For all these years, that's what we believed would happen. None of us knew the location of more than one copy at any given time, and each of us took temporary ownership of the film every few years, to consolidate the tie that binds. I imagine that you've realised that this is what you were passing on to David, when you recognised him. Something had gone wrong that day. The person you were supposed to meet couldn't make it, for whatever reason. David had to show up in person.'

'Jesus,' I said. 'I bet he enjoyed *that*.'

'Just imagine.'

Thus, light was thrown on that particular delivery. He hadn't wanted to be recognised. He'd asked his wife to leave the car and come meet me. That's why she was so evidently pissed at him. Who could blame her?

I enjoyed that thought for a while.

She sighed. 'But we misjudged Randall,' she said. '*Again.*'

Ever since those events related by the film, the six of them who'd witnessed the débâcle had recognised the implicit threat posed by the catastrophically humiliated, unquestionably deranged and unreconstructed monomaniacal autocrat they now understood their President to be.

Because they didn't want him to hurt them, they counter-threatened in return. You have to realise that none of this was ever actually *discussed* with him. Nothing like that. They just set five copies of the film in circulation. I was one of the vehicles by which the film had been circulated for all these years.

All along, they maintained a veneer of civility, of *putting it all behind them, of moving on*. But the President knew what they had done. And they knew he knew. And he knew they knew he knew. And so on and so forth.

It was like a game of chess which nobody would admit to playing.

After the President stepped down from the mechanics of Government, he naturally no longer enjoyed jurisdiction over the security services. Therefore, in order to track down and destroy all existing copies of the film which, among other things, showed him tottering from the hospital crusty with his own shit and babbling and railing like the lunatic he undoubtedly was, he would have been compelled to call in a few favours. No doubt he could have done this – he continued to enjoy profound loyalty from most of those who knew him, especially now he'd stepped aside and left some room at the goddamned *top* – but the very act of doing so would let slip to somebody, somewhere, that the President had himself a little secret. Obviously, he didn't want *that*. That would only exacerbate the problem he wanted to solve.

So, for years, it was a classic stalemate, an impasse.

Then, two months before, Oscar Petersen had a stroke. He'd long since retired. Of all of them, even including McArdle, he'd had the most trouble dealing with what they'd done. He had health problems, diabetes. Late onset epilepsy. Depression. (Who wouldn't?) So, he took his family away to farm sheep in the North-West Scottish Reclamation. In my opinion, that sounded like punishment enough. Anyway, he had a stroke and he died.

Nothing unusual about that. He was an old man. But it set them to thinking. McArdle would have none of it. He said they were being paranoid. It was all over and forgotten. McArdle yearned for it to be all over and forgotten, because he had the most to lose. But Isabel, Nathan, Frank and Ruth were of the opinion that it would never be all over and forgotten, so long as one of them was alive.

They had employed three other men like me. It so turns out that another couple of months back, one of them got himself stabbed to death in some bar-room brawl in the Sri-Lankan Reclamation. He wasn't a good boy, and Sri Lanka's a rough place. Nobody was surprised that his life should end like that. They should have expected it, but, coming so close to Petersen's death, they began to sweat a little. All their crimes of pride and deicide continued to lurk in the dark corners of their resplendent lives.

They began to think that maybe it wasn't *impossible* that old Randall had called in a favour or two. Maybe even blackmail.

Who knows. He's a clever man, wily old Randall. He always got what he wanted. And he'd had all those years to brood.

So they took consideration of the possibility that Randall had mobilised.

They still had three of us in their covert employ. Me and two others. Nominally as a precaution – as another implicit warning to Randall, *just in case* – Isabel and Nathan took a vacation. They tracked us all down. The copies of the film were set in motion. Two made it to NJC. I was carrying one. They were carrying the other when the car crashed. That left me.

'And the other two carriers?'

'Didn't make it.'

I didn't want to know the nature of their deaths, my unknown companions.

I poured a measure, downed it. I stared into the pebbling at the glass base and let this sink in for a while.

'So we're not claiming any great theological motivation,' I said. 'We're not talking about any fond attachment to the fucking truth. Nothing like that.'

She brazened that one out. I should have known she wanted something from me from the way she rode my insults like a pleasureboat on a gentle swell.

'Nothing like that at all. What we kept secret, we kept secret for the greater good.'

'The greater *good*?'

'We couldn't justify the catastrophic loss of faith in the government that would have followed the revelation of what we'd done. Not when the government was so close to achieving its goals.'

'Like saving the world?'

'Exactly.'

'Jesus, Ruth. That's such bullshit. You were all scared of what you'd done. You just couldn't stand the thought of people knowing. That's all. For Christ's sake, you have to admit *that* much.'

She shrugged. 'We took a decision. For better or for worse.'

Upstairs, there was movement. A door being opened, closed. A female voice forming a single, unclear word. A lavatory being flushed. Footsteps.

'It still doesn't explain,' I said, 'why good old Randall has chosen now to set about killing everybody.'

She thought some more. She moistened her lips with the tip of her tongue.

'After what we've discussed,' she said, 'do you believe that Jesus was treated as God by the people from whom he had to excuse himself when he needed to urinate?'

'Probably not.'

'Probably not, indeed. In fact his disciples are remarkable for the fact that, while he was alive, they just didn't *get* it. The only people who did seem to have any idea of what he might mean were the women in his life, but that's another story. The point is, the mystery of his meaning was profoundly deepened by what was said and written about him, what was *believed* about him, after he died.'

'We've seen that much.'

'You miss the point,' she said. 'Yes, there was a man. An actual man. We found his remains. There was a man who, even while he lived, was an enigma. Upon his death, those who followed him sought somehow to grasp and articulate his nature. Later generations seized on these spoken accounts, tales which passed from mouth to mouth and made written testaments of them. The generations which followed the composition of these written testaments sought to understand the written testaments, which sought to understand the spoken traditions, which sought to understand a man now long dead, who was not understood even in his lifetime. And so on.

'Jesus was made God by history – not least the vote taken at the Nicean Council in 325, under Constantine. According to what you believe, history was the mechanism by which he was either revealed as, or created God. You pays your money and you takes your choice. In this instance it doesn't matter.'

'The point being?'

'Look at Randall's life! Look at what he's *achieved*. To all intents and purposes, you're right, everybody's right: he saved the world. Who can guess at the source of Randall's cleverness? Couldn't it be God Himself? Not cleverness but *commandment*? Direct *instruction*.

'What's Randall done? He's established God's kingdom on earth. He's saved us and shown us that the True Path to salvation is through *him*. Now he's ready to leave us. He's dying. We all know he's dying. And after he's dead, what then?

'Do what Randall does. Take the long view. Don't think in terms of people. Think about the nature of history, of the origin and propagation of ideas.

'Time passes. How much time is irrelevant. Many years. Soon all who actually knew Randall are all dead. *We're* all dead. As soon as the last doctor who examined his colon, the last old man who remembers meeting him as a child, has passed away, Randall Staad ceases to be a memory, and becomes an abstraction, a notion. The world is left with second-, then third-, then fourth-hand recollections: not of what he did, that's well documented, but of what he *was*. What his nature was.'

She said, not without irony. 'Who knows what conclusions history will draw about Randall?'

I thought for a while. I lit a cigarette and smoked it.

'Aha,' I said, 'I see. The President thinks he's *God*. You should have *said*.'

She looked at me for a long time without any of the humour the situation surely demanded.

'Come on,' I said. 'Doesn't that about sum it all up? The President thinks he's God and you don't agree, he's deranged and he's pissed and he wants to kill you. Christ, you're all as confused as each other.

'Old Randall wants to be loved when he's gone. Big deal. He wants to be worshipped. Who *gives* a shit?

'He wants to play God and he doesn't think you're going to let him. He thinks you're about to blow the whistle. The celestial trumpet. Whatever. Come forth and announce the truth. Of course, he's *wrong*, but he doesn't know that. He doesn't *know* that you were more than happy just to carry on as if nothing had happened, just so long as he left you alone. But he *didn't* leave you alone because he thinks you're up to . . .'

'Pre-emptive deicide,' she said. She wasn't joking when she said it, either.

I told her the truth. I told her I didn't want to think about it. I told her I was sick, disgusted. I told her I could hardly believe they'd gotten themselves and me into such a shit-storm over a childish fantasy they were too scared to let go of.

She listened me out for a long time. Then she drained her coffee and said: 'But this is an opportunity you've never even dreamed of.'

I laughed at her audacity. I said: 'Well. *That's* a very optimistic angle from which to view proceedings.'

She looked into the empty mug. I surmised that she was finding it difficult to face me.

'It's the opportunity for revenge,' she said. 'Against whatever the source of your grievance actually is. Vengeance. Or vindication. Whatever it is you're driven towards. David knows what he's got to do. He can't do it alone.'

'Well,' I said. 'You can fuck *that* idea, for a start.'

She gazed at me over the rim of the mug. Her eyes were dead. 'I don't think you quite appreciate the gravity of the situation,' she said. 'In case that's true, let me give you chapter and verse.' She spoke slowly, deliberately, archly enunciating every syllable like an embittered and hate-wracked school marm. 'Either you help yourself – and me, and Naomi and Susan – by helping David do what has to be done, or Randall is going to kill you. Randall is going to kill all of us. Maybe not today, or tomorrow – but certainly the day after that. Or the day after that.

'But you already know that.'

She was right, of course. I had always known that. My dreams of paranoia had been dreams of prophecy. All along, it had been me who was right.

And now, if I were to walk away, where was I to go?

It was not possible to dissolve oneself within the world they had seen fit to create for us.

Staad had saved me, and in order to repay that debt it was necessary that I die for him – it was necessary that I, along with Isabel and Nathan, and God alone knew who else, was to be sacrificed in his name. In our blood would be birthed a God.

That was his will, and his will had a dreadful power. It had shaped the world to his design.

Ruth was right. I had been given the opportunity to turn my back on the demands of my saviour.

I felt curiously empty.

'The things you did,' I said.

A passing moment's silence.

'Oh, Jesus Ruth,' I said. 'What have you *done*?'

She reached out to me. She closed her small hand about my wrist. She had never done this before. One of the things I liked about her was, at least she didn't insist on touching you all the time.

She told me I'd have made a fine prophet, denouncing Mammon from the edge of the wilderness. She told me that disgust and rage had driven those men to solitude, not just the love of an unworldly and unimaginable God.

She squeezed my hand again, then let go.

A few minutes later, McArdle opened the kitchen door. In the hallway stood his wife and daughter. Their coats were buttoned to the throat against the chill. The hallway was lined with luggage. Ruth clapped her hands once, decisively.

'Right,' she said. She pushed back the chair and stood.

'This is it, then,' I said. I stooped over her like a cartoon vulture.

'So it would seem.' She extended her hand. I took it and shook it.

I didn't know what to say.

She stood looking up at me, still holding my hand. She considered for a moment, then said: 'Did you ever wonder why I singled you out?'

I shrugged. 'Of course.'

'And what did you think?'

'I don't know. I showed an interest.'

She shook her head, laughed. 'Not at all.' She let go my hand and stood back. 'Do you remember introducing yourself to me at that mess table?'

'Of course. I was terrified.'

'Well, as you did so, I was in the act of praying for guidance. Then you told me your name.'

'I see.'

'Do you?'

'No.'

'Do you know what your name means?'

Isabel had asked me that. 'No,' I said. 'No, I don't.'

She said: 'Malachi means "messenger".'

I laughed. 'Jesus.'

'I thought you were sent by God,' she smiled. 'Imagine.'

Then she said goodbye and turned her back on me.

She and McArdle walked the length of the hallway, towards the door, engaged in a muttered conversation. Once, he looked over his shoulder at me and grunted something not unakin to monosyllabic acknowledgement.

For his family I was filled with an embarrassed, shamed pity. I wanted to make excuses for myself. I wanted them to like me, despite my bursting in on their clean home in a suit stained with sweat and blood, and smelling of alcohol and cigarettes and levelling a gun at the gentle hypocrite who loved them more than he hated himself for what the love of them had made him do.

They looked at me for a few moments. The girl strongly resembled her mother. Their doubled, silent contempt was oppressive and eerie. Their eyes were devoid of anything but loathing. Although I was drunk enough to reflect that this was rather unfair, since none of this was my doing, I nevertheless wished them luck. The daughter's lip curled back a micrometre and her nostrils flared. Then they too turned their backs on me.

At the door, McArdle crushed his daughter to his chest. He buried his face in the crown of her head and drew in the scent of her. He held her at arm's length and told her he loved her. I heard him say it. I love you, honey. Then he bid goodbye to his wife. She remained stiff in her cashmere overcoat. He told her he loved her, too. Then he took his daughter's elbow and led her to the car, in the driver's seat of which waited Ruth Felton. She did not look in the rear view mirror. When Naomi and Susan were safely inside and buckled up, she started the engine and drove away.

Watching the tail-lights retreat, a process about which there is always something melancholy, I thought: 'Ruth, this is all your fault.'

I really don't think she had ever once stopped to consider that. And I really don't know why I never thought to tell her.

Fifteen *Never and Always*

All the warmth in the house left with them.

McArdle and I were left alone in the kitchen. The windows were milkily brightening at the lower edge.

McArdle bent over the basin and massaged cold water round his eyes.

'It's dawn,' he said.

I poured a glass of his whiskey and offered it to him. He took the glass in his paw and took a tiny, reflective sip.

I said: 'It was good of them to take Ruth along.'

He shrugged, dismissive. 'She's a clever woman. Naomi never even took a job. Susan's still a kid, whatever she thinks. She talks about liking guys for their minds.'

'They'll be fine.'

'Sure.'

'Where are they headed?'

'Greece. Our villa there.'

'On Crete? I know Crete pretty well.'

'Cyprus. We picked it up for a song from some bankrupt alcoholic Brit queen that lived out there. Turns out he had a broken heart. Four months after we buy the property, he takes a half bottle of *Metaxa* to the edge of a cliff and decides to keep walking.'

'They'll be fine.'

'I always felt kind of guilty about this guy. Even though he was all airs and graces, you know. Like Brits can be. He was such a supercilious asshole. It never occurred to me that he was just like everybody else. Guess being a pervert made him even more bust up inside. Jesus.'

I ruminated on this. I did not attempt to reassure him.

'Motherfucker,' he said to the window. 'You goddamn cocksucking son of a bitch. You fucking prick.'

As dawn began to establish an air of mundanity inside the house, he led me to what I can only describe as his weapons cache. Multifarious firearms were locked away in a secure cabinet set invisibly flush with one wall of the master bedroom. I allowed myself an appreciative intake of breath for the destructive power I saw ranked before me. I speculated for a grim moment upon the damage McArdle could have done me, if he had expected my arrival.

I armed myself for the days that lay ahead: a semi-automatic Heckler and Koch needle-gun with a couple of hundred rounds. A handgun in a spring-release holster at my hip. An assault rifle: the Gauss Lawman, Series III, with integrated, pump-action assisted mini grenade launcher. The crowd control weapon of choice.

Finally, a gas-mask. The familiar smell of it, the forlorn vacancy of its mournful countenance.

I looked at myself for a while, then took it off.

The weapons were signaturised. Authorising me for their use was a time-consuming affair.

Handing me the Lawman, he said: 'I hear you're pretty good with this stuff.'

I detected a note of moral disapprobation. 'Not really,' I said. 'Not especially.'

His throat rumbled. 'Whatever.'

The Gauss welcomed me with three urgent little beeps. It was my friend. It was my rod and my staff, and it comforted me.

It was past six am. McArdle sat heavily on the edge of the bed. He pinched the bridge of his nose, groaned, and pressed the heel of one hand deep into the small of his back. There followed a series of moist clicks. He stood, walked to one of the dressers – Naomi's: its surface was ranked with moisturisers and powders and bottles of scent – and rummaged in one of the drawers. His back to me, he told me that the next room, the box room, contained the house's central security command system. There were: '. . . movement detectors, heat detectors, bad *breath* detectors. I can have this house strung tighter than a southern Baptist on crystal methedrine.'

'Not too tight,' I said. 'If the house starts leaping and flashing and beeping and having a nervous breakdown every time a sparrow flies by, you'll come home to a fucking madman.'

He removed a half-empty blister pack from the drawer, popped five small white pills into his palm. He dry-swallowed them and made a face. Scowling Father Bear.

'This is an intelligent system,' he said. 'I didn't pick it up in the sales.'

I hated the fucker. 'No offence.'

'None taken.'

Because it was necessary that I be spruce and presentable the following day, McArdle offered to take my suit to the dry cleaners. Thus it came to be that I spent the day wearing a faded white T-shit which bore the grisly legend 'Chief Cook and Bottle Washer!' beneath a navy-blue, flechette-proof jacket and a pair of McArdle's old blue jeans, faded white at butt and knee, frayed at the cuff.

He told me I looked less like a stray mongrel.

I thanked him very much.

I fucking hated him.

He went to shower and shave. After administering another dose of painkiller and another couple of uppers, I went to examine the security system. It was indeed impressive; excitingly military, with thrillingly complex ranks of screens, keyboards, displays and LEDs. It occurred to me that learning how to operate it might be diverting. There was too much other stuff I was incapable of thinking about. Each time my mind settled on an aspect of it, I endured a cascading thrill of ambivalent exhilaration.

He spoke to me once more, shortly before he left for work. He was dressed in a charcoal grey, double-breasted suit, crisp white shirt and sober tie. Although he now resembled what he was, or pretended to be, he was dismayed and bewildered.

He wore wire-framed spectacles and carried a leather attaché case.

He was terrified.

He recited his cellular phone number, then instructed me not to call him on the number he'd given me. He said a lot of stuff like this. Then he said: 'I'll be back . . .'

I kneaded my brow and repeated: 'Eight, eight thirty.'

'I already said that?'

I nodded. He grunted. He reset his shoulders (they were very heavy shoulders. The rest of him seemed to be constructed with the sole purpose of supporting them). Then he strode into the crisp morning brightness. Birds were singing. The slamming of his car door and the vibration of the Mercedes engine as he reversed from the drive were signifiers of a staggering normality.

The house was locked and sealed fast. The windows were glazed with security glass. External doors were designed to withstand anything short of a point-blank mortar explosion. Internal doors were bullet-proof. Each uninhabited room was monitored by the house's paranoid, highly-strung demi-brain. The house was a prudent twerp. I set my feet on the desk (the injured leg remained somewhat stiff and cumbersome) and propped the Gauss Lawman alongside me, against the wall. I set the needle gun within easy reach of my right hand. Through the monitors, I watched the leaves and branches and blades and petals of the garden shift dreamily in the morning breeze.

My occasional slow blink became an indeterminate doze from which I awoke with a cartoon start, reaching for the pistol.

When my heartbeat had slowed to a simply neurotic pittering and pattering I stood and limped abruptly to McArdle's bedroom. I rifled through the contents of Naomi's dresser. I took a certain pleasure in this which wasn't necessarily sexual. The drawers' constituents bespoke a different world. Pretty underwear in one, practical in another. I thought about how nice it must be to have a room like this, and a wife who kept her panties in separate drawers.

I suppose the assorted boxes of pills gave the lie to this. Whatever. I discovered Naomi's uppers. The stuff she was taking was considerably more potent than the field uppers in the first aid kits. This was the kind of stuff you could buy on the black market if you were pulling a nightshift, say, or about to embark on a long journey. I took far more of them than I should.

I was wired already. I didn't want to start shooting up the house with assault weapons because the panel of a door contracted in the changing temperature, mimicking a stealthy murderer. Empty houses enjoy doing that.

But I didn't much want to sleep, either. I didn't want to do anything. I didn't want to be here.

I didn't want to do what I knew I was going to have to.

It simply is not possible to be alert all day. Even in the face of potential extinction, the mind will tend to wander. It's drawn to novelty. Repetition stalls it. Consequently, I spent most of the morning in a hypnotic reverie, reviewing the events of the past days and the events which had led to them. Time passed as I reviewed time past.

Examination of my history led me to conclude that everything that had ever happened to me had conspired to bring me to exactly this point. The very attempt at living a life I could abide was component of my predestination.

It didn't seem so strange, looking at it, that I was lurking around the house of David McArdle with a leg all busted and shot to crap, while he went off to work in preparation of the day to come, when I would be vehicle to a global revelation of lunacy and deicide. Instead, it had about it the comfort of inevitability. I felt that I had always known this would happen.

My entire life had been spent in preparation for it. I had been living a rehearsal.

I thought about the wildebeest, again, sitting passively while lions rip strips from its living flanks.

At mid-day, I took the assault rifle and shambled in a self-conscious, awkwardly spastic half-crouch to the kitchen. I opened the fridge. After downing a carton of orange juice I rooted around for something to eat that required little or no preparation. Even the microwave was beyond me. All there was, was the picked-at carcass of a good-sized chicken.

This thing I have about chickens. On Crete, I'd worked a season at one of the battery farms erected there immediately following the declaration of victory. It was the size of a small village, prefabricated and hastily ramshackle. Inside, it was like a window on hell. The things in the coop were not the size of chickens. They wanted feathers, beaks, even vestigial wings. But they had the hateful, beady eyes of chickens.

One could observe embryonic slime removed from fertilised containers, its growth to be super-accelerated. From something like a barely vital lump of mucus, to oven-ready white meat in something less than two weeks. This was part of the salvific miracle we had visited upon the world.

It is the worst insult to which I have ever been witness.

This chicken carcass was recognisably chicken-shaped. It had been corn fed. It was a rich-person chicken. Nevertheless, its corpse made gorge rise sour in my throat.

I thought of my own leg, unfolding from me like an inverted tube under sustained inflation.

I was fired from the battery farm. Eventually, I found myself working as a clerical assistant in the putative New Jerusalem. The job was low-paid, unskilled, repetitive, and provided out-of-town accommodation. Sonny Marshall lived close by, and now and again we'd meet up, reminisce over a beer or two. It made sense to share the rent on a bigger apartment, so Sonny and I became room-mates.

I met Claudia. She was a Slav, and she was beautiful. She

was a corporate technician, employed by the same body as me. She had a remarkable facility to fix anything she set her mind to. She wasn't authorised to discuss what she'd done in the war. She had a quick and wonderful smile, but was subject to passing black moods of incomprehensible intensity.

Sonny told me not to trust her. 'She's a lovely girl,' he said. 'But she's fucked up. I can see it. Just don't trust her, man.'

I told him he was full of shit and raised my hand to order us another beer. In the world beyond the military, our opinions differed radically, but Sonny and I never argued, not really. We'd been through too much to argue. There was nothing we couldn't say to one another, no opinion we shied from voicing. Our friendship had about it something fundamental. It was a friendship about which one might accurately use the word 'forged'. There had been a day when he had pressed his hands to my violently affronted flesh, stanching the intermittent gush and surge of my lifeblood. He had never once sought thanks for saving my life.

Following the war, there were many such friendships.

'You don't know anything about her,' I said.

He blew foam from his beer and gave me that big, shit-eating smile. It was winter. Although we were in the bar, Sonny had yet to remove his thick, plaid jacket with a fleece collar. Outside it was surgically cold. He scoffed: 'Says the man-of-the-world who was too chickenshit to play bury-the-bacon with the most beautiful woman he'd set *eyes* on in two years.'

'Jesus,' I sighed. '*That* again.'

His big, friendly grin, his lips all flecked with beer foam. 'Damn *right*,' he said. 'Damn *right*, that again. Jesus. I'm *bitter*. That was probably the finest good deed I've ever *done* my fellow man, and what do I get? What I get is, my fellow man is a dipshit who can't believe his luck, because he won't believe the world can be *like* that.' He sat back in his chair and as he had done a hundred times before, laughed as if incredulous. 'Sometimes people surprise you,' he mock-lectured me.

273

'Sometimes they don't do what you expect. Sometimes they do what you *want*.'

We talked in circles, round and round. I informed him that he was, once again, employing faulty rhetorical tools: he would never convert me to his doctrine of human nature by using as his device the transmutation of sexual fantasies into transparently vapid boasts of carnal adventure. It just would not stand up. (He laughed at that one.)

In return, he told me I just didn't want to hear what he was saying. It was a good-natured conversation. I never lost my temper with Sonny.

The last thing he said to me, before we were joined by the friends we were expecting, was: 'Fucked-up people don't *want* to be fucked-up. What they *want* to be is *happy*. But they won't *let* themselves be happy because they think they don't *deserve* it. They go out of their *way* to do things which fuck up the chances they get. They do it again and again, and each time they do it, their fucked-upness becomes a little bit more ingrained. Listen to me, man. Just this once.'

Sonny had problems. He was to be pitied for his fear of intimacy and his tendency to sexually objectify. Nevertheless, when I decided, what the hell, and asked Claudia to marry me, Sonny was proved right: she *was* all fucked-up in the head, *and* she was fucking someone else. To be fair, Sonny should have known, because naturally it was Sonny she was fucking.

Inside me there was a rapidly fluttering blankness, the ragged end of a loop of celluloid, clicking. The truth, as far as I was able to ascertain and understand, was this: Claudia was sleeping with Sonny because sleeping with Sonny made her feel unhappy and worthless, thereby confirming what she already suspected to be true of herself. Furthermore, given that she was unhappy and worthless, I couldn't really love her because I didn't really *know* her. As soon as I did, I'd have left her anyway. Thus she tied me up in a circle of unlogic.

The following night, after I told Sonny I knew, I went out drinking with him. It was his suggestion. He told me I probably needed it. He was right. That was the first time in my life I remember *needing* it, feeling I might go mad if I didn't get it. We took in a few bars, got ourselves pretty toasted, then headed home via the canal bridge. It was late and quiet. We stood for a while on the bridge and surveyed the sharp, icy outlines of the half-built satellite town, the frozen mud of building sites, skeletal cranes glinting pewter in the moonlight, concrete and cable, the windowless, roofless, ghostless shells of buildings to be.

The town was comprised largely of ex-forces personnel and the otherwise dispossessed. The war had uprooted hundreds of thousands, millions, and denied many of them a place to which they might return. It was a very young town and it could be a pretty rough place sometimes. There was nowhere left that couldn't be a rough place sometimes.

On the bridge, I smoked a cigarette or two, and monitored the flow of recently polluted, icy water, swirls of industrial effluent in night-time rainbows. Wordlessly, Sonny tracked the passage of satellites in the cloudless sky. We were both pretty drunk. Then we strolled along the edge of the water. Sonny wore his fleece-lined, plaid windcheater, blue jeans and these chunky hiking boots he was in love with. We all dressed like that, in functional work-clothes. I was wearing pretty much the same, except I wore a red hunting cap with the ear-flaps down and had my jaw huddled into a woollen scarf. It was cold as a bastard.

I wasn't angry. I didn't know what I was.

'What she says is bull,' he told me. He took some of the winter air deep into his lungs. 'Well,' he admitted at length. 'That's not altogether fair. It's wasting good English words on pure fucked-upness. The best you'll get is an approximation. But there we are. I told you to listen.'

I curled into myself for warmth. I said: 'I don't understand how you could do it.'

He spat into the water. 'It might as well be me,' he said. 'If she's going to be offering it round in order to push herself towards fuck-up critical mass. If it's going to be anyone, it might as well be me.'

'What about how I feel?'

He stopped for a bit, kicked his caked-up heels in the slurping, foot-churned mud of the pathway. 'I don't feel good about that,' he admitted, 'but the truth is: you were going to feel bad *anyway*. Does it make it any worse because it was me? Would you feel better if it was her goddamn *boss* or a pizza *delivery* guy or something?'

I knew Sonny's logic well. Its convolutions were a familiar cartography. I turned to him and said: 'You're the most twisted, fucked-up, evil bastard I've ever met.'

Even looking at the knife I produced from my pocket, he showed no fear, just his broad, surprised, amused Sonny face. He just gave me a big, big smile and laughed: 'Says the man with the big *knife*. Would you rather kill your best goddamned *friend* than admit to yourself that you were wrong about some woman you got all stupid over? Is it that difficult for you to admit that she might want to fuck, or be fucked by, someone other than you? Just because you're all wrapped up in this fantasy of eternal love and constancy. Je-sus, Malachi. Jesus. Come *on*.'

It was all so ridiculous, he was having a hard time keeping a straight face. You could tell he felt kind of sorry for me too, though. He said: 'Let's establish in your mind exactly who it was who told you they would never betray you, exactly who it was who told you that this wasn't true and exactly who it was who wouldn't listen. And while we're at it, let's establish exactly whose behaviour is all fucked up right at this moment. Okay?' he said. 'Let's get some perspective. Come *on*, now. *Jesus*.'

I watched breath steaming from his mouth and nostrils, like a horse.

I said: 'You're an evil bastard.'

He clapped his gloved hands. 'For *what*, exactly? What is it I did, other than try my god*damn*dest to teach you a little about how the world really is? All I ever did was prove to you how people actually are.' He squinted, read my expression. He was still struggling with laughter. 'Is that what I did or *what*? Is that it? You don't like the truth? Like, I'm to blame for the way the *world* is?'

Delighted, he clapped his hands once more. 'Jesus Christ, Malachi, if that doesn't seem a little fucked up to you, you need *help*. They've put you back together all wrong.'

I didn't lose my temper. I never lost my temper with Sonny. And I didn't kill him because he told the truth. I killed him because he was a liar.

I killed him because he was so capable a liar neither I, nor anyone I ever met, could ever prove him wrong.

I wished I hadn't thought about Sonny. I still didn't fully understand why I did to him what I did. More than once I'd drunkenly confessed to other drunks, describing what I did to him as a crime of passion, although it was not that. It was altogether passionless. It was a mercy killing. I killed Sonny because something was wrong with him. Something was missing. Upon the nature of this fundamental absence, I will not speculate, other than to record my belief that the world is better for his not being in it.

But now, as so often happened, the sun began to sit low in the sky and the shadows got long, and I could sense Sonny's presence. He was in the house with me. I could sense him giggling, just too far away to hear, over my shoulder, in the corner of the room.

As it darkened outside, I began to avoid the hallway and bathroom mirrors. I dreaded catching a glimpse of old Sonny, grinning away behind me, over my shoulder. I dreaded to hear his voice, a whisper in the far corner. A clatter in the kitchen.

Am I awake?

McArdle returned shortly after nine. Over one arm he carried my suit, shirt and tie, freshly dry-cleaned. Handing it to me, he said: 'I told my secretary a boyfriend of Susan's had been so nervous about meeting Naomi and me, he knocked over his wine glass and cut his finger to the bone trying to pick up the shards. It was a good lie, until it occurred to me half-way through the morning that I couldn't think of a single reason why the boy should have to undress and leave all his clothes behind. Still. Whatever. Have you eaten?'

He'd stopped at Burger King on the way. This was a good thing. I laid my dry-cleaned suit, still in cellophane, across the kitchen table, and placed the Gauss flat across it. The two items made for a delightfully gut-twisting juxtaposition. McArdle and I sat across from one another, biting down on Whoppers with cheese. He got ketchup and mustard smeared across the corner of his mouth. I pointed this out. He thanked me and dabbed at his lips effeminately, like an ursine but prissy maiden aunt. He placed the crumpled napkin on the table, next to the salt cellar.

He said: 'How was your day?'

I tried not to bristle at his manner.

'Fine. I watched TV mostly. A couple of movies, some sit-coms. *Jeopardy*. How about you?'

He shook his head, masticating burger. 'Everything seems fine.' He massaged his bristled jaw with the palm of a hand.

I said: 'Did you hear from Naomi and Susan? Ruth?'

He screwed his eyes shut and yawned mightily into a rolled fist. Transparently a displacement activity.

'No.'

'That's good,' I assured him. 'Really. No news is good news. And whatever.'

As a child, I had understood this to mean; news is never good. That always seemed to make more sense. It still did, if I thought about it.

'Sure,' he said.

The Presidential Address in the Temple was to begin at nine thirty the following morning. Staad's appearance would be preceded by a full programme of devotional and hagiographic

278

family entertainment before he took to the podium at eleven am.

McArdle had informed his secretary (the same secretary who did his dry-cleaning for him. Probably the woman who was charged with buying appropriate gifts for his wife and daughter come birthdays and Christmas) that he would be in late that morning because, before they left for the Temple, he wished to breakfast with his family. It was to be a special day – a day to remember joys and deprivations private as well as global. There were so many due at the Temple, he could conceive of no mechanism by which the President might be alerted of his non-arrival. And by then, it would be too late anyway.

McArdle and I were to arrive at the Callow Memorial Building at about 10.55. This allowed us ten minutes to gain access to the studio from which the address was to be relayed across Christendom in all its hushed entirety. The intent was to interrupt transmission at 11:10, by which time we confidently expected the attention of the grateful world to be fully and tearfully focused on its saviour's valedictory sermon.

Because Staad was saying farewell to the world and hello to history, the last thing anybody wanted was for some damaged nonentity to take themselves there with him by blowing out the Presidential brains. The security operation in and around the Temple was therefore both massive and highly visible. Every second usher was a secret service goon. Since its level of security was high at the best of times, and since any threat to the President was expected to derive from some latent Lee Harvey Oswald rather than an aggrieved terrorist organisation, the Callow Memorial Building had not been designated a probable target.

However, since it was the location from which the broadcast would be relayed, it naturally had been subject to comprehensive inspection and eventual security clearance. No extra security had been assigned to it. Indeed, since the day had been declared a holiday, it was actually operating with only a reduced security presence and a skeletal technical staff.

McArdle was confident that the murders of Isabel, Nathan and Shaw (and, of course, the attempted assassination of myself) had been instigated by Staad but effected on a wholly unsanctioned basis. Essentially, he believed that the President had indeed called in a few old favours, no questions asked. However, he was similarly convinced that, since Staad's capacity to execute his will was limited to the petitioning of such potentially hazardous favours, the President was all-but obliged to reckon the execution of Isabel and the others as sufficient warning to secure McArdle's silence.

McArdle had always been the cabal's weakest link. Of all of them, he had loved Staad the most. Perhaps more pertinently, because McArdle's role was characterised by such brutality, the President did not give much credence to the likelihood that McArdle could ever abide the notion that the people might see for themselves what he'd done – any more than the President could himself.

Having purchased this silence, Staad was content, temporarily at least, to leave him be. He did not consider McArdle to be a significant risk. He knew McArdle too well.

McArdle believed.

The studio itself was deep underground, approachable via a series of elevators.

To access the studio, it was necessary to be approved by three progressive levels of security. All personnel were obliged to undergo voice-, palm- and retinal-print identification.

I wondered how he expected me to walk in there alongside him.

He told me: 'That's accounted for.'

He was silent for a while. I waited for him to tell me.

When he opened his mouth, it was to say: 'Do you have a cigarette?'

I slowly widened my eyes, somewhat mockingly, and said: 'Of *course*.'

He took a Marlboro from the proffered packet and sheepishly accepted a light. He drew deep. He exhaled through his nose. He narrowed his eyes against the smoke's acridity.

He held out a hand: 'Do you mind if I see your lighter?'

I handed it to him. He looked at it and smiled.

'Isabel gave this to you?'

I nodded, exhaled. 'She did. You know it?'

'I certainly do. It was a wedding gift to her. From Randall. He hated how much she smoked. This was kind of a joke between them.' Then he said: 'Jeez. Nicotine hit.' He closed his eyes while he rode it out.

I took the lighter back, rolled it through my fingers. I read the inscription. *With thanks. R.*

I said: 'Wow. That Isabel.'

He agreed. 'That Isabel,' he said.

Then, in answer to my question, he told me this: when it came to the Callow Memorial Building, I had security clearance of a level equal to his own. Code Clearance White. The highest clearance there was.

Years previously, he didn't know exactly how many years, Isabel Beaumont had downloaded my personal data into the security clearance system of the Callow Memorial Building, which had been constructed according to her design. She had accomplished this even before the building was fully complete.

All warmth and feeling drained from my face.

This final acknowledgement of my predestination was not the oppressive matter it might have been.

Since I did not know when, I had clearly been subordinate to a will-to-purpose inestimably more powerful and manipulative than my own.

It was oddly liberating.

I began to laugh. I was going to repeat: 'That Isabel,' with something approaching awe, when I sat back again and began to think it through.

How had she come by my voice, retinal and palm prints?

I thought to recollect the night she and Nathan spent with me, back in New Winchester.

'*I know what you did,*' she said: '*I know what you did to Sonny Marshall.*'

Arrested on suspicion of murder, I was afforded a single phone call. I had nobody to call but Ruth. I lied to her. I told her I hadn't done it. I wept and pleaded with her that I hadn't done it. I told her I needed a lawyer.

Two days later, they let me go. I never understood why. There was plenty enough circumstantial evidence to send me to the chair – not least Claudia's testimony that the day her beloved Sonny was stabbed to death and dumped in the freezing and filthy river, I'd learned of her infidelity with him.

That was more than enough, but they let me go anyway. I'd been forced to attribute this to uncommonly good luck, the lack of hard evidence and a phenomenal work load. Those were very violent times.

Ruth was waiting for me. She drove me to her place, where I stayed until I got myself back together.

She hadn't been acting out of love. She had identified me to Isabel as a possible candidate for smuggling their precious film. I was no good to them if I was in jail.

They knew I was guilty and they didn't care.

By whatever mechanism, and I didn't doubt that it was corrupt, Isabel had attained my release.

To make capital from the transitory obstacle of my internment, Isabel had taken the data held by the police – retinal prints, voice prints, palm prints, whatever else – and put them to good use as a contingency plan.

She had downloaded the particulars of a murderer and scrubbed them clean until my character was Code Clearance White.

Thus I was able to isolate the moment at which I surrendered my autonomy. It was the moment I was released from custody, the moment I sat in the passenger seat of Ruth's Volvo and let her drive me to her home. I had imagined that, by some chance occurrence, I had been given my life back. I was wrong. There was no chance in it. From the moment of my release, I had belonged to Isabel Beaumont.

Ruth had told me I had no choice but to help McArdle. She wasn't exaggerating. I never had the choice.

'Jesus,' I said. 'That Isabel.'

He met my gaze. He nodded, once, by way of confirmation.

McArdle and I talked for a long time.

It didn't call for as much discussion as we allowed. There was really nothing to it. There didn't appear to be a great deal that could go wrong. I was to be there in case it did.

Simple as that.

We retired at three am. At the top of the stairs we shook hands, quite formally, and bid each other good night.

I lay, half dressed, on the guest bed in the guest bedroom. In the dark, I was able to reflect on the consequences of what we were about to do.

It is no small thing, to deprive the world of a saviour.

Eventually, I slept.

In my slumber, I heard his voice. He had been silent for many years.

A little while, and you will see me no more.

Or perhaps it was Sonny. Crouching over me in the darkness.

Sixteen   *The Code White Studio*

I rose at eight am.

Naturally, the guest room was *en suite*. I injected my leg, showered. I took my time, shaved twice with the razor that had been left next to the basin, still in its package, in case of unexpected arrivals.

It was necessary that I keep busy.

The leg wasn't bothering me too much, but I strapped it up anyway, good and firm. Naked, with my thigh all taped up, I strutted irregularly round the bedroom, stopping now and again to practise squatting and kneeling. It was impossible to walk without something of a limp, kneeling wasn't what you'd call easy and you could forget about squatting altogether, but I was pretty confident the leg would hold up tolerably well to the stresses of the day that lay ahead. Whatever they might be.

After dressing the leg, I sat on the john for what seemed like hours. Afterwards, I dressed as carefully as I was able. I knotted the tie gently at my neck.

I looked correctly sober and businesslike.

I had to breathe on my hands to warm them. Fronds shifted inside me, as if directed by a gentle current.

Downstairs, I set my jacket over the back of a kitchen chair.

The morning and the dead of night enjoy their own exclusive modes of reality. The kitchen seemed over-lit and two-dimensional, like a film set. The tiniest sound was crisp and crystalline, as if subtly amplified, coming at me in surround-sound.

The air was rich with the aroma of coffee and the bacon McArdle was frying up with some eggs.

He said: 'Can you eat? You should eat.'

'Maybe later,' I said.

The word 'later' was giddy with connotation. I smoked the first cigarette of the day, lit another from its stub. McArdle presented me with a cup of coffee.

'It's good bacon,' he said.

'Really,' I said. 'I'm not much of a one for breakfast.'

I let him get on with whatever domestic fantasy he'd immersed himself in. With the coffee, I washed down a large handful of uppers.

On the kitchen table, we laid out the day's weaponry. We engaged in a brief debate about ammunition.

I decided on a needle gun in a spring-release holster beneath my jacket, a small handgun at my waist. McArdle contended that the Gauss Lawman might attract attention, but I would not be parted from it. I argued that, since I was apparently security-cleared, nobody was authorised to give me a hard time about what weapons I chose to carry. Let them assume I was extra security, laid on to guard him on the big day. This was an argument he felt able to accept.

There were two attaché cases, inside one of which I firmly taped spare magazine cartridges. I asked him to do the same. He removed the contents of his case – pens and diaries, a personal organiser, some papers to sign – and replaced them with ammunition: two bandoleers of mini-grenade magazines for the Gauss which was my friend. I slipped a telescopic baton into my jacket pocket. We clicked the attaché cases closed in tandem and looked at one another.

'Hooo,' I said. I patted the case twice, as if reassuring it.

He looked at his wristwatch.

'Ready?'

I wiped my hands down. Patted my pockets. Straightened my tie in the mirror and fussed a little with my hair.

Then I nodded.

I followed him from the kitchen into the hallway then, blinking, into the shrill sunlight. I took the dark glasses he'd given me from my breast pocket and slipped them on. Wearing them in combination with the sharp, clean suit, the gun at my hip and the attaché case, not to mention the stupendous quantity of drugs I'd recently ingested, I felt armoured and businesslike. It was as if I'd appropriated someone else's personality.

I opened the passenger door of the Mercedes, sniffed the new car smell. Seated, I strapped myself in. I propped the Lawman before me. Exposed to daylight, it seemed to possess an extra dimension of solidity. It glinted at me with ironic complicity.

McArdle started the engine. Its quiet vibration gave my heart pause.

I watched his house retreat in the rear-view mirror, then sat back and watched the wealth go by.

After silently speculating on the prices of real estate for a block of two, I made him pull over and go buy me two packs of cigarettes. He resented making the purchase. He returned to the car with thunderous countenance. He really was a seriously hypocritical old man. He wouldn't let me smoke in the car. He was concerned about appearances.

I thought about what he'd done, and what we were about to do.

After a few minutes' sedate progress, we were caught in a temporary contraflow. There was a greatly increased volume of traffic in the city.

Because of this we didn't arrive at the Callow Memorial Building until it had passed eleven am. As we pulled into the vast, virtually empty parking lot, the President had already begun to address an eager world.

I took a moment to catch my breath and imagine the scene inside the Temple. The ranked masses in their wordless thousands. The cameras. His words. His lies.

And all the world bearing witness.

McArdle pulled the car into his designated space and killed the engine.

We sat for perhaps two seconds in silence, then stepped from the car in tandem.

We didn't speak or look at each other, even as we passed into the shadow of the Callow Memorial Building: McArdle with his big, rolling stride and me with one half-articulate limb, hobbling at his shoulder like a twisted familiar.

The Callow Memorial was an immense neo-classical pastiche, a Greek temple by way of Disneyland: pillars and smoked-glass. Intermittent art deco detail.

I couldn't imagine that Isabel had been in any way proud of it. It looked like something she'd proposed on a wet Saturday afternoon, as part of a despotic prank.

Stepping into its shadow, into the disinterested glare of its attendant security system, its many passive, recording eyes, I sensed no threat from it.

It knew me. I was inside it.

I was even a little abashed by the bulky assault rifle I had with me. It felt inappropriate, as if I'd brought along an unwanted, vulgar acquaintance.

We entered the building at 11.05. The immense, smoked-glass doorway opened to admit us, then shut with a muted, almost sexual sigh of gratification.

The lobby was cavernous, contrived in the signature components of marble, glass, leather and chromium. Ahead of us a grand, somewhat frivolous spiral staircase swept magnificently from the gallery above. Against the wall to our far right was positioned a lengthy security desk. More cameras. Behind the desk, a row of six men in blue uniforms. Right and to our rear stood two other men. They conversed quietly beside a water fountain. They paused long enough to observe McArdle and me with mannerly, unobtrusive but nevertheless implicitly barbed curiosity. One of them crossed his arms over his ID badge and gazed at me without blinking for perhaps five seconds. I stared back. I was still wearing the dark glasses. Eventually lids slid slowly over eyes and his head turned smoothly away on its axis, like an owl's.

The lobby was otherwise deserted. As we approached the security desk, our footfalls had about them an epically reverberative, theatrical quality. I wondered if, seen from above, we cast a long shadow.

Each of the guards at the desk was equipped with an earpiece and a head-mike. Most of their attention was devoted to the monitor each had set in the desk before him. Like everyone else, they were watching and listening to the President.

Nevertheless, as we approached the desk one of them was obliged to look up and process us. McArdle made a pacifying, dismissive gesture.

You go ahead watching, it said, *don't worry about me*.

Thus we walked straight through the first security check-point.

The possibility existed that somebody was doing their job and monitoring us, so we made our way down the corridor without speaking. I didn't much trust my voice to work anyway.

Behind the public facade of the lobby, the core of the building was encouragingly like every office block in which I had ever found myself. Its genus was so familiar that I sensed the oddness of its desertion. I could sense its absent personnel, how devoid the facility was of its usual milling and bustling.

We met nobody until we arrived at the second security checkpoint. It consisted of a curved desk set before a metallic double door. It was attended by two security wardens, again equipped with earpiece and head-mike. Each of them had his eyes and ears fixed predictably upon events in the Temple. They looked about five years removed from compulsory retirement. They seemed harmless enough: slow-moving, late-middle-aged men passing away uneventful lives behind a desk, doing not much of anything but chewing the fat, eight hours a day, five days a week.

McArdle greeted them both by name. They appeared as delighted to see him as they were surprised. He neither introduced me nor made any allusion to my presence. For their part, they contrived to disregard my existence with disarmingly professional courtesy.

Cordially, one of them asked after McArdle's well-being.

'I'm *late*, is how I am' said McArdle, ruefully. 'Have you seen the *traffic* out there?'

The guard had. 'Crazy,' he said. 'Plain crazy, is what it is.'

He nodded his ongoing assessment of the traffic's craziness, tapping at the keyboard before him with the practised, corporate rapidity of a hotel receptionist.

McArdle the apostate stepped abreast of the burnished metal doorway. He flattened his palm against the glass panel in the wall alongside the door. I saw the brief, blue flicker of the retinal scan. He proclaimed his name to the ceiling.

'McArdle, David.'

The door slid mightily open. McArdle thanked the watchmen and told them: 'Enjoy what's left of the show.'

They thanked him in return and assured him they would.

The door slid closed.

I was alone with them. I looked at them. They looked at me. Appraisingly; expectantly; finally, a little uncomfortably.

I was still wearing the dark glasses.

One of them said: 'If you'd like to go on through . . .'

I acknowledged the invitation with what I hoped was an assured, curt nod, not impolite, and stepped alongside the door.

As I did so, I glanced over the guard's shoulder.

On a monitor, I briefly glimpsed the President, rhetoricising away. One gnarled index finger hovered and darted aggressively before him, like a hornet.

In the far curve of the desk, to the right of the second guard, was ranged a triple column of monitors, from which it was clearly possible to observe the parking lot, the lobby – and presumably any of the many corridors, offices and suites of cryptic function of which this labyrinthine structure was composed.

It was on one of these monitors that I watched three black limousines pull smoothly to a halt in the parking lot just outside.

In the same monitor, twelve doors opened. Twelve men in black suits issued from the limousines with the creepy, spiky simultaneity of flying ants.

Their rapid progress in producing assault rifles and aluminium cases from inside the cars betrayed all the efficiency exhibited by men who are proficient in the manifold techniques by which it possible to terminate human existence.

The world rushed toward me. The strength went from my legs. I turned like an automaton from the desk and blankly offered my palm to the glass panel set alongside the door. A laser surveyed my eyes. It did not record what was behind them.

Finally, I introduced myself to the ceiling: 'Thorndyke, Malachi.'

My voice broke on the terminal syllable. I coughed throatily into my fist. I sensed the guard's interest in me increase a notch. The beam of his gaze flitted lightly, disinterestedly, across my shoulders.

I thought I might vomit.

There followed the transit of a very few interminable seconds, during which what I wanted most in the world, and what I wanted least, was to look once more upon the dire procession emerging from those long, sleek, black cars on to the tarmac parking lot a laughably few hundred metres and some minimal security away from me.

Then the door opened.

I stepped through the portal into a corridor almost identical to the one from which I'd come. Behind me, the doorway slid firmly shut.

It took me a moment to locate McArdle. He stood waiting at the open door of an elevator. He looked at me with something not a million miles away from disgust. He held his tongue until we had stepped into the elevator and the door had closed before hissing: 'What the *fuck* is the matter with you?'

I was all but hyperventilating. I rubbed my forehead. It was wet. I said: 'I think you were wrong about Randall.'

I told him about the cars.

He didn't reply. I wondered if he'd heard. Then I saw that he was chewing at his lip. His eyes were moist.

'Shit,' he said. He thought for a while, chewing at his lip. Then he tried to assure me that, if Randall had managed to have these men ordered to apprehend us, then they were authorised to do nothing more than arrest us. We would show the film, as we had planned, and then we would surrender. We would be released from custody within the day.

I did not believe him.

When the elevator stopped, he strode urgently down the delivered corridor, leaving me to limp after him as quickly as I was able. It is, believe me, not an easy thing to limp hastily without looking hysterical with fear.

We paused atop a stairwell. McArdle was breathless, red in the face. He reminded me that we had to pass a single security desk. I followed him as he marched hastily down the stairs, through a set of swinging doors, a right turn and finally into a door-lined corridor which stretched barrenly before us. At the far end, before another burnished metal door, was set the final security desk. It too was attended by two men. Before the desk were set two large cheese plants and a water cooler.

My legs were boneless. I set my full attention on the two security guards, but McArdle and I had walked perhaps half the length of the endless passage – his breath at my side, rough and asthmatic, and my own heart thrashing and pounding away inside me – before I was able to catalogue them. They were younger than the previous guards. Slimmer; muscular even. Each had about him an indefinably military air. One wore a crew-cut and rectangular, steel-rimmed spectacles. The other wore his hair short but parted to the side and a heavy, black moustache which drooped dolorously over the corners of his mouth.

Each wore an earpiece, and each acknowledged us with a brief nod before returning his attention to the screen set in the desk before him.

McArdle and I had yet to come within ten metres of them before the man with the moustache touched an index finger to his earpiece. I sensed him tense without shifting his position. His mouth, hidden by his moustache, formed a cautious, muttered sentence. Even so, I had a pretty good idea that he was saying: 'Please repeat and confirm. Over.'

McArdle and I were five metres from the desk when I saw him nod as if to himself and let go the earpiece. Acknowledging a command.

Before the men could push themselves away from the curved desk and free their sidearms, I dropped the attaché case, lifted the Lawman to my shoulder and fired five rounds at them.

The noise was intolerable.

Although the Gauss has many fine qualities, subtlety is not among them. At such close range, it would have been difficult to miss. The first two rounds caught the crew-cut guard in the solar plexus. He hit the wall like a locomotive.

The second man was halfway to his feet and in the process of drawing his sidearm. Two rounds hit his ribs, beneath an armpit. A third hit where jaw met skull. He spun through a hundred and eighty degrees. As he fell, his skull struck one corner of the curved desk.

It was all very quick.

I fell to one knee, stretching the strapped-up leg straight before me, as the roar of the rifle reverberated and rolled voluptuously along the corridor, and flipped open the attaché case. In a single, unforgotten movement, I retrieved the gas-mask and pulled it over my head. Then I stood, not without difficulty, and approached the desk, the Gauss trained at my shoulder.

Clearly, McArdle's anti-terrorist training had stood him in good stead. He had already pulled on his own gas-mask.

Astonishingly, the crew-cut guard was still conscious. He was making determined but ineffective attempts to retrieve his fallen sidearm. Crabbily, I kicked it to one side.

I was using non-lethal ammunition. The Gauss was loaded with snub-nosed, semi-solid polymer slugs known as jellies. A few dozen such rounds fired into the most raucous civil insurrection would traditionally bring about an impressively speedy cessation of violence with minimum loss of life. A couple of hits from point blank range shouldn't kill a fit man, but they would almost certainly break bones.

This guard had taken two rounds to the solar plexus at close to point-blank range. The impact trauma would have been considerable. Additionally, the impetus of his collision with the wall would unquestionably have shattered bones. But still he insisted on making redundant attempts to retrieve his firearm. Idiot.

I took the needle gun from its holster and fired once into his ass. He was unconscious in about three seconds. He could thank me for every penny of temporary disability allowance he was able to claim.

In my earpiece, I could hear McArdle breathing rapid and shallow.

My own voice was rendered thin and tinny by the integral microphone. I said: 'Can you get us into the studio?'

He leaned massively over the security desk.

He said: 'Oh Jesus. There are teeth on the table.'

I kneeled over the moustachioed guard. The difficulty with non-lethal weapons is, things can go wrong. You're not supposed to aim for people's heads. I think his neck was broken. I didn't want to move him to find out. He was spread ineptly all across the floor. I balanced myself clumsily over him and tried to reach the desk, from the surface of which I obligingly flicked some of his teeth with the edge of my cuff.

Then, with the edge of a sleeve I wiped dapples of blood from the ranked monitors.

I saw twelve men in dark suits and very neat haircuts striding purposefully down one unidentifiable corridor of the Callow Memorial Building. They carried assault rifles and attaché cases. I didn't imagine that they intended to use non-lethal ammunition. They were wearing gas-masks. How nice. We were all wearing the same face.

I barked at McArdle through the mask's internal mike: '*Open the fucking door.*'

With the Gauss' integral launcher, I fired a series of mini-grenades down the passageway. They exploded thunderously and coated the walls and floor with anti-traction liquid. Another crowd-control device. It's difficult to riot if you can't stand up.

Very sound logic. Great comic potential.

I needed to pee.

I expelled the spent shells, loaded fresh cartridges and as McArdle tapped gingerly away (blood on the whorls of his fingertips) I fired them down the long corridor. Each landed with a skid and a hiss then cracked open with an inoffensive little plop. From their interior began to bubble a veritable volcano of viscous, white foam which expanded until it had reached the height of the ceiling. Fizzing and bubbling, the wall of froth began to bloat towards us with the half-comical, half-disturbing mindlessness of a creature in a B-movie.

A siren sounded. It was urgent and terrifying. For a second McArdle and I nearly lost what composure we had struggled to maintain. The siren stood as a stark reminder that I was trapped in a corridor with anti-riot suds and a slippery floor between me and twelve men who had been dispatched to dispatch me.

The siren stopped. Somebody had cut it. It served no purpose. Everybody knew exactly what everybody else was here for.

I placed a hand on McArdle's back and urged him to hurry.

I kept my eyes trained on the monitors. I watched the men

in suits traversing a corridor. I had no means to identify which. They walked quickly, but they didn't run.

McArdle tapped a final sequence into the sticky keyboard, said something I didn't catch, and stepped alongside the security door. Again, I watched him subject himself to the passport procedure. When it was done, he called to me, and I too offered my palm, retina and voice.

The door rolled open on thousands of oiled bearings. I experienced a brief rush of triumph. It was an armoured door behind which, instead of yet another corridor, there lay a tubular elevator large enough to accommodate maybe five people, standing shoulder-to-shoulder.

We stepped inside.

'McArdle, David,' he announced at the ceiling. 'Code White.'

It was very impressive.

I faced the doors. The suds had reduced the passageway outside the elevator to the length of a few metres.

It ended in a wall of froth, in which I suddenly believed I saw the shifting, fluid suggestion of a moving form.

I lifted the Gauss to my shoulder and fired the width and height of the corridor. The noise was immense. Each round left an entry wound in the foam, which quickly closed.

The elevator door began to close. It took its time. Alone, it must have weighed five tonnes.

I couldn't hear what exactly McArdle was shouting, but I could understand it.

'They're out there,' I yelled back. 'They're fucking *out there* right now.'

The substantial door pressed fast, and the elevator began to drop in an alarmingly leisurely fashion.

As McArdle was about to finish shrieking the word 'impossible', there was a concussion whose intensity was indescribable. The impact shook us to our knees. The body of the elevator car vibrated like the skin of a drum.

I took McArdle's shoulders and drove him into the

shimmering, undulating wall. I was screaming. It was important to me that he understood the external elevator door to
have been hit by a rifle-propelled grenade.

He looked down at me through the hangdog lenses of the
gas-mask.

I bellowed: '*Jesus.*'

I made a mime of turning away in extravagant disgust. I
ejected the magazine from the Gauss and kneeled to reload. I
stuffed a magazine into each jacket pocket. I felt the lining
give. McArdle opened his attaché case and passed me a
bandoleer of grenades. I slung it over my shoulder.

Please believe me when I say it was not a comfortable or
companionable descent. When it was over, and the door
opened, I hammered vigorously but fruitlessly at the control
panel with the butt of the Gauss. It did no damage whatsoever.

I said: 'Tough fucking elevator.'

Instead, I pumped a couple of foam grenades in there.
Whoever the door opened on, they were going to get
swamped under about a million gallons of sticky spume.
Fuckers.

The environs of the Code White Studio were considerably
more luxurious than the office complex above. There was no
indication that we were so far underground, or that the entire
complex could be sealed, denying access to the putative
irradiated and starving hordes above. It was a little slice of
underground heaven. It was all very white and bright and
clean. The white tiled floor clicked under our heels. Pot plants,
drink and candy vending machines stood at junctions. We
passed a gymnasium, a sauna, a make-up room. How odd, to
be marauding such a place.

We moved as quickly as we were able. As well as the
injured leg, I was burdened by the weight of so much
firepower. Also, I kept turning to douse the floor with anti-
traction cartridges. McArdle breathed as if troubled with a
respiratory problem.

He kept glancing at his wristwatch.

At 11.17 am, he stopped, put his weight against one wall, caught his breath, and pointed:

'Third door on the right. That's the studio.'

The studio could be accessed by four corridors radiating from it like points of the compass. I fired anti-traction and foam grenades down each of them. Our pursuers would be forced to approach the Code White Studio like the Keystone fucking Cops.

I slung the Gauss over my shoulder, drew the needle gun and followed McArdle past a couple of potted cheese plants, to the door of the studio. A screen above the door indicated that a transmission was in progress. Through my earpiece, I heard him bark a somewhat sardonic laugh. Through the com-link, he announced: 'Ted, Sarah, this is David. I'm coming in. Please be calm. There's no reason for anybody to be afraid.'

As we stepped inside the door, five or six centimetres of solid metal swung smoothly and mightily shut behind us. McArdle engaged the locking mechanism. Six steel bolts slid convincingly into place.

The room in which we found ourselves was half-lit. A desk containing twenty workstations curved towards the far wall. It overlooked a long, narrow window which opened on to a studio floor. I recognised it immediately as the studio from which CTW was broadcast. Beyond inoperative cameras and other unmanned televisual paraphernalia, I could clearly see the very desk behind which Hannah daily broadcast the news to us: the desk from behind which she had announced the assassination of Isabel and Nathan Beaumont.

The long desk was cluttered with biros, crumpled memos, newspapers, empty Styrofoam coffee cups left haphazard beneath ranks of monitors, faders, microphones, keyboards.

McArdle approached the desk, leaned over it and spoke into a small microphone: 'Ted, Sarah. It's David. I'm inside. I'm coming through.' I covered him with the needle gun. Infra-red filters in the gas-mask sought the pattern of body heat in dark corners. As far as I was able to tell, the room was as empty as it appeared.

I followed McArdle into an adjacent, much smaller room. Inside there was a single desk, again set with microphones, faders, keyboards. The desk faced a rank of eight full-sized monitors, each of which described the President from a different angle: the wizened mouth and chipped-out cheek-bones, the shrink-wrapped flesh, black eyes combusting with primal intensity. The gaze he had fixed upon the future.

Because the monitors were the sole source of illumination, the room was lit with a shifting, rippling pattern of light and shadow. It felt like the interior of a fish-tank.

There were three people in there. Two sat at the desk, another stood pressed to the wall. There was a woman of perhaps thirty-five. She wore a white cotton shirt, open at throat and cuff, faded blue jeans, loafers and half-moon, wire-framed spectacles which had slipped down the bridge of her nose. She wore blonde hair in a pony tail. Alongside her sat a slightly older man in rolled-up shirtsleeves and a tie which could only have been the Christmas gift of a much-loved, if colour-blind child. His hair was a little too long, swept back, and he wore a questionable, gingerish beard.

They twisted wordlessly in their swivel chairs to face us.

Against the wall stood a somewhat skinny college-age kid in a white T-shirt and baggy jeans and expensive hiking boots. He had about him an air of immature resentment. I suspected that, since his ego was still under development, he considered McArdle and me to represent more of a threat to his burgeoning masculinity than his actual well-being. Little prick.

Light cast by the shifting multitude of Presidents reflected on their skin and clothing.

It was the woman who spoke. She removed an earpiece, laid it on the desk and said: 'Jesus, David, what's going *on*?'

McArdle paused. For a moment, I really thought he was going to explain everything. Instead, he exhaled deeply, and removed the gas-mask. He rubbed at his eyes.

I looked over my shoulder to the studio behind me.

McArdle was breathing very heavily. 'Sarah,' he said. 'I don't have time. I just need you to do what I ask.'

She held up a palm and closed her eyes. 'I need to know, David,' she said. 'There are *issues* at stake here.'

'Sarah,' he said.

The man made as if to stand. I screamed at him to fucking *sit*. It was a very shrill scream. He sat. He said: 'Jesus.'

I yelled at the woman to do as she'd been told.

The college kid said: 'Hey, fuck *you*,' and flipped me the bird.

I shot him with the needle gun. He folded and fell like a hastily discarded marionette.

The woman and the man, Sarah and Ted, exchanged glances.

He spoke to McArdle but looked at me. He made pacifying gestures.

'Please,' he said. 'It's okay. Really. Truly. Just tell us what you want, David.'

From his pocket, McArdle removed the disk. The man held it to his face as if examining a peculiar photograph.

He looked at McArdle.

I pointed the gun at him. 'Just do what you're fucking told.'

McArdle clapped me on the shoulder. 'Go now,' he said.

I went. Behind me, McArdle closed and bolted the door to the editorial suite. I was left alone in the half-lit room, overlooking the CTW news studio.

It was 11.23.

According to McArdle, it would take less than a minute to re-format the disc, rendering it broadcastable. The film we had come to show, unbelievably enough, was something less than fifteen minutes long. The critical length was just under twelve minutes. After twelve minutes, everybody watching would have seen enough.

I spent the first minute urgently but redundantly barricading the studio door with whatever came to hand; filing cabinets, office chairs, even one or two of the ubiquitous fucking pot plants.

In the act of this, I heard McArdle's voice in my ear. I could picture him, holding the gas-mask to his face, talking to the internal mike.

'Find a monitor,' he said. 'It's ready to run in twenty seconds.'

I ran to the desk and searched the length of it. I found two banks of miniature screens, one of which showed six identical images of the President. Evidently he was enjoying a moment of silent contemplation.

This is what the world was seeing.

I couldn't hear anything.

'Find an earpiece,' said McArdle. 'There should be an earpiece somewhere.'

I swept clutter from the desk and made a cursory visual search. There was no earpiece. 'Fuck it,' I told him.

I didn't need to hear it. I'd already heard it. Instead I swung the briefcase on to the flat surface and, as I watched the miniature screens, I emptied it. I cluttered the desk with magazines.

I opened my mouth to speak, but McArdle was first.

'Here we go,' he said.

Ten seconds.

Nine.

Eight.

My eyes were drawn to movement on my right. A bank of monitors alongside those which showed the address in the Temple displayed the corridors surroundings the Code White Studio. I saw twelve men in dark suits making difficult progress along a slippery floor. They were slipping and sliding all over the fucking place.

Five.

'They're coming,' I said.

'Never mind,' said McArdle, 'never mind. They're too late.'

Two.

One.

The six screens flickered. There was a burst of static. Then it was no longer Staad who addressed us, but Isabel Beaumont. It hurt me to see her.

I had come here to do Isabel's will.

Isabel faded. She was replaced by the first scenes of the dig in the Negev. My heart lurched at the fleeting glimpse of my face. Starved and burned by desert winds.

Three times I tried to speak. The fourth time, I said: 'Is this real? Is this really happening?'

A change of scene. The bones in the laboratory. Over an incomplete, ancient skeleton, stand a doctor, the President, and David McArdle.

McArdle's voice in my ear. 'It's happening.'

I wondered at McArdle's sacrifice. He was denying himself a posthumous future. Everything he had ever done, even the thing he was in the process of doing, paled into invisibility under the unbearable glare of what the world would come to know.

The world would know what they had done.

The world would know.

I endured a sudden moment of unendurable, transformative bliss. Transfigured, I gazed down upon the world, all those millions, the body politic. Finally I was come. I was come upon Christendom not to bring peace, but a sword.

I came to myself with McArdle speaking urgently into my ear. 'Do we have time?'

Trapped in that atmospherically sealed room, he was beginning to panic. This room was not sealed. Soon they would come, and they would try to gas me.

I looked at the internal monitors. 'Eight minutes?' I said.

His voice was thin and distant. It broke up a little. 'Seven.'

'We have time.'

A change of scene. An old, incomplete skeleton in a laboratory, cracked and nicotine-yellow against the pure whiteness of its surroundings. Three people: a man in a doctor's coat, David McArdle and the President. The ranked, silent masses witnessed the President, younger, with a prophetic gleam in his eye, lift the skull and weep.

I looked again at the security monitors. Wraith-like, the figures of four men began to emerge from a wall of foam.

I watched them calling to their comrades. I knew that eight others followed. I took in four deep breaths and said: 'They're here.' I took one last look at the film, gave one last thought to what I had done, gathered up the ammunition, ran to the corner, hid in the shadow of the curved console, and drew a bead on the door through which I knew they would soon gain entry.

My heart was a piston in my chest.

I waited. I looked at my wristwatch. Minutes passed.

I spoke to McArdle. My voice was distant. I had become someone else. I no longer existed. I had stepped into history.

'Three minutes.'

His voice was breaking up badly. He might have been miles distant. Strange, that we had lived such lives, had done such things. We had known each other for a matter of days, but our names would be linked for ever. In death, I would be joined with McArdle and with Isabel.

And with Him.

In a way, I would always be with Him.

'It's done,' said McArdle.

I never heard his voice again.

There was a catastrophic concussion. The mighty security door bucked in its frame. Thin rays of smoky electric light poked into the blue-lit studio.

I huddled in my corner.

After the passage of half a minute, there was a second concussion. The door exploded from its frame. It was blown, twisted and smoking, halfway across the room. It smashed into the desk beneath which I hid and came to a halt in such a way as to obscure my line of vision to the doorway. I could feel the insulted heat radiating from it.

I glanced once more at my wristwatch. Two minutes.

They didn't have time to use gas. Instead, I heard the clunk and roll of two smoke grenades, followed by the rude, extended bark of small arms fire. There was a blizzard of shrapnel. It rained on the twisted metal hulk of the door. A chunk of desk embedded itself like the head of an axe in the wall a centimetre from my head.

There was a brief silence, broken by the cataclysmic roar of a concussion grenade. I was already pressed hard into the dark corner. The blast wedged me in still further. My head struck the wall. My knee struck my face. The desk screamed and raged and twisted against its rivets. The two-centimetre thick glass of the studio window crazed and cracked. The many monitors on the desk imploded. The door to the editorial suite blew in.

I pressed myself yet firmer into the wall. I was helpless against this onslaught. My ears were bleeding.

Four men, indistinct in the smoke, moved briskly to the doorway of the editorial suite. They sprayed the room with small arms fire.

I was glad to be deafened. I had no wish to hear McArdle die.

Two of the men continued to advance upon the editorial suite. It was they who had been tasked with discontinuing the transmission of the truth. The other two retreated towards the shadows, providing cover. In the doorway, others covered them in turn.

I struggled to extricate myself from the corner into which I had been punched. The two men had reached the entrance to the editorial suite before I was able to open fire.

The first shot from the Lawman caught one in the throat. He hit the floor clutching at it. The second man was hit in the face. Even non-lethal weaponry can do satisfying things to a face at such short range. His family wouldn't recognise his body.

The other two had scattered before I was able to draw a satisfactory bead on them. The first fell nicely and clutched at his splintered knee. The other got away.

I ducked back down.

A complex lattice of laser targeting devices began to probe the smoke, searching me out.

I glanced at my watch. They were too late.

Something landed next to me. It rolled on its fat axis, like an Easter egg.

It is a concussion grenade.

I scramble from my corner, clamber to my feet. As I do so, the first round punches into my shoulder. I'm spun so quickly and so violently that I lose all sense of direction. A series of shots hit me in the shoulders and chest. I'm pinned to the wall as if by a nail-gun.

The grenade detonates. I'm lifted by the blast as if by a heavenly messenger, as if an angel has swooped down to save me.

The window to the studio shatters. Shards of glass must have reached the seat where Hannah sits. With a little more speed, I might myself have been blown right through the jagged gap. I might have spilled across the studio floor, coming to rest in a tangle of rubberised power cables.

I hit the floor like an aircrash.

I lie where I've fallen, slumped against the far wall. My legs are arranged before me in a way that should not be possible. There is no pain. I can't move, but that's not so bad. I'd hate to spoil it all by seeing exactly what they've done to me.

Oddly, I think of my mother.

Before me, the dense smoke billows and eddies. It flows like liquid through the shattered studio window. It rises to the low ceiling and rolls like an inverted ocean.

Pinpoints of red sweep over me.

One of the dark-suited men approaches me. He carries an assault rifle. He is long and louche and blond. His once neat hair is sweated into dirty spikes.

He stands over me. If I could look away I probably would. But I can't look away, so I bathe triumphantly in his hatred.

He removes the gas-mask, throws it to the floor behind him. Behind him, ragged whips of smoke are sucked towards the newly operational ventilation system.

He has hazel eyes. They narrow as he scrutinises me. He is ugly with curiosity and disgust.

I am able to meet his eyes. He does not look away, but his gaze hardens to bare contempt as he lowers the rifle. He aims at my face.

I smile. Thick bubbles of blood. 'Cocksucker,' I say.

I'm still smiling as he pulls the trigger.

Seventeen

```
File code: 100046/macd
Username: sicarius
password: ******
Last Udpated: **/**/**
```

File DMWITRES Located.

Please wait.

File DMWITRES Retrieved.

Warning: This File Has Been Cloaked. Should You Wish to Decloak, Press Return. If You Wish to Quit, Press Escape.

If You Wish to Decloak, Please Ensure That Your Software is Code Protected, and Save Any Files Recently Modified.

Please wait.

Code Accessed and Identified. Print 65385922, Licence Confirmed, Outlet Confirmed.

*** Please Note. Decloaked Files Have Been Encrypted According to a System Restricted to the Use of Government Personnel Only. WARNING. Unauthorised Use of this System of Encryption Constitutes an Offence Punishable By Law. Unauthorised Personnel Should Quit

Hello, David, How Are You?

From McArdle's journal:

Date:

This entry I make more than a year after the last.

Yesterday lunch-time, Isabel took me for coffee, something we do with decreasing frequency. The thing that brought us close together did so to the point we must drift away. Frank and I seldom meet, I still believe Petersen to be a prick and I don't mind him knowing it. Ruth I never did like and we don't much miss one another.

But I miss Isabel and Nathan. It hurts me that we are not as close as we were. I wish we no longer had this silence at the heart of our friendship. After all, we did not behave in any way of which we cannot be proud.

Still. It was nice. Two coffees. And a Danish. That's how quickly things are getting better.

It worries me that Isabel smokes so much. She told me: it concentrates my guilt.

Be born again, I told her, absolved of all your sins of inhalation.

She laughed and said: David, I've been thinking about what happened. About Randall.

She sought a response. I had none.

Something has occurred to me, she said. She sipped her coffee and set it very deliberately back in its saucer.

I said: Go ahead. I'm listening. What occurred?

What I was thinking, she said, was: what has he got left? His dreams are pretty much realised. He's all but ceded power to the legislature. So Randall's is a story which, essentially, is finished. He's living the epilogue to a great life. All he has left, (she took a long draw on her cigarette) all he has left is judgement. But I don't think it's God's judgement Randall is interested in. Not any more. But he understands History, David.

I held up a hand: Enough, I said. I know. This stuff occurs to me too.

She told me that Connors, the doctor who performed that inconsequential little act of DNA manipulation, got himself killed six months ago. She found out accidentally, and it took her a while for the name to connect, but she took the chance to run a search and, sure enough, it was him. He was a real action hero, but too old for scuba diving. He had a coronary in shallow water and died before anybody knew he was in trouble.

Now, she told me, I don't care that it's coincidence. I'm sure, I'm positively convinced it is. I mean, the man was in his mid-sixties, what on earth he expects at his age I don't know. The point is, it set me thinking. It set me thinking about protecting ourselves. Just in case.

So, although the five of us have never again sat together, at the same time, in the same room, we have a new secret.

Isabel has arranged for four key men to be strategically placed so that, should she require, she is able to mobilise them. Three of them she came across by private means. A fourth she was introduced to by Ruth. Isabel proved the seriousness of her intent by pulling some serious strings to have him released from a charge of murder first.

Isabel, I said. Such company you keep. And always such a good girl too.

She laughed and placed her hand on my forearm. I can feel it there, right now.

She said: Ruth tells me he's a very nice young man, just a little confused about his priorities.

I laughed. Oh, God, I said, what did we get ourselves into?

She gave my arm a squeeze and let go. It can't hurt, she said.

Isabel, I said.

It's our responsibility, she said. All we did was tidy up the mess for a generation, and all we can truly hope for is that things don't get so bad again too soon. But it will happen. Things will fall apart. Things always do.

Until He really does come back, I said.

She looked at me. Come on, she said. If he was ever there, he's not now. He's gone. He turned his back on us. We're all we have.

Come on, I said. No need for the weary cynic who's seen too much.

Whatever, she said. We'll see.

She got herself another coffee.

From McArdle's journal:

Yesterday Isabel died.

And thus, fully seventeen years after the completion of this journal – this *testament* – I am forced to retrieve it from its hiding place and make one final entry, not unexpected.

All along, Isabel was right: the cancer has at last come to take Randall, and Randall has at last come to take us – like a moribund emperor who fears to go into darkness undefended. With his death, ours: with our death, the assurance of a kind of eternal life for our saviour.

Because we know what we know, and because we did what we did (because *he* did what *he* did and *I* did what *I* did), Isabel always knew that one day Randall, the big, bad wolf, would come for us. I always affected never truly to believe her.

Now he is outside, huffing and puffing, and Ruth and I are

all alone against a man who would be as God to those who are yet to come. A man who would have it that our grandchildren's children perceive the first, fuzzy aura of the supernatural about his posthumous greatness.

As I type at the kitchen table, Naomi is upstairs, busily preparing for a dinner party from which I cried off, and about which I lacked the stamina to argue. My daughter is visiting with us, although I have hinted, as politely as I am able, that I think it best she does not: I tell her I will pay for her to spend her vacation broadening her mind with travel. I tell her she should see as much of the world as she is able, because it is precious. I tell her that, when she was a child we truly believed that there might not be a world for her to grow up in. Not without humour (a woman, she is still so young), she accuses me of becoming a sanctimonious old grouch, she urges me to *get a life*, and I hurt inside, I wish that what is about to occur would not. I wish that it might somehow be magicked away. I yearn for the days when my daughter was a child. Now she is grown I miss her even when she is under my roof. I wonder exactly where she has gone. I wonder where they've all gone, all those people who feature in the journal that records those unforgotten days. Even, especially, the man who wrote them.

I know Ruth is headed in my direction and with her a shadowy figure. I know it will be the one I have met before, if one could describe it as a meeting. He had about him a tension which frightened Naomi, as it frightened me, although I would not admit to it. After recognising me, I remember him looking past us, over the roof of the car, across the street. He seemed to see something that dismayed him, that rendered him incapable of movement.

I hope it's not that man again, although I suspect it will be. Soon they will come knocking on my door, Ruth and this man who has kept the truth, this anti-gospel, this *bad news*, safe on our behalf, moving it from hand to hand, from land to land. I wonder if he ever had any idea what it was he carried. I suspect not.

I hope not.

So, I must acknowledge their arrival, Ruth and this man, this dismal messenger. I will answer the door to their accusation that I sold my soul cheaply, and surely I must answer their demand also that finally I should meet my responsibility. They cry out for my atonement.

The time has come to recognise that our achievements and our crimes are a creation of a single nature, indivisible. I am very scared.

With that, I surrender this diary to the future, whatever unguessed-at form it might take. How strange to reflect that, should you be reading these words a week after I write them or a thousand years, it is of no consequence to me. Very soon I expect to be dead.

There. It's said.

I will have lived a life wherein I did not for a passing moment understand the things I believed, or why it was I came to believe them. If there is the potential of some solace in this statement, its whereabouts are a mystery to me.